Yankee Doodle Dixie

Lisa Patton

Thomas Dunne Books

St. Martin's Griffin / New York

For Will and Michael,
my most precious gifts

And to my adorable nieces,
Elise and Madeleine

This is a work of fiction. All of the characters, organizations, and events portrayed in this novel are either products of the author's imagination or are used fictitiously.

THOMAS DUNNE BOOKS.
An imprint of St. Martin's Press.

www.thomasdunnebooks.com
www.stmartins.com

The Library of Congress has cataloged the hardcover edition as follows:

Patton, Lisa.
Yankee doodle dixie : a novel / Lisa Patton. — 1st ed.
p. cm.
ISBN 978-0-312-55693-8
1. Single mothers—Fiction. 2. Female friendship—Fiction. 3. Memphis (Tenn.)—Fiction. 4. Chick lit. I. Title.
PS3616.A927Y36 2011
813'.6—dc22

2011010282

ISBN 978-1-250-00747-6 (trade paperback)

10 9 8 7 6 5 4 3 2

Praise for *Whistlin' Dixie in a Nor'easter*

"Funny, heartfelt, and ... a Patton's debut brims with pluck ... haracters. . . . You'll be whistlin' 'more, more!' by novel's end. I promise."

—Adriana Trigiani, bestselling author of the Big Stone Gap series

"Just when you think there's nothing new under the sun, here it comes. I absolutely ... g. Lisa Patton serves up ... B&B—with plenty of s ... ssy, and very entertainin ... *Last Girls*

"*Whistlin' D* ... t for and a book that k ...

—Li ... *d Einstein*

"Lisa Patton ... ully heartbreaking ye ... *tlin' Dixie* is truly a p ... ff Bridges

"Peachy-kee ... turns toward a con ... sely satisfying. Dixi ... seeing the world throu ... *s Reviews*

"A plucky de ... he weathers each sto ... dding the helpless princess persona. Her transformation is (of course) accomplished with the aid of boisterous best friends, unlikely new allies, and a heaping helping of girl power. . . . Patton's novel delivers on its feel-good moments a ... lly making it on your own."

—*Publishers Weekly*

Praise for *Yankee Doodle Dixie*

"Southern to the core . . . funny to the bone. In Lisa Patton's new novel she proves that we can go home again, and in many cases we should."

—Fannie Flagg

"Not a beat missed when we head below the Mason-Dixon Line and pick up with Southern belle Leelee Satterfield on her ofttimes riotous but always touching quest for home, friendship, and love. In this charming sequel to *Whistlin' Dixie in a Nor'easter,* Lisa Patton's voice leaves us laughing, crying, and definitely wanting more!"

—Susan Gregg Gilmore, bestselling author of *Looking for Salvation at the Dairy Queen*

"*Yankee Doodle Dixie* oozes Southern charm. From the delightfully witty dialogue and captivating characters, Ms. Patton's writing shines in this story about home, friendship, and second chances. Leelee Satterfield is a winning combination of smarts and steel magnolia fortitude, making her a heroine you can root for as she fights her way out of disaster to find true happiness. Reading this book is like sipping a peach daiquiri on your best friend's porch. So pull up a chair and stay awhile."

—Karen White, *New York Times* bestselling author

"What works is the wonderful, Southern-fictiony relationship between Kissie and Leelee and her daughters, her close friendships, and that certain sorority sister prissiness unique to Southern women of a certain age."

—*Publishers Weekly*

Also by Lisa Patton

Whistlin' Dixie in a Nor'easter

Chapter One

It doesn't take a wizard to figure out the last thing a girl should do is go running hundreds of miles away from home to Vermont just because a man asks her to do so. It also doesn't take a pretty girl with pigtails and a pooch named Toto to tell you that there is absolutely, positively, *no place like home.*

Just thinking about wizards and terriers makes me wish I were Dorothy—sleepily opening my eyes to Auntie Em placing a cold rag on my forehead. In my case it would be Kissie sitting at my bedside with a jumbo cold compress. "Wake up, baby," she'd say. "You've just had a bad *bad* dream."

It was a dream all right, it just wasn't mine.

Fourteen months and a mound of heartache later, my compass is pointing south again, and my speedometer is creeping toward eighty. Despite having three unlikely Vermont comrades helping me to find the road back, an old German wicked witch named Helga hindered that road, making it rockier than the Appalachian Trail not twenty miles from the front door of my Vermont inn. Not only did she swindle me out of both my business and my marriage, she despised my own terrier—a small, helpless Yorkie by the name of Princess Grace Kelly. Gracie couldn't stand Helga, either; probably one of the reasons her little heart finally pooped out. Even though she's forever buried up in the freezing cold North, I've got the cross from her grave sitting right here on the passenger's seat next to me on our way back home.

I can see home in the distance. The parallelogram of Tennessee on the welcome sign slowly emerges the closer I get. The February sun is setting to the right of it and as I roll over the state line my heart rate seems to slow down. A calm washes over me like a warm shot of Grand Marnier, sliding down my throat and coating my insides. It's been over a year since I've been home and I wouldn't doubt it if I've given myself early high blood pressure.

We've been driving for three days—my two little girls and me—1,473 miles *due south.* Sarah and Isabella are in the backseat and I steal another peek at them in my rearview mirror. Their little heads are resting against the sides of their car seats, the monotony of the boundless pavement finally lulling them to sleep. For the first time all day it's quiet.

Since leaving Vermont, in one heck of a nor'easter I might add, I've paid equal attention to the traffic and my heartstrings. It is a wonder we haven't rear-ended anyone, and an even bigger one that my sultry grin isn't yet a permanent fixture on my face. Between New York and Pennsylvania all I've thought about is the man who stole my heart—and who, only hours ago, sealed our months of longing with a not-so-chaste kiss in George Clark's gas station parking lot. Peter Owen saved my restaurant and my pride when my husband left me for a blond bombshell with a face and bosoms only money could—and did—buy. Helga is the one responsible for their meeting, just one of the many "wicked witch" maneuvers she employed as part of her nasty scheme to repossess our inn.

The rest stops between Pennsylvania and Virginia were punctuation marks in my romantic recollecting. A stream of consciousness brewed in my mind: when Peter and I danced to Van Morrison's "Into the Mystic," the first time I tasted his white chocolate mousse, and the moment in the kitchen after my inn's grand opening when we both knew the sparks flying weren't just from the faulty stove.

And now, in Tennessee, some seventy-two hours have passed but I'm reduced to schoolgirl antics, playing our sole kiss over and over in my mind. I've run that kiss through my head, every minute detail, a thousand times already. How he tasted, how his lips felt against mine, the way his tongue moved slowly around my mouth, and how my heart swirled and danced under his touch. I suppose I'll have to live on that memory until the first time he comes to town. Memphis in May, perhaps? That's the perfect time of year. He'll arrive for the Beale Street Music Festival and stay for the whole month. After all, May means Mud Season back in Vermont. And Mud Season, or "The Thaw" as the Vermonters call it, means there won't be any work for him there. Heck, the whole state practically shuts down during that time.

Springtime in Memphis, however, is glorious. We'll go to the Memphis in May Barbecue Festival and the Sunset Symphony together. We'll watch the ducks walk the red carpet at the Peabody Hotel and we'll hang out with Virginia and John, Mary Jule and Al, Alice and Richard, and we'll . . . the girls will die when I show up unannounced. I cannot wait to see the look on Virginia Murphey's face when I pull up in her driveway in oh, about eight more hours. I figure it'll probably be that late by the time my daughters and I go to a drive-through for dinner and take at least three more tee-tee breaks. She and John will be sound asleep but I'll call her cell and she'll answer anyway. It won't be the first time I've dialed her at one in the morning.

Of course Alice, the bossiest of the three, will wonder why in the world I didn't come to her house. Mary Jule might be disappointed, too, but she would never question any decision I make. It's hard having to choose between three best friends. The only reason I'm driving to Virginia's house is because, well, honestly, she knows me the best. You can't room with someone all four years of college, and every summer in between, and not know everything there is to know about each other. Virginia knows that I wax my bikini line, and I know about the few little hairs that grow around her nipples and how she sometimes lets them grow too long and forgets to shave them. Modesty goes out the window when you're living with someone you've known since the age of five.

Alice and Mary Jule know plenty of my secrets, too, but there's just something about Virginia that soothes me. She's got a calming effect on my soul. Perhaps that's because she's never one time judged me about anything, or maybe it's just as plain and simple as the fact that we've never been interested in the same man. Our types are completely opposite. She likes more of a girl's guy and I've always been attracted to the guy's guy. John is perfectly happy to shop with her all day long. He's also the type to wear a Lily tie or lime-green shorts. I prefer the rugged look. I'll take a man who wears a Henley shirt over an argyle sweater, any day of the week.

Virgy—that's what I call her—and I just flat-out love one another. To this day, we've never been in a single fight. Actually, that's not quite true. The closest Virginia has come to scolding me in our twenty-nine-year friendship was when I let my husband talk me into moving to Vermont in the first place. And now, truth be told, she had every right.

I got the idea from Mama. She had always told me that being a good wife meant following your husband. She claimed she didn't really want to move to Memphis, either, away from Greenwood, Mississippi, but she did it because it's what Daddy wanted her to do. "It would have been one thing," she used to say, "to move to Jackson. Several of my best friends from Ole Miss lived there." Kissie told me that she had once overheard a phone conversation between Mama and one of her friends. Said my grandfather told Daddy that he'd teach him to be a great farmer if he'd just dig his heels into the Mississippi Delta and not move to Memphis. He told Daddy that all the cotton land stretched out as far as the eye could see could be his, if he'd just lay his roots down in Mississippi and leave Mama right where she belonged, in her own hometown. Like me, Mama was an only child.

But Daddy's roots couldn't be planted in the middle of a cotton field. Daddy told him, "Mr. Grov'a, I appreciate the off'a, but I don't need your cotton fields. I've got a cotton family business waiting on me two hours naw'th of here and I won't have to get dirt under my finga'nails. I'll buy your cotton and won't ever have to break a sweat." Daddy wasn't the farmer type. He'd rather work out of his old warehouse on Front Street, or Cotton Row as they call it, right in the middle of all the buying and selling.

I was raised in a stand-by-your-man household, and I also happened to fall head-over-heels in love with a football quarterback I first saw in the tenth grade. Even though my red-and-blue cheerleading skirt barely covered my backside, Baker Satterfield never looked my way, all because my chest was flat. That all changed, though, the summer before my senior year. When I ran out onto the football field that fall, pom-poms raised high above my head, my bosoms had blossomed into a natural size D, almost overnight. That man took notice of me then, and after swapping class rings, numerous road trips from Ole Miss to UT, horrendous long-distance telephone bills, and a proposal that would make even Scarlett O'Hara swoon, we finally tied the knot a couple of years after we both graduated from college. We had, at least at first, what I would call a wonderful marriage: two beautiful daughters, a gorgeous home in Memphis, lifelong friends, great sex, and a social life that involved peach daiquiris and other succulent activities. So when my true love told me of his lifelong desire to open an inn in Vermont—well, I had to follow my man.

Turns out my man followed something of his own and left our barely opened B&B, our girls, and our dog, not to mention our dream life, in my (then) manicured hands. Leaving my beloved Memphis had been nearly heartbreaking—so when Baker fell into the arms of a ski resort owner whose cleavage rivaled her black diamonds—I nearly ran right home. But Peter, and a host of Vermonters who saved me from vampire bugs, nor'easter snowstorms, and a Mud Season that was worse than a kudzu jungle, convinced me to finally stand on my own two feet . . . and I did.

The Peach Blossom Inn became Willingham, Vermont's hot spot for tourists, skiers, leaf peepers, and anyone who wanted to try Peter's famous shrimp dijonaisse. But when an outside offer came along to buy the operation from my frazzled and overworked arms, it was an honest-to-goodness relief. I may have worn my L.L. Bean duck boots with the best of them, but my heart was always in Dixie. In just two days, I packed up like we'd never even been there and prepared to drive south to return home in surprise fashion. The only thing to temper my utter joy was the fact that I'd be leaving Peter—a man who could wear flannel shirts and jeans and look as dashing as any Southern gentleman in coat and tails I'd ever seen. In between saving my restaurant and nudging me toward restoring my self-worth, he'd become a dear friend and eventually someone I started caring about more than I was prepared for.

Even though I tried to dash away as quickly as possible, an attempt at quickly severing our ties to Vermont, on the way out of town Peter finally made the move I'd both yearned for and dreaded—and that darn kiss just made departing seem so wrong. For as many times as I'd studied his mouth with his full, perfectly sculpted cherry lips, I hadn't anticipated our kiss would happen when it did. Or that it would be so romantic or have the lingering effect it's had as I've crossed state line after state line.

As if to prove my point, a loud horn brings me back to reality and the fact that Peter's kiss has both stolen my heart and, apparently, my ability to drive in a straight line.

I adjust the wheel and my elbow hits a solid object—oh, Gracie's cross from her grave marker wedged in between a pillow and my cosmetic case. If it weren't for me she'd be lying right here in my lap, licking the saltiness off my hands. She no more wanted to move up to Vermont than the man in the moon. I didn't either but I figured it was my place. My responsibilty to Baker.

I can't help but beat myself up for bringing Princess Grace Kelly up to the frigid North, where I had to leave her body for all of eternity. I know she was old and all, fifteen to be exact, but I'm told Yorkies sometimes live to be eighteen or even twenty. I think her body gave out because her blood froze to death. I know mine did, but I'm a lot younger than she was, if you figure she was 105 in people years.

Frankly, I ought to be blaming Baker. He's the one who moved us up there in the first place. I used to be the biggest doormat in America but I am not anymore. I know, I know, I have my own mind, and nobody, not to mention a Southern woman, should do anything just because someone else wants them to. That's called codependency. Stupid's more like it. I will never let a man make my decisions for me again. Never. Well, I haven't been put to the test yet, but that's my plan.

Virginia's house is totally dark when I pull up in her driveway. Nary a light in sight. Sarah lifts her brunette head when I turn off the engine. "Where are we?"

"Virginia's house," I whisper, trying hard not to wake Isabella. Digging into my purse, I fumble for my cell. After dialing her number by heart, the call goes straight to voice mail. *What?* She never turns off her cell phone at night. I can't ring the doorbell and take a chance on waking up all three of her young children, so I call back, just in case. Same thing. After sitting in the cold only a minute I decide to go ahead and call the home phone anyhow. It rings just four times before I get the same result and pretty soon I'm starting to wonder what in the heck I'm going to do. "Well, shoot. Now what?" I say.

"Who are you calling, Mama?" Sarah asks.

"Virginia, but I guess she's asleep." I'm annoyed and Sarah knows it.

"*It is* one o'clock in the morning." She's pointing to the red illuminated digital clock next to the radio. My six-year-old, the voice of reason.

I think about trying the windows and doors but no one in Memphis goes to sleep with their doors unlocked, not to mention without setting the alarm. The last thing I need to do is scare them. John, Virginia's husband, doesn't seem like the type to own a gun, but who knows these days? The crime in Memphis seems to be getting worse and worse every year.

I try calling a few times more before finally giving up. Leaving her a message would ruin the surprise so I press the end button, toss the phone back in my purse, and back our mud-coated old BMW down the driveway, turning my car in the opposite direction.

Twenty minutes later, when I pull up in Kissie's driveway, I turn off my headlights so they won't illuminate her bedroom. At eighty-one years old the last thing she needs is to feel frightened. I don't know why I didn't plan on coming here in the first place. After all, she's the closest thing to a mother I've got. Six weeks after I was born, the baby nurse that Daddy hired, in keeping with the standards of Memphis society, placed me in the arms of my white mother, only to be passed over to the arms of my black mother, so Mama could get her beauty rest. Just thinking about snuggling up in Kissie's cushiony arms again soothes me and I open my car door.

Sarah unhinges the belt on her car seat and slides over the console in between the front seats. I step out of the car and she reaches out for me to pick her up. At six, her arms and legs can wrap all the way around me but she still likes the security of my arms. As we walk toward the front porch I notice the black iron on the front door and the windows that have been freshly painted. There's a black urn planted with pansies in front of the stoop and two black iron chairs sit on the small porch in front of the picture window. Kissie sits there during the late afternoons so she can wave to her neighbors when they come home from work. Although her house is tiny, it's made of smooth, uniform red brick and the yard, by far the best groomed on the street, is perfectly clipped and trimmed. Her old Plymouth Fury sits under a small attached carport.

Any rap on the door would be a futile attempt at rousing her elderly ears so I go ahead and ring the doorbell. Several minutes pass before I hear a rumbling on the other side of the front door. Kissie barely pulls back the heavy beige curtains covering the picture window and peeks outside. I hear the dead bolt click. The door opens slightly and her face appears just above the four-inch brass chain, which adds further protection from anyone who doesn't belong.

"Is that you, baby?" Although it's pitch black outside, the crescent moon has illuminated our silhouettes.

"I'm home, Kissie."

She unhinges the chain and opens the first door, the sash on her pink fuzzy bathrobe loosely wrapped around her large middle. The keys on her keychain jingle as she turns the last dead bolt to open the heavy iron storm door. "Lawd, have mercy alive. Who is this?" A big smile spreads across her face as she stretches out her arms. "Come give Kissie some sugar." Sarah and I melt into her huge bosoms. When I reach up to kiss her cheek, it's greasy from Vaseline, her moisturizer of choice. "Where is Isabella?" she asks.

"In the car," I say, not wanting to budge from her embrace.

She snatches her arm back and nudges me away. "You better git her inside, 'fore she freezes or gets nabbed; one."

"You have no idea what it's like to freeze, Kiss," I say over my shoulder, halfway back to my car.

Kissie's neighborhood isn't the safest place in town. Located just off Elvis Presley Boulevard, on a tiny little cove street with about nine other modest homes, her house is the pinnacle of the block. Despite the precariousness of the location, it still feels like a second home to me. She's lived there as long as I can remember and this is not the first late-night visit from me, to say the least.

Daddy paid off her mortgage right after Mama died. All fifteen thousand dollars of it. I'm sure he figured it might be an incentive for all the extra hours she'd be investing in me. The ones she's deposited in my life already should have bought her a mansion in Midtown as far as I'm concerned. If I understand the Bible correctly, her mansion's coming when she leaves here. Not to mention a crown the size of Texas.

I lift Isabella out of the car and her little cheek is red and lined from the last few hours it spent burrowed into the rough-hewn material of the car seat. She wraps her arms around my neck, her legs around my waist, and glances around in the darkness. Her voice is scratchy. "Where are we?"

"Kissie's house," I say, and rush back to the warmth.

When we step inside, Kissie reaches out for Issie who gladly goes straight to her. "How's Kissie's lil' baby doin'? Is she all right this evenin'?" Kissie uses her baby voice whenever she speaks to Issie who, at the moment, is a big mess of strawberry-blond curly hair swirling every which a way around her face. Kissie tucks it behind her ears and heads straight down the hall with Issie on her hip. I know what she's doing. She's looking for a rubber band. She did the exact same thing to me as far back as I can remember when my hair became a muss. Issie and I could pass for twins if you compare our baby pictures. Not so much for Sarah. She's a Satterfield through and through. No one in my family has thick straight brunette hair and eyes as blue as a Hawaiian lagoon.

Ponytail holders are something Kissie keeps a plenty of around her house. That's because her hair still hangs down her back. She always wears it in a braided bun, or "plat" as she calls it, on top of her head during the day, so most people have no idea her hair is that long. Kissie refers to her color as "butterscotch." She's part black, part white. Maybe even fifty-fifty. The truth is, sixty years ago, in Memphis, Tennessee, she would never have been accepted by the whites, so she had no choice but to live as a black. I mean that with no judgment. Black folks treated me with more love than some of the people in my own family.

Kissie married a black man named Frank and gave birth to a little girl they christened Josephine or Josie for short. That poor baby died of pneumonia when she was only three years old. Kissie doesn't talk about it all that much but there's a picture of Josie in a large ornate frame hung above the couch in the living room, in between one of her mother and another of me. She kicked Frank out years ago. He preferred spending his paycheck at the dog track over in West Memphis rather than on her or their monthly bills.

To me, she's the most beautiful woman I've ever known and she treats me just like I'm her own child. Her real name is Kristine "Krissie" Phillips King. When I was little I couldn't pronounce my *R*s so I started calling her Kissie. Now everyone she knows calls her Kissie, all because of me. Even her own brother calls her by her nickname.

It would be impossible to guess her age. Between her flawless complexion and her razor-sharp mind, not to mention an agility that would rival someone half her age, Kissie is as healthy as I am. In fact, I've never known her to be sick a day in my life. She'll talk about her "sugar" every now and then but I can't remember the last time she's even complained of a cold. And speaking of complaining, that word doesn't even belong in her vocabulary.

Sarah heads straight for the cut-glass candy jar in the tiny living room. I try to stop her but Kissie's already got the top in her hands. When I clear my throat, Sarah's arm has disappeared from sight. She looks back at me, pleading, "Please. I'm hungry."

"It's one in the morning, sweet girl. The backseat of my car is covered in Goldfish, and you had a big dinner."

She shrugs her shoulders, tilts her head back and shoots Kissie a wily grin. Kissie is absolutely no help. "Cain't she have one piece, baby?" I roll my eyes in defeat, which tickles Kissie to no end and she bursts out laughing.

No one on earth has a belly laugh like hers. It comes from deep, down in her gut. When you're least expecting it, she'll let it out and it's the most contagious sound on earth. I can't think of another laugh that gets me going as fast as hers—and like clockwork, despite the late hour and exhaustion, I'm chuckling and smiling along with Kissie and Sarah.

The candy jar sings as Kissie replaces the lid. That jar has been stuffed to the brim with a mixture of Brach's hard candy and Hershey's Chocolate Kisses since I was wearing pigtails, a hairdo Kissie thought more of than Mama did. After Kissie had spent a half hour "platting" my hair just so, Mama would undo the pigtails. "That's so common," she'd say, in her thick Mississippi drawl. "A high ponytail looks much more refined."

Now Kissie disappears into the kitchen and I can hear her pulling food out of the fridge. Her fondest expression of love is cooking for the ones she cares about most and before I know it the smell of bacon is wafting through the house. People in Memphis have known about her culinary skills for years. That's actually how my grandmother came to hire her. She was catering a party once and when Grandmama put one of Kissie's cheese dreams in her mouth, she begged her to come cook for Granddaddy and her. That was back in the early fifties and she's never worked for another family a day in her life.

She has this little noise she makes while she's cooking. It's a soft grunting actually, with a *hm, hm, hm* sound that she repeats in threes over and over. It's quite endearing, most of the time, unless she's disgusted with something or someone. Then it turns into an irritated chant. I've been on the other side of that peeved *hm, hm, hm* a time or two and my preference is to stay this side of it—lest I find myself in line for a big talking to.

Like the time Virgy and I tiptoed home at four in the morning shortly after we got back from Ole Miss one summer. Daddy was out of town and Kissie always stayed at our house when he was gone. Even though we were twenty-one years old, Kissie thought it highly inappropriate for a girl to get home at that hour. The beep of the burglar alarm alerted her that we were back and here she comes huffing and puffing down the hall, wearing her favorite pink nightgown. She didn't even bother throwing on her housecoat. Her hair was hanging down her back and she smelled like Jergens lotion and Vaseline. "Where you been, chile? *Hm, hm, hm. Hm, hm, hm. Hm, hm, hm.*"

Virginia and I looked at each other and tried our best to keep from giggling. We were slaphappy and quite toasted from the Long Island iced teas we consumed at Bob Wilder's booth at the Memphis in May Barbecue Festival. There was no hiding it. She could smell it on us a mile away.

"You think you can git away with such drunken foolishness?" she said, madder than a hornet's nest. "What do you think those men are gonna do when they see you like this? Huh? They'll be takin' advantage of you is what they're gonna do. *Hm, hm, hm.*"

Virgy said, "No, Kissie. We're not those kinds of girls. We *just* kiss." She pinched my arm behind my elbow where Kissie couldn't see her.

"You *just* kiss? And then what? You think they don't want a feel? Those men will be tryin' to git whatever they can. They're just like a dawg. They git off one and then git on another. You young ladies needs to be comin' on home at a *decent* hour. *Hm, hm, hm. Hm, hm, hm. Hm, hm, hm.*"

"Don't be mad at us," I told her. "There were lots of girls at the party. We weren't the only ones."

"Till four A.M.? Nice girls don't do that. You hear? You lucky your Daddy ain't here, Leelee."

Back then, Virginia and I dismissed her as being old-fashioned. Now that I'm a mother, I know she was exactly right.

It's after three in the morning by the time I slip under the covers in Kissie's spare bedroom. As is always customary with Kissie, we stayed up talking and rehashing the events of yesteryear until I could hardly hold my eyes open another second. I heard for the three hundredth time the details of my grandmother's, as Kissie calls it, "beautiful death." "I fetched your Grandmama a fresh gown when I knew she was goin' down fast," Kissie always explains. "She was layin' there like an angel. Nary a wrinkle on her face." We talked about Daddy's death, and started to discuss Mama's, too, but I just couldn't bear to go there again. Breast cancer took her when I was only eighteen. Not a very good way to start college.

For a second I think I'm in my bed in Vermont; the sheets feel like a continental glacier. After a decade sleeping next to a hot-blooded man, I'm still not used to facing the ocean of a bed alone. Baker is gone forever. . . . Peter is gone for . . . I curl into a ball for warmth and relax into the mattress. I'm asleep before my weary mind can usher in another thought.

Chapter Two

Only a tiny bit of morning light has seeped into the room when I'm awakened by the sound of my cell phone vibrating on the bedside table. Issie is sleeping sideways next to me, her feet pressed into my back. When sleeping over at Kissie's, the girls and I have no choice but to share a bed; her house has only one spare bedroom. Sarah's in with Kissie, who never wakes up before nine anymore unless she has to be somewhere. After sixteen hours of driving and very little sleep, even the sound of Virginia's voice is not enough for me to rally. I can barely eke out a whispered hello.

"Hey." There's not a trace of oomph in her voice, either. "I saw my missed calls from you this morning. Sorry. John and I went to a movie last night and I left my phone in my coat pocket."

"I tried the home phone," I say softly, ducking my head under the covers so as not to wake Issie.

"You know we don't ever answer that. Why are you whispering? Where are you, anyway?" she says, part Memphis drawl, part itching curiosity.

I'm too tired for the surprise. "I'm at Kissie's."

"YOU'RE AT KISSIE'S? Why on earth didn't you let me know you were coming home?" Virginia's voice could be heard clear across the room.

Issie stirs slightly. "Shhh. Issie's sleeping right next to me."

"Oops."

"The reason I never called is because I wanted to surprise you."

"I thought you weren't coming for another month."

"The movers had an opening and they slid me in. You won't believe how I've started to calm down. I've been back in town only a few hours and I feel like it's all just been a bad dream. Like all I ever needed to do was click my ruby slippers together and it'd finally be over."

"What about the Yankee Doodle?" she asks. That's her nickname for Peter. Having heard me babble about him like a teenager for the past eight months, she knew leaving him would be bittersweet. I couldn't wait to tell her about the kiss though.

"That's a long story. I want to tell you about it in person. But Virginia, I'm home!" I say it a little too loud, but clamp my mouth tight, paralyzed at the thought of having to entertain Issie on this deficient amount of sleep should she wake up.

"Thank. God."

"What time is it?" I whisper even softer.

"Six." Virginia's children are early risers. They inherited that from their father.

I roll over away from Issie and cup my hand over my mouth. "*Six?* I just went to bed three hours ago."

"Can you meet at the club today for lunch?" Virginia whispers back.

"I'm no longer a member, remember?" I say, half bitterly, referring to my charming ex-husband who terminated our membership.

"Oh for goodness sakes, I'll buy your lunch."

"I'll pay you back."

"Like I'm really worried about that." Virginia is very generous. She'd give me her last Coca-Cola, even if she were hungover and dying for it.

"Do you think Alice and Mary Jule are free today?" I ask her.

"They'll have to cancel their plans if they aren't. How about meeting at one? That'll give you some time to go back to sleep. Where does Kissie live anyway?"

"You know where Belmont turns into McGavock, before you get to Sycamore Cemetery?"

"You better get out of there!" she practically yells. Up until now most of our entire conversation has been at a whisper.

"Relax. I'm fine. She has iron on all the windows and doors."

"You're a lot braver than me."

"Nothing is going to happen."

"Fine, then. I'll see you at one, Fiery. Bye."

Virginia nicknamed me Fiery a long time ago. I was the only one in our class of forty girls with red hair. That was back when people would say, "I'd rather be dead than red on the head." The neighborhood boys brutally teased me about it so much when I was little that I grew up hating my red hair *and* my freckles. Not to mention my curls. I'd have given just about anything to be Marsha Brady with her stick-straight blond hair and tan skin. Now everyone wants red hair. Go figure.

The last time I'd stepped foot in the lobby of the Memphis Country Club I was married to Baker Satterfield and living the life I'd always wanted. Or thought I'd always wanted. Now, I'm walking in the door a single mother of two little girls wondering where in the world I'm going to live and how I'm going to support them.

My three best friends are sitting at a small round table in the corner of the Red Room when I arrive. Hard to believe, but the last time I laid eyes on them was last summer, May I think it was, when they surprised me after Baker left. Mud Season in Vermont was in full swing and the three of them showed up at my door with wallpaper and paint, ready to help turn my dank, Teutonic inn into a Southern showplace straight out of the pages of *Veranda*.

As is the custom, I'm late, terminally ten minutes as usual, and my Coca-Cola is waiting for me—half poured in a bar glass with small square ice cubes—and the other half still in the bottle. I run right up to the table and squeeze each of them hard enough to leave a bruise. It's a wonder all the other women in the room don't ask us to hush. Between squeals and waltz-like hugs, we've created quite a commotion, and to make matters worse, my Coke bottle tips over as I'm slipping my arm out of my jacket. Johnson, the waiter, comes running over and mops up the spillage with extra red linen napkins.

"I'm so sorry, Johnson," I say, and try helping him with the mess.

"Don't worry about this, Miss Leelee. It's just good to have you back."

"Well, thank you. It's good to be back." I hug him from the side and hang my puffy white ski jacket, one of the few purchases I made in fourteen months of living in Vermont, on the back of my chair. It was in this very spot, nearly two years ago, that all three of these girls tried talking me out of moving. Naturally, that small detail has long been brushed under the rug. To be in Memphis at this very moment, with Virginia, Mary Jule, and Alice, is heavenly enough to make me forget all the turmoil I endured.

Alice jumps right in. Even before "How are you?" or "How are the girls?," she gets straight to the point. "How's Peter?" she asks, though when she says it, it sounds more like a declaration. "What is going on with y'all?" She sips the last of her diet Coke and chews on a couple of ice cubes. I can't help noticing how pretty her hair looks. She's one of the only women I know who doesn't highlight her hair. It's plenty blond enough naturally.

"I asked her that on the phone this morning. She says it's a *long* story." Virginia puts a freshly buttered melba toast to her lips. Her French manicure glistens from the reflection of the light overhead.

"Oh good, Leelee. I knew something was going to happen," Mary Jule, the hopeless romantic of the bunch, says and rapidly claps her hands together.

I take a deep breath. "Well, I have to say, it surprised me. Remember how I told y'all that he wouldn't talk to me once I decided to move back home? He'd come in to work, head straight into the kitchen and start drinking wine with Pierre?" I can't help but remember the sullen look on Peter's face as he sipped merlot with our maître d'.

As I spoke, all three were leaning in toward the center of the table with their arms resting in front of them.

"Well, this went on the whole week before I left. He hardly said two words to me. He'd cook all the meals for the customers and then leave immediately after the restaurant closed."

"So not like him," Mary Jule says.

"I know! Anyway, the morning I was leaving, Roberta, Pierre, and Jeb fixed a beautiful breakfast for the girls and me. Pierre even went out and bought us gifts—how sweet is that? But Peter never showed up to say good-bye. They all tried to act like it wasn't weird or anything but I knew they thought it was strange. After all, we had worked side by side in the inn together for eight months, and he never shows up to at least *tell me good-bye*?"

"He was devastated. He knew he was losing you, shoog, and he was beside himself," Alice says, consolingly.

"Well, as it turns out, after I told the other three good-bye, which was very, very sad, let me tell you, I stopped at George Clark's gas station to fill up my tank one last time. Remember he's—"

"The gossipy gas station owner. We stopped there to fill up Jeb's pink Mary Kay car," Virginia reminds me, referring to my multitalented handyman who not only swept my chimneys and raked snow off my roof with some Yankee contraption called a roof rake, but tended to his own proprietorship, Jeb's Computer World. His pink Mary Kay car was a hand-me-down from his mother. They continued to split it for advertising, though, Mary Kay on the driver's side and JCW on the other.

"Oh yeah," I say. "Well anyway, my tank was full, and as I was pulling away from the pump I saw this person walking straight up to my car. At first I wasn't sure who it was because his cap was pulled way down over his head and it was snowing like crazy but the closer he got I knew it was—"

"Peter." Alice purses her lips together and nods her head.

Just that second, Johnson walks up to the table with a pad in his hand, ready to take our order. "Good afternoon, ladies." His voice is extra cheery.

"Not now, Johnson," Alice says, and shoos him away. "We're all *dying* here."

He holds up both hands, palms out. "No problem, I'll come back," he says, with an amused grin.

"Oh Johnson," Mary Jule calls after him. "Please don't mind us. Leelee had a *Casablanca* moment and she's giving us the blow-by-blow." Alice can be embarrassing sometimes but she never really means to be short. Johnson's already moved on to the next table and seems unaffected.

"Keep goin'," Alice says impatiently, and sweeps her hand in my direction.

"Where was I?"

"The Yankee Doodle is walking toward you at George Clark's with his hat pulled way down." Virginia loves all the little details.

"Oh yeah. So, he came up to my car and I jumped out. We stood there not knowing what in the world to say to each other. I mean it was so awkward. And then, out of nowhere, he asks me what CD is in my player. I tell him I don't think there is one. Then he sits down on my front seat, says hi to Sarah and Issie, and finds Van Morrison's *Moondance* in my CD case. He slips it into the player and skips through until he lands on 'Into the Mystic.'"

"That's the song y'all started to dance to the night you got the call with an offer on the inn!" Mary Jule's eyes twinkle. She, like me, absolutely loves a romantic cliffhanger.

"Yes! And remember we never finished the dance?" I say, recalling the night my relationship with Peter went from not-so-platonic to nothing-really-happened-but-we-are-definitely-not-platonic.

"Because you didn't just let the stupid phone ring and once he learned it was an offer he got so upset about the sale that he left the inn right then and there," Alice says, finishing the story I'd told them fifty times by now.

"Well, we *finished* the dance right there in front of God and everybody at George Clark's gas station. *Underneath the falling snow.* With a nor'easter headed our way."

"You did not!" Mary Jule nearly screams.

"Shhhh," we all say, looking around the room to see who's peering in our direction.

"Yes, we did," I tell her.

"That's the most romantic thing I've ever heard in my life," Mary Jule says decisively, plopping her glass of ice tea on the red linen as if rendering a verdict.

"Did he kiss you?" Alice asks with raised eyebrows. Although she tries to appear calm by sipping her Coke, she can hardly contain herself, either.

I nod my head and visualize it for the fiftieth time since driving over state lines. "It was . . . incredible."

"It should be a movie, Leelee, I swear to God. It should be a movie." Virginia sits back in her chair and rakes her hands through her hair. "Who should play you?"

Alice turns to Virginia and waves her hand. "Hang on a second." Then she turns back to me. "And then what happened?"

"We said good-bye and . . . I drove off." I close my eyes and feel the sadness returning.

"WHAT?" Alice practically yells. "You didn't stay with him?"

I gape at her. There are no words. I don't know how to explain to them what I was feeling in that moment. That as hard at is was to leave Peter, my heart was already in Memphis when he finally made his move. Now, of course, I would do anything to make that kiss last longer than it did.

"I would have stayed," Alice says definitively and reaches for a saltine.

"Would you listen to what you're saying, please? You're telling me that you would have stayed in Vermont even though all your furniture was on the way to Memphis, not to mention all your very best friends and everything else that is familiar in your life."

"But your man was in Vermont," Virginia says.

"He was *not* my man. He *is* not my man. Never once before that moment had he told me he cared about me. Not once. I cannot even believe y'all. First you tell me I'm crazy for moving to Vermont. *In this very room.* Then you call me every week for fourteen months and ask when I'm coming home. When I finally get here you're asking why I didn't stay?"

"Of course we want you home, honey. We just want you to be happy," Mary Jule says.

Johnson strolls up to the table again and Mary Jule politely asks him to give us two more minutes.

"I just knew Peter had it for you from the moment I met him," Alice says. She always thinks she has everything figured out. It's the control freak inside her.

"Well he never told me that. *And,* even if I had known, what was I supposed to do? Stay in Vermont because *another* man in my life tells me to do so? I made the decision to come back to Memphis *for me.* I followed my own heart for once. Sure, I'm crazy about him but suppose we didn't work out? Then what?"

Alice sits back in her chair and lightly taps her fingers together. "You're right. You're absolutely right. I haven't thought of it that way."

"Thank you," I say. "Plus, y'all won't believe this. Guess who bought the inn?" I'm hoping to distract them with a bit of Vermont gossip.

"Who?" they all say at once.

"Helga and Rolf."

A uniform look of horror spreads across the table.

Helga and Rolf had been the previous owners of our B&B. They had made our lives unbearable from the moment Baker and I arrived, insisting on overseeing our new management of the inn—which was then called the Vermont Haus Inn. But eventually, I threw them out, and replaced their tasteless Germanic décor (if you can call it that), scrubbed away the years of Helga's cigarette smoke, boxed up her hideous collection of ceramic hippo figurines and created the Peach Blossom Inn. Along with being a symbol of sweet Southern goodness, peaches also signify long life, so I thought it a highly appropriate name. Its immediate success drove Helga, in particular, mad—and I knew she had been devising a revenge plot, I just didn't know what it was.

At the time, Baker had been gone for two months, shacking up with the ski slope seductress Helga had initially introduced to him. I had successfully reopened the inn—thanks to an intervention from the girls—and things were actually going well. But I was lonely, desperately so, and all I wanted to do was run back into the arms of Memphis. So I told our real estate agent, Ed, to put the inn back up for sale. I had proven I could stand on my own—I just wanted to be in sandals, not snow boots.

I never expected the inn to sell as quickly as it did—but to my credit, I had turned it from a bleak B&B with limited dining options into a warm and cozy Southernized inn serving some of the region's most acclaimed cuisine . . . thanks to Peter. What I didn't know was that Helga and Rolf, bitter at my success, coerced my realtor into secretly selling them back the property.

"That smarmy Ed Baldwin—that's my new Yankee word I learned, *smarmy*—never told me they were the buyers. And I would never have known if I hadn't had to go back to the inn. The girls and I were just outside of town when I remembered Princess Grace. I knew I couldn't dig her back up but I at least had to go back for her grave marker. That's when I saw Helga's hippo collection on the mantel, well Sarah did. She was playing with one when I came back inside from digging up Gracie's marker."

"That witch!" Alice says.

"Did you smash the hippos in the fireplace?" Virginia wants to know.

"No."

"Why not?" Virginia is ready to kill me.

"Because. I don't know. I guess I just didn't care at that moment. I wanted to come home."

"Did that make it even harder to leave, knowing she had bought back the inn?" Mary Jule asks.

"Yes and no. Roberta (my beloved housekeeper) and Peter already had new jobs up at Sugartree, the local ski resort. And Jeb had plenty of work on his own with JCW and his snowplowing business. I didn't feel like I'd be letting anyone down."

"Yeah, plenty of business all right. Jeb's Computer *World*—all twelve square feet of it." Alice shakes her head. "Bless his heart." JCW is housed inside a tiny lean-to in Jeb's side yard.

"Anyway, I figured Pierre would be able to get another job anywhere. He's the best maître d' in all of southern Vermont. I wasn't worried about him. But I just didn't have the strength to fight Helga anymore. I mean why bother? I'd put up with her crap long enough. That wicked witch can have it."

"I wonder how long it will take her to paint back over the peach paint and undo all the other changes we made." Virginia loves the way the inn looked after they came up to help me remodel.

"Do you think she'll change the name back to the Vermont Haus Inn?" Mary Jule asks, choking out the cold, Teutonic name.

"Of course she will. When I drove back up I noticed the Peach Blossom Inn sign was down. She had thrown it in the trash pile. I snatched it back up and made room for it in my car. There was no way I was going to give her the satisfaction of thinking she had thrown away my beautiful sign."

"Who cares anyway?" Alice says.

"That's my point!"

"I'm glad you took it. You might just need that sign one day," Mary Jule says.

"I'm going to hang it in my rec room. When I find a place to live." Thinking about that reminds me of all the tasks I have ahead of me and I start to feel terribly overwhelmed.

"Leelee, I am so proud of the way you've handled all this."

"Thank you, Virgy. I really think I've changed. I'm not ever going to let another man make all my decisions for me. Let's eat, though, I'm dying." I pick up the red linen napkin and place it in my lap.

Virginia motions for Johnson who comes right up to the table. "Ladies, what looks good today?" he asks.

"You know what I'm getting, Johnson. My usual," Virginia says.

"Chicken salad stuffed in an avocado." He smiles and puffs out his chest.

"Yes, siree." She unfolds her own napkin and places it in her lap. "Plus I need a little more tea." Virginia taps the top of her glass. "When you get a minute." Then she announces, "Y'all might as well get what I'm getting because I'm not giving out any bites today. I'm starving."

We all agreed to follow her advice. Chicken salad avocados all the way around.

By one fifteen in the afternoon, most of the lunch crowd has dissipated. Not so, however, for a few women seated around a couple of bridge tables in the corner enjoying a lingering lunch. I love cards. Don't get me wrong. It's just that a table full of older women with granny glasses on the tips of their noses, a cigarette or two in the ashtray, and a gin and tonic at 1:00 P.M. grosses me out. They're always there, though. The beau monde of Memphis.

Nearby I spot the only other occupied table—a four-top with Memphis social elite at either side, each with her pearls and respective Vera Bradley accessories. Tootie Shotwell is a former Tri Delt president at Ole Miss. (I was a Chi O.) I catch her studying me out of the corner of her eye before leaning into the other three women at the table. With a subtlety gained from years of practice, four sets of eyes tactfully flit in my direction, but are always ready to glance away lest they be caught staring.

"Did y'all just see Tootie Shotwell turn around and gossip about me?" I lean into the table, talking under my breath.

"What are you talking about? How in the world do you know what she's saying?" replies Alice.

"It's obvious. Who else could she be discussing?" I say indignantly. I knew my return to Memphis Baker-less would not go unnoticed . . . but I had hoped to make it twenty-four hours at least.

Virginia says, "Uh-oh, here she comes." Tootie's group has just finished their meal and have to walk by our table in order to reach the club's exit.

Alice speaks first. "Hi Tootie, how's it goin'?" she says with feigned interest.

"Greaaaaaat," Tootie says, with a plastered smile. "How are y'aaaaaall?" She looks around at all of us and steps back when she notices me, mustering up a phony look of surprise. "Leelee! What are *you* doing home?" *Excuse me while I gag a maggot.*

I start to answer but Mary Jule jumps in before I have the chance. "We've convinced her to move back. We just couldn't stand having her that far away." She kicks me under the table and half smirks at Tootie.

"Really? Was Baker okay with that? He was the one who just *had* to make a change, wasn't he?" she asks, with her three sidekicks all gawking at me like I'm some new zoo creature.

"He's getting used to the idea," I say. Not a lie, just not fessing up to the whole shebang. Even though I've made my peace with the situation, it's quite another to declare oneself a divorced, single mother of two, homeless and jobless to a gaggle of Memphis's most cunning gossips. I'm simply not ready to reveal to the outside world what's going on in my life. Admittedly, I should have thought of that before I agreed to meet everyone at the club.

"Oh, well tell him hi. Trey will be thrilled he's back in town. He'll have another golf buddy."

I force a smile.

"Bye y'all." Tootie flips us a ta-ta wave and sashays out the door.

"I can't stand her," Virginia says.

"Nobody can," Alice adds. "But let it go. You can't control people. You can only be responsible for your own actions. I learned that in therapy. Well, actually, Richard did. But he tells me everything."

"You *think* he's telling you everything," Mary Jule says.

"Whatever. First things first, where are you going to live?" Alice asks, turning to me.

"With Kissie," I say.

They all cut their eyes at one another. I can tell it's disapproval time.

"What's wrong with that?"

"It's not that there's anything wrong with it, honey," Mary Jule says, and touches my arm, "it's just . . . far away."

Virginia takes a more *direct* approach. "You can't live in that part of town. What are you gonna do? Use that address for Sarah and Issie on the Jameson application?" All four of us attended Jameson, the elite all-girls school, from kindergarten through twelfth grade. Kissie's neighborhood has never seen the light of day on a Jameson School application.

"Maybe," I say, a bit stubbornly.

"Come on, Leelee. I'm trying to be the voice of reason here," Virginia says. "Not only is it a bad part of town, but what about when your date comes to pick you up? And you might as well start thinking about dating, you know. Especially if you're giving up the Yankee Doodle."

"I haven't given up the Yankee Doodle. He's coming for a visit in May." A slight exaggeration since I haven't actually invited him yet. . . . "Dating other men is the last thing on my mind."

Before I can say another word Alice speaks up, despite the fact that she has yet another saltine in her mouth. She holds her hand in front of her lips so the rest of us aren't exposed to the mush on her tongue. "I have a therapist I want you to talk to. Richard's been talking to her all about his childhood crap. She's helping him a lot."

"So I need a therapist because dating is the last thing on my mind?" It comes out far more defensively than I had intended.

"No, because of everything you've been through. That's why you need a therapist," she says, and swallows the last bit of her saltine as if to punctuate her thought.

Somehow I knew that would probably be a good idea but it wasn't something I was ready to jump into right away. "I'll think about it. But right now, all I can think about is, where is my furniture going in four days? How am I going to support myself? Where is Sarah going to school next week?"

"These things will all work out. They always do." Virginia tears open another melba toast and looks back at the kitchen door. "Where in the heck is our lunch?"

After staring in deep thought at the ceiling for what seems like hours, although it's only been thirty minutes, I glance over at my cell phone plugged in on the bedside table. I reach over and hold it for a few minutes, turning it over and staring at the keypad. I'd resisted the temptation for three days already but now I punch in the numbers to Peter's phone . . . and hang up before it starts ringing. *Oh this is ridiculous. Just call him.* I dial back but it goes straight to voice mail. His recorded voice tells me that he's away from his phone. "Leave a message and I'll get back with you," he says.

"Hi. It's Leelee. I just wanted to tell you that I made it. I'm here. Back in Memphis. Safe and sound." I want to tell him I miss him but I'm afraid. "I . . ." I pause and change my mind. "I hope you're good. Hope to talk with you soon!"

I'm disappointed that he didn't answer. And a tiny bit afraid to wish he would have.

Chapter Three

"Leelee, today is the first day of the rest of your life," I speak into the mirror and tap my toothbrush on the side of the sink. Who actually said that? I wonder. I remember hearing those words for the first time when I was in high school and not giving it much thought. It sounded corny back then but today is different. I'm starting my life over and it sounds like it ought to be my mantra, or at the very least my thought for the day.

I stroll into the kitchen around eight thirty and Kissie's got her old griddle heating over two eyes of her gas cooktop. She's stirring pancake batter in the same yellow mixing bowl I've seen her use a hundred times before. "Good mornin', sweet," she says from the stove. "Did you sleep well?"

"I always do when I'm here." I detect a faint amount of body odor while reaching around her middle and kissing her cheek. "I hope Sarah didn't toss and turn too much."

"That baby did fine. You know I sleep like a rock anyway. What's on your agenda today?"

"I'm not really sure where to start, to tell you the truth. A house? A job? School for the girls?" I sound exhausted already. "And I can't wait to get a new dog." I've already decided the only way I'll ever move past the ghost of Gracie is to go ahead and replace her.

"Ooo-wee. You've got lots of business that needs straightenin' out." She sighs heavily while unwrapping a large package of Tennessee Pride sausage. I watch as she lines the entire iron skillet with sausage links all the while wondering who in the world is going to eat all this food.

"Tell me about it. I feel like my head might bust off my neck." Glancing around her kitchen I say, "Have you brought in your paper yet, Kissie?"

"No baby, it's still layin' out there in the driveway."

"I'll be right back."

I throw on my robe and head on out the front door. Her next-door neighbor to the right waves to me. Mrs. Clark, another kind old lady, knows all about my family and me from living next to Kissie all these years. They have been next-door neighbors as long as Kissie has worked for our family. I wave back and smile, pondering just how safe these two elderly ladies really are. As much as I hate to admit it, it scares me a little. After grabbing the paper I practically run back to Kissie's front door.

While Kissie turns the sausages and flips the pancakes, I sit at her small dining room table scanning the want ads. Even though I'm in another room, she's not but a few feet away and watching her cook gives me absolute peace. It reminds me of when I was little and I'd be at our kitchen table working on my homework while Kissie prepared dinner for our family.

Issie and Sarah are in the next room watching *Sesame Street.* Sarah's not too happy about it but cable is not a service to which Kissie subscribes. "When are you going to get cable? You'd love it." I have to raise my voice so she can hear me over the crackles and pops from the sausages.

"What do I need cable tee-vee for?" she hollers back.

"The Food Network for starters."

"The network stations are all I need. Long as I can watch my stories during the day, I'm just fine."

I fold the want ads in half and open up the rental section, grab a pen, and join her in the kitchen, which quite honestly is almost too small for the both of us. Glancing around the room it dawns on me that it could fit inside most of the closets of the homes built today. Despite their age, the avocado-green appliances still sparkle. And you could eat off any of the shelves in her fridge. "I thought you loved staying up late watching TV," I say, nestling into a corner near the sink.

She answers me without turning around from her stove. "Now that Johnny Carson's gone, I don't care all that much about it, to tell you the truth. I read my Bible at night anyway." Kissie's is a tattered and worn old King James version and even with her tenth-grade education, she seems to have an inherent grasp on all of the Bible's great truths. It's beyond me how she understands the Old English language but she does. "After Jesus comes into your heart, that Bible goes from black and white to color," she's always telling me.

With the morning sun streaming in through the window over her kitchen sink I can't help staring at her complexion. You'd never in a million years know she's eighty-one. That's one attribute the black lady has hands down over the white lady. Here I am, almost thirty-four, and wrinkles are already cracking my face.

Nothing looks too promising in the rental section, further adding to my dismay. "How long can we stay here?" I ask her, sighing heavily.

Kissie whips her head around. "What kind of question is that? My house is your house, Leelee."

"I know. But you have your own quiet life. Sarah and Issie make plenty of noise—"

"Listen here." She waves her spatula in the air as she emphasizes her words. "You've been through a ha'd time. You can stay here long as you need to. I'mo always take care of you and your little girls." Kissie turns back around tending to the sausage—apparently the matter is settled.

Tears pool in my eyes. Standing in her kitchen, smelling her cooking, feels as good and safe as any moment I can ever remember. The stress of the last fourteen months, for right now anyway, has evaporated along with the water in her grits. I have a sudden urge to hug her so I walk up and reach my arms around her waist from behind, dissolving into her fat back. She taps my left arm with her free hand. "You've always been my baby, Leelee. Just cuz you're older don't mean that's going to change. Kissie's here to help you get your business straight. Why don't you go sit down at the table and make those calls? You've got a plenty to do this mornin'." Giving her one more squeeze—my arms won't even fit all the way around her—I leave the kitchen in search of a phone book.

So what's the first task at the top of my list? Actually, that's an easy one—Sarah needs to be in school . . . yesterday. Besides that, we need a house to live in and all the utilities turned on, a new checking account, new health insurance, new telephone service and of course, I need a job. With so much ahead of me, I'd like to cave under the pressure but somehow I decide to take it "one step at a time." Maybe I do need to see a therapist. I'm beginning to sound like one. After all, who wouldn't feel completely overwhelmed if the chores on their plate were stacked as high as mine? Just as I start to wonder how I'll ever clear them off Tootie Shotwell's toothy smile pops in my head, and my pride takes over. I will balance that plate high above my head and in one hand, by gosh. I will not allow someone like her to cause me to crash and break into a million pieces.

Both of Kissie's telephones are antiquated, rotary dials. One hangs on the kitchen wall and the other rests on a portable telephone table, with an extra long cord that reaches all over the house. I find it in her bedroom and after searching through one of the phone books tucked in the slot on the phone table, I dial the number to the Jameson School. While talking to the admissions director it's clear that they are not at all open to Sarah entering this close to the end of the year. She can make the move over in the fall, the woman says, provided she passes the admissions exam, but not now.

I try to convince her again that it's only for three months—and I'm an alumna to boot. She doesn't relent a bit, instead suggesting a few private tutors who could assist Sarah until the fall. I can't bear to tell her that I'm homeless, jobless, and on a budget . . . a budget that does *not* include private tutoring. Instead I politely say thank you, like any trained Jameson girl would, and put the phone back in its cradle.

I start to consider how much a tutor might cost—it can't be all that hard to come up with—when a brilliant idea suddenly comes out of nowhere. Why can't I homeschool Sarah? Surely I can manage teaching kindergarten for three months. Adding the thought of living with Kissie for a while and having her around to take care of us makes the idea so lovely that the more I think about it, the better it becomes. I grab my cell phone and run out to the car to call Virgy. It's a topic that might be better discussed away from Kissie. I sit down in the front seat and dial her number.

"I've got a great idea," I say, as soon as she answers.

"What?"

"First off, I called Jameson and there's no way Sarah can start until the fall."

"I'm not at all surprised," she says bluntly.

"It kind of makes me mad, actually, after Daddy paid for thirteen years of tuition."

"Oh forget it. You've got plenty of other stuff to make you mad. What's your great idea?"

"I'm thinking of homeschooling," I say, feeling more and more proud of myself.

Silence.

"Are you there?"

"I'm here," she says.

"Why aren't you saying anything?" I say.

"Because I'm trying to remember when you went back to college for a degree in education."

"*Virginia*." I'm nervously tapping the steering wheel.

"What?"

"There are only three more months left of school. It's *kindergarten*," I tell her.

"Do you honestly think you're the homeschooling type?"

"Maybe."

"Poor Fiery. She's temporarily lost her mind."

"I have not. What's wrong with homeschooling?"

Virginia's back to the silent treatment.

"I'm serious."

"Dogwood Elementary is supposedly a real good school out in Germantown. Just rent yourself a house near there. Or send them to Germantown Elementary. Either one."

"What do you have against homeschooling?"

"Nothing. It's . . . it's just not for me. I can tell you that," Virginia says.

"It might be for me."

"Tell me something. How are you going to support yourself and homeschool Sarah? Don't you have to get a job?"

Upon hearing the *J* word, the reality of my life screeches back in and swaps places with the denial that has been taking up residence for years. "Details, details," I say with truthful resignation.

"Details, details," Virgy's voice mocks back at me.

I lean back against the headrest and sigh. "I'm getting mad at Baker again."

"See, I told you that you had plenty to be mad about."

The idea of living with Kissie seems to be fading fast. I would have lived with her, though, despite what anyone else says or thinks. "Why don't you go with me today to look for a rental house?"

"I wish I could but I don't have a sitter. I doubt you'll want three extra little children tagging along with us."

"Probably not."

"Just call me when you get back. Will Kissie keep Sarah and Issie or do you need to bring them over?"

"They can stay here."

"Okay, get going and call me later. I can't wait to hear all about it."

I hang up with Virginia and sit in the car a moment longer. The more I think about it, she's right. Considering the small amount of money Baker sends every month, I do have to go back to work. And heaven knows I'd never want to be the cause of Sarah being unprepared for first grade at Jameson. Homeschooling probably is not the most realistic option. Okay. Decision made. I will rent a house in Germantown and put Sarah in school. She started kindergarten at a public school in Vermont; I suppose she might as well finish the year at one.

When I get back inside, Kissie's left arm is wrapped around Issie who is hanging on her hip. She's holding a fork in her right hand, scrambling eggs.

"How is Kissie suppose to cook, baby girl?" I say, reaching out for her.

Issie moves over into my arms while Kissie finishes. By the looks of the food she's preparing, you'd think she's feeding the whole neighborhood. Besides the eggs, pancakes, sausage, and grits, there's a big bowl of fruit on the counter.

"Will you please put cheese in my eggs?" Issie says.

"Of course I will, baby." Kissie has to turn sideways to get past us on her way to the fridge. "Y'all sit down. The table's already set."

I put Issie at one of Kissie's dining room chairs but not before covering the seat with a kitchen towel and a couple of the old phone books she never throws away. "Breakfast is ready, Sarah," I call, as I'm getting Issie settled. She runs in and finds her own spot at the table.

Once all the food is ready, Kissie places the feast, which is on big platters, in the middle of the table. After she's finally seated at the head of her table, she asks Sarah to say grace and we bow our heads.

"God is great, God is good, let us thank Him for our food. And for Kissie," Sarah says, in her cherubic prayer voice.

I raise my head and notice Kissie's head is still bowed. "And Lawd," she says, "I thank you for bringin' my babies home safe. Please help Leelee today. She has so much ahead of her and needs that peace that surpasses all understandin'. And please Lawd, bless my body so I can have the strength to always be a help to her. In Jesus' name I pray. A-men."

"Amen. This looks delicious," I say, spreading my paper napkin across my lap. "Thank you for making this beautiful meal. Isn't Kissie the best cook in the world?" I look over at the girls just in time to grab the bottle of maple syrup out of Sarah's hand. She has just poured half a cup onto her plate and her pancakes are now floating. As I'm dripping the syrup on top of Issie's pancake she says, "I sure miss Gracie. When are we gonna get another puppy, Mommy?"

"You said we could get one as soon as we move to Memphis," Sarah adds. "And we're in Memphis."

"I said we'd get one as soon as we're settled. It wouldn't be fair to Kissie to bring a dog into her house."

"Why? Don't you like dogs?" Sarah asks Kissie, with a big bite of pancake in her mouth and syrup dripping off her bottom lip.

"Honey, please don't talk with food in your mouth," I say, and pat her lips with my napkin.

Kissie, who has enough food on her plate to feed all four of us says, "I like dogs. I just don't have a place to put one. There ain't a fence in my backyard."

"We could build you one," Sarah says, innocently.

Once Sarah's comment sinks in, Kissie explodes in hysterics. Her hearty, infectious laughter bubbles up from the depths of her gut—a window to her inner joy. She lightly slaps the table. Already I'm grinning with her. "You gonna build Kissie a fence? That's so sweet, baby." I'm sure the image of Sarah and me operating a post-hole digger is better comedy than anything she sees on TV.

"Then why don't you get a hamster?" Issie says, with a squeal. "You could keep his cage in your bedroom."

Kissie nearly falls off her chair. That one little remark from Issie puts her over the edge and she holds her stomach, rocking back and forth in her spot at the table. I'm forever amazed at her ability to derive joy from the smallest of things. She calls it the "Fruit of the Spirit" and says that I can have it, too. All I need to do, she says, is dedicate my life to the Lord.

Of course it's impossible for me to watch the tears streaming down Kissie's face and not double over myself. And hearing my daughters laugh along with us reminds me of how Kissie describes heaven.

"There's gonna be music with singin' and dancin', and lots and lots of laughin'," she's always telling me. "The Lawd gonna make sure of that. Heaven gonna be full a' all the things that make us happy."

Summer had barely started when a man dressed in a business suit rang our front doorbell. My parents, who weren't home that day, had taught me never to answer the door by myself so I followed behind Kissie into the foyer. She peeked through the side window aligning the front door and instead of opening it she paused and looked at the floor, as if she was considering not answering at all. Several moments passed before she finally cracked the door, using her body as a shield between the outside and me.

From the sound of Kissie's voice I knew something was horribly wrong. "There's a speed limit on this street," she said, muttering "hm, hm, hm" *over and over, as if she were disgusted with the person on the other side of the door.*

"I'm sorry, ma'am," a male voice said. "She ran out in front of me."

Panic crept all over me, an emotion I had not yet felt as an eight-year-old. I clutched Kissie's waist. "What's wrong? Kissie, what's wrong? Is it Daisy?" A ten-pound white fur ball with big black eyes, she was a birthday gift from Daddy—a Bijon from the litter of one of his clients.

"Wait just a minute, baby," she said, turning around. "I'm tryin' to talk."

"Can I help you? I feel terrible about this," the man said.

"Just leave her right there on the step. No, second thought, wait here, please. I'll be right back."

Kissie grabbed my hand and pulled me along with her.

"What's wrong with Daisy? What's wrong with Daisy?" When Kissie didn't answer, I started to wail. I tried collapsing on the floor but she wouldn't let me. She held on to my hand and dragged me out to the garage, searching through a pile of rubbish. When she spotted a box, she held it with her left hand, all the while clutching my hand in her right so tightly; it would have been impossible for me to move, impossible for me to run away to the front porch. When we got back into the house, she instructed me to sit on the couch in the den and not move a

muscle. The tone of her voice was stern. It confused me, but because of it I minded her. I could hear her in the entrance hall, whispering to the stranger. "If you put her in the box, that would help us quite a bit. I don't want my little white girl to see her dog layin' there dead. Hm, hm, hm."

"I'm very sorry, ma'am," the man said.

"Well, all right then." Kissie shut the door and hurried back into the den. She sat down on the couch and scooped me into her arms. "Daisy's in heaven, Leelee."

Pulling away from her I flailed my legs, kicking and screaming, crying so hard I wailed with each sob. Pretty soon I had sucked up enough air to keep me gasping for each breath. Kissie pulled me onto her lap. Rocking me back and forth, she patted my head and pushed the hair away from my watery face. With the lapel of her uniform she wiped away my tears as I pressed into her bosom. "You'll see her again one day, baby. She's much happier now, anyway. She's up there with the Lawd. Runnin' around, barkin', no cars to worry 'bout." Kissie's smile took up most of her face. "Nobody gonna tell her she cain't."

"I want to go there," I told her, when I saw how happy she looked. "I want to be in heaven with Daisy."

"I know, baby. But it ain't your time."

"When is my time?" I asked between sobs.

"Only the Lawd knows that." She kept rocking and rocking until my sobs turned into whimpers.

Just thinking about Daisy and Gracie, and having to bury them both is almost enough to keep me from sinking my heart back into another dog. But the only way over one is to love another. That I know for sure. Just like the birth of your first child, it's hard to imagine that you'll ever love another as much as you love the first, but of course you do. And I will.

Once I've helped Kissie clear the table and wash the breakfast dishes I settle back down at her dining room table, determined to find us a place to live. After circling several homes in the For Rent section of *The Commercial Appeal*, I set up three appointments to see houses in the Germantown area—having decided to take Virgy's advice and pick a house in a neighborhood with a good school. Growing up, Germantown used to be considered "the country." Mary Jule and I rode horses out there and only a handful of people from Jameson School lived out there, but today it's considered a suburb. For the most part my friends live in East Memphis or Midtown. Unfortunately though, some of the elementary schools around there leave a little to be desired. So moving out to Germantown is my only option, for the next few months anyway.

After placing a large basket of freshly dried towels on the floor next to the table, Kissie pulls out a chair, sits down next to me and starts folding. She can tell I'm frustrated because I sigh loudly after hanging up the phone and run my fingers through my already unruly hair.

"One thing about life is always true. Things are always changin'," she says. "You don't have to live there forever. Just do what you need to do right now for your little girls."

"I know. You're right. You're always right," I say, and bury my face in my hands.

"The Lawd will bless you for puttin' them first." Kissie stretches one of her fluffy yellow bath towels and expertly pinches the corners together.

"I'm gonna start calling you Aristotle," I tell her.

"No, baby, I don't want that name."

"How come? Aristotle was a genius."

"That might be but he thought women weren't fully human," she says matter-of-factly as she plops the perfectly creased towel on the table.

"What!" I sit up in the chair.

"That's right."

"How do you know that?"

"I read it somewhere. I may not have a degree but when I read somethin' I never forget it. You know my memory is just like an elephant's," she says, snapping the wind out of one of the towels.

I make a mental note to look up Aristotle and check the validity of Kissie's claim. Then I change my mind. She always knows what she's talking about.

Right after lunch, Kissie keeps the girls while I head out to Germantown to check out the rentals. The first house I tour is drab and depressing. A faint mildew odor permeates the air the second I step inside. After living in BO-infested surroundings in Vermont for fourteen months and endlessly ridding the Inn of Helga's lingering cigarette aroma, there is no way I would ever entertain the idea of living in a stinky house. It has to smell good on the front end or "nothing doing" as Mama used to say. To Daddy, the man who bragged about having "the keenest olfactory senses known to man," there was nothing worse than a home with houseitosis. I'll never forget the time he helped me search for my first house. When the real estate agent escorted us to the front door of a little home on Alexander, Daddy, dressed to the nines in his custom-tailored suit and cashmere overcoat, stepped inside the foyer, turned to the woman and said, "I'll meet you back at the car, thank you very much. I don't want to go back to the office smelling like mothball soup."

The second house, only a couple of blocks from the first, is not much better. In fact it's even more dark and dingy on the inside, making me think both of the houses must have been taken off the market and turned into rentals because they were too hard to sell. Discouragement reeks from every corner. Thinking about the house I left in Memphis before we moved to Vermont, I'm not sure how I can't be discouraged. That bright, cheery, odor-free house, only a few blocks from all of my best friends, is fifteen miles away in the other direction, now occupied by happy people living my Memphis dream.

The unfairness nearly keeps me from starting the car and moving on but I've already set up the third appointment. I figure I might as well go ahead and keep it—this one can't be much worse than the first two. *They are rental houses,* I keep telling myself. *Don't be expecting perfection.*

Ten minutes later, I pull up in the circular driveway of 2247 Glendale Cove and from the driveway, the view actually isn't bad. The small front porch has a nice wooden Chippendale-style railing on either side of the steps. Boxwoods run across the front of the home and there's even a picture window off to one side. Two dormer windows poke out of the black shingle roof, which appears to be a story and a half. I know from the ad that the home has three bedrooms and two and a half baths.

Since the owner has yet to arrive, I walk around back. There's a nice backyard, fenced for a pet, and there's even a swing set. It's old and a bit rusty, that's for sure, but at least it exists. The best parts about the house are that it's affordable, it's in the Dogwood Elementary School district, and pets are allowed.

Once the owner arrives and shows me around the house, I'm positive that this is the place for us. The three bedrooms are downstairs next to one another and there's a nice-size kitchen with a large picture window that looks out over the quiet cove. Not too many cars passing by—a perfect situation for little ones. Upstairs has a large attic and a big playroom that sits over the garage in the back. There's a living room and dining room just off the wide foyer and a small half bath. Carpeting runs all through the downstairs. I'd have preferred hardwood floors but if that's the worst part of it, I can certainly live with beige rugs.

I write out a check for the first month's rent plus a deposit and the owner hands me two keys. What a relief. While it may not be "home, sweet home" yet, at least the moving van now has an address to deliver my belongings.

Before returning to Kissie's, and after a stop at Dinstuhl's candy store for a white chocolate chunk, I head over to Seessel's grocery to fill my new pantry. Seessel's went out of business years ago, it's actually called Schnucks now, but in the same way that I call Macy's, Goldsmith's, I'm never going to be able to stop calling Schnucks, Seessel's. Extinct hometown landmarks die a slow death, especially in the South.

I leave my shopping cart for just a second and as I'm returning with an armload of items I forgot from the previous aisle, I notice there's a woman trying to get past my cart, where I've left it a little too far into the middle. By the time I recognize the face, though, it's too late to turn around. Cissy Green, the absolute last person on earth that I'd ever want to see—well, besides Tootie Shotwell—is looking dead at me. Her perfect taupe-eye-shadowed eyes bug out of her head when she sees who's at the other end of the displaced cart. "*Leelee?*" she says, with perfectly executed astonishment, as if she hadn't already heard through the grapevine that I had returned to town, with no Baker, no job and—well, thank the Lord I have a house now . . .

I feel my hand flitter in a fake, glad-to-see-you wave, and already know a polite smile is creeping onto my face.

"What in the world? I thought you were in Vermont?" she says, with a phony shrill to her voice.

"I *was* in Vermont, Cissy. But I'm so happy to be back in Memphis. The Northeast is overrated; let me tell you." I can hear myself babbling even though my insides are screaming at me to *shut up*! Even *I* think my voice sounds obnoxious.

"Why? What happened? I thought—"

I interrupt her on purpose. I can't take whatever it is she might say next. "The girls and I *froze* the entire time we lived there. It's just hard to be Southern and live that far up there. Last month it never got above negative five for three weeks straight. Can you believe that?" I exaggerate a tad. But I need her to think that my move home was all about the weather.

"I had no *idea* it got that cold," she says, with emphasis on "idea," as if I had just suggested the formula for permanent Botox.

"Me, neither. I can promise you that. Alaska maybe, but the continental United States? It never once crossed my mind."

"What does Baker think about it? I mean he was all gung ho to move. Is he okay about coming back?"

"Oh, he's dealing with it." Again, not entirely a lie . . . but certainly not the whole story. Why on earth can't I just tell her the truth?

She pushes on. "I remember somebody telling me he was sick of the insurance business and that was the reason he wanted to move away. Will he go back to Allstate with Mr. Satterfield?"

"It's actually Satterfield State Farm. And we aren't sure yet." At least *that* was the truth.

"Well, he'll be great at whatever he does."

Baker gets all kinds of passes because he's good-looking and a former UT football star . . . one of the many perks of Southern football majesty. The truth of the matter is Cissy cares way more about Baker than she does me, it's *his* happiness she's after.

"Oh, yes. Baker is great at lots of things," I say, knowing that list now includes cheating on your wife and abandoning two daughters. If there could be a way that I could make my cell phone ring right at this moment I would give up my right baby toe. Since it doesn't, I take matters into my own hands. "Cissy, do you happen to know what time it is?"

She glances at her diamond Rolex Oyster Perpetual. "One thirty."

"Oh my gosh, I'm late. I have to have Issie to a doctor's appointment in fifteen minutes. I've got to run *right now.* Bye Cissy, good to see you." I back up my cart and turn around and leave it, two aisles over. I'll do my shopping closer to Kissie's house where I, the great liar, can be completely anonymous.

I grab my cell to call Alice and whisper into the phone as I'm exiting the store. "It's starting."

"What's starting?"

"I just ran into Cissy Green, of all people. She kept trying to dig all the scoop out of me she could get. What am I going to do when people start finding out that Baker and I have split up? And even worse that he has a fifty-year-old girlfriend with silicone implants. Or maybe they're saline. How can you tell the difference anyway?"

"One is softer than the other. You know, better to the touch," she says.

"Well shoot, Alice, I didn't manage to fondle her boob while I had the chance . . . what with trying to keep our livelihood intact I forgot to feel up my husband's mistress." My sarcasm reeks of wounded pride.

"Leelee, listen. You're gonna hold your head up and deal with it. Who cares?"

"*I* do. I hate my life."

"Don't ever say that again. Everything is gonna be fine in the long run. It's hard as hell right now but you'll be yesterday's news tomorrow."

I start to protest when she butts in, "Leelee, you have five more seconds of this pity party and then I have to pick up the children from mother's day out. Miss Becky passes out candy like it's as healthy as spinach and I have to save my patience for whatever sugar rush they're on."

"You're right, you're right."

We hang up, laughing, and as I'm running out to my car I hear my name called from across the parking lot. Acting as if I don't hear the person, I bolt inside my car, my heart running so fast it might as well be the engine. There's no telling how many cell phone calls Cissy Green has already dialed from the inside of Seessel's, and I know all too well the rate of speed at which Dixie gossip blasts down the highway. Just as I ram the gearshift in reverse, I hear a knock on my window. I want to pretend I don't see the person for fear it's another Baker-lover but I notice Natalie Walker's kind smile in my peripheral view. We graduated together at Jameson and she's as nice a person as you could ever find. I roll down my window and hug her through the opening.

"Hi, sweetie," she says, genuinely happy to see me. She was at my going-away luncheon and would have to be burning at the stake before she'd ever say a mean word about me or anyone else. Something about her gentle hug and soothing voice brings tears to my eyes. The Cissy Green incident shook me senseless. "Are you okay?" she asks.

"*No.*" I sit back in my seat, feeling the tears pour down my cheeks. She hurries around to the other side of my car and I toss all the junk from the passenger seat into the back between the girls' car seats to make room for her.

Natalie reaches over and wraps her arms around me once she sits down. "What is it, Leelee?"

There's no sense in lying again—so I let loose. "Vermont was a disaster. It didn't go well from the minute we arrived. The move turned out to be catastrophic for our marriage." I pull away from her and look her in the eye. "Baker and I split up."

Natalie's face contorts into a grimace. "Ohhhh, sweetie, I'm sorry." She nervously nods her head up and down. Here she thought she was coming over to say hi to an old friend and now she must feel as uncomfortable as a portly girl lying out with a bunch of size fours at the beach.

"I'm sorry for crying," I stutter in between embarrassing sobs.

"Don't be silly. It's okay. Is there a way I can help you?"

"There's nothing you can do, Natalie, but I appreciate it." I'm nervously rubbing the leather on the steering wheel when something reminds me of how well connected she and her husband are in town and it gives me an idea. "Actually, there might be something." I look in my rearview mirror and notice the mascara smudges under my eyes. "Oh look at me. I'm frightful."

Natalie reaches over and gently pushes my face away from the mirror. "No you are not. Now tell me what I can do."

I fumble around for a Kleenex and all I can find is a dirty McDonald's napkin lodged in between the seats. It's been stepped on and is full of grime but without a better option, I spit onto a corner and gently pat the mascara away from under my eyes. "I need to work," I say through sniffles, turning my head toward her. "As soon as possible. You and Tim know everyone in town. If you hear of any job openings will you please let me know?"

"Of course I will. I don't know of any right offhand but I'll think about it."

"Preferably somewhere fun. I mean, I don't mind working. Honestly. I've just run a restaurant all by myself. Well, actually, I had a partner but that's another story. With all that's gone on, I can't help but wish I could just work at a place where I would feel excited about getting up in the morning."

"What's your degree in? Remind me."

"Communications."

"Oh sure. Ole Miss?"

I nod my head.

"Tim works in TV. You know WZCQ down in Midtown? He's the sales manager there."

"I'd forgotten that," I say, a glimmer of hope returning.

"It houses FM 99 and AM 59, too. Would you like him to check to see if there are any openings?" she says, with genuine interest.

"Yes! That would be great."

"Okay, what's the best number to reach you on?"

We exchange cell phone numbers and promise to get together in the next week or two.

"We'll find you a job, sweetie. Don't you worry," she says.

I hug her once more and watch as she walks to her car. Why can't there be more Natalie Walkers and less Cissy Greens in this city? For gosh sakes.

Later that afternoon, no more than two hours after leaving Natalie, my phone rings. I'm driving back to Kissie's after slipping into a Kroger closer to her house. I grab my cell, in hopes of seeing a certain Vermonter's number, but am disappointed when the area code reads "901"—Memphis. I answer anyway. "Hello."

"Hi Leelee, it's Tim Walker. How are you, girl?"

"Hi Tim, I'm fine. How are you?"

"I'm great. Doing fine. Natalie says you need a job." He's down to business but friendly.

"I do. I *really* do."

"They need an assistant over on the FM side here at ZCQ. You'd be answering phones, handing out prizes—you know, the items that people call in to win on the radio?"

"Sure. I won a prize on the radio once. But it was a long time ago."

"You'd do a lot of that and some administrative work. Plus you'd be assisting the program director and the promotions director. Sound like something you might be interested in?"

"Definitely," I reply, hoping my desperation doesn't sound too unprofessional.

"I don't know how much the pay is, but I do know it's the kind of place where you can work hard and move up in the company."

"That sounds great, thank you so much, Tim."

"No problem. Glad to help you."

Tim told me to call an Edward Maxwell to set up an interview. I jot down his phone number on a piece of scratch paper I find in the console. "I'll call him when we hang up," I say.

"Okie doke. Hope it works out. Lemme know."

"I sure will. Thanks so much, Tim."

"My pleasure."

After hanging up with Tim I almost want to scream I'm so happy. I'm confident I could be wonderful at that kind of work. I have a real love for music and to be among radio and music personalities sounds like a dream job. WZCQ is always throwing rooftop parties at the Peabody Hotel and their promotions van seems to be everywhere—car dealerships, Memphis in May, charity events. My mood lifts just thinking about the job. I hang up from Tim and call Mr. Maxwell right away.

After talking with him, I agree to come in for an interview. I'm intrigued to meet him; during the phone conversation he sounded a bit strange, arrogant almost. After working for Helga, I'm determined not to have another boss who makes my life miserable. That said, lord knows I need a job, so I really can't be too choosy.

Ed tells me that he needs a copy of my résumé, which I decide to drop off first thing in the morning. I could email it but I don't want to chance it ending up in his spam folder. It's six years old. I know what I'll be doing till the wee hours of the morning.

Wednesday afternoon I walk in the front door of WZCQ for my interview, oh my goodness five minutes late, and I feel a mixture of excitement and anxiety. After checking in with Jane, the receptionist who I had met earlier when I dropped off my résumé, I take a seat on one of the outdated couches in the lobby. A man wearing dark makeup walks by and says hello with a deep, familiar voice. It's Stuart Southard, the weatherman on channel 12. A regular Memphis celebrity. I get a little warm in the cheeks and involuntarily smile; I can't help but be a wee bit starstruck.

"Ms. Satterfield?" Jane says, after I've been seated for ten minutes or so. "You can go back now. Straight down the hall to the left and you'll run right into the FM 99 offices. Good luck!" If the size of her smile could determine my chances of getting the job, I'd be a shoo-in.

"Thank you." I grab my purse and the folder containing an extra copy of my résumé, hot off the presses, and head down the hall, my mind ablaze. I'm already fretting about how much this job might pay, combined with doubts about my alimony arrangement with Baker. I'm still not so sure I made a good decision, opting for a quick solution with less compensation rather than a long, painful negotiation with a bigger settlement. If Daddy were alive, he would have made sure I hired the finest lawyer in town and had run Baker across county lines. Since that wasn't the case, I'm living with the fact that I have to be away from Sarah and Issie all day long because of money.

As I'm wandering around shyly, not knowing where I'm headed, a rather cute-looking guy stops me. "Can I help you?" he asks.

"Yes, thank you. I'm here to see Edward Maxwell. I have an interview at one." I glance at my watch and see it's one fifteen. "Actually, I've been waiting in the lobby for a while. I was here right at a couple minutes past."

He shrugs his shoulders before a well-rehearsed smile spreads across his face. "Hi, I'm Paul." I'd know his voice anywhere. He's the afternoon deejay at FM 99.

"Nice to meet you," I say.

"I'll get Edward for you." He disappears down another hall and leaves me standing in a small area with a coffeemaker and fridge. It's not really a break room; it seems to be more of a reception area. I sit down on one of the chairs with a black plastic seat and steel frame and glance around the room. The walls are lined with gold and platinum records stacked on top of each other and running all the way down the hall. I recognize Bon Jovi's gorgeous face from across the room and can't resist the urge to walk over and inspect it.

Presented to WZCQ FM 99 to Commemorate
RIAA Certified Sales of More Than 500,000 Copies of the
Mercury Records Album *Slippery When Wet.*

Each plaque says the same thing but with a different artist and record. Bonnie Raitt's *Nick of Time,* Tom Petty and the Heartbreakers' *Full Moon Fever,* Don Henley's *The End of the Innocence,* Kim Carnes's *Mistaken Identity,* Bette Midler's *Beaches.* Mariah Carey's *Mariah Carey*—they all bring back a flurry of memories and without realizing it, I've traveled quite a ways down the hall inspecting them. The sound of a man's voice startles me away from thoughts of the past.

"Miss Satterfield?"

I whip my head around.

"Hi. Edward Maxwell." He smiles, sort of, and keeps his hands at his side.

Smiling back, I instinctively offer mine. "Hi Edward. Nice to meet you."

After a weak shake he says, "Come on back," and turns down another hall, which is lined with even more gold records and award plaques. Edward doesn't walk alongside me; instead he's keeping pace in front. We pass a large window that lends a full view of the broadcast room and as I stroll down the hall of a radio station that has been around since the forties, I'm struck by how rich the music scene truly is in Memphis, Tennessee. I suppose, having grown up here, I've taken it for granted all these years. Beale Street was the birth of the blues, for goodness sake. And between B.B. King, Stax Records, Sun Studio, Elvis, Carl Perkins, and Jerry Lee Lewis, Memphis has as much to brag about as Los Angeles or even New York for that matter. Why in the world we lost the Rock and Roll Hall of Fame to Cleveland, Ohio, is still a mystery to me.

Once Edward reaches his office door he heads on in front of me. When I finally arrive he gestures toward a chair in front of his desk and asks me to take a seat. "Pretty cool, huh?" he says, as he's walking behind his desk.

"Excuse me?"

"The gold records. The platinum records. All the awards."

"Oh. Yes! Wow. Y'all have so many."

After sitting in his chair, he scoots himself all the way up so he can rest his elbows on the desk. "That's what happens when you're number one. No lonely number there."

I tilt my head a little to the side.

"Three Dog Night?"

"Oh! Sure. 'One Is the Loneliest Number.'"

"If you hadn't known that one, this would have gone to the bottom of the pile." He holds up my résumé, which is in the center of his desk. "You've passed the first test."

"That's a relief," I say, and mean it.

Edward combs his short but full beard and peers down at my résumé. "You went to Ole Miss?" He looks up with a blank expression on his face. "I've heard that's a big party school."

"Well, sure. It had its moments." *That's an odd question.* "But I didn't do all that much partying." Okay, I lied.

The combing of his beard continues. "How fast do you type?"

"I think about forty words per minute. I took typing in college and I'm actually pretty good at it."

"This job would be answering the phone calls that come into the station. You'd be assisting me and the promotion director, who you'll meet before you leave." Every time he lists a job responsibility, he holds up another finger. "You'd distribute the prizes to the contest winners." *One finger.* "You'd coordinate with traffic and make sure they have all the info the jocks need." *Two fingers.*

I look a bit confused at the term "traffic."

"The traffic department generates a daily log that lists everything from the songs that will be played during a certain shift, to the ads that will air, to the station promo spots, to the live ads the jocks read. That kind of thing. In short, the jocks need a log that tells them exactly what's going on during the day. They need to know precisely what time to give away a certain prize." He drops his voice to a slightly elevated whisper. "Jocks are basically idiots. We have to give them the ABCs of everything. Tell them what they need to keep the contests straight."

That's rude, I wish I could say.

"You'd be sending out FedEx packages." More listing on his fingers, we're at three fingers and a thumb now. "Plus you'd be helping me with my letters and stuff. Do you have a problem with getting coffee?"

"No," I say, shaking my head. Lie number two.

"Just kidding." He breaks into a frightful smile, his full cherry-red lips have several wrinkles, resembling sun-dried tomatoes in between his mustache and beard.

I have to force a grin.

"Does the job sound like something you'd be interested in?"

"Absolutely. It's exactly what I'm looking for." I lean in toward him. "I'm really good with people and I'm honest." Well, I may have lied about not partying much in school and not minding getting coffee, but basically I am very honest.

"Okay, let's give it a chance. I'll send you upstairs to HR and you can talk to Janice about benefits. We have the usual. Health, dental, and life as an option. 401(k) matching after you're vested—that's five years, I think."

"Honestly? You're offering me the job, already?" I say, without thinking. Uh-oh, I hope I didn't sound too eager.

"Careful, this trial period is part two of the test."

"What's part two?"

"How quick you are. You don't look like a blonde to me."

I practically have to bite the sides of mouth to force out another grin.

"I'm assuming a redhead can add some fire to the job. I'm giving you a chance to prove yourself."

What a total weirdo. "Well, thank you. I appreciate that. I do a very good job."

"The job pays thirteen an hour. That's $27,040 a year if you work a full forty-hour week . . ." I tune him out as he goes on to discuss vacation days and sick time and personal leave and dress code. All I can focus on is that I have a job offer.

Okay. I'll take it. But shouldn't I be negotiating my pay? Isn't that what educated people do? Yes, of course it is. I'll play hard-to-get and try to act like they'd be lucky to have me. *Just say it. Ask for more money. Do it. DO IT.*

"You said the job pays thirteen an hour, right?"

"I did."

"Actually, thirteen dollars an hour . . ." I'm scratching my head. "Thirteen dollars an hour is . . ."

"All I'm going to pay. Take it or leave it."

"Oh! I was just hesitating because I wanted to tell you how nice that is. Thank you, Edward. I'm thrilled to get that kind of salary." *Way to go, Leelee—that showed him. Lord, Sarah would have negotiated better.*

"Oh and one more very important rule. We have quite a few celebrities who come in an out of this station. There's no room for star fu—uh, stargazing. I don't want my staff hounding the stars."

"I understand. I'm not like that anyway."

"It's a real no-no, Leelee. I don't run that kind of ship."

"No worries at all, Edward."

"So when can you start? Can you be here at eight thirty Monday morning?"

I'm so not ready for this. How in the world will I ever get the girls dressed, fed, and ready for school, and be in Midtown by eight thirty? But it's not like I have a choice—I have to have a job. And I'm certainly fortunate to have found one so quickly.

"So you'll start Monday?"

"Yes. Of course I'll start Monday. That's no problem at all!" Lie number three, or four—I can't keep track—comes out easily and with high-pitched enthusiasm. What the heck? That's only five days from now. Of *course* I can have my rental house completely unpacked, Sarah and Issie enrolled in school, and my new life completely figured out in that amount of time.

"Before you head up to Janice, I'll introduce you to Kyle. He's my promotion director."

"Okay, sure. I'd like to meet him."

Once again I trail behind Edward Maxell on the way to Kyle's office. The man walks so fast it's hard to catch up. I decide not to even try. Kyle is sweet, probably about my age, not much to look at but he's a frosty bottle of Coke compared to the program director. That Edward is an odd bird. Oh *boy* is he an odd bird. And that might be the nicest thing anyone's ever said about him.

Chapter Four

Moving day arrives, bright and early on a Saturday morning, and it's mixed with all kinds of emotions. It makes me happy to think that I'll be settled again in a home that's all mine. A home where the girls don't have to whisper. A home where there's no wicked witch waiting on the other side of a flimsy door ready to bite their heads off for raising their voices. But, I'm moving into a bedroom all alone. No husband with whom to share my bed, to reach over and pull me close, stroke my hair, share our love. I haven't been sleeping alone for nine years. And even during those last months in Vermont, I may have been alone, but Peter was always close by in the kitchen, not to mention in my thoughts.

As I'm dressing for the day, I'm struck by the fact that I've been home for five days now and haven't heard a word from Peter. Something is not right. It's not like him to ignore my phone call . . . phone calls, really. At the very least he'd want to tell me he's glad that Sarah, Issie, and I made it back safely. It doesn't make sense.

Before I know it I've let my mind run away with me, conjuring up all kinds of neurotic scenarios. I'm picturing him stranded on the backside of a black diamond with a broken leg, screaming for someone to rescue him. That boy can ski anywhere, and he ventures into uncharted areas where he has no business. Maybe he sped too fast over a patch of black ice—I was always telling him to slow down. That little truck of his doesn't have enough weight in the back to warrant speeding down a bunny slope much less a mountain. Oh gosh, suppose he hit a moose?

If he's in the hospital somewhere he'll wonder why in the world I haven't checked on him. What's the matter with me? Punching in his number, I dial it so quickly that the line doesn't connect, causing me to have to hang up and start over. My fingers are practically shaking as I dial again. After four rings, there's still no answer. And then . . . voice mail. *What?* He should be answering his phone. It's—I glance at my watch—7:30 A.M. in Vermont. Uh-oh, that's way too early to call a chef who works nights.

Even still, I leave a message trying hard not to sound desperate. "Hey, it's me," I say, my voice happy and shrill. "Gosh. I, I'm just checking on you. The girls and I are here. We made it safe and sound. Kissie's helping me to move into a new house this morning. It's nice and spacious with *plenty of room for guests*. Hey"—I lower my tone—"will you please call me? I want to know you're all right. You know how my head gets going, worrying about things that might not be true. I want to make sure Helga hasn't hijacked you and forced you to become her boy toy. Now that's an image I'm sure you'd rather not have planted in your brain," I say, with a giggle. "Seriously, call me. I can't wait to talk to you."

After hanging up the phone I analyze every word I said. It sounded motherly. Too desperate. He'll think the joke about Helga was stupid. On the other hand, my lightheartedness might convince him to dial my number. Oh lord, Peter. Please just call me back.

Kissie and I drop off Sarah and Issie at Virgy's so we can be at the new rental house by seven, or at least soon thereafter. There's a whole lot of cleaning to be done before we meet the movers who are due to arrive around ten.

After kissing the girls good-bye and shutting Virgy's antique mahogany front door, I notice Kissie in the passenger seat as I walk back to the car. No matter what I say to try and convince her to stop wearing her white uniform, she won't do it. I tell her all the time that it's old-fashioned and completely unnecessary and that I want her to be comfortable when she's at my house but it doesn't do any good. She insists on wearing a white dress with three-quarter-length sleeves and a puckered waistband in the back that she's spent time ironing the night before. Her hose are wrinkled around the ankles, and she wears white, lace-up orthopedic shoes, which are bulging over the outsides of the soles, just as they always have been. You can't cook like she does and not keep on an extra few pounds—and heaven help anyone who mentions dieting. There aren't enough *hmm, hmm, hmms* in the world to express how Kissie feels about restrictive eating. When she bends over too far, her white girdle shows. It extends way down on her thighs, which can't help but bubble out around it. It's the kind of girdle with snaps to hold up her stockings. I bought her a pair of tennis shoes for her birthday three years ago and although she was ecstatic when she opened them, she won't dare put them on unless she's in her own home.

For the last sixteen years, she's been out at her mailbox waiting on the postman the exact day her Social Security check is due to arrive. I try to pay her when she's helping me but she flat refuses to take my money. "We are family, Leelee," she tells me. "I ain't takin' no money to help you move, or to take care of your little girls. You ain't got no mama; no daddy, neither. Who else is gonna help you? Alice and them have their own hands full. They've got their own children. They can help you sometimes, but ole Kissie is here for you all the time."

That leaves me no choice but to go out and buy her groceries. Or sneak and pay her light bill. Or ask to take her car when we go out and fill it up when she's buying her toiletries in Walgreens. The truth is, if she charged for it, her loyalty and support would bankrupt me and there's no currency besides love to repay all that she's done.

Kissie's not spent much time in Germantown and as we drive down Poplar Avenue she's taking in the sights. Every once in a while she'll make a comment. "I catered a party one time down that street there," or "that's the nursery where your daddy bought that dogwood tree that stayed in our front yard on East Chickasaw Parkway." I love to take her driving, it reminds me of when I was a little girl and Daddy would take us all out for a Sunday drive, which always included a trip to our family plot at the cemetery. He and Mama would be in the front seat and Grandmama, Kissie, and I would be in the back. Looking back on it now, it makes me wonder when Kissie ever got a weekend off.

When we pull up in the driveway on Glendale Cove, Kissie oohs and ahhs. That's until she gets inside. My new rental house is nice but it's certainly not clean. At the last second before leaving her house, Kissie remembered her Hoover. That's after we had already put her broom, mop, toilet wand, and all kinds of cleaning supplies in my car. If it weren't for Kissie, I'd have no idea how to cook, clean, or remove any sort of stain out of a blouse. She's the one who taught me that hot water sets a stain—a fact that got me through college at Ole Miss and then through two messy toddlers.

With a deadline fast approaching, we get right to work—starting first with the foyer, and then moving deeper into the home. After we clean the bathrooms, I head on in to the kitchen to start lining the cabinets with shelf paper. Kissie's in the front living room vacuuming when she spots the big eighteen-wheeler out the front window. "Movin' van is here, baby," she hollers, after turning off the motor.

"Just in the nick of time," I say, under my breath, dashing out the front door to meet the two men in the driveway. I direct the movers while Kissie finishes lining the kitchen cabinets. "You need to get your kitchen done first," she says. "Your little girls need three meals a day." Each time she gets another box marked "Kitchen" Kissie has it unpacked in minutes.

Once the movers finally set down the last piece of furniture, right at four hours later, I write them out a check and shut the door. Kissie and I collapse on two of the wooden chairs at my breakfast room table.

"How 'bout a Coke?" I ask her, knowing that the first thing she stocked in the fridge was two six-packs of the little green-bottled Cokes. "Let's rest a second before we make lunch."

"That sounds delicious, baby." She slightly pushes her chair away from the table.

I clutch her arm. "I'll get it. Don't you move a muscle." I'm halfway to the fridge when I remember bottles have caps. "Oops, we don't have an opener."

"Oh yes we do. I unpacked it already." She points behind her. No one in the entire world can set up a kitchen like Kristine King. She's got an innate method of organizing each kitchen tool in relation to the stove, the sink, or the fridge. "Church key in that drawer right there beside the box. Second one down." She shortens "icebox" to "box." After finding it right where she said it would be, I reach into the fridge and take out two ice-cold beverages. I set one down on the table in front of her. "Here you go."

"Thank you. Sometime there ain't nothin' any finer than this right here." She holds up the bottle and takes a long swig. "Ahhhh. I thank the Lawd every day He lets me have another."

"The only problem with these is eight ounces isn't always enough. I'll get you one more."

"No, baby. I can't have but one. My sugar's been actin' up *any*way."

"I thought it was better."

"One day it is. Next day it ain't. Dr. Jones says I need to lay off my sweets." Kissie loves pies, cakes, candy, and especially Hershey's Kisses. She says she loves the way they melt on her tongue.

I close my eyes and sigh; the last thing I want to hear is that anything is awry with her.

"Kissie is okay—"

A loud knock on the door interrupts her sentence.

"Who in the world?"

"Maybe the movers forgot somethin'," she says.

I shrug my shoulders. "Finish your Coke, I'll be right back."

When I open the front door there's a man with dark brown hair beaming at me. He's wearing a black and turquoise windbreaker with "Tupperware," of all things, written across his right breast. One hand is shoved in the pocket of his khaki pants and the other is holding some sort of orange-colored cleaning product. He's not bad looking or anything but his hairdo makes me think he's in the military. It's a little longer on the top and from what I can tell it seems to be buzzed in the back. "Hi," I say hesitantly.

"Hi! I'm, Wiley. I live in the house next door." He takes his left hand out of his pocket and switches hands with the cleaning product before reaching out his right hand to shake mine.

"I'm Leelee Satterfield. Nice to meet you." I respond as pleasantly as possible when you're covered in dust and have been cleaning and moving all day long.

"And this is Luke." He points to the dog at his side. Luke's not on a leash but he doesn't move from his perch.

"Hi Luke," I say, and bend down to pat his head. The pooch looks up at me with appreciation. "What kind is he? A Lab?"

"Half Lab. Half something else, maybe." The man leans in closer, lowers his voice and speaks out of the side of his mouth. "I got him at the pound. Had a feeling he might be put to sleep."

"He's so sweet." I scratch the dog under his chin and down his back. "We never would want you put to sleep, Luke, never."

"Watch what you say. He's pwetty smart."

"Oh. Gosh. I'm sorry."

"It's okay. I named him after Luke Skywalker." Upon hearing his name, Luke peers over at his master. "I see you're moving in." He pokes his head in my door and glances around at the living room on the left and the dining room on the right side of the foyer. "Would you like some help?"

"Oh no. You're nice to ask but you don't have to do that."

"I insist. Let me just go put ole Lukey boy up and I'll be back. Second thought, can he stay in your backyard? That way I can look out on him."

"Actually . . . Wiley," I say, trying to politely come up with an excuse as to why all I want is some peace and quiet.

"It's not Wiley, it's *W*iley."

I tilt my head.

"With an *aar*."

"Oh my gosh! Excuse me. *Riley*." How embarrassing. I feel just awful. He's obviously got a speech impediment. Now I *have* to invite him in. "You can let Luke out through the patio door in the den, if you want."

"Oh no he cain't!" Kissie hollers from the kitchen. "I just finished vacuumin' those carpets. I don't want no big dawg trackin' mud through this house."

"Oh he won't bwing in mud." Riley puts his hand aside his mouth, and calls from the front door, leaning in toward the foyer, "It's not wet outside."

My coy smile lets Riley know that I'm humoring Kissie and I ask him to please take Luke around back. Within a minute flat, Riley's knocking on the back patio door. Kissie's closest so she lets him in.

"Kissie, I'd like for you to meet my next-door neighbor, Wiley . . . I . . . I mean *Riley*." *Gosh, Leelee, what's the matter with you?* "Rrriley, this is Ki- Kri-Kiiissie." At this point I'm so flustered I can't get anybody's name right.

Kissie says, "Why hello."

Riley says, "Hello."

I say, "What's your *last* name, Riley?"

"Bwadshaw," he says.

Instead of simply leaving well enough alone, I just have to say, "Well, isn't that just the nicest name? Riley Bwadshaw."

It's not until Kissie looks at me with her eyebrows raised that

I realize my latest faux pas. "I mean Bradshaw." I close my eyes and shake my head, completely disgusted with myself.

"I bwought over a housewarming pwesent for you." He hands me the orange cleaning product he was holding earlier.

"How nice." After looking at it a moment I place it on the coffee table. "Thank you."

"Mind if I take off my jacket?" he asks.

"Of course not," I say. "Where in the world are my manners? Here, I'll hang it up for you." I'm so mortified, the man could ask me to buy his house and I'd do it; probably overpay him for it while I'm at it.

Riley removes his jacket and hands it over. Kissie and I, at the exact same time, can't help but stare bug-eyed at the shirt he's wearing. It's the bowling kind with vents on the sides. His is black and the lettering on the breast pocket reads, "Tupperware products can change your life! Ask me how!" To be honest, I've never seen the word "Tupperware" on a piece of clothing in my whole life. Nor did it ever once cross my mind that Tupperware clothing even exists, not to mention the life-changing kind. I do everything I can not to look at Kissie; I know one moment of eye contact with her will send me into a laughing attack and lord knows I've already offended the man enough.

After a minute or so of unsubtle gestures like poking out the right side of his chest and scratching just below the logo, Riley not-so-inconspicuously turns around, so we can read the writing on the back of his shirt. "TUPPERWARE ROCKS!" is embroidered in all caps and it's underlined with several red lines, also embroidered. After he stares at the blank wall and makes a comment about how much he likes the beige paint color, he turns back around. It's obvious that he's studying our faces, which, rest assured, were quite blank. "I can tell you ladies are dying to know how Tuppa'ware can change your life."

I'm not dying to know at all, but of course I lie and say, "How can it change my life, Riley?" Out of guilt for my previous faux pas, I nod my head and act like I'm interested. Kissie, on the other hand, doesn't act in the least bit interested. In fact, by the perturbed look on her face, I can tell she's well on her way to a stupor.

"All I had to do to get started was give two parties and weport four hundwed dollars in sales," he says. "Today, I'm at the top of my game. I've been on luxuwy vacations, I've got a bwand-new car." As he's listing, he's counting on his fingers. "And you should see the furniture I've collected over the years. I'm the only male selling in Germantown"—he lowers his voice and closes his eyelids—"it's a gweat way to meet the ladies."

Kissie slowly turns her head in my direction. Her eyebrows look like upside-down crescent moons. Between the look on her face and Wiley's face it takes everything I've got to keep my shoulders still.

"Either of you ladies intewested in holding a Tuppa'ware pawty?" Riley takes the jacket back out of my hands and holds it up to show us. Bless his heart. "Professional Tupperware Hunter" is in big neon green letters on the back.

"Just for having one, you can get a stylish Twi-Mountain Highland Jacket like this one. It features a nylon zipper fwont, waglan sleeves, elastic cuffs and waistband, and twin pockets with safety flaps." He's pointing to each jacket feature, while holding it up to give us a better look. "See this hidden hood concealed in the collar? For added comfort, it's got a vented yoke and mesh upper lining. They come in sizes wanging fwom small to double X large." He turns his glance toward Kissie. "Or, if you'd rather have a bowling shirt, you can get that, too. Are you a bowler?" he asks her.

I'm looking at Kissie out of the corner of my eye. Although her butterscotch face doesn't get red, I know it is anyway on account of her pursed lips and squinty eyes. Riley has her completely unnerved.

"We've got a stellar ladies' team."

At this point, she's glaring at the poor thing. "*Hm, hm, hm.* Do I look like a bowler to you? *Hm, hm, hm. Hm, hm, hm.*"

"You'd be surprised at the vawiety of women on the Tuppa'ware team."

"I'm goin' back to the kitchen," is Kissie's response to that. "Either there or Bolivar," she mutters up under her breath as she's walking off.

Bolivar is home to an old Tennessee mental institution. You can't grow up anywhere near Memphis without hearing about how so-and-so is going to end up in Bolivar if they aren't careful. Anytime I'd get in trouble Mama used to say, "You're gonna send me to Bolivar." The funny thing is Bolivar is just the name of the town that houses the Western State Mental Hospital. Everyone has just shortened it to Bolivar.

Riley never stops talking. Instead of helping me unpack he strolls around my house analyzing every piece of furniture I own. Since I don't know him all that well, I figure I better stay right with him. I mean, who's to know? When he walks through the dining room he halts in front of my antique sideboard. "Wow! That's an expensive piece. Where'd you get it?" He runs his hand over the top and examines his fingers for dust.

"That came from my grandmother," I tell him.

"Pwetty darn nice. I tell you what, though. It could stand a good coat of polish. I'll be wight back." He heads out the dining room door that leads through the kitchen where Kissie is, and sprints right back through holding my housewarming present. "This is a bwand-new bottle of Owange Glo wood polish and conditioner. 'It's got a bwilliant luster that fills the air with the natural scent of fwesh owanges.'" He holds up the bottle, squirts a bit into the air and sniffs.

As soon as the words leave his lips, Kissie's *hm, hm, hm*ing again. I can hear her all the way in the kitchen. "No, Riley." She's in the doorway now with her hands on her hips. "I ain't puttin' no Orange Glo on Miz William's mother's sideboard. We've been usin' Harrell's Paste Wax long as I been workin' here." She strolls over to her stash of cleaning supplies and brings over her own can of Harrell's to show Riley. "I'mo do it myself. *Hm, hm, hm.*"

Riley says, "How much did you pay for that Hawell's?"

Kissie says, "Something like twenty-three dollars."

Riley says, "This Owange Glo retails for six ninety-nine," and an ear-to-ear smile spreads across his face.

She squints her eyes again and pops her hand on that big hip of hers. "That's cuz it's so *cheap*!"

"It's even cheaper if you buy it by the liter." Riley chuckles and snaps his fingers in the air, completely clueless to Kissie's dismay. "It cleans and shines wood finishes thwoughout your home in one easy step. It contains pure Valencia owange oil to wevive your wood, westore its luster, and wemove dirt, gwease, and wax buildup. It's also gweat on stainless steel, cewamic tile, and fiberglass to wemove gwease, soap film, gum, and stickers."

Kissie is so quiet, she's seething through her teeth—I know she's mad when her voice drops low, "Who are you anyway? A salesman for Orange Glo?"

"Not at the moment. But I can't say it won't be in my future!"

"*Hm, hm, hm,*" Kissie chants, loudly. "*Hm, hm, hm. Hm, hm, hm.*"

"You are wight about one thing, though. I am a salesman. Tuppa'ware and Cutco, both. Ever had a Cutco demonstwation?"

Kissie is flat done with Riley. "No, and I don't want one, neither. We have lots of work to do in this house, Riley. Now if you'll excuse us, we *need* to be gitting back to our unpackin'."

"I'll be glad to help."

"No *thank* you." Kissie places her hand on Riley's shoulder and leads him to the back patio door where Luke's nose is pressed up against the plate glass, smudging up the sliding door that Kissie cleaned earlier with Windex. "You go on back home now, you hear? Come back another day." She slides the door shut behind him and flips the lock.

I wave at him through the glass.

"Do you think we've hurt his feelings? I bet he won't be back here any time soon," I say.

"Not only will he be back, you won't be able to git rid of that man. You wait and see if ole Kissie ain't right."

Kissie is right about one thing. We still have hours of work to do. And if the sound of my stomach gets much louder I'll have to eat that horse Kissie's always talking about.

"How about a late lunch?" I ask her.

"I'm so hungry I could eat a horse," she says.

"You always say that."

"That's cuz my people always said it."

Chuckling to herself, Kissie reaches in the fridge and pulls out turkey, lettuce, tomatoes, and a new jar of Hellmann's. She makes my sandwich first and sets it down in front of me. Strolling back to the kitchen counter, she finds a cutting board and places it down on the Formica. With a knife she's expertly filed on a sharpening stone, she begins to slice a medium-size sweet onion.

Slicing Vidalia onions isn't the only way they make me cry. Just their scent brings tears to my eyes.

I'm not sure which was redder, my face or my hair. The shorter strands around my forehead had fallen out of my high ponytail and were damp with perspiration. When I pushed them away from my eyes I could see Kissie's large frame ambling toward me.

"Leelee. Leelee. Come here, chile."

I stomped my foot when she caught up with me. "No, Kissie." The last thing I wanted to do was leave the neighborhood dodge ball game.

She was holding a wet towel in her hand that had been soaking in a bucket of ice water. Grabbing me by the arm, she pulled me over to the side. "Sit down a minute."

Reluctantly, I fell to the ground.

Kissie leaned down over me and wrapped the cold cloth around my neck. Right away I could feel my body temperature start to fall. "It's ninety-eight degrees out here. Either you take a minute to cool yourself down or you're gonna come inside for good." Her face was right up in my face, the remnant of lunch on her breath. The onions from her favorite sandwich—raw Vidalias, tomatoes, and homemade mayo on Wonder bread—stunk to high heaven. I reared my head back to escape the odor.

My arms were crossed over my bent knees and the grass tickled the backs of my clammy thighs. I scowled and pouted at Kissie as I watched the game going on without me.

It seemed like forever but only five minutes passed before she removed the towel from around my neck. "Go on back now."

Before running off, I wrapped my little arms around her waist.

I can't slice, chop, or smell a Vidalia onion without thinking about that day. Or how much I love her. Kissie took better care of me than my own mother.

As I'm watching Kissie fix her favorite sandwich, the corners of my eyes moisten and a tear seeps out of my eye, trickling down over my chin onto my neck.

I bet I've checked my phone ten times today. Why hasn't Peter called me back? It's not like him, I keep thinking. Only seven days ago we shared a spellbinding kiss and I heard the words, "I've wanted to tell you for months how much I care about you. And how beautiful you are, inside and out." Surely, there's no way he could have forgotten his words.

Virgy brings Sarah and Issie over around six and Alice and Mary Jule are right behind them with plenty of takeout from Pete & Sam's, Daddy's favorite restaurant and another famous Memphis landmark. I'd been craving their barbecue pizza and garlic spinach for the last year and a half. Even Sarah and Isabella like the spinach—the garlic and parmesan cheese hiding any bitterness the spinach has otherwise.

As I knew they would, the girls approve of my new rental and promise to help me decorate in the weeks ahead. Alice even offers to drive Kissie home, a proposal I can't refuse. By eight o'clock, the two of us can hardly hold our eyes open. I had to insist she lie down earlier, after we ate our late lunch. After all she's almost three times my age.

Sarah and Issie love their new room. Today is quite a contrast from the day they first eyed their new bedroom in Vermont, which could barely fit twin beds with one nightstand in between, let alone a dresser. Baker, who had arrived three weeks before us, had not bothered to make their beds or arrange any of their toys. In this house, the bedroom is plenty large enough for both girls. We have painting to do, that's for sure, but at least the beds are made, their clothes are in the closet and Barbie's 3-Story Dream Townhouse is in the corner. Barbie and Ken are fully clothed and their wardrobes are hung in Barbie's trunk. The stuffed animals are stacked in the corners and their Fantasy Vanity is set up with makeup, nail polish, and hairbrushes in place.

Speaking of bedrooms, mine looks like Hearst Castle, compared to the shoe box I slept in back in Vermont. I will never ever forget, no matter what happens to me when I'm old, the look on Alice's face when she first saw that my great-grandmother's canopy bed was the only stick of furniture that could fit inside my bedroom. In this house it fits perfectly and I have a nightstand on either side.

After the girls are asleep, I crawl on top of the mattress and try watching a little TV. When I turn on the ten o'clock news, a tranquility washes over me and I can feel the tension in my body start to subside. There's Al Blakley and Lisa Murphey, both twenty-five year veterans at WZCQ, welcoming me back to town with their warm familiar faces. Only a few minutes pass before a commercial airs and I'm back to the world inside my head.

His kiss was just as I'd imagined it would be. At first I was embarrassed and shy. With George Clark and all of Fairhope, Vermont, watching who wouldn't be? But when he reached up and held my face in his hands, after ripping off his gloves, the outside world melted away. I'd been staring at those perfect teeth and supple, pink lips for months, all the while wondering what it would be like to have them touching mine. Would his kiss be tender? Or would it be frantic, imbued with abandon? I'd thought about it over and over. But I didn't want to go too far with my thoughts. Suppose he didn't want me? Suppose I was merely his friend—a platonic liaison. And now, I've not been able to think of anything else but his kiss. His face moving in toward mine plays over and over in my head. I can see his eyes, as blue as the inside of a lovely conk shell, hovering before mine—and the tenderness of their story. He wanted me. He needed me. It was real. So why hasn't he called me back? It scares me to think that he may have been just another man telling me just another story. Using me to get what he wanted. After all, he did work for me. I was the one paying his salary. No! Peter is different.

I rise from the bed and search for paper to write him a letter. Among the boxes and clutter I'll be lucky to find an old receipt to pen my thoughts. Then I remember who helped me move in. I dash into the kitchen and throw open the drawers. Sure enough, a lined yellow legal pad sits in the top drawer under the phone so I grab it and hurry back to my bed. My purse is always kept on the floor beside me and I reach down, plop it on top of the covers, and rummage for a pen. I'm tired of wondering, tired of keeping all this to myself. As I place the pen's point down on the page, any ill will about his feelings for me vanishes.

Dear Peter,

I'm not sure if you got my messages or not. Sometimes voice mail can be unreliable. I knew you'd want to know that the girls and I made it back to Memphis safe and sound! It was a long drive, but I'm happy to say we weathered the nor'easter. Somewhere around Scranton, Pennsylvania, I stopped at a Target store and bought a portable TV for the car. We had played all the car games I could think of and the girls had had their share of little arguments. I knew a movie would keep them quiet for a few hours at a time, so I splurged on a small TV with a car adapter and put it on the console in between the front seats. It has a DVD player inside and I loaded up on several new movies. That one purchase turned out to be my saving grace. I hardly heard a peep out of them the rest of the trip. Several exits down I got the brilliant idea to buy two headsets for the girls so I could listen to my own music up front.

There were a few bumps but all in all it was a very pleasant road back.

You'll never believe this: Helga bought back the inn. After I left you at George Clark's gas station I remembered Princess Grace's grave marker. As you might guess, I turned around for it. When I got back to the inn, Helga had already placed her hippo collection back on the mantel. I thought about staying and calling off the whole move but then I realized you already had a new job. I didn't want to run the Peach Blossom Inn without you. So, I went ahead and left.

Tell Roberta hello for me when you see her at Sugartree. She'll be great at her new job. So will you. I hope to talk with you soon. I can't wait for you to come to Memphis. How about May?

Love, Leelee

P.S. Guess what? On the way home, the girls and I actually saw a moose!!!!!!

After I punctuate the last of the letter, I fold it into a spare business-size envelope—it's not one of my nice embossed ones, but I'm too desperate to wait on unpacking boxes in search of my personalized stationery to share my feelings with Peter. I don't seal it yet, and fumble through my oversize purse for my Day-Timer and flip over to the address book. "Owen, Peter" is the third entry under the *O*s but there's no address. Only a phone number. Why in the world I never wrote down his address I'll never know. I make a mental note to call Roberta and get it from her. Surely she has it and if she doesn't, I'll send her on a GKA assignment. The GKA, our acronym for the Gladys Kravitz Agency (named after the one and only from *Bewitched*) is the means by which Alice, Virginia, Mary Jule, and I get our information. It's how we know things. For instance, if it weren't for the Agency, we'd never know how many times Alice's husband, Richard, plays golf every week. Although he's got his secretary trained to say he's on a sales call, all we have to do is park out on Greer, the street next to the Memphis Country Club, and wait on him to round the seventh hole. It's covert. It's crucial. And it's certainly credentialed. We've been charter members since the seventh grade, the year of the Agency's founding.

Moving and unpacking, the stress of this past week, have rendered me utterly exhausted yet I take the letter from the envelope and reread it five times, making sure it sounds okay. I start to fold it up and place it on my bedside table when it crosses my mind to give Peter another call. As I'm mulling it over, my chin hits my chest. I haven't yet made the bed, and my linens are still in boxes—but with no one to crawl toward under the sheets, I fall asleep on top of the bare mattress, clutching my cell phone.

Chapter Five

The music on FM 99 blasts from the white Bose alarm clock across the room. "Every Breath You Take" by the Police is not a bad way to start my Monday morning but the tiny bit of natural light poking through the blinds certainly is. I can't think of the last time my alarm has been set before dawn. *Get up and turn it off. Otherwise you'll lie in bed and daydream about Peter an extra thirty minutes. Or an hour.*

When I walk into Classic Hits FM 99 for the first time as an employee, Edward Maxwell's door is closed. It feels a little awkward, not knowing anyone, so I sit at my desk and start poking around the small office. A vast collection of old vinyl records, alphabetized by artist, is squeezed into floor-to-ceiling cabinets behind the desk chair. I can't help but pull a few out to examine. With each album I touch my mind flashes back. Steppenwolf's first self-titled album with "Born to Be Wild," Virginia and I, each dancing like a wild child, down the long hall in front of her bedroom. *Chicago,* Jay Stockley and I slow-danced to "Colour My World" in Alice's parents' basement. The Cars—Mary Jule and I screamed "My Best Friend's Girl" at the top of our lungs in her Mustang with the windows rolled down almost every night the summer before we went to college.

When I get to the S section my eyes are drawn to the blue spine of one of our favorite childhood albums. *Diana Ross and the Supremes Greatest Hits*. If only I still had that gorgeous pastel poster of the Supremes that came inside the album. I check to see if it's in this one and it's not. Gone to the same place as the posters inside the Beatles *White Album* and James Taylor's *Sweet Baby James*. Probably ripped off a bedroom wall and wadded up inside a trashcan by a mom who's desperate to redecorate once her child goes off to college.

"Alice always gets to be Diana Ross," Virginia whispered in my ear, and jumped so high her head hit the canopy over my bed. One more jump and she landed on the carpet with a big thud. I bounced to the mattress on my butt first and then sprung off the bed behind her. We hooked arms and skipped down the hall out to the den where Alice and Mary Jule held their noses and shimmied their butts down to the floor. "Come swim, y'all," Mary Jule called while moving her arms over her head as if she were crawling across the pool.

Virginia ripped into the jerk. I stood there, eyes traveling back and forth between the two, wondering which side to join. Virgy looked at me like she'd kill me if I didn't follow her. Not wanting the other two mad at me, either, I decided to go out on my own and pony around the outskirts of the room and back down the hall. It was Saturday afternoon and American Bandstand *was on the TV. We'd waited all week to dance along with the teenagers. As ten-year-olds, teenagers were our greatest infatuation and we copied their every move.*

The console housing the television took up one side of the wall in our den. Alice stood just two feet from the screen holding one of the finials from my four-poster bed in her hand. Mary Jule, Virginia, and I stood a few feet behind her, singing into our own finials. Clad in striped polyester mini dresses and white go-go boots, the four of us sang and danced our hearts out.

"I'll sing Diana's part, and y'all be the Supremes," Alice turned around and instructed. None of us was gutsy enough to protest the fact that she was always *Diana, so we took our places behind her. The music started and I felt the goose bumps rise as Diana and the other two appeared on the* Bandstand *stage. When they started to sing, we hummed and oooed along with them, swaying our bodies and snapping our fingers. Alice turned around to us again and put her fingers over her lips. When Diana opened her mouth so did Alice. "Stop in the name of love, before you break my heart," she sang into her pretend mic, while the rest of us only got to echo, "Think it oh, oh-ver."*

Whether it was Diana Ross, Martha Reeves, or the head WHBQ Cutie, Virgy, Mary Jule, and I had no choice in the matter. We were always the Supremes or the Vandellas. Just one of the background Cuties. Never the star. If we had been little when the Dixie Chicks first burst on the scene, Alice would definitely have "called" Natalie Maines.

WHBQ was *the* radio station back then. There was a little window on the outside of the building where people could watch the deejays inside. We'd walk several blocks in the summer just to be able to take a gander at George Klein, the morning deejay, best known as Elvis's closest friend from high school. Back home we'd hole up in front of the TV every Saturday afternoon before *American Bandstand* to watch him host the local dance show, *Talent Party,* starring the WHBQ Cuties. I don't think there was a girl in Memphis, Tennessee that didn't dream of one day becoming a Cutie.

I'm so engrossed in reliving my past, that when the phone rings I don't pay much attention. After several rings, though, it dawns on me that it's most likely my job to answer so I pick it up and say, "Classic Hits FM 99 radio, may I help you?" I say it with confidence. Charm. Oomph. Like I'm a twenty-five-year radio veteran. I'm feeling so good about myself; a little chill runs down my spine.

"I see the pandas!" a man says, excitedly.

"Excuse me?"

"Two of them in the field. Yeah, baby. I can see 'em from my car. I'm pulled off on the shoulder of I-240, right near Christian Brothers High School. *I've spotted them,*" he says proudly.

"O-kaay."

"Oh, there one goes! He's heading into the woods. Nope. He's coming back out. Tell Johnny Dial he should come on down. It's crazy. Oh yeah. More cars are pulling off the interstate and parking right behind me. They see 'em, too. I'mo hang up now and call the zoo. See ya later."

"Thanks for calling," I say, with absolutely no clue of what's just happened.

"Sure. Glad I could help."

I hang up the phone, stunned. What in the world is this guy talking about? Pandas on the interstate?

The faint melody of a song emanates from the clock radio on my desk. I reach over and turn up the volume. Surely it's okay to listen at work. This is, after all, a radio station. The phone rings again. Once more I answer it the same way. "FM 99 radio, may I help you, please?"

"They are so *cuuute,*" a girl says, squealing.

"I'm sorry. What's so cute?"

"The pandas. I'm down here at Christian Brothers High School and I can see them right next to the woods."

"Really? How many are there?"

"Two. Two adorable little panda bears. Do you know when the zoo people are coming to rescue them? I'd hate to think they might get hit by a car."

"I'm not sure, actually. I'm just getting in to work."

"It's quite a sight out here. I bet there are one hundred cars lining the interstate and a hundred more here in the school parking lot. There's nowhere else to park. Oh. Here comes the fire department. Maybe they can help catch them."

"Do you know what happened? How the pandas got loose?" I say, feeling panicked, too.

"Yeah. Johnny Dial's been talking about it on the radio all morning. You know how the Memphis Zoo just got the pandas? They were taking them around to different places in the city to show them off. Johnny Dial called it 'The Panda Bear Field Trip.' They accidentally got loose and people started spotting them near Christian Brothers High School."

"Oh my," I say, feeling just as concerned as she. "I so hope they'll be okay. I didn't even know the zoo was getting panda bears. I've just moved back to town and I'm still not up on all the Memphis news. I dearly love pandas."

"Oh me, too, girl. Their names are Ya Ya and Lee Lee."

"Leelee? That's my name!"

"You should come down here and see her for yourself."

"I wish I could but I better stay put. It's my first day. Oops, the other phone is ringing, thanks for calling." I hang up from her and spend the next thirty minutes talking with more callers about the loose panda bears. It's hard to imagine the zoo would be so neglectful, I can't help thinking.

A guy strolls by my office and glances inside, whistling as he walks. We briefly catch eyes. He gets a few feet past my door before taking a few steps backward. "Hellooo, gorgeous," he says.

"Hi," I say shyly. *Oh dear.*

"And you must be the new Sallie," he says, with a wink. I'll admit his voice is captivating, although I'm not so sure about his personality.

"Was she the old assistant?"

"That she was." After stepping into my office he holds out his hand. "Hi, I'm Stan. Stan Stallone. Midday jock." He winks again and nods his head deliberately, like he's sure I already know exactly who he is—which unfortunately I do, though thankfully never this up close and personal.

"Nice to meet you," I say out of habit.

Stan leans in closer till he's right in my personal space, so close I can smell his coffee breath when he talks. It's black and it's nasty. "And you are?"

An involuntary jerk of my head causes me to hit the album cabinet behind me. "Leelee." I reach up and rub the back of my head. "Satterfield."

"Careful there. Are you okay?" Now his nose is almost touching mine.

I plop down in my chair to escape the odor. "I'm fine," I say, although it sounds more like a squeak, and I decide to breathe through my mouth only.

"Well, welcome aboard, Leelee Satterfield."

"Thanks."

His eyes travel from my face down to my feet, with a pause at my chest. *Double nasty.* I'd heard his voice on the radio for years and had conjured up an image of what he might look like. Gorgeous voice, gorgeous man, I'd always believed. Not Stan, bless his heart. A large bottom on a woman is fine but it's a different story altogether when it's on a man, especially when his waist is much smaller. "Ever worked in radio before?" he asks and squats down level with my face.

There's not much room in the tiny office, but I drop my pen on the floor and use my feet to "accidentally" push my chair back as far as it will go. "No. But, I love music," I tell him.

"A top prerequisite for the job."

"My girlfriends and I have seen just about every artist who's come to Memphis for the last twenty-five years. We know a lot about music."

Stan's eyes are focused right on me as he pushes the stapler and tape holder out of the way and makes his large self at home on top of my desk. "*Really?*" He crinkles his mouth to the side and nods his head. "Hang on. I'm good at this. Who holds the record for the most number ones in the seventies?"

"Oh, I'm not good at that kind of music trivia. I just mean I'm good at recognizing songs and knowing who sings them." I nod my head.

"All right then. Who sang 'Diamond Girl'?"

"Seals and Croft." *Duh, duh, duh.*

"'Nights Are Forever Without You'?"

"England Dan and John Ford Coley."

"Not bad, not bad."

Ask me about a good song why don't you, Stan the Man?

"Okay. Hit me up. I like the obscure ones. Nothing too easy," he says, and honks the mucus in his nose way back inside before swallowing it.

I'm so grossed out by what he just did that I'm having a hard time concentrating. "Let's see, 'Gimme Shelter'?" I say. It's not obscure, but the first one that comes to my repulsed mind.

"Was it in the sixties or seventies?" he asks.

"I'm not sure."

"Oh yeah. I've got this one." He's nodding his head up and down. "You were trying to stump me, weren't you?" He points his finger straight at me. "Duran Duran."

"No. That's not it."

"Yes. It is. 'Shelter.' It's a Duran Duran song."

"It may be, but I'm talking about 'Gimme Shelter.' By the Stones. I don't know all that much about Duran Duran."

"What? They were *the* super group of the eighties. 'Rio'? 'Hungry Like the Wolf'? 'Is There Something I Should Know?'"

I'm lightly shaking my head.

"Oh come on. 'Planet Earth'?"

"I remember 'Hungry Like the Wolf' from the radio but I never bought a Duran Duran record."

"You never owned a Duran Duran record? You've gotta be kidding me."

I shrug my shoulders. "Sorry."

Stan rolls his eyes like he's the only person alive that knows anything about music. "I knew 'Give Me Shelter.' Just didn't hear you say 'Give Me.' So. Have you seen Eduardo yet?"

I shake my head. "His door's closed."

"I'll knock and let him know you're here."

"Oh no, you don't have to bother—"

By the time I stand to protest Stan's already off the desk and hustling out the door. *Bang, bang bang.* "Eduardo, Ms. Satterfield is out here waiting on you."

Edward's voice booms through the walls. "I'm on the phone, Stallone. Tell her I'll be with her when I can."

Stan sashays back inside my office. "Well, you heard the boss."

"Actually, I'm fine. I've got plenty I can—"

The phone rings and Stan springs to answer it, deliberately brushing my left shoulder with his arm. "Ninety-nine," he says into the phone, practically hanging on top of me. "Edward's on another line. Is there a message?" Stan scribbles out a note on the pink pad on my desk and at this point, he's *fastened* to my shoulder. "Okay. Have a good one. Buh-bye . . . why yes it is!" He straightens back up—thank the Lord. "You must have recognized my voice. Aren't you kind. I sure will. Good to talk to you, too." Reaching back over me to hang up the phone, he hovers yet again on top of my shoulder. "Grady Walker from the zoo. He's a frand."

I lightly shake my head. "A frand?"

"Part friend. Part fan. Get it?"

I arch my eyebrows and feign a smile. Kissie must be rubbing off on me. I just might have to start *hm, hm, hm*ing myself.

Stan turns toward the door. "I'll be back," he says in an Arnold Schwarzenegger voice, hits the door frame and disappears down the hall.

Oh double dear.

Not having any idea about what to do next, I busy myself by reading the various folders in the file cabinet. In the first two hours since arriving for my first day on the job, I've talked to at least ten people about the pandas, taken several phone calls from station winners inquiring about their prizes, and jotted down messages for all kinds of people I've never met. I have no idea how to transfer a call but surely Edward has planned for someone to train me. I'm just hanging up from another winner when I see Edward standing in the doorway.

"Good morning, Leelee. I see you're finding your way."

"Hi, Edward." I smile and tuck my hair behind my ears. No denying it. He makes me nervous. "How are you this morning?"

"Dealing with the usual morning team crap. But fine."

"Did you hear about the pandas?"

One barely squinted eye glares at me. "I've been dealing with the pandas all morning. Would you hand me my messages, please?"

"Sure." I reach over and grab his stack of pink message slips and pass them over.

Edward flips through the stack and stops when he sees a certain name. "Damnit." He rolls his eyes. "Grady Walker is calling from the zoo. I'm sure he's not happy." He looks up at me. "When will the idiots in this town grow a brain?"

I furrow my brow. Not sure what he means.

"Johnny Dial is in the business of ratings. He's the master prankster. People fall for his pranks every single time. And I'm the one who has to wipe up his mess. To think hundreds of people mistook two guys dressed in panda suits for real pandas is asinine."

Now I'm the one who feels like an idiot. Not only did the rest of the city fall for the panda prank, I was right there with them. "What's wrong with people these days?" I say, and shake my head in disgust. "They just get more gullible by the year."

Edward's the fidgety type. He can't sit or stand still. I notice him tapping his thumb on his messages and looking around the room.

"I have some questions for you," I say, with plenty of oomph in my voice, trying to show him my excitement about my first day on the job. "Nothing big. Just a few technical ones."

"I'll try to answer a couple but with all the crap I'm dealing with this morning, I don't have much time."

"Oh, no problem. I can ask the person who'll be training me if you'd rather."

Edward hesitates. "Quite frankly, this job is not rocket science. You're a college graduate. I doubt you'll have any issues."

My stomach falls to my feet. *Aren't you being a little harsh? I'm simply asking if someone can show me the ropes. Lead me around a little on my first day.*

"I will tell you this. Sometimes our winners become angry if they arrive to pick up their prizes before we actually get them into the station. That's why I demand that we never go on the air with a promotion until the prizes are in house and in the prize closet. Sales is terrible about that. They want to please their clients so they promise them the moon."

I nod in agreement.

"I need you to be aware of their schemes. The sales people will try all kinds of things to butter you up. They'll want you to be their best buddy. They'll try to tell you the prizes are on the way. But don't believe them. They're liars. All of them."

Edward's face darkens till it's beet red. "Each and every on-air promotion has to be cleared by me," he says, enunciating every single syllable for emphasis.

I could tell he was excitable in the interview but now I'm positive he's the type that could blow at any moment. Dear God, just tell me he's not another Helga. That's all I need, one more job where I have to tiptoe across another glass pond.

"Would you like to see the prize closet?" Out of nowhere a huge smile replaces his sour expression.

"Sure," I say, trying not to sound too excited *or* too scared.

"Follow me."

We head down the hall and stop just outside a door that has an on-air light that, at the moment, is bright red. Edward removes his keychain from his pocket and fumbles through several keys before finding the exact one. He jerks another door open and steps forward. Inside is a vast collection of FM 99 paraphernalia. Hats, T-shirts, mugs, key chains, bumper stickers, and plastic cups—perfectly organized on the shelves. CDs from different artists heard on the station are perfectly stacked and alphabetized. There's a label on one of the shelves marked "Concert Tickets" with a box on top. Edward grabs it and flips through the different labels. "Whenever you enter this closet, be sure to keep this out of sight from the jocks. They'll try to sweet talk you out of the tickets for their friends and family." There's a box marked "Gift Certificates," which Edward explains is for cruises, airline tickets, and hotel vouchers—all the prizes that are given away on air. "And especially this box." He taps the top. "It's very valuable."

He closes the door, secures the dead bolt and stuffs his keys back in his pocket. After glancing into a small window on the door of the room with the on-air light, he heads back down the hall while I follow behind. Instead of turning into his office, he turns into mine.

"Where's Dial? He's not in the control room."

Although I've not met him I know exactly what he looks like. Johnny Dial, *the* morning disc jockey, has been on the air since before I went to Ole Miss. Blond hair, blue eyes, and cute as a bug. He's on TV all the time promoting the local Toyota dealership. Every single year *Memphis Magazine* names him best local celebrity, best deejay, and sexiest Memphian. If I'm thirty-three, he has to be at least forty. "I haven't seen him. Sorry."

"He better not have left yet." Edward scowls and scurries out of my office. I hear him slam his door.

Ten minutes pass.

"Pssst." I look up to see Johnny Dial poking his adorable head in my office. He's motioning to me. "Come here a minute."

I point at myself. "Me?"

"Yeah. Come here." His voice is barely a whisper.

I hurriedly follow him down the hall, out the FM side of the building and into the AM side. A pair of headphones is in one hand and he's carrying a briefcase in the other. Every time we turn down a new corridor he looks behind and shoots me a sparkly smile. "Just a few more feet. I'm not a weirdo. I promise." Finally he ducks into an empty office, pulls me inside and shuts the door. "Sorry about that. There was no time to explain."

My grin assures him that he's safe with me. "Is there something wrong?" I ask.

When he chuckles I recognize his laugh from the radio. He's known for it. "No. Not at all. I'm just trying to avoid Edward. Not only is he mad at me about the pandas, he wants me to record this stupid-ass promo today for the Spring Sweeps. I'm supposed to be on the golf course in fifteen minutes. Way out at Windyke."

"Windyke? You better hurry."

"I know. Can you cover for me?"

"How?"

"Tell him you took a message that said I had a dentist appointment at ten thirty. If I start on that stupid promo now, he'll have me in the production studio for the next two hours. I'll do it tomorrow."

"Sure. I'll tell him that." What is it about this guy that makes me so willing to lie for him ten seconds after meeting him? Who am I kidding—he's got charm like Baker and confidence to boot.

"Thanks. You're the best." He puts his hand on the doorknob. "I owe you one."

I nod in agreement. Maybe I should tell him that he fooled me, too, with the panda prank. Nah. I'm way too cool for that.

Johnny gestures for me to walk out ahead of him. "Have a great day. Bye, cutie." He goes one way and I go the other, toward my office. Several feet down the hall he calls after me. "Hey, what's your name anyway?"

I turn back around. "Leelee."

"Glad you're working here, Leelee." He starts to walk off but changes his mind. "Have you met Stan yet?"

"Oh yeah."

"What do you think?"

I smile slightly and shake my head.

He snickers again, walking backward as he speaks. "You and me are gonna have some fun."

"I sure hope so," I reply, with a grin that surprises even me.

"Done deal. See ya tomorrow." Johnny waves and turns the corner.

I head back to my office, pondering my weakness for beautiful men.

After the panda ordeal finally settles down, the rest of my day sails along fairly well. Kyle, the promotion director, takes time to answer all my questions and then details all the promotions that he's got going on. There's a bachelor auction for the Kidney Foundation, and Stan will be auctioned off to the lucky lady who writes the largest check—it takes all my strength not to guffaw at the thought of actually paying for an interaction with Stan. There's a movie premiere at the Malco Ridgeway Four and a rooftop party at the Peabody Hotel, all this week. I can tell by the messages I take for him that he's the busiest person on the floor. Part of my job is to assist him, he tells me, and to show up at some of the promotions. Edward never bothered telling me any of that.

Around four o'clock I notice Edward passing by my office. "I'm going flying," he says, as he moves swiftly past. No point in commenting. He's already halfway down the hall.

Once the five o'clock whistle blows I am so ready to go home I can't stand it. And I'm sure Sarah, bless her heart, must be antsy and ready to get the heck out of after-care. By the time I get to Dogwood Elementary, she's crying. The poor little thing is hungry, cranky, and not liking the fact that she hasn't seen me all day. It doesn't help one bit to have to pick her up during the dreaded bewitching hour. The after-care teacher tells me that Sarah likes the other kids and that she has played with them very well until now. As adaptable as she has been to all the change in her life, I'm sure she has her breaking point.

The drive home is awful. I reach over and grab the first CD I can find, hoping that it might help.

"I don't like that CD," she says about Raffi's *Bananaphone*.

"You used to like it."

"It's for babies. Like Issie."

"Is there another one you'd like to hear?" I ask, as I'm picking up speed, cruising five miles over the speed limit.

"No."

"No, ma'am?"

"No, ma'am." Her voice is barely audible.

"We'll be home soon and you can watch *cartoons*," I say, hoping to console her.

Instead of answering me she stares out the window. I figure it's best not to bring up anything else about the events of the day.

When we pull into the driveway, I'm ready to cry myself. It's a little before six and I haven't even thought about supper. Since Kissie's been keeping Issie all day, I feel like the least I can do is treat the poor thing to dinner. I'll call the Germantown Commissary, the best barbecue joint in town, and order takeout for all of us as soon as I get inside.

I stop in front of my mailbox and as I'm getting out to check my mail I notice, out of the corner of my right eye—Riley—in his front yard raking leaves, even though it's almost dark. He's wearing his Tupperware windbreaker (I can tell by the turquoise) and what appears to be a white painter's cap. Luke, perched in Riley's driveway, which is separated from mine by only four feet of grass, is keeping watch over the cove.

Goodness gracious, I'm not at all in the mood for Riley. I jump back in the car, acting as if I don't see him, but it's no use. He's in my driveway now, motioning for me to roll down my window.

"Who's that man, Mommy?" Sarah wants to know.

"Our new next-door neighbor. Hi Riley," I say, as my window lowers.

"How was your first day at work?"

How in the world did you know that? I've only met you once. "Oh fine. Thank you."

He notices Sarah in the backseat. "Is that Sawah?"

"Yes." *And how did you know my daughter's name?*

"Hi Sawah. I'm Wiley."

"Hi Wiley," she says.

"Actually it's Wiley with an *aar*," he tells her.

I turn back around and smile at Sarah who, unlike her crazy mother, keeps her mouth shut and simply waves at him.

"I have a pwoposal for you." He tips his painter's cap.

"What kind of proposal?" I ask hesitantly. *Oh dear. Why did I roll down my window?*

"I noticed when I was in your house the other day that your guest bathwoom needs painting."

He's right. The color is terribly drab. A pale, ugly gray. "No kidding. I hope the landlord lets me repaint it."

"You pick out the color and I'll get the job done. It's on the house. Neighbor helping neighbor."

"Oh no, Riley, that's not necess—"

"I insist. I could have it done in a couple of hours. While you're at work. You could come home to a bwand-new bathwoom."

"Don't you have to work?" A reasonable question, I think.

"My hours are flexible. That's another perk about my line of work."

I consider when exactly I would have time to paint my bathroom and Riley's offer suddenly seems pretty good. I speak before giving it another moment's thought. "I suppose that would be okay."

"I can do it tomowow."

"Oooh, that's too fast I think, but . . . okay." As soon as I say it I regret it. "Actually, on second thought, I won't be able to get the paint that fast."

"You could head over to Home Depot wight now."

"Oh no no no. Sarah will never survive the car ride. She is ready to be home. Plus, I would rather get my paint at Porter or Benjamin Moore and I have a feeling they're closed by now."

"Why buy fwom them when Home Depot is so much cheaper? It's just a wental house."

He has a point. "That's true."

"Say, I could go to Home Depot for you."

"That is so nice of you but I'll have to pick out a color, and by then the girls will be ready for bed." *Why am I telling him all this?*

He pulls out a paint sample book from his back pocket and hands it through the window. "I've alweady thought of that."

"Well my goodness, Riley. You are so thoughtful." *And a little creepy. Is there something more to this offer? It seems too good to be true.*

"Thanks."

"I'll take a look at it and let you know." I reach to put the car back in drive but he keeps talking.

"Why don't you go ahead and call my number now? That way it will alweady be in your cell phone. It's 901, of course, 555-5897."

Before I have time to think about the ramifications of what I'm doing, I dial Riley's number. The University of Memphis Tigers' fight song blasts out of a cell phone holster on his belt. He grabs it, flips it in the air, and pops open the flip-top without the use of his fingers. "Got it."

"Alrighty then. Thanks, Riley. I'll let you know when I've picked out a color."

The minute Sarah and I walk in the door, I smell food. Not just any food. Kissie's food. Pork chops, macaroni and cheese, lady peas, homemade yeast rolls, and black-bottom pie for dessert. The feeling of euphoria that washes over me is enough to make me want to collapse on the floor.

Issie runs up and grabs my waist—so happy I'm home. "Mommy, where have you been?" I scoop her up and she pats my hair. "It's been ages since I've seen you."

"Ages? I know it feels that way, baby."

I lean over and kiss Kissie's cheek. She's holding Sarah in her arms.

"Let's do a group hug," Sarah says, and extends her little arms toward Issie and me.

"It smells heavenly in here. I was just about to call the Germantown Commissary for takeout," I tell Kissie.

"Save it for another night. Anytime you're ready, we can eat," Kissie says. For some reason, she's walking around the house closing all the curtains and shutters.

"What are you doing?"

"I don't want no Peepin' Tom lookin' at us in here. I want to eat my dinner in peace. Every time I'd get back to my story or my ironing, here comes a rap on the door. I'll give you one guess who it was."

"My next-door neighbor?"

"Mmm-hmm."

"Bless his heart. What did he want?"

"*Nothin'*. He's just comin' up with some excuse to be here, that's all. Doesn't he have to work himself?"

"He was in the driveway when I drove up." I reach into the cabinets and pull out the dinner plates, lining them each side by side.

Kissie spoons the food onto the plates as she talks. "Lawd have mercy, that boy is so *nosy*. First he wants to know where you are workin'. Next, he wants to know the girls' names. Then he'd be acting like he wanted to help me but all he did was talk. He'd tell me he was gonna fix this and paint that. I finally had to shoo him out the door."

"He wants to paint the half bath in the hall."

Her eyes bug out. "You gonna let him?"

"He says he'll do it for free."

"Unh-unh, Leelee. There ain't no such thing as free. There's always a string attached."

"Oh don't be silly. What in the world could he want from me?" I say, while walking over to the table with the girls' dinner plates.

"Your hand."

I stop dead in my tracks and look at her straight on. "My hand? Don't be silly. Never going to happen."

"That ain't gonna keep him from wantin' it."

"Oh Kissie. He's harmless," I say, and call the girls to the table.

"Might be. But he's irritatin'." She has a point.

"I feel sorry for him, actually."

She's reaching in the fridge for the milk carton. "I don't."

"Why not?"

She shuts the door to the refrigerator and turns around with a serious look on her face. "He's got a nice house. A nice car. Nice clothes. Nothin' wrong with him but the way he talks, and that ain't all that bad. *Hm, hm, hm*."

"Maybe he's just lonely," I tell her, pondering the fact that he's an almost forty-something, living alone and selling Tupperware for a living.

"And that's exactly why you need to be careful." She puts our plates down on the table and goes back to the counter for the butter dish.

The next afternoon I'm sitting at my desk. I've only been back from lunch a little while when the station phone rings. "May I speak with Leelee?" a man says.

"This is she."

"Hi Leelee. It's Wiley."

"Oh hi, Riley," I say, a wee bit frustrated. There's a no-personal-calls policy at the office, or so Edward insists, and Riley is not someone worth bending the rules for.

"Say, I need to ask you something. I'm coming along nicely in the bathwoom. But I was wondering if you want me to wemove your hardware."

I feel the need to whisper in case someone overhears me. "That's funny you should ask. I've been thinking of replacing it with something cuter. But since I'm just renting the house I'll want to put the old hardware back on when I leave. You can remove it but save it for me, please. Just put it in one of the drawers in the vanity if you don't mind."

"I didn't want to get paint on it."

"Of course not."

"Why are you whispewing?" he says.

"Because I'm not supposed to take personal calls at work."

"All wight," he whispers back. "I'll get back to work myself."

"Thanks, Riley."

"No pwoblem."

I can't help but think about Kissie alone with him all day. My hope is that he'll be so busy, that he'll leave her alone. Besides, Kissie can easily put Riley in his place. Surely she's just being overprotective. After all, how much trouble can he really cause?

When I drive up from work, Riley's not in the driveway. The minute Sarah and I step in the door I run to the guest bathroom to see the transformation. I'd been thinking about it all day. I even stopped by Restoration Hardware on the way home and found some beautiful green glass knobs to replace the old tarnished brass handles. With the honey-wheat color paint I had picked out, I just knew the bathroom would look gorgeous.

"Hi Kissie," I say as I dump my purse on the kitchen table. "Does the bathroom look good?"

She looks up from her ironing board but doesn't say a word.

Issie's watching TV in the den. Running past her I reach down and kiss the top of her head on the way to the guest bathroom. There's a little flutter in my heart I'm so excited.

Throwing open the door, Restoration Hardware sack in hand, I switch on the light. I've been picturing a cute new soap dish with fragrant soaps, monogrammed guest towels that pick up the green in the new handles, a pretty wicker wastebasket, and my water lily painting that I'd bought from a Memphis artist at the Pink Palace Crafts Fair, hanging over the commode.

Before I even have a chance to inspect the paint job I'm taken aback. There's a large gaping hole in the wall, right next to the toilet. After a deep gasp, my hands shoot up to cover my face. What in god's name? I bend down to examine it further and peek inside the hole. Studs, wires, and insulation are all I can see. When I glance around the rest of the half bath, two smaller holes, to the right of the sink, are my next clue that Riley Bradshaw's definition of hardware must be synonymous with toilet paper holders and towel racks. Not to be confused with the brass, ornamental kind, his idea of hardware means the white porcelain holders built into the drywall. I have to admit I'm wondering if poor Riley has his own loose screw.

Just for the heck of it, I pull out the drawer to the vanity and sure enough, right where I told him to put it, is "my hardware." It barely fits in the drawer due to the big glob of drywall cement protruding out of the back of each piece.

Out of the corner of my eye, I happen to catch a glimpse of a certain butterscotch face. And it's not happy.

"*Hm, hm, hm. Hm, hm, hm,*" she hums, extra loud.

I have no words . . . or hums.

"I declare. I ain't seen a man so uncoordinated in all my life. He's all thumbs. *Hm, hm, hm.*"

"What was he thinking?" I say, whisking my hand across the bigger of the two holes.

"That's just it. He doesn't think." She waves her arm. "Look at the size of that hole."

"Bless his little heart."

"His little *brain* is what you need to be blessin'."

"Oh Kissie, that's awful. Okay, bless his little brai—" I can hardly get the words out because my shoulders have started to shake.

When Kissie sees me she belts out one of her deep, wonderful guffaws and all of a sudden the situation is completely hilarious.

"He was just trying to be help . . . ful," I say. "No telling how much his *free* paint job is going to cos—" Words are hard to come by when Kissie gets me going. We hoot and teehee until tears are streaming down our faces. For a solid five minutes we howl and point at the holes in the wall, bending over, holding our stomachs. The only reason I can let up at all is because my face hurts so bad.

Kissie points to the floor while holding her stomach with the other hand. "At least, at least the toi—toil—toilet paper is in go—good shape."

At the sight of the lone toilet paper roll sitting on the tile floor beside the toilet, I fall to my knees, avoiding the painted walls and collapse onto the floor, shrieking and snorting until I'm sure we've alarmed both the girls.

"Wait, baby, I'm fixin' to wet. Move out of the way." She pushes past me and tugs on her girdle before plopping down on the toilet. I push my way back up, shut the door to give her privacy and stammer out to the den. Falling down on the nearest chair, I can hardly contain myself. I'm doubled over in the fetal position. Watching me roar gets

Sarah and Issie going, so the three of us continue to fall out laughing until Kissie comes back from the potty. Now all four of us are a mess.

If not for a loud knock there's no telling how long our sides would continue to split.

"Uh-oh. Here he comes now," Kissie says, keeping her backside firmly planted on the sofa. "The un-painter."

I stand up to answer the door.

"I wouldn't answer that if I were you," she says.

"He knows I'm here. I'm going to have to open it eventually." I sling open the door and sure enough, there he is. No longer wearing his painter's cap, a billowy white chef's hat now rests on his head. He's holding a magazine and hands it to me straight away. It's all I can do to keep my composure, especially at the sight of the poor thing in his new hat. "What's this, Riley?" My face is wet with tears.

"I thought you might need some pwoducts for your new kitchen." He doesn't even mention the bathroom, much less the holes in the wall.

It's not a magazine after all, it's a catalog and one glance tells me exactly why he's wearing a chef's hat. "You're a Pampered Chef salesman." I glance up at him with a grin, biting the insides of my cheeks.

"A Pampa'ed Chef *consultant.* Just got my kit in the mail today. You are the first person I thought of to host a Pampa'ed Chef pawty."

"Hmmm. Well—"

Sarah and Issie run up to the door and stand on either side of me. He leans down to their level. "Wouldn't you girls like to host a pawty?"

"Yes." They're jumping up and down. "Can we, Mommy?" Issie asks.

Now I'm in a fine mess. Who do I disappoint? My daughters or my next-door neighbor? I turn around to Kissie who has not even bothered to budge off the sofa. Her big lips are puckered and she's shaking her head.

"Can I have a day to think about it?" I say, rubbing the tops of both my girls' shoulders.

"What's there to think about, Mommy? I love parties," Sarah says.

"Me, too," Issie says.

"You could invite all your friends, *and* their mommies!" Riley says.

I don't even bother looking behind me. The pitiful faces of my little girls are all I need to decide. "I guess we're *having a Pampered Chef party*."

"Would you like to set a date?" asks the consultant.

"Not right now, Riley. Can I get back with you about it?"

"Oh sure. We'll talk about it tomowow."

I can just picture Alice's face now when the Pampered Chef Party invitation, hosted by Leelee Satterfield, arrives in the mail. She'll have a heyday with that one, not to mention her first introduction to Mr. Riley Bradshaw.

Later that night, after crawling under the covers, I reach over for my book, which is resting on the nightstand. When I notice my cell phone, I'm reminded to charge it for the night and as I'm reaching to plug it up I notice the voice mail icon on the screen.

In haste, I dial my voice mail box and wait for the prompts.

"Hi Leelee. It's Peter. I'm, well I know it's been a while since we've talked. Thank you for your messages letting me know you made it safely to Tennessee. I don't know why I didn't call you back. I . . . I don't know . . ." He pauses a moment. "It just feels a little weird. You're there. I'm here. I'm not sure what's going on. My job is working out well, though." He laughs. "They've already given me a raise. Anyway, I hope all is well. Tell Sarah and Issie hi for me. Call me when you get a chance. I . . . Take care, okay?"

I play it again. And again. Analyzing every inflection, every word. Why has it taken him over two weeks to call me? There's just no explanation for it. I mean, what about our kiss? What about our darn kiss?

Mustering up all the courage I can find, I dial his number. Even though our schedules are completely different—I work during the day and he at night—I take a chance that he'll pick up his phone. When it goes to voice mail, I'm terribly disappointed but I leave him a message urging him to call me, no matter the time.

When I hang up the phone my heart beats, well *blasts,* inside my ears and it's nearly impossible to rest. I try reading but my mind is clearly not on Mr. Darcy, no matter how much he's changed. Jane Austen's prose, although beautiful, doesn't seem to be able to hold my attention.

The TV helps a little, a mindless episode of *All in the Family* seems to do the trick, followed by reruns of *The Jeffersons* and *The Nanny.* I must have fallen asleep sometime between *The Nanny* and *Roseanne* because it's after midnight when I hear my phone ringing. I fumble around; it's somewhere tangled up in my covers. Four rings later, I barely catch it before the call goes to voice mail.

"Hello." There's a bit of desperation in my voice.

"Hi." *It's him. It's* finally *him.*

"How are you?" I ask, my voice lifting upon hearing his hello.

"I'm fine. How are you?" Something about his voice is different. I can't put my finger on it, but fear screams inside my gut.

"I'm pretty good. Just trying to get myself settled," I tell him.

"I bet."

"So much has happened, Peter, you wouldn't believe." I sit up in bed, propping a few large pillows behind me. "I don't even know where to begin. Helga, the ride home, my new house—oh my gosh, you won't believe my neighbor, bless his heart, he reminds me of Jeb. And my job. Wait till I tell you all about my job."

"You've got one already, huh?"

"Yes, it's a miracle how it worked out. See I ran into this old friend of mine whose husband works at this TV station here in town and she called her husband . . ." I ramble on and on. I'm not sure why I'm doing it but . . . "And then he called me to tell me about a job opening on the radio side and I called the program director, who basically offered me the job right on the spot. It's turning out to be pretty fun, actually."

I tell him all about it and he tells me all about his job and how he's really enjoying it so far. With every word he speaks, though, I'm growing more and more leery of the diffident tone in his voice.

"Leelee?" he says, seizing a pause in our conversation.

"Yes?"

"I'm happy for you. I truly am. You deserve all the happiness life has to offer."

"Thank you. So do you." *What are you saying? You're sounding like this is good-bye.*

"You are the sweetest most wonderful girl I know. I've been thinking about us every day since you left. You know, about you living in Tennessee and me living here in Vermont. And honestly, I don't think it's fair to you, to keep you tied up in a long-distance deal."

I close my eyes and fall back on my pillow, unsure how to respond. Cautiously I say, "But, what about our good-bye, just a little over a week ago? Didn't that mean something to you?" I reach up and pinch my lip, rubbing it nervously between my fingers.

"Of course it meant something to me. It means a lot to me. But think about it. We are something like fifteen hundred miles apart. I don't see you ever moving back up here; like I told you when you left, you're not meant to be a Vermonter. You're happier back down South. I would never want to be the one to take that away from you."

I can feel my eyes fill with tears and every one of my nerve endings seems to have caught fire. Not only are my feelings hurt but I can actually feel the pain seeping through my pores. "So, you don't think . . . you would . . . ever be able to come here?" I say. By now my sinuses have started to close and I'm sure he can hear the affliction in my voice.

"*Move there* you mean?"

"Well, yeah. I think you'd like it down here."

"It's not a matter of whether I'd like it or not. I'm just not the kind of guy that can move somewhere without a job. I guess maybe I'm a bit practical when it comes to that." He chuckles slightly but I know him well enough to know it's out of nervousness. He doesn't find that funny at all.

I honestly don't know what to say. The awkward pause in our conversation grows even longer. He finally breaks the silence by changing the subject. "My new job up here is pretty good, actually. Besides the raise, I'm designing a new menu."

"That makes me happy for you." My voice cracks and I'm sure he can tell I'm crying.

"I always want to be your friend, sweetheart," he says. "Always. I never want to lose touch with you. This is not about me not thinking you are the perfect girl. It's about me not thinking I can give you what you deserve. Can you understand that?"

I shake my head no, even though he can't see me.

"I'll always be here for you if you need me. Okay?" His voice is tender, one of the things I love about him the most. "Please tell me you'll be okay."

"I'll be okay," I manage to eke out, even though I don't think I will.

There's more silence in our conversation. Honestly it's because there's nothing more to say. It's not like I can beg him to move here. And it's not like I'm ready to talk about life as his friend instead of his girlfriend. In the end instead of sealing our relationship, our kiss killed our friendship.

"I'll talk with you soon," he says.

Instead of responding, I'm silent.

"You can call me anytime, Leelee," he says.

I can barely speak. "Yes, we'll talk soon," I manage to say.

"Bye, Leelee."

"Bye, Peter."

And then he's gone. Our phone conversation is finished and I suppose, so is our relationship. Lying flat on my back with my arms straight down at my side, my bed feels like a coffin. Why is it that even though we never really had a long romantic relationship, I feel like I'm dying? Love seems to be screaming at me from the other side of the room, *Why can't you hold on to me? What is it about you that can't keep me alive?*

It's not my fault! I want to scream back. *How can I argue with him about not wanting to move down South to a place he's never even visited?*

Peter Owen, the boy from New Jersey, the finest chef I've ever encountered, the dad who lost a baby to SIDS and had his wife leave him for his baby brother, the wonderful man that I just happened to meet and fall in love with, doesn't see himself as anything but a true Yankee. He might not know it, and I suppose that's just the way it is, but I'll always think of him as the best thing about the North. He'll always be my Yankee Doodle Dandy.

Chapter Six

Six weeks later, I'm a little sorry to say that my beloved Memphis seems to be letting me down. The weather is freezing for the end of March. Normally everyone would have shed their jackets by now but the chill in the air won't seem to let go . . . it's hanging on as steadily as my somber mood ever since Peter told me that he wanted to be "friends."

It's hard as heck waking up in the mornings but by the grace of God I'm doing it. The girls are getting to school, almost always on time, and they're getting used to the after-care. It's not the perfect situation but it's manageable. Thank goodness for the preschool program I found for Issie. She seems to enjoy her school even more than Sarah does.

More surprisingly, I'm getting to work on time and despite Edward and Stan both, I'm starting to feel comfortable. I'm gaining confidence and I can feel my self-worth returning. As Johnny predicted, the two of us are having fun together. He's quite a prankster, that one, continually hoodwinking poor unsuspecting souls (like me), naïve to his tomfoolery.

One morning during a rare early March snow shower, Johnny told the listeners that the morning show was broadcasting live from a parking lot on Mt. Moriah Road. Jack, Johnny's sidekick, recorded an ad, or promo as they say in radio, inviting folks to "Ski Mt. Moriah." People actually showed up ready to ski, wearing ski clothes and hats and toting their snow skis, even though the snow accumulation was merely a dusting. Mt. Moriah Road is as flat as a pancake, just like the rest of Memphis. The station phone never stopped ringing all day. I was the one taking the calls, explaining to the folks that it was just another of Johnny's signature stunts. "Sometimes people just have a hard time using their noggins," Mama would have said. Daddy, never having much of a tolerance for ignorance, wouldn't have been quite as kind. "They don't have enough sense to get out of the rain," he would have said.

The big buzz around the office is that Liam White himself is stopping by the radio station for an interview. Liam White, at least to my girlfriends and me, is the equivalent of Sting or Jackson Browne or possibly even Jon Bon Jovi. Maybe not quite as famous, but he's certainly *our* definition of eye candy. His mellow, harmonic voice has captivated me since I was first old enough to appreciate the bliss of rock 'n' roll. Around the age of eight or nine, I discovered the wonder of "Miss Thing" (one of his very best songs in my humble opinion), on the radio and when I became old enough to study his album covers I discovered how thrilling it can feel on the inside when a handsome face stirs the female desire.

To think he'll be coming to the radio station where I'm employed is, well, it's just unimaginable. I've been looking forward to it all week. Truthfully, I haven't been this giddy since *American Bandstand*. I even went out last night and bought a new dress for the occasion. I mean, why not? How many times does a girl get to see a celebrity of that caliber in person? Even if I just watch him pass by my office I still need to look nice. Besides, Johnny swears he'll make sure that I get to meet him. If left up to Edward, he'd just prance Liam White right on past me without so much as a wave. After all, he made it perfectly clear that he doesn't want his staff "hounding the stars."

Each jock, on every shift this week, has been promoting Liam's appearance. They've been giving away a pair of concert tickets every day and the grand prize winner gets entered into the pot to win a chance to speak with Liam on the phone when her name is announced. Not only that, she also wins two backstage passes to meet him in person after the show. My job is to deliver the tickets to the winner once she shows up. Now I realize the winner might be a man, but it would be a crying shame given Liam's delicious looks.

Liam is due in around nine thirty to catch the tail end of the morning drive time audience. That way Johnny can talk about it all morning, play Liam's hits, and keep the listeners hanging on till the end of his shift. I can tell Stan is plenty peeved that he wasn't asked to conduct the interview. From what I've been observing, Johnny gets way more breaks than Stan. It all comes down to the difference in their two personalities, if you ask me. One is fun. The other is, well, not in the least bit fun.

If truth be told, I've been twitchy and flustered all morning, literally counting down the minutes to Liam's arrival, not to mention the flurry of texts to the girls. So when the control room door swings open (I can hear it from my office) and Johnny pops his head in my door seconds later, I practically jump out of my skin. "Hey kiddo," he says, "White's in the lobby and Edward just left to go down to get him. Make up an excuse to be in the control room after say, five minutes. I'll make sure you get to meet him."

Breathe Leelee, breathe. "I'm a wreck," I blurt out.

"What?"

"I'm nervous," I say, tucking my hair behind my ears.

"You'll be fine." Johnny rubs the top of my head with his knuckles and smiles. "Hey, why don't you put all the ticket winners' names in a hat and bring that in with you? White can draw the grand prize winner from there."

"Seriously?"

"Yeah. Why not?" he says, with a shrug.

I slightly shake my head. "Edward is why not."

"Forget that buffoon. It's a perfect excuse for you to be in the control room."

No doubt about it, meeting Liam White is definitely worth the risk. "Okay, but now I'm even more nervous."

Johnny cracks up laughing. "You'll be fine." He holds up a hand with five fingers spread apart. "Remember . . . five minutes." Then he's gone. *That adorable laugh. I could listen to it all day long.*

The sudden appearance of a certain face only makes matters more tense. I flat don't have time for Stan. "Mmm, mmm, mmm, mmm, mmmmm," he mutters from the doorway. He must like my new dress. It's somewhat sexy, admittedly, a V-neck, light blue, with a small, thin ruffle running from the right shoulder down to the hem on the left side. It's fitted at the waist with three quarter length sleeves.

Stan, despite all evidence to the contrary, thinks he is one hot hunk of burning love. I remember hearing his voice for the first time on the radio, and I distinctly recall thinking, *Now that's the kind of disc jockey that I could hear in my sleep, the kind that would make my heart melt. That man's voice could lure me anywhere.* But after getting to know him, he couldn't even lure me into an all-expense-paid shopping spree at Saks Fifth Avenue.

He strolls into my office acting like he's looking for something on my desk. He's looking for something, all right, he's looking for information. And he thinks he's incredibly sneaky, glancing at all the messages I've taken for the other jocks. I can see his eyes staring at the little pink notes even though he's pretending to be in search of something else. "Where . . . is my *highlighter*? I could have sworn I left it right here." He's pushing the messages, which are neatly stacked in piles, off to the side but furiously scanning them at the same time.

I'm absolutely dying to ask him why he feels the need to be so dang nosy all the time but of course, I wouldn't dare. "What color is it?" I ask, casually.

He's a crafty one, that Stan. After a short pause he answers, "Orange. I'm a UT fan."

I slide open my drawer and hold up an orange one. "Here, take mine. I'm not using it right now."

"Aren't you kind."

I tilt my head and grin.

"Thank you, Ms. Satterfield." Plucking it out of my fingers he glances at my chest. "Nice dress you have on today," he says, now standing much closer to me, his breath a looming stink bomb on the horizon. To make matters worse, he honks his snot up into his nose so loudly I'm just sure it can be heard clear down the hall.

"Thanks, Stan," I say. I can't help but wince as I take a step backward. I'm on the verge of vomiting from the sound of him swallowing all that gunk in his nose.

"Well. What's the occasion?"

I shake my head and shrug my shoulders. He's the last person I want to know about my premeditated wardrobe purchase. Even more importantly, though, I don't want him to notice how flustered I am about meeting Liam White.

"You're not fooling me."

"What do you mean?" *Uh-oh. I'm busted.*

"Liam White? A huge star? Right here in the halls of 99."

I scoff. "It's not like *I'll* be talking to him." Hopefully, I sounded convincing. I'm not about to let him in on Johnny's scheme.

"Yeah, but he'll pass by here on his way to the control room. He might just look your way. You never know."

Just at that moment, Edward's full-mouthed self can be heard all the way down the hall. My heart sinks to my toes just thinking about the fact that I'm actually within fifteen feet of Liam White. I can hear Edward bragging about the FM 99 award plaques and gold records. Funny thing is, he's the only one talking. Stan hears him, too, moves into the doorway and stands there with his neck craned down the hall, just about as conspicuous as a car mechanic at a deb ball.

I'm not trying to be ugly, but Stan's heinie or "honkus" as Virginia calls it, is too wide for the both of us to be in the doorway. My plan, all along, has been to pretend to be reading the phone messages when

Liam White walks by. Now *I'm* the one having to stand sideways and peer out the doorway to try and get a glimpse of the arriving entourage. And it's *my* office. Not Stan's.

When I muster up the courage to peek out the door, Liam is standing with his arms crossed and Edward is still blabbing away about his stupid plaques. There's another guy who looks as bored as Liam. I notice him glance at his watch. "We should get on with it," he says.

Edward looks offended, but only for a second. "The control room is around the next corner," he says, and continues talking incessantly as they meander down the hall. I'm sure Edward has never walked so slowly in all his life but to him, the observance of his vanity wall by a big star is well worth the stroll. "Johnny Dial will be the jock conducting the interview," Edward says. "I'm sure you've heard of him. He's won more R&R awards than any deejay in Memphis."

Of course Edward never bothers to introduce me; he marches right by my office without so much as a glance in my direction. As planned, I look up from reading the phone messages and smile nervously at them anyway. By luck, I manage to catch Liam's eye while in the small sliver of space between Stan's rotund left hip and the doorjamb . . . and he smiles back. My pulse stops. The other guy doesn't look at me, and Edward certainly doesn't. Our boss never introduces Stan, either, but that doesn't stop him from hollering out to Liam as they pass by. "Mr. White. I'm Stan Stallone. Middays. Huge fan, huge fan." He trails pathetically behind them toward the control room, pronouncing huge as "youge."

Liam White is even better looking in person than he is on his album covers. I've seen him on TV before, *Soundstage* and *Austin City Limits,* but boy is he a drool up close. Blondish hair with a receding hairline—much like Sting. His close-cut beard and mustache give him a bit of a rugged look. So do his blue jeans. His flannel shirt is untucked and rolled up at the sleeves, and he's wearing a pair of white Nikes. A brown leather jacket is draped over one arm. I could have drooled all over him.

How in the world am I ever going to get rid of Stan? I keep thinking.

He could thwart my entire plan. I have to race down the hall to the copy machine, make a copy of the winner sheets and have the names cut up in strips and placed inside an FM 99 ball cap, all within a matter of minutes. As nosy as Stan is, he'll be watching my every move. I grab the folder marked "Liam White Ticket Winners" on my desk, tuck it under my arm and head down the hall, leaving Stan in the doorway.

Stan spots me and calls out, "Where are you going?"

"To the copy machine. Gotta work," I say over my shoulder.

"Have fun," Stan hollers back.

When I return from the copy room, I notice Stan's sitting in the other control room across the hall from my office. It's the room where the traffic guy, Michael, broadcasts the morning traffic report. There's a window from there into the main control room and that sneaky Stan has nabbed a ringside-seat for the interview. He sees me walk by but doesn't invite me to join him. Little does he know I've got other plans.

I can hear Johnny from the clock radio on my desk and it doesn't appear that he's started the interview yet. There's a seven-second delay, in case someone accidentally cusses, but it sounds like he's simply announcing the name of the last song he played, "Dancing Hearts." One of Liam's biggies.

I fumble for a pair of scissors and hurriedly cut the winners' names from the sheet into strips. When I rush to the prize closet to pull out an FM 99 ball cap another idea comes to mind. If there's one thing Edward dearly loves it's all this FM 99 paraphernalia, or "swag" as he calls it. If I dare enter the control room during the Liam White interview, I better have enough swag to warrant my presence. It's risky, but as Virginia would claim, worth getting fired over. I grab enough shirts, hats, and coffee mugs to outfit Liam's entire band.

My heart is blasting out of my chest while waiting for the on-air light to go out. When it finally shuts off, I slowly push open the weighted door. Liam is on the far side of the control room across the board from Johnny and by the way they're laughing I can tell things are going well. I see him glance over at me, making eye contact for the second time. Johnny shoots me a mischievous smile but then continues his conversation with Liam.

The other guy, the one accompanying Liam, is standing in the corner, clearly relegated to that location because Edward's backside is taking up residence in the only other chair in the control room. When Edward first sees me, I can tell by the way he squints his eyes that he's peeved. But after observing the abundance of swag in my arms, his scowl transforms into an expression of pure elation. He gets up out of his seat and starts grabbing the stuff away from me, passing it out as if it had been his idea all along.

"Here's a sweatshirt for you," Edward says to Liam. "And a T-shirt and a hat." He leans over and plops a ball cap down on Liam's head.

Liam calmly removes the ball cap and lays it on the desk next to the mic, an act that hardly deters our program director.

"What else do you want? A coffee mug? We can load you down," Edward tells him. "Look at the quality of this stuff. First rate. Sure to last." He's feeling the material of one of the sweatshirts with one hand and bouncing a coffee mug in the air with the other.

"If it means I get to meet the redhead, I'll take it all," Liam says with a Memphis drawl that is as smooth as Jack Daniel's Tennessee whiskey and just as lethal.

My knees go weak.

Edward whips his head around in my direction. I can tell by the puzzled look on his face that he's in a conundrum. His strict policy about his staff not rubbing elbows with the stars is battling with the fact that one of the stars actually wants to meet his programming assistant. Edward's introduction is lame at first, then he wises up and all of a sudden I'm his best friend. "Leelee is our wonderful programming assistant," he says, with an artificial smile.

"It's a pleasure," Liam says and stands up. He tries to squish around Edward but there's no room. Edward never bothers to move so Liam gives up and extends his hand around him.

"Thank you. Nice to meet you," I say, positive he can feel my hand shaking.

"Programming assistant? You must run this ship," he says.

Out of nowhere, I'm suddenly shy. I can hardly say a single word when I realize I'm actually shaking hands and talking with Liam White. All I can manage is a timid head nod, reduced to the awkward social habits of my six-year-old.

Johnny, who senses my stage fright, does his best to intervene. "Hey Leelee, have you got the names of the winners?" One side of his headphones is pushed away from his ear.

"Right here in the hat." From somewhere outside of my body, I can feel myself walking over to Johnny behind the control board, handing him the ball cap.

"Hang on a second," he says under his breath as he readjusts his headphones and pushes a button on the board. "We're talking with Liam White, our guest in the Classic Hits FM 99 studio today. He's in concert tonight at the gorgeous Orpheum Theatre downtown. Have you ever performed at the Orpheum?"

"No. Tonight's the first time." Liam's wearing headphones as well.

"You're in for a treat."

"So I've heard."

To watch Johnny Dial converse on the radio, you'd never know there's a mic in front of him. His hand gestures and body language give the impression he's talking with someone in his own living room. He'll scratch his head, rake his fingers through his hair, and even sneak a crotch scratch while he's talking. "It's been through several renovations," he says. "The last one was just a couple of years ago when they increased the depth of the stage to be able to host larger Broadway productions like *Phantom* and *Les Mis*. The sound in the place is state of the art. That must be pretty important to you."

"Sound is everything," Liam says with a nod. "I'll keep sound check going an extra hour just to make sure the mix is right."

"I've heard other musicians say the same thing."

"If a guitar is too loud, and the audience can't hear the background vocals, that's a problem. They can't experience the full show."

"Or your voice. That would be an even bigger problem," Johnny says, and rests his chin inside his right palm.

Liam laughs. "I suppose. We travel with our own sound guy, and our own sound equipment. The board doesn't look much different than the one you're using."

"I'd like to apply to be his sound guy. I give good board," says a voice out of nowhere. It's Stan on the mic in Michael's traffic room. All heads turn toward the window between the two control rooms but not a word is spoken. Johnny never acknowledges the comment. Neither does Liam. *Poor Stan.*

"We've been giving away tickets to your show all week and one of our lucky winners gets to go *backstage* and meet you tonight," Johnny says, and waves me closer.

"I'm looking forward to it," Liam answers. He seems sincere. At least he does to me.

"Our lovely programming assistant, Leelee"—he reaches out his arm to pull me close to him—"has all of the names in this FM 99 ball cap. Liam, if you'll do us the honor of choosing a winner, we'll get this show on the road." He motions to me to hand the cap over to Liam.

Edward jumps up, snatches it away from me, and hands it over to Liam himself.

I feel Johnny press his left elbow into my side, just like Virginia would do if Edward did something stupid like that in front of her. With his other hand, he pulls the mic closer to his lips. "That's it, Liam. Mix up the names really well."

Liam digs inside and pulls out a strip of paper, which he unfolds. He leans into his mic. "And the winner is . . . Kathy Warren."

Edward initiates a phony round of applause.

"Kathy Warren, if you're listening, call in and talk to Liam White. He's right here waiting to talk to youuuuu." Johnny cuts to a commercial.

There's a conversation going on during the commercials between everyone in the control room except me. The girl who's never, one time, been at a loss for words is suddenly dumbstruck. My eyes dart around the room and without knowing it fixate a little too long on Liam. Edward notices and I can clearly read the "that's enough" look on his face. I weigh losing my job against standing there just to be in the presence of Liam White. Even though I've already mastered the art of surreptitious gawking, my head, in a rare moment, actually wins out over my heart. So I turn around and leave.

About ten minutes later I hear the control room door swing open, and Edward's voice is drowning out all the others. This is my last opportunity, I'm thinking. My last chance to talk with Liam White. After all, never in my life have I been this close to a "real" celebrity before. Unless, of course, you call Jerry the King Lawler or Tojo Yamamoto celebs. Alice's high school boyfriend, Tim, would round a group together every Saturday morning for the wrestling matches at the WZCQ TV studio, to whoop and holler at the fake blood splattering all over the ring. We weren't but ten feet away.

Plus Memphis has had its own list of famous people and if you're lucky enough, you might have a sighting. Rufus Thomas, the Funky Chicken himself, was walking down Beale Street one night and Virginia dared me to ask him for his autograph, which of course I did, with no hesitation or fear. Alice rode an elevator with Cybill Shepherd once and she's told the story so many times I feel like it was me on that elevator. Mary Jule and I attended Al Green's church one Sunday and when I was little I saw Elvis in his front yard at Graceland. But never have I actually carried on a conversation with a real star. Until now.

When I hear them leaving the control room, I charge out to the little reception room down the hall. Tidying the coffee area has not yet become a task I aim to do on a regular basis, but today I'm considering it a fine part of my job description. I'm rinsing the coffeepot (even though it's full) when I hear them approaching. When I sense he's only a few feet away, I turn around. "It's nice to meet you, Liam."

He stops right in front of me. "You, too, Leelee."

I cannot believe he remembers my name.

"Are you coming to the show tonight?" he asks.

To have to tell a famous singer with whom you're carrying on a conversation that you haven't bought tickets to his show is beyond embarrassing. I had not anticipated this wrinkle in my well-executed plan. "Actually . . . well, I thought I didn't have a babysitter so I didn't get tickets, but now I do. So I'm planning on looking for tickets," I say, not missing a beat.

He turns to the other guy with him. "Do you have any tickets with you?"

The man reaches in his pocket and pulls out a small stack wrapped in a yellow rubber band.

"How many would you like?" Liam asks me. "Two, four, six?"

It's all I can do to keep my eyes from bugging out of my head. "Seriously? Are you—are you sure?"

I can feel Edward's eyes burning a hole in my left cheek. *This is it, I'm fired.*

"Of course," Liam says.

Between Edward's piercing eyes and Liam's offer I'm as nervous as a Chihuahua stuck inside a room with a pit bull. I pull my hair back into a ponytail and twist it into a knot. My weight shifts from one foot to the next. Despite Edward's dissecting stare, and knowing full well I could be fired I say, "Well, I have three best girlfriends who would kill me if I went without them."

The guy with Liam counts out four tickets and hands them to me.

"Now you have four tickets," Liam says.

"Thank you. That's very, very generous of you," I tell him, avoiding Edward's eyes at all costs.

"Give her backstage passes, too," Liam says.

The hair on my arms stands straight up.

Once again the man with Liam reaches into his coat pocket. He pulls out stickers with Liam's picture and with a Sharpie writes "Memphis 3/31" in a blank space, followed by the letters "A/S."

"Hi, I'm Leelee," I say to the guy while he's writing. All of a sudden, I'm Chatty Cathy.

He looks up at me. "Deke."

"Nice to meet you, Deke."

He grins. But just slightly.

Liam takes the passes from him and hands them over to me. "Leelee. What a great name. I've never known a Leelee. Family name?"

I nod my head. "My grandmother was a Leelee."

"That's lovely. Will I see you tonight?" His sexy, yet tender smile has turned me into jelly.

"Yes, you will. Thank you again." It's highly possible that I might just faint.

As he's walking off he winks. *Just like Peter.*

Edward escorts Liam and Deke to the door before asking me to join him in his office. I lag behind on purpose as we're walking down the hall, like a kid trailing behind her teacher on the way to the principal's office.

When I turn into Edward's office he's standing in front of his desk with his arms crossed. There's a scowl on his face. No doubt about it, I'm in big trouble. "Let me see your tickets," he says, well, demands.

I hand them over. Oh well, so much for the concert, so much for the backstage passes, so much for my job! Why oh why do I do the things I do?

Edward walks behind his desk, takes his seat and fans out my tickets, laying them right next to his. After studying them intently he looks up, eyes piercing. "Yours are in double D. That's way behind row Z. Never mind." Scooping up the tickets like a card shark he reaches across the desk. "Here." There's a smirk on his face. He's *not* firing me. He is also *not* mentioning my backstage passes. Could that glaring invitation possibly have eluded him? I'm not getting my hopes up.

I'm not sure whether to keep my mouth shut or stroke his ego. I decide on the latter. If nothing else, I'm slowly learning how to steer my way through the cesspool of his pompous malarkey. "I bet yours are fantastic seats, Edward," I say, with a huge smile.

"Let's see." He bends down and glances at his tickets. "Row R.

Center. On the aisle of the eighteenth row." The chair squeaks as he leans back and puts his feet on the desk. "Perfect."

"Wow, those really are good seats."

"Of course they are. A gift—actually a *bonus*—from White's record label." All of a sudden he yanks his feet off his desk and sits straight up, leaning toward me. "There are no gifts in radio. That would be payola and Classic Hits FM 99 does not engage in such illegal activities." He points at me for some reason and then relaxes again. "Sony always takes care of me. It's good to be the PD." He crosses his arms behind his head, closes his eyes, and cradles his head into his palms.

Hoping he's finished with me, I start to head for the door but my movement startles him. After commanding me to have another seat, I'm made to endure a fifteen-minute lecture about "radio protocol" and the way I'm supposed to behave when a star is around. I manage to convince him that I was only trying to promote FM 99 and promise to mind my p's and q's while at the concert. I'm off the hook this time but as I leave his office and step out onto a sea of eggshells I find myself tiptoeing back to my office.

Chapter Seven

"You mean to tell me that we not only have free tickets but we're going backstage to meet him? *Tonight?*" Alice shrieks into the phone, on a four-way call during my lunch break. I'm darting into the grocery store to pick up a few things for dinner, anything I can do to keep from having to drag the girls through here after school. Of course the drawback to shopping at lunchtime is I can't buy anything that might spoil. So today I'm shopping for macaroni, pizza sauce, bread, fruit, granola bars, coffee, and anything else that will keep in my car until I get home.

"You're lying," Virginia says.

"Would I lie about something like this?"

"Yes," they all answer in unison.

A lady pushing her grocery cart out to the car overhears my conversation and shoots me a funny look as I pass by.

Cupping my hand over my mouth, I whisper, "Well, this time I'm not."

"Thank god you have this new job," Mary Jule says. "It's the best thing that's ever happened to us." Mary Jule is, hands down, the most excited of the three about my job. Deep down inside she probably wishes it were hers. None of my friends actually have to work but I know there's a teeny envious streak in all of them.

"I was just thinking the same thing. Hey, can everyone get a babysitter?" I ask.

"What do you think husbands are for?" Alice says.

"As you know, I never had that luxury with Baker when I was married," I say, as a gorgeous bunch of white lilies distracts me. "Y'all hold on a second, I need to find out how much these lilies cost."

"Where are you?" Alice asks.

"Seessel's. In the flower department. Hold on," I tell her. "How much are these lilies, please?" I ask a lady who's arranging yellow roses and baby's breath in a tall vase.

Virginia says something else, but I'm not really listening.

The lady stops what she's doing and pushes the lilies aside so she can read a tiny price tag on the bucket. "These lilies are four dollars each, ma'am," she says.

"Okay, thank you. I'll probably get some next time," I say to the lady before rejoining my phone conversation. "Flowers are ridiculous this time of year," I tell the girls.

"It's Easter," Mary Jule reminds me.

"Oh yeah. Wait, Virginia, what did you say a second ago?"

"I said Baker is a *loser*."

"That is something I'm finally well aware of. Hey, speaking of husbands, do you think John might watch Sarah and Issie tonight? I almost hate to ask Kissie, she's been spending so much time at my house lately. I'm sure the poor thing could use a break." John is the most likely husband to keep my children. He does anything and everything Virginia asks.

"If I tell him to he will," Virginia says, matter-of-factly. "What time does the show start?"

"Eight."

"Bring the girls over around seven. Wait a second. Why don't we all go out for a drink before the concert? I've heard about this great new place down on South Main. I think it's called the Cocktail Garnish." Virginia Murphey has been looking for any excuse to extend the party since we were fifteen, back in the days when we'd steal bourbon out of our parents' liquor cabinets.

"Woah, woah, *woah*. I'm not sure I can be ready by then," Mary Jule says. "I haven't even found an outfit yet. I've got to run up to the mall right now. If I can't find anything, I can't go." Mary Jule is not kidding when she says this. Her entire closet is full of clothes she's only worn once. She can tell you to what special occasion she wore each outfit, but rarely will it see the light of day twice. I keep telling her that eBay should be her new best friend but so far she's never taken me up on my advice.

"And I've got to find a pedicure appointment or I can't go, either," Alice says.

"What? Who's going to see your toes? It's freezing outside," I say. "Wouldn't you know it? I've been waiting for warm weather since last August in Vermont and Memphis gets a record cold snap."

"Well, at the very least I have to get my nails done," Alice says.

"I got mine done yesterday, thank goodness. What are you wearing, Fiery?" Virginia asks.

"I'm not sure yet. Maybe jeans or this new dress I have on. I bought it last night because even if all I got to do was catch a glimpse of Liam White I figured I better look cute. It's adorable."

"I was gonna wear jeans and a long top—to cover my gigantic stomach," Virginia says. "What do you think?"

"You don't have a gigantic stomach," we all say.

"Everyone gets a big stomach after babies. Everyone but Fiery," Virginia says.

If I've heard that once, I've heard it a thousand times. "Virginia, I told you why my stomach isn't big. It's from all those years of ballet." Mama had me in ballet shoes before I knew my ABCs.

"Yeah, yeah, yeah," Virginia responds.

"I do not have time to listen to this," Alice says. "I'm hanging up so I can find someone to do my toes."

"Wait, Alice," I say. "I'm thinking of wearing jeans, too. What do you think?"

"Absolutely not," she says. "Wear the dress. It will look like you came straight from work and didn't take the time to dress up for him. Play it cool."

"Maybe he's single," Virginia says. "Do you know?"

"No idea."

"Did he have on a wedding ring?" Mary Jule asks.

"I never looked for that."

"You have lost your edge, Leelee Satterfield. Where's your Kravitz spirit?" Virginia says.

"I'll Google him and see what I can find out," Alice adds.

"Google him and find out? Aren't you getting a little ahead of yourself? I highly doubt the guy has any ideas about me other than a random act of kindness."

"Whatever," Virginia says. "Just refuse a date with a rock star if it makes you happy."

"That is completely ridiculous. I have to get back to work now. See y'all tonight."

Six hours and eleven wardrobe changes later, four peach daiquiris, one pedicure, two manicures, and an incident with a curling iron on the fritz, the girls and I pull up to the Orpheum Theatre, where there's a long line into the parking lot across the street. We take a chance on a garage a little farther down on Beale and luckily someone's pulling out of a spot on the first floor—a "lucky Jimmy" Daddy used to call it. He claimed the good parking spots waited on him and that he never had to walk more than a few feet to where he was going. When I asked him who Jimmy was and why he was lucky, he told me about his lucky college roommate, Jimmy, who kissed more pretty girls than any other boy at Ole Miss.

This unseasonably cold weather is wreaking havoc on my Southern soul. Having endured Vermont's glacial conditions for fourteen long months, only to come home to spring temperatures under the fifty-degree mark is disheartening to say the least. As we hustle down Beale Street to the theater, huddling next to each other for warmth, the wind off the Mississippi rips through our hair. I try tucking my long curly locks inside my jacket but it's no use. My hairdo has already been blown to hell in a handbasket.

Once at the front door, I pull out our comp tickets and hand them, along with our backstage passes, to the girls. We all follow Virginia's lead and pin our passes to our shirts. The ticket taker, an older man with a bow tie, smiles when we hand him our tickets and sees our passes. He's been working here as long as I've been patronizing this theater. "Enjoy," he says and shoots us his best Polident smile.

"Oh we will," Virginia says, and prances inside with her jacket over her arm, proudly flaunting her backstage pass on her voluminous chest.

If you ask me, the Orpheum, originally built as an opera house in the Roaring Twenties, is the prettiest theater in the South. The lobby, opulently decorated with tasseled brocade red draperies, enormous crystal chandeliers, and gilded moldings, has a grand double staircase that leads to the mezzanine. I couldn't count the number of times I've been here to see Broadway shows, ballets, and concerts if I tried. These red velvet seats have been witness to childhood memories like Jameson class trips to the opera, my one and only bobbed hairdo (which made me look more like a coiffed French poodle than a preteenager), and even summer dates with Baker to see old movies on the big screen.

Tonight the lobby is filled with people our age and older. Not too many twenty-somethings, let's put it that way. Virgy and I each order a chardonnay and Alice and Mary Jule order beer. While glancing around the lobby I notice another girl wearing a backstage pass but she and her date are wearing theirs on the thighs of their blue jeans. "Look how that girl is wearing her pass," I say to the rest. "Should we move ours down to our legs?"

"NO. Leave it right where it is. He'll have to look at your bosoms."

"*Virginia*. I don't want him to do that."

"Of course you do," Alice says. "They're one of your best features."

"Suppose he's *married*?" I say, and use my fingers to indicate little quote marks for the word "married."

"Suppose he's not," says Mary Jule, looking me straight in the eyes with a cocked brow.

Inside the theater, more gilded molding and a tremendous red velvet curtain hanging in the wings enhance the proscenium. There are 2,500 seats in the Orpheum and several boxes on both the mezzanine and the balcony. I've always dreamed of getting to sit in one of those boxes for a concert or a play. The mighty Wurlitzer pipe organ, played before each movie in the summer, usually sits majestically on a hydraulic lift, just to the left side of the orchestra pit. Tonight it's in its cradle, tucked safely away under the stage.

After handing our tickets to an usher, we follow her down the center aisle. I can't help but wonder if she's even heard of Liam White. I'm guessing she must be at least seventy. Alice, who always walks like she's on one of those moving sidewalks, is blazing down the aisle when someone reaches out and touches her on the leg. She stops and leans down toward the seat. The closer I get, a very familiar profile comes into view. Tootie Shotwell, dear lord almighty, is blabbing away to Alice. I stop, dead in my tracks, and whisper to Virgy, "I'm turning around. I'll just walk down that other aisle." I point across the theater.

"And deprive her of seeing your backstage pass? You are not."

She has a point.

Mary Jule, Virginia, and I pause long enough to wave at Tootie (and slightly push out our chests so that she sees our passes) before continuing behind the lady usher. Closer and closer, we creep to the front of the stage. It's got to be a mistake, I'm thinking, when she leads us past the front row and into the orchestra pit, which has been raised from the bottom and is now level with the rest of the seats. Virginia goes in first, followed by Mary Jule, then me, and finally Alice. Once we're settled into our row, after exchanging titillating looks, Alice leans forward and asks the couple in front of us about our seating.

"They open the orchestra pit when the show is otherwise sold out. It's a way to fit in more people. Kind of cool, huh?" the lady says.

I'll say. So here we are. The four luckiest girls in town. Fourth row, center seats. Free seats, no less, right up under Liam's nose.

Mary Jule holds up her beer. "To Leelee. The best excuse for a new outfit I've ever had." I'm not really the Talbots type, but on Mary Jule, the new brown and pink wraparound looks adorable.

The concert begins seconds later, with a roar from the crowd. Liam White strolls out on stage and the audience goes berserk. No introduction. No warning. No musicians who walk out first and take their places behind their instruments. Just Liam. He's got to be forty-five, I'm thinking, even though he doesn't have a gray hair on his head. He's so close I can see his dark chest hair poking out of the top button on his flannel shirt.

"That's exactly what he was wearing today at the radio station," I yell to my friends over the applause, as the crowd rises to their feet.

Virginia reaches down to her purse and pulls out a pair of binoculars. She's bending them to fit her face when I lean over Mary Jule and pull on Virgy's blouse. "What are you doing with binoculars?" I have to keep yelling over the screams. "We're practically on top of him."

"No wedding ring," she yells back, and tries handing them over to me.

"I don't need those. I can plainly see his ring finger," I scream back over the roar of 2,496 other ticket holders.

She says something else but I can hardly hear her.

"Huh?"

"I said, wouldn't you rather I made sure?" Virginia yells back.

I'm cupping my hand over my mouth and talking very loudly. "This is not about me going out with him. It's about enjoying the show and getting to meet a rock star that we've loved for years."

Virgy shrugs her shoulders.

When the applause dies down Alice asks me why Virginia was using binoculars.

"She was looking to see if he's wearing a dang wedding ring," I say, with exasperation at my lovingly relentless friend.

"Rock stars don't even wear wedding rings," she says with a shrug.

Three guitars circle a stool in the middle of the stage. Liam picks up the guitar nearest him from its stand and strums a few chords. We're so close that as he turns the knobs on the side, I can read the word "Taylor" on the tip of the guitar head. He chats freely with the crowd, completely comfortable alone on the stage. "How's everybody doing tonight?" he says with one foot on the floor and the other resting on the footrest of the stool.

People scream and whistle.

"Happy to be here in Memphis," he says, before belting out the first line of one of my favorite songs. "I know a young lady who lives down the hill." Once again the crowd goes wild. "Please Be Mine" is one of the biggest hits of his career. Virginia, Alice, Mary Jule, and I sing along with him to every word, as does everyone else in the audience.

For the first three songs Liam enchants, acoustic only, alternating between the three guitars circled around him. Finally he puts down the third guitar and stands to welcome his bandmates onto the stage. They all take places behind their instruments. The guitar player sure is cute, I'm thinking. So is the saxophonist. There's even a girl in his band—the keyboard player.

Our preshow cocktail hour has brought out the best in every one of us. Mary Jule thinks she's Jennifer Beals in *Flashdance* all of a sudden and Virginia is singing so loudly, people are staring at the poor thing. I'd never tell her to her face, but she sings off key worse than Alfalfa from *The Little Rascals*. Alice's wine keeps sloshing over the top of her cup as she sways to Liam's melodies. As for me, I can't take my eyes off the handsome singer who personally invited me to his concert.

Two songs later Liam lifts the guitar strap off his neck. I see him notice someone in my direction and smile, followed by a wave. I turn around behind me to see whom he's waving at, as does everyone else in the first three rows.

A lobster claw reaches over and pinches a chunk out of my arm. "He's waving at you, Fiery. He is waving at YOU!" Mary Jule nearly deafens my eardrum with a high-pitched squeal in my ear.

I whip my head back around. "No way." Alice grabs my knee.

When he continues staring straight at me I slightly lean into Mary Jule. "Oh my gosh, I think he might be." Shyly, I wave back. Just in case.

Fifteen minutes later, the guy sitting next to Alice taps me on the shoulder from behind and points toward the center aisle. I turn my head in that direction and as God as my witness, Edward Maxwell and family are standing in a single-file line. He's beckoning me out of my seat. Virgy and Mary Jule are so busy dancing they don't even notice. I whisper in Alice's ear, "Oh crap. There's Edward."

After a quick glance toward the center, she mouths two words. "You're. Lying."

"Excuse me, excuse me," I say to four people who all have to get up and move into the aisle so I can pass around them.

"I'm switching seats with you," Edward simply says, once I'm in front of him and hands me his ticket stubs.

What am I suppose to say to that? *No, I refuse? Over my dead body? We like our own seats, thank you very much?* I have no choice but to turn back around, ask the same four people to please move out to the aisle, yet again, so I can grab my purse and my best friends and leave our orchestra pit fourth-row seats.

Three minutes later, we're seated back in row R.

Alice Garrott is fit to be tied. She taps me on the shoulder and screams over the music. "What a jerk!" I just shake my head. There's no point in my making a comment. Besides, I've already told them every detail about my bombastic bully of a boss.

Liam White plays for a solid two hours. When he returns for

a third encore, every single person is on their feet hollering for him to continue. "'My Turn,'" someone yells. "'Turn It Up,'" another person calls from the audience.

His final song, a version of "Heartbreak Hotel," sends the crowd home happy. While on Elvis's turf, many a singer feels the need to pay homage.

When Liam does leave the stage for the final time the house lights go up and most in attendance head out the exit doors to our right. I have no earthly idea where the backstage entrance is located so I flag down another elderly usher. "Excuse me, please," I say, "do you happen to know where we're suppose to go with these passes?" I point to my chest.

She throws her thumb over her right shoulder and turns her head. "The far right of the stage. See those folks?"

I glance around.

"They're all doing the same thing. They want to meet Mr. Liam White, too. Might as well get in line."

The four of us move to the back of the long line, ironically right behind the grand-prize winners from the radio. Kathy Warren recognizes me and after introducing her to my friends the six of us can't stop chatting about the phenomenal concert. I'm right in the middle of telling Kathy the story of meeting Liam at the station when I spot Edward. He and his wife and two kids are at the very front of the line. He must have left his fantastic seats early to ensure his spot. Edward seems very peeved that he has to wait to see Liam like the rest of us (I can tell by the way he's shaking his head while talking to the head usher) but he's not given any preferential treatment whatsoever.

When we're all finally escorted back, almost everyone stops to admire the backstage area. Signatures from stars who have performed at the Orpheum are all over the place. Logos of Broadway shows have been meticulously etched on the walls and cast members have signed their names all around them. *Les Misérables, The King and I, Phantom, Rent, Cats,* they've all been here. Eddie Murphy, Carol Channing,

Hal Holbrook, Cary Grant, Mickey Rooney, Stevie Ray Vaughan, Jackson Browne, Michael McDonald, B.B. King, Christopher Cross, Jay Leno, everywhere I look there's an autograph from another one of my favorites. Still firmly planted in the front of the line, Edward and family never bother moving around the room to admire the artistry.

Deke, the guy who had been with Liam earlier, appears at the head of the line and leads everyone into a large green room where he explains that Mr. White will arrive shortly. A laminate hangs around his neck, designating his authority. He glances in our direction but doesn't say hello.

Finally, Liam moseys in. I notice right away that he's changed his shirt. Edward runs right up to him and appears to be introducing his family. Liam shakes hands with Edward's wife and two kids but I can tell by the way he's looking around the room that he's not exactly thrilled to see them. I can't help but wonder if he noticed Edward exchanging seats with us.

"There's *ole Eduardo,*" Virginia says, speaking softly, as if Edward might hear her from across the room. "The first one to talk to Liam White."

"Has he no shame?" I say. "He's the one telling me not to hound the stars."

"He's a joke," she says.

"The other day he asked Johnny Dial if Aruba was part of Spain."

"He did not," Mary Jule says.

"Honestly, that's what he said," I tell her.

"Maybe you should apply for his job," Alice says.

"Never going to happen. It's a man's world among program directors. But you can't help but wonder how he got the job in the first place."

Liam continues to work his way down the meet-and-greet line, signing autographs and posing for pictures. Every once in a while he scans the crowd.

"Wonder if he's looking for you, Fiery?" Virginia says.

"Nooo," I say. "What time is it anyway?"

Mary Jule glances at her gold Ebel watch. "Eleven thirty."

"Is everyone good to stay?" I ask.

"Al's probably expecting me by midnight," Mary Jule says.

"Then you need to tell him to come get you. We're not leaving until we meet Liam," Alice says, indignantly.

"Oh Alice, I'm sure we'll be home close to midnight. Look, he's almost to us," I say.

When there are only four more people in front of us, Edward strolls up, never mentioning the seat exchange. "Enjoy the concert?" he asks me.

"Oh my goodness, yes," I tell him.

"He didn't play 'Shaking All Over.' Disappointing," he says.

What about the great ones he did play? "I was a little sad he didn't play that one, but he has so many. I thought the show was amazing."

"He should have played it," Edward says definitively.

"Oh well, maybe next time." Hoping to get off the awkward topic, and after a prolonged and uncomfortable moment or two, I ponder introducing him to the girls. I'm honestly afraid of the look Alice might give him, but I see no other way around it. We're all standing here like statues. "I'd like for you to meet my best friends," I say lightly, touching his arm. Once I introduce each of them to Edward, he nods and in turn introduces us to his wife, Shelly, and their children, Edward and Shelly. They proceed to plant their feet right there in line with us.

Seconds later, Liam's walking up to us, well he's walking straight up to me. *Oh my god. Oh my god. Oh my gooooood.*

"Hello, Leelee," he says, with alluring charm.

"Hi, Liam," I say assuredly, his earlier wave from the stage has heightened my self-confidence. If my thoughts were played on a TV monitor right now, I'd never be able to show my face in public again.

There's an awkward moment of silence before Virginia nudges me. "Oh! Sorry, this is my dear friend, Virginia. And my other dear friends, Alice and Mary Jule." Am I supposed to reintroduce Edward? He's staring at me like I should. I decide against it.

Virginia says, "Nice to meet you. Thanks for the tickets."

"Yes, thank you so much," Alice says.

Mary Jule just smiles. I can tell she's about to lose it. In fact, her smile appears a little contrived. That happens when she's nervous or flustered. Like the time her mother-in-law, who she's a little embarrassed of, gave her a homemade potpourri tower at her wedding shower. I'll never forget it as long as I live. When she opened that gift—a tall glass vase, with white lights swirling through a mound of stale, apple-scented potpourri—Mary Jule had a look on her face that was phonier than a knockoff Gucci purse.

"You're welcome. I'm glad you guys could make it. Did you enjoy the show?" Liam asks.

"Oh yes. It was incredible. We have all your records. I just love 'Miss Thing,'" Alice says, not knowing what else to say to a famous musician.

"Me, too," Mary Jule says, her voice shaky.

"You guys couldn't have been more than eight or nine when that song came out."

"But we listened to the radio all the time," I tell him.

Edward, who's not been acknowledged by Liam yet and is standing there like a bump on a log, chirps up. "Where's your next stop, man?"

"Florida. We're in several cities there, as a matter of fact," Liam says politely, after taking a deep breath.

"Did you hear that?" Edward says to his son, who appears to be around eight. "Mr. White is headed to Florida."

Edward Junior's eyes are practically closed and big Shelly is holding little Shelly in her arms. Clearly this outing is past their bedtime, though Edward Senior seems oblivious. Edward grabs his son's left shoulder and shakes him so hard the poor little thing almost loses his step. "Florida? Your favorite place? Shells, the beach, boogie boards?"

Little Edward just stares at big Edward and Liam, smile-*less*.

"What city do you land in first, buddy?" Edward asks him.

"Jacksonville, I think."

"I love Florida," I say, my head darting at the others for confirmation. Clearly I'm still nervous myself.

Alice can tell and she tries to help. "Oh yeah, Destin is our favorite place. We've spent many a crazy day on that beach. Have you ever been there?" she asks Liam.

He shakes his head. "I don't think so. That's on the Panhandle, right?"

"Yes. With the whitest beaches in the whole world," I say.

"Wait a minute, I take that back. I had a gig in Panama City once. Isn't that close to Destin?"

"That's in South America," Edward says, drawing out each word, like he's the only person with a brain.

A very long silence follows.

Liam cocks his head and gazes at him. Alice, on the other hand, can't help herself. "No it's not. It's in Florida. An hour from Destin. Not far from Seaside."

"I've heard about Seaside," Liam says, completely ignoring Edward. "Isn't it a community of pastel houses and restaurants right on the gulf?"

"It's this side of heaven," Alice tells him, her Southern drawl painting quite the scene. "*Unbelievable* restaurants. And the homes are to die for."

Liam starts to comment but is interrupted by Edward. "I'll have to fly down there sometime," he says, shoving his hands in his pockets. "Is there a private airport nearby?"

We all look at each other and shake our heads. How on earth would we know that?

"I'm a pilot." He rocks from the balls of his feet back to his heels several times, determined to impress Liam.

"Cool," is all Liam says and changes the subject right back to Seaside.

All of us stand there chatting about Florida for about five minutes, during which Shelly, holding a sleeping child in her arms, intermittently asks Edward if they can go home. When Edward finally decides to honor her request, he pokes Liam with his elbow and says, "I'd love to chew the fat all night, buddy, but"—he sighs deeply—"got to get these kids to bed."

Liam simply nods his head.

"See ya, champ," Edward says and then turns to me. "Are you leaving soon?"

"Oh. In a few minutes," I say.

"I'll see you bright and early then." Edward and family finally stroll off.

As soon as my boss is only five feet away, Liam leans his face close to mine and under his breath says, "What was up with him taking your seats?"

I shake my head and shrug my shoulders. "They were better than his."

"What an idiot." He turns around to Deke, who's been hovering behind him the whole time. "Let's get out of here. Come with me, ladies, I'll buy you a drink."

Next thing we know the four of us are being led through the lingering crowd, out the green room and down another hall. I can't bear to look behind me. The image of Edward—hands on his hips, eyes narrowed, and lips pressed together is as haunting as my memory of Daddy the morning he stumbled upon his brand-new Lincoln sitting in the garage with a large dent in the trunk. Oh well. I'll worry about it tomorrow. I'll make sure to get to work bright and early. Not a second late.

"This is not happening," Alice says under her breath as we make our way down the long hall. "What are the odds?"

When we reach a dressing room with a large gold star on the door, Virginia scoots up behind me and pinches the back of my arm. I practically have to pinch myself, too—Liam was our teenage idol, something about him makes me feel like a young girl again.

Once inside, I'm taken aback by the cornucopia of food spread out on the counter below the large makeup mirror. It's the kind with big clear lightbulbs spaced two inches apart, tracing the outside of the mirror. Fresh cantaloupe, honeydew, mango, red grapes, raspberries, blackberries, and kiwi—arranged to resemble the petals of a flower—circle a bowl of poppyseed dressing. A gorgeous platter of imported cheeses with goudas, cheddars, époisses, and havarti looks like a still-life painting next to assorted crackers, apple slices, and breads. Jumbo shrimp spills out over a small ice sculpture shaped like a guitar. There's a bar set up in the corner.

At first, it seems a little awkward to be in his dressing room. Knowing what in the world to say to a rock star can be a little bit intimidating. Fortunately Alice and Virginia have no problem. Earlier trips to the bar have aided that predicament. Even still, Mary Jule and I are a bit more timid.

Liam is a gracious host. He shares his magnificent food and pours his expensive wine freely. Rombauer chardonnay. I recognize it immediately, and seeing the antiqued white label with gold embossing brings back a memory so sudden it hits me in the gut. For a moment, I'm not in Liam White's dressing room . . . but back in front of the fire at the Peach Blossom Inn, with Peter's inquisitive mouth swirling the buttery wine on his tongue. When I hired him as the chef, we spent long hours revitalizing the menu and wine list—and paired with his braised scallops, the Rombauer was as close to bliss as you get, considering it was winter in Vermont.

Once we've each partaken of a dainty plate of food, Liam offers us a seat. There's a sofa in one corner, where Mary Jule and Alice settle onto the downy cushions. I sit down on a less comfortable chair. It's metal, but the seat cushion is at least padded.

Virginia settles back in one of the overstuffed club chairs and crosses her legs. "Leelee knows all about wine," she tells Liam, as she swirls the chardonnay in her glass. "She used to be an inn owner in Vermont."

"Vermont?" He glances at me from the bar, where he's pouring himself a glass of Rombauer. "For real?"

"For real," Alice says. "She had a four-star restaurant up there." She points to the ceiling as if that's where Vermont is. "And you should have seen the wine cellar. Lord have mercy."

"Four stars? That's saying something. Wish I could have eaten there." He pops a shrimp into his mouth. "I would imagine that was quite an adjustment. Memphis, Tennessee, to Vermont."

"Trust me. It wasn't her idea," Virginia says.

Liam must be wondering if I even talk.

"Really." He pulls a chair out from the makeup area, it's like the one I'm sitting in, and sets it down next to mine. He swings his right leg over the seat and sits on the chair backward. "Tell me more."

"Well, let's see. I only lived there fourteen months. My life became one big nor'easter and then—"

"She got the hell out of Dodge," Alice says, taking another sip of her wine.

A cute smile follows bright eyes. "Why? What happened?"

"Oh, one thing after another really. I—"

"For starters, she had to fire this German witch of a bitch, whom she bought the inn from, and then the witch turned around and swindled it back, right under Leelee's nose." Virginia's gotten into the habit of talking for me, well, they all have.

"That's no fun," he says.

Mary Jule, who has been practically mute until now, suddenly sits up in her seat and turns on her Dixie charm. Not only does she have on a new dress, she made emergency appointments for a blow-dry, manicure, and a spray tan—and now she's determined to make them work for her. Her vowels have never been as long as they are tonight. Even Scarlett O'Hara never worked that hard. "Theen, her huusband leaves her for an *oolder* woman who Leelee finds out has had oodles of plastic surgery."

Liam finds Mary Jule's comment so hilarious, he spits out his wine.

I, on the other hand, stare her down like she has lost her ever-loving mind. My face turns as red as the big curtain on the stage and I have a pretty good idea of how that looks next to my fiery hair. Not only do I have no desire to discuss this tidbit of information with superfluous people like Tootie Shotwell, discussing it with a rock star who has invited us to his show is way worse.

When she sees my face and realizes it has embarrassed the fire out of me, she tries her best to recover—minus the exaggerated accent. "But Leelee didn't do anything wrong, though." She waves her hand in front of her face as if she's fanning away a bad smell.

This unfortunately gets Virginia going. She stands up, tops off her wine at the bar (it's sloshing over the top it's so full) and prances right up to Liam, chatting to him like they've been buddies for years. "She was rich as all get out though, and Baker—that's Leelee's ex—fell for her wiles. But Fiery did not let that stop her. Oh no. Once he left she turned the inn into a romantic *Southern* getaway. Well, we all did." She sweeps her free hand, palm up, toward all of us. "We surprised Leelee when that asshole left and helped her redecorate the inn," she says, with an emphasis on "ass" and a prolonged vowel to put Mary Jule to shame.

Alice stands, raising her voice over Virginia's so she can now be the center of attention. "New paint, new wallpaper, we even changed the name of the place from the Vermont Haus Inn to the Peach Blossom Inn. Right after she fired Helga."

"Helga?" Liam's eyes dart from one of us to the next, trying to keep up with who's on first.

"Yeah. Who names their child Helga? And let me tell you, she fit it, too. Six feet tall, hair slicked back in a tight gray bun. Mean as a snake. Leelee couldn't stand her," Alice says.

"I can't stand her myself," Liam says, chuckling.

Mary Jule chimes in again. "We even got rid of her hippos."

"Okay, now you've stumped me. Her hippos?" He looks directly at me, with a delicious grin and an amused smile on his lips . . . clearly he's charmed by my friends.

I shift in my chair and sit closer to the edge, uncrossing my legs, and attempt to make any bit of sense out of the insane fragments my tipsy friends have sputtered out during the last ten minutes. "Her pride and joy. When she sold us the inn, there was a collection of about twenty ceramic hippos that she insisted could not budge off the fireplace mantel. Several months later, when I dared to replace them with my own Herend china figurines, she flipped. I thought she might spontaneously combust, she was so angry."

"We were there, witnessed the whole thing," Mary Jule says and sweeps the hand that's holding her wine through the air. Of course a little spills onto the floor. "Oops," she says. "Sorry."

"Princess Grace even hated her and she loved everyone," I tell him, finally loosening up.

"Okay. Now you're killing me. Who in the hell is Princess Grace?"

Virginia, who never really liked Gracie, rolls her eyes and sighs loudly, purposefully bringing attention to herself.

I roll my eyes and shake my head in Virginia's direction. "She was my precious little Yorkie who died in Vermont after her blood froze to death. Don't even get me started on that one. I didn't think I'd be able to bury her. Vermonters don't bury their dead in the winter, you know." I sit back in my chair and cross my arms.

"What?" He swings his leg over the back of the chair and heads to the bar, filling his glass almost as full as Virgy's. "You guys are moving so fast, I can't keep up with you. What is this about Vermonters not burying their dead?"

"I'm serious. Vermonters can't bury people in the winter. Guess why?" I say.

"I have no idea," Liam says—and means it.

"Because the ground's frozen," I tell him.

"I'm a California dude. Never thought about that."

"Neither did I!" Virginia and I both say at the exact same time.

"But it's true, shoog," Alice says.

"What happens if some poor soul kicks the bucket in January?" he asks.

"He lies in a mausoleum until *The Thaw*. That's the term the Vermonters use for spring, which, by the way, actually doesn't even exist, but that's what they call it. I'm getting riled up just thinking about how quirky Vermont is," I say.

Liam takes another sip of his wine. "You girls are a hoot. This is the most fun conversation I've had in years."

Deke, who has poked his head into Liam's dressing room twice already, says to him, "We're almost ready to pull out, man."

"Give us five more minutes," Liam tells him, still laughing.

Everyone, and I mean everyone, in the room is well on their way to finding themselves three sheets to the wind, or "toe up" as Virginia calls it. Everyone, that is, except me. With a mother who preferred vodka to water, I'd learned early on what my limits were . . . not to mention what that can do to a family. For as long as the four of us had been stealing sips from our parents' liquor cabinets, I have been the designated driver.

After Deke comes in a fourth time, Liam looks at him and waves. "Okay, I guess we have to be on our way. Where are you guys parked? We'll drop you off."

"Right down on Beale Street, in a parking garage," Virgy tells him and I can tell by the way she's flaring her nose that she's tingling inside. This night is one for the Gladys Kravitz Agency history book, that's for sure.

When I glance at my watch, I'm shocked to see it's almost one o'clock in the morning. As we pass back by the green room I can't help but peek in, scanning the place for Edward in case he's somehow resurfaced. Fortunately, he's gone and so are all the instruments that once graced the stage. A few of the men who must have cleared all Liam's gear are still milling around.

Liam guides us out the stage door, down to his bus parked on the side of Beale Street and the four of us step onto Liam White's tour bus like we own the joint. Almost as if it's a reflex, I look around to see who's watching. Although I'm acting like a groupie, I certainly don't want anyone to think I'm one.

The minute we enter the bus, the hair on my arms sticks straight out and I can feel myself shivering. Thank god I'm wearing a padded bra. I notice Alice doing the same thing. The temperature inside is not much different than the climate outside.

"Welcome to Alaska," Liam says.

"Gah-lee, why do y'all have it so cold in here?" I ask him. "I might as well be back in Vermont."

"Because he's got control of the thermostat." Liam points to his bass player.

"Hey. It's not only me. Dan likes it even colder," the guy says.

"Dan's our driver," Liam says. He looks behind him and points to Dan, who's sitting at the wheel with a big piece of pepperoni pizza in his hand. "Phil's talking trash about you, dude."

Dan swallows in haste. "I heard him. Not true, not true."

"Let me show you guys around." Pausing to introduce us to his bandmates, he says, "Hey everyone, meet Leelee, Alice, Virginia, and . . ." He hesitates. "I'm sorry, is it Mary Jane?"

"It's Mary Jule. But don't worry about it. Happens all the time," she says.

The Liam White band members have all changed into sweats and long-sleeved T-shirts. No one is wearing shoes but all of them have on heavy socks. His keyboard player, the only woman, has on a zip-up fleece.

Some wave, some say hello (none of them stands) before turning back to the show they're engrossed in on the tube.

They're all stretched out on black leather, deep comfortable sofas that face each other on either side of the bus. The windows are darkened. A huge flat-screen TV hangs from the ceiling in the corner. I notice two pizza boxes with the tops open sitting on a banquette table which is right next to a small stove with four burners. A sink, fridge, and a microwave make it a mighty cute little kitchenette.

When we walk through the kitchen there's a piece of paper taped to a door to the left. "You Dump, You Pump," it says. All of us notice the sign but Alice is the only one who acknowledges it. "I wouldn't want to be the one to break that rule." She giggles and raises her eyebrows.

"Trust me. You certainly wouldn't," Liam says, chuckling.

He holds open a door, just past the kitchen, and we walk through a hallway with six individual curtains on either side of the bus. "These are our bunks." He pulls back one of the curtains on the middle row to show us the inside. "There's a TV in each bunk and we use these headphones so we don't disturb one another." He picks up a pair and throws it back down on the bed. "The TV rarely works, but the DVD player usually does. The woes of a bedroom on wheels."

"So y'all have a satellite?" Alice asks him.

"Yep, we sure do."

"I've always dreamed of riding on one of these," Mary Jule says, glancing around.

"Come go with us," Liam says, still chuckling.

"Unless I want to find myself huusbandless, chiiildless and with all grandmotha's silva' sold to a pawnshop when I get back, I bett'a not." *Here go the vowels again. Okay, Scarlett, that's enough.*

Liam bursts out laughing. It's obvious that he finds Mary Jule completely hilarious.

One more door, leading to the back of the bus is the only place left to view. "This is my room," Liam says, opening the door. "But I only use it to sleep." There's a queen-size bed with a large mirror above it, another big flat-screen TV and a whole stereo system built into the corner. One of his guitars is resting underneath the window.

"This is really nice. Do all y'all share the same bathroom?" Virgy wants to know.

"Yep, no big deal, though. We don't shower here. We always have hotel rooms in every city."

Deke pops his face into the room, which barely fits the five of us anyway. "Hey, man. We need to know where to drop off the girls."

"Okay. We're done here," Liam says, and asks us to go up front to show the driver where we're parked.

When we get to the parking garage, Liam hops off the bus and makes sure we make it safely to our car. "Who's driving?" he asks.

"I am," I say, as I'm digging for my keys. Once they're in my hand, I hit the open lock button on the remote.

Virginia leans over and whispers to him. She doesn't think I can hear her (that always happens when she's tipsy). "She won't tell you this part. But she's a champion. Leelee turned that whole inn around and made it work. The only reason she left is because she was so homesick."

He whispers back but I can hear him, too. "There's something about a redhead that intrigues me. Something that tells me she's got fire on the inside. Enough to make all kinds of things happen. I can just tell that about her."

"You don't know the half of it," Virginia tells him.

He opens my door and steps aside for me to sit down in the passenger seat. "Cute car."

"Thank you." I put my hands on the wheel and lean back in the seat. "It's a miracle she made it through a Vermont winter, but she's a tough ole cookie." I tap the steering wheel and tuck my hair behind my ears. I feel like I'm telling my date good-bye after the eighth-grade dance, with the parents watching.

After we're all inside the car he bends down outside my door. "Great meeting all you girls."

"You too, Liam," everyone says.

"Be good." He winks and shuts the door.

All of us watch in awe as he slowly ambles away from my car. Once we're sure he's out of earshot, we erupt into high-octave screams.

I turn around to the backseat. "Did that really happen?"

"It was history in the making," Alice says.

"I'm serious. Did Liam White honestly invite us to his dressing room and then give us a ride on his dang tour bus and then walk us to my car?"

"I'm framing this dress," Mary Jule says. "I'm asking Al to do that for me for Christmas."

"So are we groupies now?" Virginia asks.

"No. Groupies wouldn't have gotten off the bus," Alice says.

"What is it with me and guys that wink?" I say, placing my car in reverse.

"What do you mean?" Mary Jule asks, leaning up from the backseat.

"He winked at me twice. Peter always did that."

"Peter who? He's a loser, too," Virginia says.

Stopping my car in the middle of the parking lot I turn around to look at her. "No, he's really not a loser at all. He's wonderful. He's just no longer interested in me, I suppose." Even though we've just had the time of our lives, the mention of Peter's name always makes me sad.

Mary Jule massages my shoulders from behind as I drive out of the garage. "It's not that he's not interested, Leelee. He doesn't want to tie you up with a long-distance relationship. He's a man. He's got the job he's always wanted and he's getting paid well to do it. That's hard for a man to do."

"What's hard?" I ask her, picturing him with a sauté pan in one hand, a grill pan in the other, hunched over the stove at the Peach Blossom Inn with a bandana wrapped around his forehead sponging up the sweat from his brow.

"To leave his job with no guarantee of another one."

"I guess," I say, wishing for the first time since returning home that I was back in Vermont.

By the time we get back to Virginia's it's one thirty in the morning. The thought of having to be up in four and a half hours is worse than a Vermont black fly bite on the back of my neck. Well, maybe not that bad. But it's a miserable thought all the same. I keep the car running while I run in to get the girls who are sound asleep on a palette on the floor of Virginia's playroom. John carries Sarah and I carry Issie out to the car. That John, nothing ever bothers him. Virginia can stay out all night with a rock star, and instead of being bugged (as Baker would have been), he's elated. There's nothing he won't do for Virginia or for any one of us. Baker would have been sound asleep wearing earplugs.

As I'm driving off, I can't help but fantasize what it would be like to be on the arm of a real rock star. As great as it sounds, the thought occurs to me that, like everything else, it must have its downside. There's got to be a drawback to his lifestyle. It's fun to dream about, though, so I indulge in the fantasy most of the way home.

By the time I tuck the girls in their own beds though, my fancies have already turned into angst. I have to face Edward in six hours.

Chapter Eight

All hell's broken lose at FM 99.

When I walk in the front door of the station Jane waves me down from the receptionist's desk. "Thank God, you're here," she says. "This phone has been ringing off the hook."

Four more lines buzz. She presses a button and holds up her hand. "Hold on."

My heart sinks. Paranoia in all its irrational glory bombards my mind. Could it have something to do with me joining Liam White in his dressing room and staying there till one in the morning? Could Edward have possibly found out about the tour bus ride?

Jane answers each line and immediately puts all the callers on hold. Pushing aside the small microphone that stretches from the headset across her cheek, she closes her eyes and sighs heavily. "Oh girl. Johnny Dial is at it again. He's giving our entire listening area, which is close to three hundred thousand people, emergency routes out of the city. He's telling folks in downtown to get on the interstate at Riverside Drive. Then he's telling people out in Germantown to hop on I-40 at Germantown Road. To the folks in Midtown he's recommending they take 240 and loop around the city. But he's not telling folks why. People are in a panic. Fire engines have been dispatched and that's creating pandemonium. I just transferred the mayor to Dan Malcomb's office." Dan Malcomb is the general manager of FM 99.

"Oh good lord," I say.

"I've been handling all these calls myself. Now that you're here, I'm sending them up to you, girlfriend."

"I was on the phone instead of listening to Johnny on the way in. The one morning I don't listen, this happens."

"It's a good thing. You may have headed out of the city yourself. He fooled me this time."

"What exit route did you take?"

"No, girl," Jane lowers her voice. "He fooled me when I got in. I don't listen to FM 99. I'm a K 97 girl, but don't tell nobody." The phones start ringing again. I imagine the callers probably got frustrated, hung up, and are calling back.

"Your secret's safe with me." I can't help but shake my head. "That Johnny's crazy. Cute, but crazy."

The buzzing of more phone lines causes Jane to throw her hands in the air. She simply nods her head and waves.

As I'm running up the back stairs to my office, a thought crosses my mind. There is some good that's come out of Johnny's latest prank. It means that Edward's attention will be elsewhere. With any luck, last night's concert will be the furthest thing from his mind.

I can hear both of our station lines ringing when I step into the FM hall. I fling my purse down and answer line one, slipping down into my chair. I don't even have time to remove my coat. "Classic Hits FM 99, will you please hold a minute?"

"NO. Transfer me to the control room. Dial's not picking up."

"Sure, Edward," I say, and a chill creeps up my spine. It's hard to dissect his mood, the tone of his voice no different than usual.

After transferring him into the control room, I answer another call. "Classic Hits FM 99, may I help you, please?" The background noise lets me know it's a cell phone.

"Yes. Why are people leaving the city? I'm in Germantown and the line to get on the interstate must be two miles long. Will it be that way all the way to Nashville?" I can hear a slight amount of panic in the man's voice.

"Well it's—"

"Or am I supposed to go towards Mississippi? Or Arkansas?" His panic is growing. "Should I be taking the new bridge across the river or the old one? I'm confused."

"Well sir, actually . . . it's a joke."

"What's a joke?"

"That Johnny Dial is at it again. He's just pulling your leg," I say lightheartedly.

"Pulling my leg my ass!" His voice is growing louder. "Does he think this is funny?"

"Well, sir, I've actually just gotten to work and I'm—"

"What's your name?" he says, sharply.

"Huh?"

"Your name. I want your name."

"Leelee." I'm coy when I say it.

"Okay, *Leelee.* Let me tell you something. I'm sick of this bullshit. This is the very last time I'll ever turn on your damn radio station." (Actually he says "g.d." but I don't even like to repeat it.) "You tell that Johnny Dial that I'm going to beat his little ass the next time I see him. You got that?"

I don't say anything.

"You got that? Because if you don't tell him, I'm gonna let the air out of your tires. Now I don't mean that as a direct threat. It's an indirect threat. Because I'm assuming that you, little darlin', are going to make sure that this is the last time that little weasel is allowed to do something like this. I hope they fire his ass!"

Just at that second, Stan strolls into my office, whistling and snapping his pudgy fingers. I glance over at him, frustration all over my face.

"Okay, sir, I will give him your message."

I hang up, sigh loudly, and stare at the phone. Almost immediately another line starts blinking. Five rings later I'm thinking of letting it ring off the hook.

"Aren't you going to answer it?"

I look up at Stan, who's flipping through the mail on top of my file cabinet. Honestly, I wish he'd just go away, especially when he snorts his snot again and swallows it seconds later. "I'm not sure," I say.

"Here, I'll take care of it." He stretches his big self around me from behind and leans into my back while reaching for the phone. Seeing that I'm not at all in the mood for Stan, I wriggle out from underneath his embrace.

"Classic Hits FM 99 radio, may I help you?" he says, before an artificial smile forms on his face. He nods. "I feel your pain. Yes. I un-der-stand. Edward is . . ." He looks at me and I shake my head. "Not in yet. Why yes it is! I'm just helping out my secretary here."

Oh, so now I'm your secretary.

"No, not my style. I'm not into that foolishness. Straightforward Stan. That's my name. Okay. Talk soon. God bless. Buh-bye." He settles his overgrown rear on my desk and dramatically drops the phone into its cradle. (Stan wouldn't even consider pulling a major prank. Behind his back, Johnny calls him "Stan the Brown Nosing Wussy Wus Man." Or sometimes just "Wussy Wus" for short.)

"Dial is in trouble now." I detect a bit of a smirk upon his face, the disdain for his chief competitor seeping through.

As soon as the words leave his lips the hall door bangs and hits the wall. Dan Malcomb rushes past my office, heading straight toward the control room. Even though the room is supposed to be soundproof, Stan and I can hear muffled screams. The large window across from my office gives us a pretty good view into the control room.

Moments later, Edward runs by and once again I hear the control room door open and shut. More screaming. Nosy Stan slides off my desk, knocking several of my pens onto the floor, and slips across the hall to Michael's traffic room. He must have pushed a certain button because all of a sudden, the conversation out of the main control room is blasting through Michael's speakers.

"We could lose our license," Dan Malcomb screams. "*What the hell were you thinking?*"

"I've tried to warn him. A thousand times." Edward's calm but sickening voice makes me ill.

"Go on the air right now and tell them it's a damn joke," Dan Malcomb screams even louder.

Then total silence. The sound of Michael's door closing is the last thing I hear. That Stan has shut me out, though I have to admit I was a willing eavesdropper.

Two weeks ago, when the *Delta Queen* was docked down at the Mississippi, Johnny told the listeners that the state of Tennessee had decided to legalize gambling on the boat for twenty-four hours only. So many people showed up at the steamboat to get into the casino that the captain had no choice but to pull away from the dock, leaving a thousand people screaming to go on board. All Johnny got for that one was a talking-to. He told me later that Mr. Malcomb secretly loves all the PR but has to at least go through the motions and act like a good general manager. Johnny's ratings are so high, I bet he could rob a bank and not get fired. I bet they'd just move the broadcast straight on down to the jail. But high ratings or not, this time there's no doubt about it, he's in trouble. Big time.

Like I had hoped, Edward is far too concerned about what Johnny's doing than what I'm doing or, more importantly, what I did last night. The suspense of the evacuation prank is killing me, though. It's that part of me that loves a confrontation, as long as it has nothing to do with me. When I hear Edward's office door slam, I muster up all my courage and wait at the control room door until the on-air light fades. The morning show is almost over for the day when I slide inside. When Johnny sees me, he laughs. One side of his headphones is off his ear.

"Are you okay?" I ask him.

"I'm fine."

"Do you still have a job?"

He nods his head.

"Thank goodness. I was worried there for a second."

"I may have taken this one a bit far but it's April Fool's for god's sake."

"You're right. I forgot all about that until just this second."

Johnny shakes his head. "Not to worry about me. I'll survive." He flips through his log sheets and pushes several buttons on the board. For the life of me I can't imagine how anyone learns to operate one of those.

"Oh, by the way," I say, "thank you." There's a bit of sarcasm in my voice.

"For what? Don't tell me you followed 240 out of the city."

"*No,*" I say with a giggle. "Actually I was on the phone with my girlfriend on the way here this morning and missed the whole thing. I want to thank you for taking the heat off of me."

"Why? What did you do?" His blue eyes twinkle and a huge smile spreads across his face.

"I'm taking it as a good sign that you don't know."

"I don't know anything. Do you, Jack?"

Jack, Johnny's sidekick, is seated on the other side of the control board typing on his computer. "I know na'zing," he says in a German accent, like Sergeant Schultz on *Hogan's Heroes*. "I know na'zing."

"Are y'all pulling my leg?" My eyes travel between the two men.

"No," Johnny says. "I swear to god. We know nothing."

I feel the warmth from the hall, all of a sudden, on my back as the door swings open. It's always freezing cold in the control room due to all the heat from the equipment. Stan breezes right past me.

"Good morning, everyone." He files in all chipper-like and places his briefcase next to Johnny's on the credenza behind the control board. He loves nothing more than entering the control room fifteen minutes before his shift starts. I feel like he does it just to bug Johnny.

Now I can't finish my story.

"How was the concert?" Stan turns around and asks me. "I heard you got up close and personal with Mr. Liam White." He winks several times to alert me that he's the one in the know.

"Who told you that?" I ask him.

"A little birdie."

Before I can say another word the little birdie comes charging through the door. He glares at me with mean in his eyes. My heart starts racing like I've just jogged four miles and by now I'm ready to dive in a hole. The blood rushing to my head makes me feel as though I might faint.

"We would have enjoyed an invitation to wherever you went with White last night."

Oh no. "Edward. Honestly, I meant no harm. When he asked to buy us a drink, I had no idea we'd go to his dressing room, much less his tour bus." As I hear the words leaving my lips, I'm ready to shoot myself. If Virginia had been with me, she would have shot me already. When under pressure, I've been telling on myself my whole life.

"You went on his *tour bus*?" Stan says, and bobs his head like a bobblehead doll. "Hubba hubba."

"Did you sleep with him?" Edward asks.

The room goes perfectly silent. My heart takes a nosedive and I can feel tears bubbling behind my eyes.

Johnny's mouth pops open, and his eyes bulge. "*Dude!* You shouldn't say that. Isn't there something about sexual harassment in there?"

"*You* have no room to say anything today," Edward says. His heels come off the floor as he points at Johnny.

I'm not sure how to respond. It's the biggest insult I've ever received, bar none. "Of course not," I finally say with an indignant look on my face. "What kind of a question is that?" I bite the inside of my mouth to keep from crying.

"A direct one," Edward says and strokes his beard. I watch as he moves behind the board and picks up the logbook.

"I'm sorry, Edward. I think I just got carried away in the moment.

My friends and I have been listening to Liam White since we were eight or nine." I hold my hand out to indicate how tall we were back then. The fear in my voice, I'm sure, must be evident to everyone. "We were just excited to get to talk with him. I meant no harm by it. I promise."

"See that it never happens again. I don't want it to look bad for the station."

"How could it possibly reflect poorly on the station?" Johnny says. "We have a hot radio assistant and he likes her. I would think that would look good for the station." The great thing about Johnny is Edward doesn't scare him a bit.

"Not necessarily," Edward says, as he's flipping through the log. "He just wants to get in your pants. Can't you see that, you silly girl?"

The tears I'd been fighting back well up in the corners of my eyes and all I want to do is run as far away from FM 99 as my legs will carry me. I refuse to let him see me cry so I gnaw down on the inside of my mouth even harder. The metallic taste of blood lets me know I've succeeded. "I would never allow that to happen. I realize that you don't know me very well, but I'm not that kind of girl."

"That's what they all say, until they get around the stars. They're called star fu—"

The sound of me gasping for air cuts him off before he can complete the word.

Edward shifts his feet, jams his hands in his pants pockets, and looks me in the eye. "That's a saying, Leelee." Now his tone has shifted from harsh to patronizing. Even he knows he's stepped over the line. "I don't mean it literally. It's what those of us in the business call people who hang around the stars—people who are obsessed with the stars—male *or* female. It refers to the people who are so impressed with a star's success that they make fools out of themselves backstage. Like you've done. Trust me, I've been in this business a long time. Make sure you stick to your job description."

Now I'm not only hurt, I'm incensed. "I have no intention of *ever* becoming a star f— . . . a star f—*fornicator*!" I say, with a shaky, but loud voice. "Besides Liam White has no intentions or interest in me. He was just being nice to us. When would I ever run in to him again anyway?"

"Well, I suppose that's true. He's halfway to Florida by now." Once again, the tone in his voice changes and this time he's half nice. "I bought his tour T-shirt at the concert last night. Jacksonville is his next stop. See." He turns around so we can all see that he's wearing the shirt. Like a true psychopath, Edward's gone from crazy to calm in no time at all—and I'm left watching him walk out of the control room, tasting the blood in my mouth.

Johnny points behind Edward's back and mouths the words, "He's the star fornicator," and uses his fingers as quotation marks.

There's no way I'll be able to get to the end of this day. I've got another hour until lunch and I'm not sure I'll be able to make it that long. Edward's accusation has hurt me to the core. Seriously. I'm devastated. I would never sleep with a man I didn't know, much less a rock star. This is the most frustrated I've been since Baker took up with the silicone snow bunny. Even though I'm distracted by answering phone call after phone call about Johnny's evacuation escapade, my tears won't stop. I can't help but look up at the clock every few minutes, counting the seconds until my break.

When the phone rings again, I'm tempted to pick it up and scream, *What? It was a joke. If you don't like it, don't listen.* My voice is completely flat when I answer the phone. "FM 99" is all I say, with no affect.

"What an idiot." It's Johnny calling from his car. Just hearing his voice makes me even more emotional. I wish he were single.

"Don't cry, baby. He's as sick a pup as they come. Try not to let him get to you."

"He's so *mean.*"

"Yeah, but he's just an insecure bully. He does this to every girl in your position. We must have had fifty programming assistants since

I've been working here. Well, I'm exaggerating. They're on to him in HR, though. Just try to ignore him."

"I don't know that I'll ever be able to ignore him. That's not my personality."

"Just focus on how stupid he is. He asked me the other day if Bonnie Raitt was white or black. And he's supposed to be the program director of this station. For god's sake."

"Are you in trouble?"

"Yeah, but don't worry about it. They'll get over it. Here I get them coverage on all the major TV stations. *Free PR*. And they're pissed."

"Oh well."

"Plus, most of our listeners thought it was funny. I had tons of calls on the request line from people who were like, 'Dial, this is great. How do you do it?' Leelee, I swear you should have seen the veins in Malcomb's neck. They must have been an inch in diameter. He was screaming at me, telling me we could lose our license." Johnny busts out laughing. Still has his sense of humor, despite the amount of discord he's caused.

"I bet it was touch and go," I say, sniffling.

"Yeah, but if they want another wuss like Stan, they should hire one."

"Oh gosh, don't even say that." At the sound of his name, I glance out my office and can see him through the window of the control room.

"Speaking of, he's so happy I'm in deep shit. Did you see the look on his face when we were all in the control room earlier?"

"Oh, the poor thing's just jealous of you. Did you know he listened to y'all's conversation? He went into Michael's room and pushed a button so he could hear it."

"I figured he would. That nosy little wussy wuss. Listen, I have an idea. A way to get back at him. Are you in?"

"I don't know. I'm in trouble, too. I have to be careful."

"You won't get in any trouble. I just want to mess with him, that's all. Have some fun."

"I'm always up for fun," I say slowly, sniffing away the last of my pathetic tears.

"Great. You know how he's always reading everybody's phone messages?"

"I caught him doing it again yesterday."

"Here's what I want you to do. I'm emceeing the Miss Memphis Pageant. Stan's done it for the last five years in a row. For free. They've asked me to do it this year and I want to mess with him a little bit."

"How?"

"Write out a message to me from Lyn Simpler at the Miss Memphis Pageant. In the memo line write, 'Wants to know if a thousand dollars is okay for your talent fee.'"

"Johnny Dial, you are *so* bad."

"Put the message on your desk where he'll see it. He's gonna go ape shit." He falls out laughing again and that gets me going.

"Are you ever going to tell him it's a joke?" My tears have given way to laughter and I can't help but picture Stan's poor face when he reads the part about the thousand dollars.

"Hell no."

"As long as he doesn't find out I'm the one who set him up I'll do it. But only for you."

"He ain't gonna find that out. Just put out the bait. Trust me, he'll fall for it hook, line, and sinker."

From my radio, I hear Stan sign off. "And remember, Memphis, don't forget to wish upon a star. You never know what kind of *trouble* you might get yourself into." When he says the word "trouble," he over emphasizes, making it sound enticing. Once, when I asked him what his sign-off meant, because honestly I had no idea, he said, in this condescending tone of his, "Leelee, think about it. You know how people say 'Let me see what kind of *trouble* I can get into'? Meaning they're looking for fun? That's what it means."

That's a toe-curler if I've ever heard one. Why not sign off in a cool way like Johnny does. "Keep rockin'," he says. Or Paul, the afternoon jock, who signs off by saying "Good night Dancing Jimmy, wherever you are." Dancing Jimmy, God rest his soul, was a good-hearted drunken homeless man for many years who hung around Midtown in Memphis. He'd raise his arms out to his side and spin around as fast as he could, dancing "the helicopter" for beer money.

From the inside of my office, the sound of a vile, extra-loud snort-snot out in the hall, nauseates me to the point of gagging. It also alerts me to the fact that Stan will be standing at my desk in five, four, three, two, one second, "Hi Stan," I say, without taking my eyes off my computer screen.

"How did you know it was me?"

There's a big part of me that is dying to ask him if he needs a Kleenex. I mean isn't that better than keeping all that gunk inside? "Lucky guess," I say, turning around to smirk at him head-on.

"Well gorgeous, how are you this afternoon?" *What do you mean how am I? I've just been slaughtered by Edward Maxwell, right in front of you, and you have the nerve to ask me how I am?*

"I'm okay. How are you?" I say, wryly.

"Fantastic," he says, and nods his head for emphasis.

Like clockwork, he strolls up behind me and peers over my shoulder. The bait is laid out before him on my desk, out from Johnny's message pile, as if I haven't filed it yet. Just like Johnny instructed, I had written out a message to him from Lyn Simpler at the Miss Memphis Pageant. In the memo line it reads, "Is 1K okay for your talent fee? Let her know by . . ." The rest is left blank. And right on top of the note I've laid my pen, as if I'm not finished writing.

"Sneaky" is Stan's middle name. First he starts with a friendly back rub. The way he's kneading my shoulders, not too hard, not too soft, feels pretty good. Before I know it my eyes droop and my chin drops to my chest. Truthfully, I'm starting to feel a wee bit guilty for my willingness to trick him. Sometime during the middle of the massage, I feel him lift one hand off my shoulder and lean down over me. He's fingering the phony note from Miss Memphis when his other hand stops abruptly, his fingers digging deep into my shoulder blade.

"Ow, Stan. That hurts," I say, rolling my chair away.

"Did you take that message?"

"What message?" Lord, this job is turning me into a big fat storyteller.

"The one to Dial from the Miss Memphis Pageant."

I don't say yes and I don't say no. If I have to lie it might as well be by omission, for goodness sake.

"This is bullshit. Total *bullshit*." He slaps his hand on the desk and storms out of my office toward Edward's.

I am in so much trouble.

Now what? I will never let Johnny talk me into anything like this again as long as I live.

"That snake in the grass," Stan says, two seconds later, after finding Edward's door closed. "How does he manage to con them out of a grand for doing the exact same thing I've done for free? All these years?"

I'm keeping my mouth shut. He picks up my phone and starts dialing.

"What are you doing?" I ask him, panic setting in. I swear to Buddha I'm going to kill Johnny Dial for hoodwinking me into this.

"I'm calling Lyn Simpler."

My mind is racing. "I wouldn't do that if I were you." My bottom lip hurts from biting down on it so hard.

"Why not?" Stan says, with the office phone in his hand.

"Because . . . you'll look greedy. After they pay Johnny all that money, they'll wonder why they did it. I mean, you'll look like a saint. Think about it. Johnny will be the one they think less of. You'll be more popular than you've ever been. I wouldn't doubt it if they write an article about you in the paper, heralding your devotion to philanthropy." Those words could have only been one thing. Divine inspiration.

He hangs up the phone. "You've got a point, Ms. Satterfield."

"Of course I do. You be the rose, not the thorn."

"Absolutely."

"After all, you've said it yourself. You don't like foolishness. You're the good guy. The one who's up-front and straightforward."

"I will be there for them when they call me back next year. After they've realized the mistake they've made."

"Atta boy, Stan. You're making the right move," I say, standing up, hoping he'll get the hint to leave my office.

Somehow my edification of him replaces the guilt for what I've done. Sort of.

Right before leaving for the day, and after the phone calls have finally stopped, I have a minute to myself. Not a sound, not even the radio broadcast can be heard in the halls of FM 99. As usual, my thoughts drift onto Peter, especially after the day I've had. I miss him so much; it feels as if each of my freckles have been pinpricked. Leaning back in my chair, I exhale loudly, as if I can't bear to take in another breath. The loss I'm feeling is not much different than what I felt when Daddy died. Or even Mama's death—although, hers didn't seem as hard at the time. At seventeen, after suffering through years of alcoholic rage, even a breast cancer diagnosis is not sufficient to wipe away a buildup of resentment.

Peter Owen would never have treated me disrespectfully. In fact, his behavior ranked on the opposite end of the spectrum from that of Edward Maxwell. He took care, beautiful care, of me. And right now, my heart feels like a knife has sliced one of its chambers and it can no longer bathe my lungs with oxygen.

When I hear Edward leaving early for his weekly "flying lesson," I pull out a legal pad and reach inside my drawer for my nicest pen. Letters seem to be the only way I can talk to Peter and let him know how I feel.

Dear Peter,

I'm sitting here at my desk, at my new job, and I can't help but think about you. It's going very well, for the most part, but my new boss is, well I might as well say it, he's a jerk. Can you believe it? After all the struggles I went through in Vermont I'm working with another Helga. I don't mean to complain. The job has its upside. It's fun and I'm enjoying most *of the people I work with but it's nothing like it was when we worked together.*

Did I ever tell you how much I had wanted to kiss you? When we were sitting by the fire that night at the inn, just a few weeks before I left, I could not stop looking at you. I'm sure you never noticed, but I was looking. Noticing every little thing about you. Your clothes—that ivory-colored corduroy shirt you had on, the one that you had rolled up at the cuffs, your faded blue jeans, the T-shirt you wore underneath. In fact, I noticed your arms that first day you came to the inn for an interview. I remember exactly what you had on—a T-shirt and blue jeans—and I could see the little veins in your forearms, so strong.

That night, when you came up from behind me and took my Corona and placed it on the table, my heart sunk down to my toes. Then, when you took my hand in yours and spun me around so we were face to face, I thought I would melt right into you. Could you hear my heart beating? And then the call came with an offer on the inn. I didn't want to answer that phone. I wanted you to stop me. I wanted you to hold me. I could practically taste your lips. Don't you know I would have loved to let it ring?

I had no choice but to come back home when I got the offer to sell the inn. What was I going to do? We weren't committed to one another.

I hope you are doing well. If you get a chance I'd love for you to write me back.

Love always,
Leelee

I fold the letter and hide it inside my purse. It feels good to get it out, say the things that I've longed to tell him. I'll just put it with the other unmailed letter in the drawer of my nightstand. Maybe I'll mail it. Probably I won't.

If someone had told me a year ago that I'd be picking up my young daughters from after-care, Monday through Friday at five thirty in the afternoon after having left home at seven thirty in the morning, I'd have said, "Never in my lifetime." But as John Lennon said, "Life is what happens when you're busy making other plans." I was busy all right. Busy helping Baker make *his* other plans.

Once the girls are in the car, the thought of going home and dragging out pots and pans, spending an hour in front of a stove, and then cleaning up the mess, makes me consider Bolivar, the loony bin, as a viable option.

I'm tired. I'm lonely. And if truth be told, I'm depressed—an emotion that surfaces very rarely for me. Who wouldn't be depressed after the berating I received from Edward? And in front of Stan of all people.

When a woman is depressed what does she do? Besides stuffing her face? She goes shopping of, course. Most women might go to the mall, but this girl is headed straight for the pound. I've been without a dog long enough.

When we pull up to the Memphis Animal Shelter, the girls bound out of our car. I've been thinking about another Yorkie and I'm still not sure that I won't do that in the end, but Alice about has me talked into adopting a mutt. Virgy thinks I should get a lab or a golden but I want my pooch to be able to sleep with me. Especially now that I've got the bed to myself. Virginia has always teased me about my yappy little dogs, so this time I'm thinking of going up a size. As much as I'd like to have a pedigreed pet, I've started to come around to the animal shelter motto. Riley would be so proud.

The moment we walk inside the front door, I'm knocked over by the smell. Issie lets go of my hand and pinches her nose. Sarah tugs on me to lean down and puts her hand aside her mouth. "Maybe we should go somewhere else," she says, whispering in my ear.

Squatting down between the two of them, I pull each daughter close to my face. "Don't worry about it. This is just the way all doggie shops smell." After letting the lady at the desk know we're here to adopt a dog, we only have to wait five minutes before a woman in uniform arrives to take us back to where the dogs are kept. The funny thing is, the cage area smells better than the reception area.

The girls and I walk hand in hand following the woman in uniform down a long hall. Down the first aisle, twenty sets of black eyes seem to be saying, "Take me home, Mommy. I'll be a good girl." The faces of the dogs are almost too hard to bear—big black eyes and noses, long pink tongues hanging out the sides, ears flopped over, others poking straight up, brown, black, white, spotted . . . I don't even want to think about the fact that these beautiful little faces might not make it past the weekend. It makes me all the more determined to take home a small bundle of joy today.

It's nice to see that each cage has plenty of room. Divided into two parts, the front, where the food is kept, is for viewing and there's another part of the cage behind with a bed. Although each animal is separated, they can still peer at one another.

"Can we get a puppy?" Sarah says. "All these dogs are big."

"No honey, we can't get a puppy," I say. "I wish we could but I don't have time for house breaking."

"What does 'house break' mean?" Issie asks.

"Potty training for dogs," I say.

The woman in uniform overhears me. "We can find you a dog that does his business outside. Guaranteed."

"Thank you," I say, before turning back to the girls. "We don't have to get a big dog, but she has to be an adult. She must know how to potty *outside*."

"Princess Grace doo-dooed inside when we lived in Vermont," Issie says.

"Of course she did. But that's only because she had no choice. Would you want to put your bottom down on four feet of freezing cold snow?"

Issie and Sarah both laugh. "No," they say at the same time.

"Well, Gracie didn't want to either." The *Willingham Gazette* found a new subscriber the day I moved to town. Spreading out newspaper in every corner of our apartment was the least I could do for the poor old thing. "Our new dog has to use the backyard at our new house. That's all there is to it."

All kinds of adorable faces beckon us to take them home. I imagine each one saying, "Pick me, please. Oh pretty please. I'll make you happy. I'll be the loyal one in your life if you'll just give me a chance." Issie and Sarah stop at every cage claiming the one inside is the one they want.

About halfway down the second aisle, in the corner of one of the cages, is a smaller cream-colored, shaggy dog with floppy ears and big black eyes. She can't weigh more than twelve pounds. Although she doesn't come up to us like the others have, for some reason just the sight of her, all shaggy and overgrown, makes me swoon.

"Is she a puppy?" I ask the lady.

"Nope. It's full grown."

"Any idea what kind she is?" Her fur is pitifully misshaped but I could give her a good clip and she'd look like a beauty.

"Let's see, looks like a terrier mix to me," the shelter worker says. "I can tell by her curly tale."

"Can we see her? Or is she a him?" I ask.

"Let's see here." The woman checks a card fastened to the cage. "It's a him."

"Oh, I don't know about a him," I say, disappointed. "I've never had a boy dog."

"I would like a boy dog, actually," Sarah says. "He could be my little brother." When I see the longing in her sapphire eyes I reconsider. I imagine this guilt thing, as a single mother, won't ever change.

"Okay, we can look at him," I say.

The woman opens the cage, attaches a leash to the little dog's collar and pulls on him. He slides on all fours out of the cage and once outside, cowers.

"Ohh, he's so scared." I bend down on my knees and my daughters do the same.

"Come here, baby," I say.

"Come here, baby," Issie says.

"All you do is copy everybody," Sarah tells her. "Copycat."

I press my lips together and toss Sarah a stern gaze. "Say you're sorry."

"I'm sorry," she says, barely audible.

"Sorry who for what?"

"I'm sorry, Issie, for saying 'you copy.'" If her tone dictated the amount of sincerity in her heart, it's not much of an apology. I suppose it will have to do for now.

We all reach out our hands to the little dog. "Can we play with you?" I say.

After several seconds the little pooch edges closer, finally close enough for a little pat on the head. He licks my hand.

"He must have been abused. You can tell by the way he cowers," the officer says.

"That is terrible. Who in the world could have hurt this little man?" I pick him up and place him in my lap, kissing the top of his head.

Sarah says, "Can I hold him?"

"Sure, be very gentle," I say, and hand him over.

"I want to hold him," Issie says, and strains to pick up the little guy. He wriggles away from Sarah's lap. Undaunted, she goes after him again. He never snaps and seems not to mind being chased.

"I was holding him," Sarah says, picking him back up.

"It's still Sarah's turn, Issie. Just wait another minute and then you can hold him, too," I tell her.

"Does he have a name?" I ask the lady.

"Nope, we don't give them names, only numbers. It would make it too hard when we have to . . ."

With eyes bulging and lips pursed, I leer at her in a desperate attempt to stop her from saying another word.

She reads me loud and clear. Instead of finishing her sentence, though, the officer goes mute. I can tell by the look in her eyes that she's scared to say another word.

After pondering his fate for only a moment I ask, "Is he close?"

She nods her head up and down, slightly pursing her lips.

That's all I need to hear. "What do you think, girls? Should we take him home? It might be nice to have a boy around the house."

An hour later, after waiting for the microchip to be inserted into our new addition's shoulder blade, the adoption papers are signed and I've written out a check for sixty-five dollars. It ensures he's been neutered, flea-dipped, dewormed, and vaccinated.

Once we're in the car, the little shy dog who'd cowered away from us jumps back and forth between the seats as if he's finally been emancipated. His little back legs dig into my left thigh, as his tail spins faster than a whirlybird, and he peers out the driver's side window as if to bid adieu. Once he finally tires from darting all around the car, he curls up on my lap and licks my elbow. "What should we name him?" I ask the girls, while stroking the top of his head.

"How about Cotton?" Sarah says.

"Cotton, huh? I like that." I really don't, but I have to tread lightly. "Sometimes I think it's nice to name a dog after a person. After someone you love or admire. Take Gracie, for instance. She was named after the most elegant woman who ever lived. Princess Grace Kelly was not only a movie star, but a classically beautiful, sophisticated woman and princess."

"How did she get to be a princess?" Sarah wants to know. Through the rearview mirror, I can see her eyes growing larger.

"She married a prince, of course. The Prince of Monaco. She was my favorite movie star; I used to daydream that I was her. I would fantasize that I had blond hair and blue eyes and wore her elegant clothes and diamonds. Not to mention kissing all those gorgeous men in the movies." This elicited a few chuckles from the girls. "Naming Gracie after her was quite apropos."

Issie says, "I think we should name him after Roberta."

"No Issie, Roberta is a girl's name and we have a boy dog," Sarah says. I can see her shake her head through my rearview mirror, like her little sister is the dumbest person on earth.

"Actually girls," I say, "there are plenty of people out there with androgynous names. Just look at all the Jordans or the Taylors of the world. Both boys and girls have that name. Alex, Sandy, Aubrey, Madison—there are a million of them." Suddenly the most famous of all androgynous names pops in my mind. "I forgot about Alice Cooper, he's the king of all them all!"

"Who's Alice Cooper?" Sarah asks.

"A rock star from the seventies. He had a song called 'School's Out' and on our last day at Jameson School, in our senior year, Mary Jule, Alice, Virgy, and I rigged up a sound system and blasted it all throughout the school. You should have seen us dancing in the halls in our Alice Cooper tight pants with black stars painted around our eyes. If we had done that any other day, we would have all been expelled."

"You were crazy, Mommy," Sarah says.

The more I think about naming this little dog Roberta, the better it sounds. "In the olden days people even called their boys Meredith," I tell them. "My friend Karen Perrin had an uncle Meredith. He was the nicest man, always taking the time to talk with us and help Karen with her math homework. If his mother could name him Meredith, why can't we call this precious dog Roberta?" The little man peers up at me with longing. "We can start a new trend. Maybe once we call him Roberta, other people will start naming their sons Roberta."

I look back at Sarah and she's staring out the window pondering that thought. By now, she's used to the whims of her wacky mommy.

All this talk of Roberta's name makes me miss my dear friend. If someone had told me the day I first stepped foot in Vermont that my little five-foot-tall, roly-poly housekeeper who wore plaid skirts with flowery tops would become my best friend I would have highly doubted it. Even better, she's the type of person who would get a huge kick out of having a dog named after her, girl *or* boy. I think I'll call her when I get home and tell her.

Sarah looks over at the mutt and says, "Come here, Roberta." Giving her a slight cock of the head, he prances to her lap and nestles into a spot, resting his head on the door's armrest. Apparently it's decided. Roberta it is.

Chapter Nine

When I flip on the radio, after I get back in the car from dropping off Issie at school, "Fire and Rain" pours out of the speakers. It's so vivid—almost like James Taylor is on the morning show in the control room, singing directly into the mic. I can hear a guitar but the other instruments are missing, the ones that give the song its full rich sound. FM 99 is not known for playing acoustic versions of songs (Edward would never allow a song to be played that hadn't originally reached the top ten on the Adult Contemporary Billboard chart), but even still, I'd swear it was James himself.

"Thought I'd see you one more time again. Nah, nah, nah." After the music fades, there's clapping. *Control room* clapping! I nearly hit another mother exiting the preschool parking lot.

"All right, all right. *JT.* That was awesome," Johnny says. "It's great to have you back."

"Thank you. Glad to be here." That's his voice. I'd know it anywhere. It really is James Taylor!

"You're in concert tonight at Mud Island," Johnny says.

"That's right," says JT.

Okay, what in god's name is going on? Why am I the last to know that Sweet Baby James himself is at FM 99 today—only a few feet away from my office? It's only been two weeks since Liam White was in the studio and now we have an even bigger star. I truly am going to kill Johnny Dial this time. I look down at my outfit and consider turning back around and heading home. This dress has been hanging in my closet for five years. I'd have thrown it away a long time ago but it's one of those outfits that can pass in a pinch, when everything else is dirty. It's the kind that you'd never wear to something special, though—and this is better than something special. One glance at the clock tells me I better keep driving forward and accept the fact that I'm going to meet *the* James Taylor looking like I just left the Dress Barn.

"You've played Memphis what, six or seven times, and every single time I see you, you seem to get better," Johnny says. "Your voice is smoother now than it was the first time I saw you back in 1970, I think it was."

"The *Sweet Baby James* tour."

"That's it. One of the best shows I've ever seen at the Mid-South Coliseum. I still remember you came out on the stage wearing a flannel shirt, sat down on a stool and opened the show with 'Sweet Baby James.'"

JT laughs, and it's unmistakable.

I remember that shirt! I was there. One of my very first concerts. I fumble through my purse and punch in the numbers to Alice's cell. When the answering machine comes on I'm practically squealing. "Turn on FM 99. JT is in the control room talking about the Sweet Baby James concert at the coliseum when that man in the crowd screamed out 'Walking Down a Country Road.' Remember that, Alice? Oh my gosh. I have the coolest job in the world." I push the end button and throw the phone back in my purse.

What woman isn't obsessed with James Taylor? Actually, with Alice and me, it's not as much of an obsession as it is an infatuation. We're enthralled with his love life. I mean, what man writes the kind of lyrics he does without the kind of magnetism, charm, and seduction that drives a woman crazy? Carly Simon was so lucky.

"I'll tell you what I wish I still had," Johnny says. "That poster that came inside the album. It hung on my bedroom wall with thumbtacks in the corners for years."

"I've had many people tell me that."

I'm weaving in and out of the lanes, speeding down Union Avenue in rush-hour traffic, praying with every fiber of my being that I make it before he leaves. If I don't get to meet him, maybe I'll bump into him on the way out. Or at the very least catch a glimpse of him from ten feet away.

When I finally pull up to the station, by the grace of God, he's still talking to Johnny. I'm late, my normal five to ten, so I hightail it up to my office, not even pausing to wave to Jane on my way in. Through the window in front of the control room I can see the back of JT's head. He's wearing his signature newsboy cap! I am literally just five feet away from the one and only James Taylor.

When the phone starts ringing, I reach down to grab it, never taking my gaze off the window across the hall from my office. I can see James scratching his neck. Now he's putting a coffee cup to his lips. Now he's leaning down and picking up his guitar. He's about to play another song. I *must* think of an excuse to get inside that control room!

"Hello," I say into the phone, after it rings only once. My giddiness is hard to conceal.

"Is this FM 99?" a man asks, puzzled.

"Oh. Yes it is. I'm sorry, I was distracted. May I help you, please?"

"Sure. This is Steve Conley. I'm the stage manager on James Taylor's crew. We're down here at Mud Island loading in his gear and our tour itinerary says he's not due into Memphis until four o'clock. We're all a little confused down here and I can't get JT's road manager on the phone. Do you know if he's by himself or if he has someone with him?"

"Hold on a second, let me check." This is it! My great excuse to mosey into the control room.

"Actually, it looks like . . . ," I'm craning my neck across the hall to survey the inside of the control room as best as I can, "he's alone. But why don't I get your phone number and give Mr. Taylor a message to call you as soon as he comes off the air?"

"That would be great."

I jot down the information and kiss the pink note in my hand. With my purse hanging over my shoulder I tear down the hall to the ladies' room. Because I'm nervous, when I reach for my blush compact it slips out of my hand and crashes to the floor. Just my luck. Now it's in tiny pieces all over the black tile. With no other choice, I sweep up the peach tinted bits with the enclosed brush and use it anyway. This should teach me to come to work without taking the time to fix my makeup and style my hair. At the moment my hair's in a ponytail, but I quickly tear out the rubber band and fluff it in the mirror. Once I finish brushing on my mascara I notice brownish black dots below my eyebrows. Ripping out a paper towel from the holder I hurriedly dampen it in the sink and wipe the residual fluid from my eyes. When I take one last look at myself in the mirror, it occurs to me I look like Goodwill Strawberry Shortcake, minus the striped leggings.

On the way back down the hall I notice Edward's door. It's shut, thank goodness, and after bending down I can tell he's not made it into the office yet. No light is peeking out from underneath the slit. Taking a deep breath, I turn the corner to the control room. Even though my stomach feels as though I've just stepped off the Zippin Pippin at the fairgrounds, I've already convinced myself to try and remain calm. Cool. Collected. I can do this. I can be in the same room with James Taylor and chat with him like a normal human being, nary a star-struck bone in my body.

The on-air light fades. Mustering courage and charisma, with pink phone message in hand, I courageously push open the control room door with my shoulder, ready to hand the note over to JT himself.

Johnny's in his regular position working the board, Jack's on the other side as usual, in front of his computer, and JT is . . . nowhere to be found. I glance behind me in the unfortunate instance that I may have just missed him.

"*Where's JT*?" There's panic in my voice.

They both glance at each other before bursting out laughing.

"What? *What*?" My voice is climbing. "Did he leave down the back steps while I was in the bathroom?" I look behind me again and cover my face with my hands, exhaling loudly. "How could this have happened?"

Jack reaches over, picks up James's newsboy cap resting on the counter next to him and places it on his head. "Good morning, Leelee," he says, in a perfect, and I mean spot-on, JT voice.

All I can do is stare at Jack. I can't utter a single sound. My face must look as forlorn and pitiful as Lucy's did that day in Hollywood when Ricky wouldn't let her meet John Wayne. Of course both guys, at this point, are falling out of their chairs from laughter, all at my expense.

"It's not funny," I say, and inadvertently stomp my foot. "I believed y'all. I almost turned around and drove all the way home to change out of this tacky dress." I look down and squeeze the fabric between my fingers. "But I was afraid I'd miss catching a glimpse of JT. And now I find out it's all *a joke*?"

Johnny stares at my dress. "That dress really is tacky."

Blood rushes to my face.

"I'm just kidding you, girl."

"And how is it that I don't know that you sing?" I say to Jack, throwing my arms in the air.

"I don't know how you don't know," he says, chuckling.

"You sounded exactly like him." Now it all makes sense. Jack can talk exactly like George Bush, Bill Clinton, and Ross Perot. He's imitating them all the time on the radio. Of course he can talk and sing like James Taylor.

"Why aren't you rich and famous like, like that guy who does Richard Nixon and all the other presidents' voices? You're just as good."

In a dead ringer for the voice of Howard Cosell, Jack says, "Because Rich Little's not stuck in Memphis, Tennessee, working for a boob like Edward Maxwell."

"I'm devastated. I was just sure you were JT."

"What do you need James Taylor for? Didn't you see the note on your desk?" Johnny asks.

I whip my head in his direction. "What note?"

"I put a sealed envelope on your desk. Go read it. Just don't let Edward see it."

"What's it about? Am I in trouble?"

Johnny giggles that giggle. "Go look at it."

When I get back to my desk, there's a long FM 99 envelope with my name on the front, sealed shut. I'd been so eager to get inside the control room that I hadn't even noticed it before. I tear it open and inside there's a pink telephone message, folded over twice. Before reading it I glance over my shoulder. Unfolding the message, I notice it's to me from Liam White. *Liam White?* He called at 8:00 A.M. and there's a phone number. In the notes part, Johnny writes: "Wow, girl. Looks like you've got a suitor."

My heart zooms down into my black leather pumps. At the bottom of the note is another message from Johnny: "Make sure 'you know who' doesn't hear you call him back. Be discreet about it and btw, I've copied down White's number to sell to the *National Enquirer.*"

On impulse and before I have time to consider the validity of the situation, I go running toward the control room and bump right into "you know who."

"What's your hurry?" Edward asks, holding his briefcase, FM 99 silk bomber jacket slung over his shoulder. (It's not even chilly outside.)

"Oh nothing. I, I'm just checking one of the liner notes on the log. I might have written something down wrong."

He slightly opens the control room door and pops his head inside. "Good job with the JT bit, buddy," he says to Jack, and then heads straight to his office and shuts the door.

As I'm stepping inside the control room, the den of radio sin, reality grabs me by the tail and shakes me good and hard. All of a sudden it's so obvious. Johnny Dial *is lying*! Now I've become a victim of his monkey business. *Hmmmm.*

Instead of allowing his out-and-out Judas kiss to bamboozle me, I remember the new Leelee, the girl who shed her pushover exterior and stood up to Helga the Horrible in Vermont. With all the confidence of Jamie Lee Curtis daring to go gray in her late thirties, I push open the control room door and march inside. My tongue is pressed firmly on the inside of my cheek, my eyebrows are raised and my arms are crossed in front of my chest. "Okay," I say, undaunted. "I admit it. You've gotten me once today. But it's not going to happen a second time. Nope, I'm not falling for it."

"You're pretty cool, girl. Got a celebrity calling ya," Johnny licks his index finger and extends it my way. "Sssss," he says. "You're hot."

Uncrossing my arms, I say, "You are making that up and I don't appreciate it."

"No, I'm not. I swear. Liam White called here looking for you."

I reach back and wind my hair into a knot. "Did he say what he wanted, O Master of the Mischief?"

"No. He just wanted to talk to you. He called the hotline. Tyler the intern took the call."

"And then what? Let me guess"—I pop my finger toward Johnny—"Liam White told Tyler that he wants to marry me. Where is Tyler? Maybe I should get it straight from the horse's mouth." Knowing full well he's nowhere close, I look all around the control room for effect.

"We sent him downtown to Union and Second. He's passing out morning team bumper stickers," Jack says with a chuckle.

"How convenient," I say.

"I swear." Johnny's laughing, too.

I shake my head and leer at him.

"Okay. I can see how you might not trust me," he says between chuckles.

"You think?"

"Here's exactly what happened. White calls early this morning. He asks to speak to you. Tyler tells him you aren't in yet so he leaves his number. I swore Tyler to secrecy. I told him he'd be fired if he breathes a word to anyone. Except Jack. He heard it, too."

Jack holds his hands up, palms out. "Your secret's safe with me, kid." Now he's Humphrey Bogart in *Casablanca*.

"Hmmm. Johnny Dial I have to say, you are so good at taking a plausible situation and stroking it just enough to make it sound real."

"If you don't believe me, call the number yourself. You'll see," Johnny says.

I stare at the number a few moments. "If you're kidding me . . ."

"It's the truth." Johnny draws a cross on his heart. "Hope to die."

Instead of calling Liam White I rush into the ladies' room to call the one friend who might support me if this story is real. Sure enough, Mary Jule starts screaming when I tell her. The believer in all things fairy tale (nothing has ever really gone wrong in Mary Jule's life; both of her parents are still living and Al is completely devoted to her) tries to convince me that Johnny is indeed telling the truth. We talk a few minutes more before she persuades me to hang up from her and call Liam White right this minute.

After pondering the risk of calling from my desk or the bathroom, I decide to put it off until lunchtime. Part of me is counting down the seconds and the other part of me is still dubious. And rightfully so. The more I think about it, the crazier I think I am for believing Johnny Dial. But when the clock strikes twelve noon, I race out to my car.

Just as I'm about to punch in his number, Alice's name comes up on my cell phone. When I answer she screams into my ear. "DO NOT CALL LIAM WHITE BACK."

Surprise, surprise. The pipeline has sprung a leak.

"Why?"

"Haven't you learned anything?" she says. "A: You're being way too eager. B: We still don't know if he's married or not. And C: He might have a dang disease."

"Alice! I'm not going to bed with him. I'm just returning his call."

"Can't you let *him* call *you* back? Hold on, I'm getting Virginia on the phone with us."

When Alice explains to her what's happening Virginia's just as adamant. "Absolutely not, Fiery. Let him call you back."

"But suppose Edward finds out? I'm already taking a risk as it is."

"No, let him chase you. You be the *one* girl in the world who doesn't call him back," Virginia says.

"There's something I haven't told y'all. I admit it. I kind of can't stop thinking about the guy," I say.

"I don't care. Let him call you back." Alice is unbending.

"Easy for y'all to say. Suppose you two were single, in love with a man who's decided that he lives too far away from you to make the relationship work, and a dang rock star calls, albeit probably just to say hello, but still—he calls. What would you do?"

They both reiterate it again. Neither would dial the number.

"Okay. I won't call," I say, throwing in the towel.

"Good. I'm proud of you," Alice says.

"So am I." Virginia is such a liar. She'd be calling him back so fast, in fact she'd have called him back an hour ago.

"Whatever," I say, "but I've got to go now. Bye."

I pick up the pink piece of paper again. Read it twice. Three times. Next thing I know, I'm dialing the number. While it's ringing, I picture Alice with a big ole scowl on her face. Next I see Virginia, not mad, just a little shake of the head as if to say, *Couldn't take it?* Quickly, I push the end button on my phone.

Then I imagine Mary Jule with a sweet smile on her face. "Leelee, of course I'd have called him back. I'd have done the exact same thing as you." That's when I pick up the phone again and start dialing.

After four rings he answers. "Hello." His voice is low, like he's just woken up from a nap.

"Hi, it's Leelee Satterfield," I say. The contrast in our voices is the difference between a first soprano and a baritone.

"Who?" His tone is abrasive and abrupt. I consider hanging up on him.

"Leelee Satterfield," I say again. Now my voice is coy and meek. I'll be surprised if he even heard me.

"Oh hi, Leelee," he says, no affect.

Now I'm wondering why in the world I didn't follow Alice's advice.

"What can I do for you?" he asks, quite businesslike.

"I'm actually returning your call. I got a message that you called me earlier this morning."

"No, I never called you."

Knife inserting into heart. *I hate you, Johnny Dial.* "Really? Johnny said he talked to you."

"Who's Johnny?"

"The morning deejay, here at FM 99."

"I never talked with him," he says curtly.

"Actually I meant to say it was Tyler, our intern, who took the message," I stammer, humiliation lacing my voice.

Silence.

This is all a very bad dream. "Sorry to disturb you. I'm sorry to have called. Bye—"

"How did you get this number? Seriously."

"I told you." I can hear my heartbeat thumping inside my ears. "Johnny Dial gave it to me." What a sick joke he's played on me. This one is just cruel.

"Well, I've gotta jump," Liam says.

"Okay, well. See you later," I say.

"Yeah."

Then the call is over. The line is dead. I stare at the phone in disbelief. What in the world just happened? I burst out crying. How have I been so fooled? Just two weeks ago, Liam White had been a perfect gentleman when he invited us backstage and dropped us off at our car. It just doesn't make any sense. That's it. I'm done with

Johnny Dial. The guilt I felt yesterday about playing the trick on Stan is suddenly much worse. I've been playing on the wrong team.

After another long day at the office, I pull up in my driveway and the Tupperware/Cutco/Pampered Chef consultant himself is, as always, in his front yard with Luke. I'm starting to think he times his yard duties to coincide with my arrival from work. I simply wave—I'm so not in the mood for Riley—and head around back to the carport. Once I throw the car in park, I hurry my daughters out of the car. Roberta's in the backyard pawing on the fence and the girls blast through the gate to play with him and climb on the rickety old swing set.

After hurrying inside, I throw open my fridge and reach for a Coke. The chilliness of the bottle in my hand seems to somehow take the edge off. When the doorbell rings, seconds later, I don't even have to wonder who it is. Popping the top on my Coke as I go, I stroll over to the front door and peek through the peephole.

There he stands, holding something new in his hand. As much as I'd like to ignore him, there's no use.

After sucking in a deep breath and exhaling slowly, I throw open the door. "Well, Riley. How are you?"

"Just fine." Seeing it's the middle of April, he no longer needs a jacket. Today he's wearing a big button on his Tupperware golf shirt that reads, "Discover the Chef in You . . . Ask Me How!"

He hands me a part of the newspaper that's been folded in two.

"What's this?" I ask, not even bothering to unfold it.

"Your Wednesday circular. You wan over it when you dwove in the dwiveway."

"Oh, that's okay," I tell him, sweeping my hand across of my face, "I don't usually pick those up until they've been run over several times and are soaked in rainwater."

Riley shakes his head and squeezes his lips together. "You shouldn't do that. You're missing out on some gweat deals." Reaching over to grab the circular back out of my hand, he opens it to show me. "You won't believe what Kwoger's got on special this week. I've just gotten back with a big load of gwocewies. Let's see, I got deals on toilet paper, toothpaste, dog food, Wagu—"

I slightly tilt my head to the side.

"Haven't you ever bought Wagu?" he asks me.

"I don't think so."

"You should twy it. It's the best wed sauce in the world."

"I'll have to do that, Riley."

"Say, I noticed last night that one of your fwont porch lights is out." He's pointing to the right side of my stoop.

I move outside to peek at the lantern. "Oops." Stepping back inside the foyer, I flip on the light.

"See."

Sure enough, one of the four small twenty-five-watt crystal lights is burned out on my lantern. "Don't worry about that. No biggie," I say. "The rest of them still work."

"I'm pwetty big on always keeping my lightbulbs changed," he says, ignoring my comment, and reaches up to unscrew the dead bulb. "I've switched over to the CFLs. They save all kinds of money per year. I happen to have one wight here."

When I see the white, curlicue lightbulb he's removing from the pack I say, "Oh no, Riley. That's not the right kind."

"What do you mean?"

I'm not sure how to break the news to him. I might use one for a closet or the pantry but never where someone could see it. "I appreciate it, really I do, but I'll just get one at the grocery store. Don't worry about it." I reach out and pat his arm.

"Like I said, it'll save you quite a bit of money in the long wun. Actually, you should weplace all your lightbulbs with these."

As long a day as I've had, I can't hold back from telling him the truth, whether it hurts his feelings or not. "I'm going to be honest with you, Riley. That's not the kind I use. I mean, I'm not sure those CFLs are meant for the decorative light fixtures."

"Listen, twust me." He leans in closer and talks—like he always does when he's trying to make a point—out of the side of his mouth. "It's the better choice."

It's not worth arguing with him. I'll just replace it with a crystal bulb later. "Okay, go ahead."

"Alwighty then." It takes him a minute, but once he's completed his chore he wipes his hands on his shirt, right underneath the large button. "Say, I was wondering, have you had a chance to put your list together for the Pampa'ed Chef pawty? I would like to do a cooking demonstwation for your guests."

"Honestly? I have not. My house isn't close to being ready. I couldn't have a party here anytime soon, even if I wanted to. I've got way too much to do in this house." I have to admit I'm a little disappointed with the poor thing.

"Like what?"

"For starters, I've got curtains and pictures to hang, silver to polish, and several more boxes to unpack. There's no way I can have a party right now." Really, I'm dying to say, *Where are the guests supposed to use the bathroom, Riley? I've got two gaping holes in my powder room wall.*

"I could help you get your house weady."

"That's really sweet of you, but it's just stuff I need to do myself. I appreciate it, though." Now I'm backing inside my house and slowly shutting the door.

He steps forward as the door is closing, unrelenting. "Why don't you host the pawty at my house?"

Oh my stars. I can't even squeeze that into my brain. "That's very nice of you to offer but I don't think so. Tell you what, if you have a party with your own friends, I'll be happy to come over and buy something."

Honk honk. Honk, honk, honk. Speaking of friends, here come mine, hanging out the car windows.

Riley whips his head around. "Looks like you've got company."

Virginia screeches her car to a halt halfway up my circular drive and all three bop out of the car. Alice holds a deck of cards over her head and waves. Virginia's got the wine and Mary Jule is holding a pizza box under a big sack from Pete & Sam's. I wave back from the porch.

Virginia has left her car radio on and is out in the yard dancing. She puts the wine bottles down and twists till her bottom barely touches the grass. "Twist and shout, twist and shout," she sings at the top of her off-key little lungs. "Come on, come on, come on baby now." Alice and Mary Jule join in, "Come on and work it on out, work it on out."

From out in the yard, Virginia spots Riley's blue Tupperware golf shirt. "I bet you're Riley," she calls from the grass, still dancing.

"I bet you're wight," he calls back and turns to me. "Are you having a pawty tonight?"

"Oh no, Riley. They are my best friends. We don't have parties at each other's houses. They're just dropping by."

"With wine and cards?"

"We don't need an excuse to get together. It's just what we do." I race out to the grass to join them, leaving Riley on the porch. How do you explain a twenty-nine-year-friendship to a guy like Riley in only a few words? Four women who have known each other since kindergarten and, if lined up barefooted among hundreds of ladies all in a row, could pick out each other's feet. Not to mention our belly buttons or bare bosoms.

With an overexaggerated motion of her arm, Virginia beckons for Riley to join us. "Can you dance, Riley?" she yells over the music.

"Of course I can," he yells back, cupping his hand aside his mouth.

"Then what are you waiting for?" she yells back.

Riley bounds off the front step and races out to the yard. Virginia shimmies on over to him. "Do you pretzel?"

"You bet I do." With that, the two finish the rest of "Twist and Shout" pretzeling through my front yard.

After the song is over, Alice, I can tell by the way she's studying Riley, is absolutely chomping at the bit to ask him about his button.

She shuffles right up to him, reads his chest and says, "How can I discover the chef inside me, shoog?"

"Funny you should ask!" Riley says. "I just happen to be performing a cooking demonstwation at a Pampa'ed Chef pawty tonight. It's a blast."

"Well good for you," she says, completely uninterested in Riley's plans. "Let's go inside, y'all."

One look at Riley out of the corner of my eye tells me that he's not about to let the conversation drop. I can just tell by the way he's twitching his face from side to side, as if he's frantic to come up with a way to hawk his wares. "And I'd be happy to do the same thing at your house. If you'd like to host a pawty, I'll teach you all about discovering the chef inside you." Riley walks along beside her and never stops talking.

"Let me think about it, shoog," she says and helps Virginia carry the wine. "Where's Roberta, Leelee? I'm dying to meet him."

Once inside, we hole up in the kitchen. Mary Jule heads straight for my pantry and pulls out paper plates and napkins. After doling out the food and calling the girls and Roberta in from outside, something else on Riley's shirt catches her eye. She studies it a bit longer before her curiosity gets the best of her. She strolls over right beside him and glances toward his neck. "How *do* you get your collars to stay down like that? My Al's golf shirts are always turning up on the edges."

"It's one of my best-kept secwets," Riley tells her.

"Do tell, shoog, do tell," Alice says, and walks over to Riley to get a better look.

"Well, it's actually vewy simple." He inverts his lapel—just under the collar—to further explain. "I tack down my collar edges with thwead. That way, they don't curl up anymore."

Mary Jule can't stop herself from reaching up and touching the tip of Riley's collar. "If that isn't the most, well the most *domestic* thing I've ever seen. My Al wouldn't sew a button even if his life depended on it. Good for you, Riley," Mary Jule says. "Okay everyone. Let's eat. I'm starving."

After Riley finally leaves for his cooking demonstration, and once the girls are in bed—after four rounds of spades, I fess up about my phone call to Liam White. As expected, the girls are none too pleased. Mary Jule takes the blame though, and tells the others it was all her fault. I try to put it back on me, helping her not to feel bad. After all, she was not the one dialing his number.

Naturally, the conversation comes back around to Peter. Even though his name seems to be part of my past, they are still willing to talk about him as long as I feel the need. I tell them about the letters I've written but never intend to mail. And, as is always the case, they try to convince me that the reason he's not here in Memphis has nothing to do with me—but everything to do with his job. Mary Jule has beaten me over the head with the same words time and time again. "Men need stability," she says. "They don't just do things irrationally; they need some kind of guarantee as to what's on the other end." It all makes sense, but my heart can't seem to let go. I wish I knew why I'm still missing him as much as I do.

The next morning I'm actually early to work, ready to face Johnny Dial and have the chance to say my piece. It's still hard for me to believe that I've become the latest object of his teasing—when he fooled me the first time the shame was on him, as they say, but now that it's happened twice, I suppose I'm the bigger fool.

The control room is, as usual, a sloppy mess of half-empty coffee cups and Coke cans. With an aloofness that Alice could pull off even in her sleep, I go about picking up the trash acting cool and distant. It's not part of my job necessarily, but it's an excuse for me to be behind the on-air light legally. After pitching over a dozen empties into the corner wastebasket, I stroll over to the audio console, pretending to check his daily log sheets. Johnny, who seems to be oblivious to the fact that I've been indifferent says, "Talk to White?"

"Very funny, Dial," I say, eyes down, flipping agitatedly through the pages. "Har-de-har-har-har."

"What are you talking about?"

I shove the log back over to him. "Don't give me that."

"Whoa. That doesn't sound like the sweet Leelee I know." Normally Johnny prefers to stand while operating the board, but he slowly lowers himself onto the rolling stool. His eyes look like saucers.

"The big hoax you played on me, *that's* what I'm talking about."

"Why would I do that to you?" he says with very convincing sincerity.

"Because that's what you do. You make a living playing jokes on poor unsuspecting people like me. I don't know why I ever trusted you," I say, stepping toward the door.

"I swear to you. I didn't do that." He removes his headphones and moves toward me.

"Then why did Liam White act like he never called me?"

"I don't know." He turns around to Tyler, who's across the room. "Hey Tyler, are you sure you talked with Liam White? Are you sure he called for Leelee?"

Tyler turns around from where he's stacking old records, which are spread out all over the place, leftovers from Stan's lunch hour requests. "Yeah. I'm sure."

Johnny shrugs his shoulders.

"Then I just don't get it," I say. "He acted perturbed with me for even thinking he would give me a call. I'm telling you, the guy was downright rude. I just wish you could have seen how nice he was to my friends and me at his concert. I mean it, Johnny. Virginia swears he was flirting with me."

"I don't know what to tell you, sweetheart. I'm sure that's hard for you. But think about it. He gave out his phone number. How else would you have been able to call him back? Obviously he's psycho. You're much better off knowing that right now on the front end."

"I've already had one jerk in my life. Why would I want to get in line for another? Oh well. Maybe God's looking out for me." I pull open the door of the control room and head back to my office, just in time to collide with Edward.

"Good morning," he says, in his usual insolent tone of voice.

"Good morning to you, Edward," I reply, and duck into my office.

The morning jumps off to a busy start with a flurry of activity swarming around my office. Several winners flood by to pick up their prizes. Kyle spends a half hour explaining the promotions he has on the calendar for the week and Edward has an appointment with a Mercury Records rep who seems to want to spend more time with me than with Edward. When I glance at the clock I'm surprised to see that it's close to ten. Stan the Man hasn't even shown his face yet.

I'm on the phone explaining our winner policy to a woman who Johnny just told can only win one prize a month, when he comes busting into my office. "White's on the phone again."

I place my hand over the receiver and whisper, "*What?*"

"Put that person on hold," he says anxiously.

"Would you please hold a minute? I'll be right back," I say to the lady and press the hold button. Then I turn around to Johnny with a suspicious glare.

"White's on the request line asking to speak to you. Stan's up next, though, and since he and Edward are like this," he holds up two fingers, "I'm giving him the office line and having him call you in here."

"What makes you think it's really him? What'd he say? Is he in a good mood? Was he nice to you on the phone?" I say, running all queries into one big sentence.

"What is this? Twenty questions?"

"Just trying to protect myself here, I mean, after what happened yesterday . . ."

"Then what do you want me to do?"

"I don't know," I say. "How can you be sure it's really him? Maybe it's someone Edward's planted to catch me." I'm burying my face in my hands and shaking my head. "It's too risky. I could lose my job. Tell this person that I'm not interested in talking to him." By now I'm so flustered I can hardly think straight.

"Okie doke." I can tell by the sound of Johnny's voice that he disagrees. He bangs the door frame and runs back to the control room.

As he's leaving for the day, Johnny stops by my office to check his messages. I can't help myself. "So what did *Liam White* say?" I twirl my index finger next to my head as if I'm referring to a crazy person.

"He asked why not, and I said, I don't know, man. I don't get involved in love quarrels."

"*Love quarrels?* Why did you say that?"

"I don't know. I think this whole thing is weird."

"Well that makes two of us that think it's weird. Let's just forget it ever happened." My phone rings and I pick it up while Johnny's standing there glancing over his phone messages. "FM 99, Classic Hits, may I help you, please?"

"Is Leelee there?"

"This is she."

"Hi Leelee, it's Liam White," he says in a cheery voice.

What in *the world* is going on? I'm shocked and confused all at the same time. Just a weak, "Hi," is all I manage to say before mouthing to Johnny, "It's him," and pointing to the receiver in my hand.

"I wish I had known I was calling the request line. That's all they gave me in information. I finally wised up after it rung two hundred times before your deejay ever picked up the phone."

"Okay."

"Did you get the message that I called yesterday?"

"Yes, and I called you back." Now it's my voice that's sounding icy. Well, maybe just a little icy.

"When?"

This guy really *is* psycho. "Okay, well. It's nice talking to you again." I look over at Johnny, who flutters his fingers in an amused wave and leaves my office.

"Are you hanging up?" He sounds shocked.

"I'm at work and I can't really talk," I whisper back, and pivot my chair around so I'm facing the corner, just in case Stan or Edward walks by. "Besides, you weren't interested in talking with me yesterday, and honestly I don't understand why you want to talk with me now. You certainly didn't seem happy that I had your phone number." I say the last little bit more loudly—my tone rising as I explain my feelings. At the very least, I can be proud I stood up for myself, and to Liam White of all people—this is a very different Leelee than the pushover who was left to fend for herself in Vermont.

"I never talked with you, hon. I don't know what you're talking about."

This guy is very strange, Leelee. Just hang up the phone. "Well, I talked with someone and he didn't want to talk to me, so I—"

"Wait a minute. I bet you talked to Deke. Shit. I gave your deejay Deke's phone number by mistake. And I forgot to tell him."

"What are you talking about?" I say.

"I am truly sorry. I'm in the habit of giving out Deke's phone number instead of mine since he handles most of my business. He doesn't trust me to write things down," he says, with a chuckle. "Sometimes I can be a bit flaky. Here, let me give you mine."

I'm stunned. But I'm still not sure whether to believe him or not. In a rare moment of silence I hold my tongue, waiting.

"Have you got a pen?"

"Yes," I say, reaching across my desk.

He gives me his number. "Leelee, I am so so sorry. Was Deke rude to you? He's got a real abrupt manner to him sometimes."

"He was pretty rude."

"It's his job to look out for me. This is my fault. Honestly, he didn't know I called you."

After spending a miserable evening last night, beating myself up for not listening to Alice and Virginia, I don't quite know what to think or say. "Well, then, how are you?" I say, for lack of something more creative.

"I'm feeling pretty good. Got a day off today in West Palm Beach. It's eighty-four degrees and the hotel we're at has a killer pool. Have you been to West Palm before?"

"Yes, but it's been a while."

"We're headed to Boston next week. Then I'm in New York for a couple of days. I'd fly you up there if you wanted to come."

I'm so completely stunned by his words I cannot speak. Could I have actually heard him invite me to New York City?

"Hello. Leelee, are you still there?"

"Yes. I'm here."

"I think you are adorable. I'd like to get to know you better."

All right. That's it. I've lost it. Bolivar here I come.

"If it's the room you're worried about, that's not an issue. I'll get you your own."

I'll say you will. I have a million questions I'm dying to ask him. Like *Are you married?* for starters. Alice's silly qualms have now started to alarm me. "Gosh, I haven't been working here all that long," I say. "I don't think I have any vacations days coming to me." It's more of a thought than an answer.

"Oh, well another time then," he says matter-of-factly, but with obvious disappointment in his voice.

"Oh! I didn't mean that I *couldn't* come, I just mean I'll have to ask. That's all."

"Okay. I get that."

We'd been talking a whole two minutes when Edward slides into the room. "Leelee? Would you come to my office please?"

"Oh sure, Edward. I'll be right there," I say, pushing the receiver away from my mouth.

Instead of turning around and walking back out the door, he stands there waiting for me.

"Thank you so much for calling," I say in a very professional tone.

"I'll make sure the tickets are mailed to you when they come in." This time, *I* hang up on Liam White.

I peer up at Edward, guilt written all over my face.

"Who was that?" he asks.

"A sinner. I mean a *winner*," I say, and follow him into his office. A half hour later I emerge numb and weary from the droning instructions Edward gave me about our latest promotion—reiterating again all of the particular rules about contest giveaways, prize distribution, and the sneaky salespeople who will try and coerce me into giving away products that haven't yet arrived. But not even his dull tone could spoil the adrenaline rush from Liam White's telephone call.

So what now? A rock star has just invited me to join him in New York City. And I *hung up* on him. What are my best friends going to say? I send them all a text asking if there's any way they can meet me for lunch at Molly's, a Mexican restaurant close to the station.

The girls are already seated at the table when I show up a little after twelve. With large, bifolded menus covering their faces, they don't even see me slip into my seat.

"Y'all are going to scream your head off when I tell you this," I say, as soon as I sit down.

All three menus close at the same time and six eyes stare at me, accented by high-arched brows. "What!" they all answer at once.

"Guess."

"It's something about Liam White," Virgy says. "I know that look on your Fiery face."

Mary Jule lays her menu down on the table and folds her arms on top of it. "Oh, Leelee. I still feel bad about the advice I gave you. I should have told you not to call him back."

Alice says, "You never listen to me, do you?"

"Liam-White-just-invited-me-to-New-York," I say, trying hard to contain myself, but running all my words together regardless.

Mary Jule stands right up at her seat, balls her hands into fists, and moves her arms around and around in circles, swaying her hips. "I knew it. I knew it," she sings.

"Okay. I don't usually do this, but I'm putting a stop to this right now. After the way that asshole talked to you on the phone. Give me his number. He's deranged," Alice says.

"It wasn't him I talked to." I explain the whole story about how I'd really talked with his road manager, Deke.

Alice is skeptical at first. Mary Jule is dreamy-eyed. Virginia, in a total about-face, is beside herself. "Fiery, this is so you. I don't know anyone else in the world that would get an invitation from a rock star to go to New York. When are you leaving?"

With her right arm, Alice slices the air to form a large *T*. "Time out," she says. "We don't even have any proof that he's not married. And even if he's not, how do you know he doesn't have a disease?"

"Oh my gosh. I just thought about something," Mary Jule says, ignoring Alice's last comment. "Remember that movie, *The Banger Sisters* with Goldie Hawn and Susan Sarandon?" She glances around the table, waiting for all of us to confirm that we remember. Then she leans into the table and lowers her voice. "They take plasters of those rock stars' members." Stirring her Tab with a cocktail straw, she leans down to take a small sip.

"I swear to god, Fiery, if you don't at least take a measuring stick," Virginia says.

I stare expressionless at Alice and Mary Jule. "Did she just say what I think she said?"

"She said it," Mary Jule says, and her artful smile melts into laughter.

"I am not finding this funny," I say.

"I'm sorry," Mary Jule goes on, "but I have this mental picture of you digging in your purse for one of those soft measuring tapes, 'Hold on, Liam, Virginia needs to know your measurements.'"

I slap my hand on the table. "Would you please listen to yourselves? I mean, seriously now. Y'all already have me sleeping with the guy."

"I'm only teasing," Mary Jule says.

"I'll tell you right now he's going to expect you to," Alice says.

"No, he is not. He told me that he'd get me my own room."

Alice looks off to the side, as if she's pondering my potential for a sordid life. "You're right. I'm sorry. I'm getting way ahead of myself. Of course you're not going to bed with him. But you have to realize how vulnerable you are."

"Plus, what about Peter?" Mary Jule asks.

"What *about* Peter? Everything he said at George Clark's parking lot, when I left Vermont, was just a show of emotion. He doesn't care for me that way. If he did, he wouldn't let not having a job stand in the way."

Alice says, "I don't believe it."

"Then why don't I hear from him?"

"He told you he didn't think he could handle a long-distance relationship. And more importantly, he doesn't have a job *here*. Maybe it's too hard for him to call you. Why don't you call him?" Alice says.

"I don't know. I'm trying to let him go."

"Have you heard from Baker?" Virginia asks.

"He calls the girls every couple of weeks, and all he talks about is how great things are going for him in Vermont. He says he wants the girls to spend their summers there. They aren't going to want to leave me to spend their summers freezing to death. He's dreaming."

Virginia chews and swallows the tortilla chip she's just dunked in salsa. "Okay, back to Liam White. How will you get off work?"

"I'll have to call in sick. There's no way Edward will let me go, nor could I ever tell him. I'll have to sneak."

"I'll call this afternoon and get you an appointment for a spray tan." Mary Jule reaches over and looks at my fingers. "And a manicure."

"Will Kissie watch the girls?" Virginia asks.

I look at her like she's crazy.

"I was just going to offer, that's all," she says.

"I know, thank you," I say, patting her hand. "But Kissie's here, thank goodness."

When I get back to the office, I start pretending like I'm not feeling all that well. With the fake flu coming on I figure I better start the symptoms now if I'm going to accept Liam White's offer. And the thought of that offer, spending a fantasy weekend with him in New York, has got to be the most surreal notion that has ever crossed my mind. It's hard to imagine that it's even a notion to begin with. Six months ago I was in Vermont fighting off black flies, nor'easters, and snowdrifts; eight months before that I was still in my Memphis dream home with a loving husband and two daughters. It's all too much to take in sometimes, and when an opportunity like this comes along—to escape, really escape—well, I'd be a fool not to take it. It might be only for two days but it's been a really long time since I've done something fanciful and entirely for me. Heck, it's been years since anyone's pampered me. I'll call Liam White and accept his invitation as soon as I leave for the day. Sure it's a little indulgent, but it is New York City after all. I can think of no better place to bask in extravagance.

Chapter Ten

Kissie's rooting around my kitchen when I get home. Actually she'd call it "rambling" around the kitchen and by her chants and the tone of her voice, I can tell she's quite peeved. Riley's not around, it's not hot outside, and there's a Democrat in the White House. That leaves only one thing or one person she could be irritated at—me.

When I had called a few days ago to ask if she wouldn't mind staying with Sarah and Isabella next weekend because I had an invitation to go to New York from a *rock star* she hardly had two words to say. Personally, I thought she'd be thrilled, as much as she loves Duke Ellington and Louis Armstrong. "Hmm," she finally said, and sat there on the other end of the phone, like she was holding back what was really on her mind. After I said, "Isn't this wonderful?" she only said, "All right," with a tinge of irritation. Although she held her tongue on the phone, I knew good and well the discussion was far from over.

I had only been home a little while when she gave me that "Kissie glare." It's a look I've seen many times before, and one that at my age I thought I'd outgrown. She stared at me an extra long moment, puckered her lips and finally said, "How old is this man you're runnin' off to see?"

"I don't know." That's the response Kissie has always taught me to say when you don't want to commit yourself to something.

"Huh," she says, and lowers herself slowly onto a chair at the breakfast room table, staring into my eyes. It could only mean one thing—Leelee lecture time.

When my doorbell rings twice consecutively, it only makes matters worse. Besides sending Roberta into a barking frenzy, it sets Kissie's nerves on fire. Because she's absolutely positive who's ringing it, she shakes her head and says, *"unh-unh."*

I mosey on over to the foyer and peep through the peephole. Sure enough, there's Riley with a large box in his hand. He has to hold it over to one side so he can see in front of him. I fling open the door. "What's this, Riley?" I say, as he hands it to me.

"I happened to be in the yard today when the FedEx man dropped it off. I didn't want it to get stolen so I bwought it over to my house. It's to you from someone in New York City."

Peering at the top, I scan the label to see whom it's from before shaking it. I don't recognize the sender.

"It's a little heavy," he says, reaching out to touch it again. "Maybe it's a new pair of boots. Or possibly a food basket."

I shake the box a time or two.

"I twied bwinging it over when I saw Kissie dwive up with the girls but she didn't answer the door."

I lean in closer to him, whispering, "She probably didn't hear you. She's a little hard of hearing." I fibbed. So he wouldn't feel bad. In truth, the minute she gets to my house now Kissie closes all the blinds. Since the big picture window in the kitchen has no covering, she drags the ironing board into the den. I don't think it's because she doesn't like Riley, necessarily, he just drives her crazy, or as she says, gets on her last nerve. Kissie says by the time you turn eighty, you no longer need to worry about whether people think you like them or not and if you don't feel like talking to someone, you shouldn't have to.

Riley seems a little hurt when I don't invite him in, but after a whole day of Edward, not to mention the firing squad Kissie has planned for me, an evening of Riley is simply out of the question.

I hurry back to the kitchen, where Kissie is searching through the pots and pans, grab a knife out of the drawer and slice open the top of the box. When I peek inside, it's full of styrofoam peanuts and a card bearing my name is resting on top. I quickly rip open the envelope and pull out the card, which has a picture of a girl on the front with the New York skyline behind. "Living reckless and loving it" it reads, and it's signed "Liam." I glance over at Kissie, who is now busy at the stove, pretending to be uninterested in my package. I can't help wondering what she'll think about him, now that he has sent me a present.

After digging through the foam bits, which have partially spilled onto the floor, I pull out a box from the Magnolia Bakery. Twelve cupcakes, all different flavors, are a wee bit squished from the journey south. There's also a T-shirt with "I ♥ NY," and several brochures from tourist attractions: the Statue of Liberty, the Empire State Building, and the Staten Island Ferry. When I had called Liam back, he had asked me what I liked most about New York. Besides Broadway shows, which are my very favorite thing about New York, I had told him that although I'd visited several times, I'd never been out to the Statue of Liberty or ridden the Staten Island Ferry. He even included a Statue of Liberty bobblehead and an umbrella with logos from all the famous Broadway shows. Opening the box feels like Christmas, only better, because it's the first time a man has bought me presents in a long, long time.

"*Hm, hm, hm,*" Kissies chants, while she's taking a stick of butter out of the fridge. "*Hm, hm, hm.*" Now she's back at the stove checking her rice. Her gravy's starting to boil and she's still not saying a word, although I've caught her peeking at me when she doesn't think I'm looking. I know dang well she's interested in what's in this box. When I stroll up behind her with my T-shirt held up to my chest, she turns around with her wooden spoon in her hand. Her head is slightly shaking, her bottom lip tight, as she chooses her words carefully. "I ain't studyin' no rock star." What she means by that is, *I'm not interested in him*. Or, in other words, *I'm not impressed.*

I'm confused. What is it about Liam White that's got Kissie so upset? She's never met him so she can't have any reason not to like him. She has no idea of his music so she can't have an opinion on that. Finally it dawns on me. She thinks I'll be sharing his room.

"Kissie," I say, nonchalantly, as I'm picking up the foam peanuts from the floor. "Just *in case* you're wondering, Liam has reserved me my own beautiful room in New York."

Standing right there in front of the stove with the steam from the rice moistening her face and without turning around she says, "Nobody else knows that. They'll be thinkin' you are shackin' up with him."

Before I have the chance to respond she keeps talking with the top to the rice in one hand and a fork in the other. "What do you think those little girls in there will be thinkin'?" Sarah and Issie are in the next room on the couch in front of the TV with Roberta squeezed in between. Kissie extends the rice top in their direction.

"They don't have to know the details. I won't be gone that long. It's just a couple of days," I say. Reasoning with her is normally a futile experience.

Instead of answering me she moves over to the drawer and counts out the silverware. After she finishes setting the table and she's had time to give the situation more thought, she places both hands on her hips. "Life has thrown you a curveball, baby. But it don't mean you need to throw all you know out the winda' neither. The Lawd is gonna give you another chance at love but you must be smart about it."

"I am being smart about it."

"How do you call runnin' off to New York with a man every woman in the world wants to be with smart? That's what you did the first time around. Picked yourself a man every woman in Memphis wanted to be seen with. And what did that git you? Nothin' but heartache. *Hm, hm, hm.*

"Now I sat back and watched it happen the first time but I ain't gonna keep my mouth shut this time." She opens the oven and removes a pan of her yeast rolls. The smell normally sends me into a state of bliss, but tonight I'm in the middle of a reprimand.

"Kissie, he's getting me my own room. He's not even going to try to take me to bed."

"That's cuz he has any woman he wants tryin' to take *him* to bed!"

I thought about that for a moment. "That might be, but I'm different. You know I'm not like that."

"What do he want with a woman half his age anyway?" she asks while drizzling clarified butter onto the top of her rolls.

"I'm not half his age."

She continues on as if she didn't hear me. "That's what happens to men when they get older. They want to be seen with young women. Lust is real funny, Leelee. And you are very vulnerable. You never can predict what might happen when a man with all the right words and a real pretty face is sweet-talking you. You might think you are strong enough to resist him, but that ain't always the case. Ole Kissie knows what she's talking about." She heads back to the stove and turns off all the burners.

Following right behind her I say, "I am not going to let him sweet-talk me into anything. I realize now Baker was like that, but I'm not going to ever let that happen to me again. I'm a new person."

"New person? When a handsome man is buyin' a woman things, taking her on trips, tellin' her how pretty she looks, he's *ha'd* to resist. *Especially* if he's rich and famous. The Lawd wants you to flee from the devil. Not run right into his arms."

"He's not the devil, Kissie. Of all things."

"I'm not sayin' *he's* the devil." Her voice is shaky and her lips are pressed tightly together. "I'm sayin' it's the devil hisself who puts the temptation in your path in the first place. *Hm, hm, hm.*"

"So what do you want me to do? Cancel my trip?"

"I'm not gonna tell you what to do. I'm only tellin' you how you need to be thinkin'. Settin' our minds on what's right is the best way to beat that ole devil at his own game."

I open my mouth to comment but she interrupts me.

"I know what I'm talkin' about," she says, pointing to her chest. "I didn't get to be eighty-one years old without plenty of stumbles in a whole lot of potholes. I'm just tryin' to save you from another big scrape on your knee." Her voice is softer now. If there's one thing I know about Kissie, she only wants the very best life has to offer me.

"I know. And I appreciate it." Wrapping my arms around her I rest my head on her shoulder. "I promise I'll be careful. I'll know if he's not a nice person."

She squeezes me into her large frame and strokes the back of my head. "Well, there's gonna be plenty of clues along the way. Just make sure you keep your eyes wide open."

One big fat fib to Edward and a few days later, I'm standing in the check-in line at the Memphis International Airport ready to board a Delta flight to the Big Apple. My nails and toes are pale pink and I've been sprayed a fake golden brown. (It looks marginal at best considering my lily white skin could no more get this tan than an albino's could, not to mention the orange in the tanner clashes with the orange in my hair. The girl at Tan-tique talked me into medium when clearly I should have opted for extra light.) I've got on a darling outfit, though. Mary Jule picked me up bright and early Saturday morning and we spent the whole day running back and forth from the Laurelwood Shopping Center to the Oak Court Mall until we found the perfect dress—a pale yellow sleeveless sheath with a wide stretchy black belt, black leather peep-toe pumps, and a short black cardigan with tiny, knotted buttons to match. Mary Jule thought it was the cutest ensemble she'd ever seen and told me not to be surprised if she copied. Looking at myself now, here in the airport, I'm wondering if I don't look more like a bumblebee.

After struggling to place my extra large, overstuffed piece of luggage on the scale, the woman behind the Delta counter smiles when she hands me my boarding pass. At first I thought she was being friendly, but when I'm seated in row three and the flight attendant passes me a warm wash cloth with a silver tong, it hits me. I'm flying first class to meet a dang rock star in New York City. Right before I have to turn off my phone I text Virginia: "Loving my seat on the plane. Can't decide between the filet or the snapper." There's not a full meal offered today but she'll get the picture.

Two hours, a bowl of warm mixed nuts, and an emergency glass of wine to calm my nerves later, the flight attendant announces on the overhead that we're only fifteen minutes from the gate and the butterflies in my stomach come alive. My heart catapults back and forth against my chest as I ponder what's ahead and the possibilities the weekend might bring.

I step confidently off the plane and as I'm walking down the corridor toward the baggage carousel I notice a man holding a sign with my last name. I walk on past, never dreaming it could be for me, when something tells me I might as well ask. Just for the heck of it, I look him square in the face and say, "You're not here for *Leelee* Satterfield are you?" When he tells me yes, and that he would help me with my luggage, I'm tempted to scream.

Moments later, my coachman is whisking me away in a black Lincoln Town Car to the Mandarin Oriental hotel. As we weave in and out of the traffic, amid the honking and the near misses of cars colliding, my face is glued to the window. I'm fascinated by all the people outside, scurrying as if each is running their own personal race, trying to beat the clock.

When we pull up to the hotel, after rounding Columbus Circle and edging into a spot right in front of the curb, the doorman opens the rear door of my coach and a bellman takes my bag. Deke is waiting for me under the porte cochere when I step out of my carriage and as I dig in my purse for cash to tip both the driver and the doorman, he stops me. "I've got this," he says, deadpan, and hands the doorman a five. "The car company will bill us. You can put your money back."

"Well, thank you. You didn't have to do that," I say, as I stand face-to-face with Mr. Grouch.

"No problem," he says. I can't help but wonder how he's feeling about me now that I'm here as Liam's date.

"So how are you?" I ask. There's no reason for me to be ugly just because he's a mean ole grump.

"Not bad." There's a Liam White laminate around his neck with a penlight and a Sharpie clipped onto the lanyard. "Liam's at sound check. He wants me to bring you up once you're situated in your room." He hands me my room key. "I've already checked you in."

"Okay," I say, and shrug my shoulders. "Thank you." I wonder if he's planning on apologizing for how mean he was to me on the phone.

"I'll meet you back here in the lobby in, what, ten minutes?" He glances at his watch. "Is that enough time?"

"Oh, my goodness, yes. I'll be back in less."

When I open the door to my room, my eyes are first drawn to a floor-to-ceiling picture window covering an entire wall. I hurry over, tear open the sheers, and peer down below. From the twenty-second floor, the tops of the trees in Central Park form a canopy of green, resembling clusters of broccoli. A white loveseat sits in front of the picture window with a desk off to the side. There's a white coverlet on the king-size bed with large shams bearing the hotel's monogram. When I turn around, I notice my suitcase is already set up on a luggage rack in the corner. I practically float over to the bathroom, which is equally elegant. The oversize sauna tub is underneath another large picture window and there are two sinks with flower vases containing birds of paradise at either end. A separate black marble shower, with dual shower heads, invites the imagination to run wild.

The big question is whether or not I should meet Liam in my bumblebee suit. After staring at myself in the full-length mirror for a full five minutes, pivoting my foot and trying desperately to see my backside, I decide to go ahead and keep it on, minus the sweater. Hurriedly, I fluff my hair and reapply a little blush and lipstick.

Exactly fifteen minutes later, I'm stepping out of the elevator into the lobby, ready to greet my rock 'n' roll prince.

Deke's on the phone. He waves me over but talks the whole time we're walking together. It sounds like he's speaking with someone at a hotel, something about an early check-in. We step back onto another elevator and take a ride to the thirty-sixth floor. Although he's now finished with his phone conversation, Deke and I stroll in silence down the hall and stop in front a wide set of doors. He moves through ahead of me into a beautiful ballroom with floor-to-ceiling windows covering three sides of the room. The Hudson River is on one side, Central Park is on the other, with Columbus Circle underneath the third set of windows. The tables are elegantly set for a formal dinner, each graced with topiaries as centerpieces. Liam is on a short stage in the middle of the room singing and I recognize the same band members who were with him in Memphis. I know the song, "Dusty Love." Once it's over, he lays down his guitar and happens to spot me standing with Deke in the middle of the room. He leaps off the stage and heads straight over, reaching out his arms.

"Hi, baby," he says, once his arms wrap around me.

Baby? Normally, I would think a guy was sleazy for calling me that so soon but coming from him it's the sexiest thing I've ever heard.

"Hi, Liam," I say, entirely convincing myself that this is what it felt like the first time Grace Kelly met Prince Ranier.

"You look gorgeous." He takes a step back and I watch his eyes travel from my hair down to my toes.

"I do?"

He slowly exhales. "Yellow is your color. It looks great with your hair," he says, lifting a long lock off my shoulder and holding it in his hand. "Wow. So beautiful."

"Thank you." I smile coyly.

Reaching out for my hand, he leads me to the stage where he helps me up onto the platform. "Hey everyone, remember Leelee from Memphis?" They all nod and say hello. He wraps one arm around my waist and speaks close to my face. "Why don't you sit at one of the chairs at that table," he points to the foot of the stage. "I'll be finished here shortly and we'll go for a drink."

"That's fine," I say, still quite shy in his presence.

Once seated I send a three-way text to the girls that reads: "Sitting at a ballroom table with a penthouse view of Central Park on one side and the Hudson River on the other waiting for Liam to finish his sound check. He just called me 'baby.'"

Virginia immediately writes back, "Might leave John for a band member. I want the guitar player."

Mary Jule writes, "I'm so jealous."

Finally ten minutes later, Alice responds. "I admit it. I would KILL to be there. Have fun." I can't help but smile to myself at Alice's admission while glancing toward the stage where Liam is playing the first bars of "Miss Thing."

The second sound check is over Liam grabs my hand, walks me through the ballroom, and whisks me out the door. We step onto an elevator, and it seems to stop on every floor on the way down. With my hand clutched tightly inside his, he scoots me farther back to accommodate each person. Once we reach the lobby he leads me through to the bar, where he heads straight for two empty bar stools.

He throws his leg over his stool and pats the one next to it. "Have a seat, young lady."

It's higher than most stools and since my pale yellow sheath hasn't much give in the skirt, I have to wriggle my way onto the seat.

"You gonna make it there?" he asks jokingly, while reaching over to help hoist me up.

"Yes, I've got it now," I say, awkwardly scooting my backside into the chair. Clearly there's a disadvantage to a sheath, though I'm sure this wasn't the scenario my mother had in mind when she told me a good sheath dress would be indispensable. With all the maneuvering my dress has twisted and the back is now around the front. I try smoothing it back around, slowly hiking up one hip after the other, all the while looking like a seal writhing about in a chair. I don't have to look into the mirrored bar to tell my face is on fire.

I catch him looking at me as I'm situating my purse over the back of the stool. "How's your room, Leelee Satterfield?" he asks me confidently.

"It is *beautiful*. And the view? I had no idea," I say as gracefully as possible, considering I've just been squirming in the seat like a five-year-old being forced to pose for a portrait.

His green eyes sparkle as he speaks. "I know. My room has views of both Central Park and the Hudson. It's definitely an advantage of these corporate gigs."

"What do you mean by that?" I say, slightly out of breath from my unexpected workout.

"Some of the larger companies have events or conferences for their employees, say once a year, and they hire guys like me as their entertainment. The best part is that they have big budgets, so the fee is great, plus they're usually held at a wonderful hotel like this one. But, like everything, there's a downside." He looks down the bar and tries to attract the bartender's attention. "The audiences are terrible."

"I'm not sure what you mean by that, either," I say, when he looks back at me.

He smiles and chuckles a bit. "For one thing, they never stop talking. And they're usually shit-faced by the end of the night. They're not paying to see us, so they normally aren't too attentive."

The bartender finally arrives and Liam orders a Heineken. "And for the lady?" the Asian bartender asks.

"Do you have peach daiquiris?" I say.

"No. But I could make you a peach bellini martini."

"What's in that?" I ask.

"Peach schnapps, vodka, peach nectar."

"Hmm, that sounds a little strong for me."

"It's very good, though," he says, wiping his hands on a bar cloth.

"Maybe I'll have . . . a . . . okay, I'll take it," I tell him.

When our drinks are served Liam leans over and holds up his Heineken bottle for a toast. "To Leelee, who looks like a Southern belle in her yellow dress, with peach bellini-daiquiri-whatever-you-call-it, and who puts all these Northern women to shame." He never takes his eyes from mine, and gently taps our drinks together.

I deftly lean in to sip from the precarious rim of the martini glass, and lower my eyes away from his. The first swallow melts deliciously down my throat—a dangerous combination of peach and fire and deep, deep warmth. I make a futile mental note to watch out for these concoctions . . . not to mention the man I'm sitting across from.

Noticing the warmth spread in my cheeks, Liam leans back and chuckles—a confident grin spreading across his weathered face. He takes a relaxed pull from his bottle and laughs. "Lightweight," he says teasingly.

We spend the next hour engrossed in conversation. Everything from why Deke is gruff (Liam says that's the way most road managers act), to my job, and onto Alice, Virginia, and Mary Jule. He tells me he thinks they are hilarious and wonders why they don't have their own TV show. I tell him all about Kissie and how she's keeping my daughters, and how I hope and pray Riley's not driving her crazy.

I lose count after the sixth fan who interrupts us, recognizing Liam and then asking him for his autograph. The first time I don't really understand what's going on—Liam is so conditioned to the occurrence that he barely has to pause our conversation to sign the cocktail napkin. I can't help but bask in the thrill of being the one on his arm, as the admirers glance over at me while Liam is signing his name. It's one of those pinch-me-quick moments, when you're not sure if it's a dream or not. But after a while it becomes a nuisance; our conversations are too readily upended and the thrill I got from being gawked over now seems like an invasion of privacy. Especially when the women smile and bat their fake eyelashes. I suppose that little fashion accessory is back but Mama always said it makes a woman look common and cheap.

Every once in a while, when Liam touches my knee or puts his arm around my shoulders, I'm reminded that it is not a dream at all and I'm living my own fairy-tale moment. He may not be Daddy's definition of a Southern gentleman, but Liam is a very nice person with a great deal of respect for me. Kissie is dead wrong this time.

"Are you getting hungry?" he asks, when a highly enhanced blonde wanders away.

"Sort of." I'm not about to act like it, but actually I'm starving.

"I don't normally eat until after the show, but I'd be happy to order you something." Seeing my confused face, he continues. "It preserves my voice," he says, clearing his throat. Even though I'm not familiar with what in the world he means, I shake my head in agreement and smile.

"I have to head on upstairs in a sec, but my goodness, Leelee Satterfield, it's hard to get up and leave you right now," he says with such simplicity and directness it stuns me.

"Gosh, you are so complimentary. Thank you," I say, tucking my hair behind my ears.

"You're just a doll, baby. I'm stoked you decided to come up." He kisses my forehead before glancing at his watch. "Deke's probably getting antsy about now. He'll start calling if we're not backstage on time. We better head."

As we're strolling through the hotel, my mind is ablaze with possibility. The way people are smiling at us gives me the impression that they think I'm his girlfriend. Or even better, his wife. This is the most regal moment of my life; I can't imagine anyone could blame me for considering what might become of it.

Deke greets us at the ballroom and shows us back to a small green room set up outside Liam's dressing room. Once inside, I notice the elaborate spread of food and drink, exactly as it was backstage at the Orpheum. The decadent jumbo shrimp chilling on top of an ice sculpture fashioned after a treble clef, an assortment of exotic fruits fanned out on a silver tray with a curry dip in the middle. Brie, calumet, and other fine cheeses nestled inside red, green, and purple grapes. Once again a bar is stocked with Coke, Sprite, Perrier, Heineken, and wine. My eyes zero in on the green bottle with the blue foil top and the familiar antique white label, barely visible amid the ice in the wine cooler. It's the Rombauer Chardonnay again—and as much as I'm determined not to think of him, all I can see are Peter's perfect lips. I can practically hear him calling my name from the kitchen.

"Leelee, are you with me?" When I feel Liam touch me on the shoulder, I'm startled back to our conversation.

"Oh sorry. I spaced out there for a second." I lightly shake my head as I bring myself back to the present.

"Would you like a glass of wine, baby?" he asks.

"Not right now, thank you, though. Is all this food for you?"

"Yeah. It's a terrible waste, huh? Surely, the hotel must give it to their employees after I leave."

"Don't your band members help you eat it?"

"Believe it or not, they've got their own dressing room food. That's the business, though. My manager insists I keep it on my rider."

"What's your rider?" I take the liberty of popping a shrimp into my mouth. At this point, I'm ravenous.

"It's part of my contract. It tells the promoter what I need for each show. Aside from all my technical specs like how many inputs and outputs I need for my mics, amps, monitors, and such, it also spells out what kind of food I'd like to have backstage. I've thought about taking some of it off but my manger is convinced that there will come a night when I really want it. So I just leave it in."

Deke knocks on the door to let Liam know he's got fifteen minutes before show time and that he better get changed. Five minutes later, when the bathroom door opens and I catch sight of my date standing in front of me wearing a dark suit and pale blue dress shirt, he nearly takes my breath away. He's knotting his tie as he walks toward me.

"I have to dress up a bit more for these corporate gigs. Don't want to stick out like a sore thumb," he says. "Hey, Deke, show Leelee to her seat out front, will you?" He leans in and kisses my cheek. I know I'm blushing, but can't do anything to prevent it.

On the way into the ballroom, I see everyone is in cocktail outfits. Now I'm the one sticking out like a sore thumb. I politely excuse myself from Deke with a lame excuse about needing to check my phone messages, and go running back to my room to change. I had a feeling I'd need a cocktail dress so naturally I packed my favorite. It's a vintage pale pink, strapless organza, tea-length made in the 1950s. The best part about it is, it was Mama's—part of her trousseau when she was betrothed to Daddy.

By the time I get back the show has already started. The people at my table glance over at me, the strange single woman sneaking in without a name tag. A few minutes later, in between songs, the man sitting next to me asks whom I'm with.

"I'm with Liam," I say, and point toward the stage.

His eyes bulge. "Are you his wife?"

"No, girlfriend," I hear myself saying, shocked not only that I said it, but by how quickly the words tumbled out of my mouth.

"Really?" I watch him place his hands on his wife's shoulders and whisper to her from behind. She looks back at me and leans all the way over her husband. "You're with Liam? What it must be like to stare into that face!" Within minutes, the word has spread around the table and all of them want to be my new best friend. Normally I'd be pleased with the attention and newfound camaraderie; but it's clear they're only interested because I'm with Liam. And I'm not really "with" him. This must be what it feels like to be royalty. Rock 'n' roll royalty, anyway.

Liam was exactly right about people talking during his show. I notice many folks standing at the back of the room, their chatter causing an underlying background noise that continues throughout the whole show. It affects the music, but I suppose if you hadn't listened to every album like I had, you might not notice the difference. When he hits the final chord, the couples at my table jump up to clap for him, all the while looking over at me. For all they know we could be deeply in love. Love. What would that feel like, to be really, actually, in love with Liam White? Little do they realize, I am nothing more than a working mom Cinderella enjoying a weekend away from my reality. It's not as carefree, this fantasy, when you know it's really not true. We all continue clapping and a few whistles come from the back tables—where the cocktails have started to fuel rowdy behavior. I wonder if Cinderella was able to enjoy her time at the ball, knowing that there was a ticking clock hanging over her head. I look at Liam who is now making final waves to the crowd, and he catches my attention and issues a heart-stopping wink in my direction. He certainly makes a convincing Prince Charming.

When the lights come up, I see Deke beelining it over to my table. He motions for me to follow him quickly. As I'm walking away I hear one of the ladies say to another, "What I wouldn't give to be her right now."

The door to Liam's dressing room is shut when we make it backstage and his bandmates are milling about, eating their own food. I linger outside chatting with his drummer, Danny, exchanging pleasantries, commenting on the noisy audience and raving about the hotel's views. When he asks me how I like Liam's suite, I immediately bristle and feel the blood rush out of my head. Shame rushes through me. I don't feel like Cinderella anymore.

"I haven't seen his suite," I say as politely as possible. "I have a lovely room, though, that overlooks the park."

He smiles slowly, but nods his head like he doesn't believe me—as if my propriety is just for show. For the first time since I've arrived, it feels ugly.

At last, Liam's door opens and I notice he's changed back to the casual clothes he wore earlier. In a brief flurry, he asks how I liked the show but can barely stay for my answer; much less comment on my change of dress or even hug my neck. I walk next to him down the hallway as he explains that he has a quick meet-and-greet that he must attend. Deke whisks him away down another corridor and I find myself all alone. I turn around and walk toward the green room, resigned to making small talk with his bandmates, who all think I'm sharing his bed.

A solid forty-five minutes later, Liam returns carrying a white teddy bear dressed in a pair of see-through black thong panties. All the guys in the green room whoop and holler at the sight of sexy lingerie.

"What's that?" I ask shyly when Liam strolls over to me.

"A fan gift," he says, and shrugs his shoulders.

"Wow," I say, and raise my eyebrows a touch.

"What's new?" Jerry, his guitar player, says while he's stuffing one of Liam's jumbo shrimp in his mouth. "I keep telling White I want to see his collection."

I must have had an inquisitive look on my face because Jerry says, "What can I say? His fans want to shop for him."

"Let's head," Liam says to me as he throws the bear to Jerry and wraps his arm around my waist. "I'm ready for a drink. And I could eat somebody I'm so hungry." The guys whoop and holler even louder.

As he holds open the door, Liam peers down at me. "You changed."

I am still stuck on his last words but quickly adjust, feigning a coy smile. "Everyone in the audience was dressed up," I say. "So I ran back to my room for a quick change."

"You look gorgeous."

"Well, thank you." I look down at my dress.

"Good enough to eat," Jerry says.

When I whip my head around and give him a dirty look, he backs away and holds up his hands, palms out. "Just joking."

A few of the guys snicker, and I turn to Liam expecting support but instead find him in the midst of a grin.

In an instant Liam White has fallen off his pedestal.

A limo is waiting to whisk us off to a restaurant a few blocks away. After the uncomfortable situation in the dressing room, I am grateful for the short trip and the many excuses to look out the window and gawk over the streetscapes. My rose-colored glasses may be off when it comes to Liam, but it's no reason not to enjoy the remainder of the evening—and to his credit, he's apologized three times for his crass bandmates. I guess that's the problem with fairy tales—there's no room for humanity.

When we step inside the door, just past eleven, the maître d' asks if we have a reservation and Liam says, "Yes, White."

The man looks down at a book resting on a podium. "I'm sorry, Mr. White. Could it be under a different name?"

"Longfellow?" he says, and looks over at me. "Deke's last name."

Again, the man looks through his book. "No, sir. Another name?"

"Satterfield?"

The same thing happens again.

"I guess we don't have one." There's a chill in Liam's voice as he digs his phone out of his jacket and punches in a number. "Deke," he says, angrily, "there's no reservation here at Marea. Okay." He hands the phone to the gentleman.

Next thing I know we're being shown to a table and the maître d' pulls out my chair. Liam sits down next to me. "We'll take a bottle of the Dom," he says, as he's scooting his chair up to the table. The gentleman smiles and disappears into the back.

I've only tasted Dom Perignon one other time when Virginia, Mary Jule, and I each pitched in forty dollars to celebrate Alice's graduation from graduate school at Emory. Of course, that was a while back and we purchased it directly from a liquor store. Here at this restaurant in New York, I'm sure the cost is quadruple that.

"So, tell me," he says, after the sommelier has poured us each a glass of champagne. "How is a girl like Leelee Satterfield single?"

After a deep breath, I tell him all about Baker. I start with how we met in high school and how it was me who first had a huge crush on him. I tell him how we came to be married. We talk a little about the divorce and how Helga, the ruthless shyster, had masterminded a scheme to swindle him away from me.

He reaches over and takes my hand, raising it to his lips, and kisses it tenderly. I love how attentive he is to me, listening to my every word. Once he even says he'd like to slap Baker around a bit and that one comment instantly endears him to me. It's nice to think someone cares about my life and how I'm doing, rock star status aside.

"Any boyfriends since you split up?" he asks.

"No. Well, I take that back, sort of."

"A sort-of boyfriend?"

"There was this guy in Vermont. The chef at my restaurant."

"Helga's brother?" I had told him all about how we came to purchase the inn from Helga and Rolf in the first place.

"No, this was after Rolf left. I advertised for a new chef and he applied. He came in and added a new menu—he was amazing, actually. He looked after my girls and me and if it weren't for him, I don't know what would have happened to us. Peter, that's his name, and I made that place into a remarkable little getaway."

"But he was your sort-of boyfriend." His eyes travel away from me and look around the room.

"He never was my boyfriend. But we cared about each other more than we wanted to admit. Until I was leaving—then he finally admitted it. But that was after he acted terribly rude to me when he learned I was moving back home." I whisk my hand in front of my face. "It's complicated."

Abruptly, without waiting for the wine steward, he pours us each another glass of champagne. Then he raises his glass and holds it next to mine. "What do you say we toast to me and you?"

Me and you? I'm sitting across from the man whose album covers I've drooled over since I was twelve; someone who's surprisingly easy to talk to and even kind. I've spent collectively less than twenty-four hours with him, it seems vastly premature to be discussing "me and you." "Okay," I say, "I'll drink to that," totally ignoring my rational internal dialogue. It didn't seem right to spoil the moment, I suppose.

"Tell me about you," I say, the champagne finally loosening my tongue.

"What about me?"

"I don't know, just anything about you. Do you have children?"

He nods his head in affirmation. "I have a son, twenty-seven."

My eyes open wide.

He smiles as he sips the champagne from the glass and swirls it around in his mouth. "I was a bad boy."

I tried calculating how young he was when his son was born. Alice had already found out that Liam is forty-four. "So you were . . ."

"Seventeen," he says. "And no, we never married."

"Have you ever been married?" I ask.

"Nope."

"Gosh, that's hard to believe." That may have come out wrong. I change the subject back to his boy. "Is your son a musician, too?"

"No. He's a whole lot smarter than his old man. He actually works for a living," Liam says with obvious pride in his voice.

"You work for a living," I say, and pat his arm.

He laughs. "Not like him. He's a craftsman. Like in the old days. A damn good one, too. You should see the work he does. Gorgeous cabinetry, millwork, moldings."

"Where does he live?"

"Northern California. In Napa Valley. Ever been there?"

"You know, I haven't. Someday, though."

"You should come with me some time."

Edward's scary mug suddenly pops into my mind—unfortunately causing me to cringe about the big fat one I told him about having the flu. "I'd love to," I say, now accustomed to these hypothetical open invitations of Liam's.

When we finally get around to ordering it's very late. Probably close to midnight. I look around and notice there are only a few stragglers left in the restaurant. The waiter politely explains that the kitchen will be closing shortly and that he needs to take our order. We haven't even looked at the menus and Liam tells him to please come back in five minutes. When the poor thing returns and we still haven't looked at the menu, Liam scans it quickly and orders the halibut. I decide on the sea scallops.

Throughout the dinner, my cell phone keeps beeping and after the fifth time Liam says, "Someone is desperate to get ahold of you. You might want to see about it."

"It's just my crazy girlfriends. No worries," I say. When I glance down at the phone I have five text messages.

We talk all through our meal. He tells me about the record he's due to record in the next few months. We talk more about his son and the fact that he doesn't see him much. He confesses that he's a grandfather and laments that he would like to see more of his grandson. I tell him about Roberta, Jeb, and Pierre and that being only four hours away from them makes me miss them all the more. I get so lost in talking about Vermont, recalling the zany predicaments I'd been in—from shoveling my car out of five feet of snow to overbooking the inn—that I don't even realize who I'm discussing. He stops me when I mention Peter.

"Tell me more about this Peter dude, your *sort-of* boyfriend. It sounds like you still like him."

I'm not really all that keen on giving any more details but when he presses me unrelentingly, I go ahead. "Well, there's not that much more to tell. He was a really great chef and he helped me out of a really tough spot. We became good friends over the months that we worked together and then I got an offer on the inn."

"Did he want you to stay?"

"It was too late. I'd made my decision to come back home. It was a decision I made for me, and not anyone else. It would have been hard to change my mind at that point."

"You made the right decision."

"You think so?"

"I know so. You made a decision based on your needs and not someone else's. I like that. And I like you."

"I like you, too," I say, less shyly this time.

Then he leans in to kiss me. Right there at the table. It's just a peck, but it's still a kiss. When he smiles the crow's-feet in the corners of his eyes crease, revealing the difference in our ages. It startles me, quite honestly. Eleven years is a big difference, even if he is a rock star.

He picks back up his fork and dabbles at his fish. "So you and Peter have unrequited love? That can be a powerful thing." If I didn't know better, I'd swear he was jealous.

"Can we please not talk about Peter? He lives in Vermont and I live in Tennessee. There is 1,473 miles between us and I'm never moving back there and apparently he's not moving to Tennessee."

"Why not?"

"Because he doesn't have a job in Tennessee. And he's from New Jersey. And, well, I don't think he would like Memphis. I don't know, it's a moot point." The sharp tone to my voice must let him know that I'm done talking about Peter because he finally lets it drop.

We are the last two people in the restaurant at one o'clock in the morning. Our poor waiter is lurking around our table, no doubt ready to go home. The thought crosses my mind that they are keeping the place open only because it's Liam. Thankfully Liam notices, too, and signals for the check—which is calculated and paid with swift efficiency. Never seeming to have broken eye contact, Liam asks, "You ready?"

"Yes," I say, smiling back at him—caught up in the absurdity of the moment, the extravagance, the bottles of champagne and wine, I know I'm practically swooning. I break eye contact and take a deep breath.

"Why'd you do that?" he asks.

"Do what?"

"You went from a smile to a funny look all of a sudden."

How do you tell a celebrity that you're on a date with that you have just caught yourself acting starstruck? I can't tell him that. "I'm fine. Don't mind me. This whole thing is just, surreal. *Crazy.* It's just so . . . this isn't my life," I say with an audible sigh. There it is. The one thing we've both been pretending all night to ignore: he's famous and I'm just another dreamy-eyed woman.

When we return to the hotel, Liam's holding my hand as we stroll casually through the lobby—my fairy tale suddenly melts into a puddle of reality right in front of the elevator bank. As we're headed back to our *respective* rooms, the thought goes through my mind: What's going to happen if he invites me up?

Well, I'm going to tell him that I'll see him tomorrow when we tour the Statue of Liberty. If he wants to have breakfast first, then fine. Surely he knows my intentions for this relationship, and that I want to take things very slowly. But then again, does he? After all, the girls and I hung out backstage at his show in Memphis for over an hour. I flew up to New York on a whim, just because he invited me. I've shared a lot of personal information with him, shared a kiss and practically agreed to visit his son in Napa. I can't say I haven't sent some mixed messages. But I'm steely-eyed and determined to say right back: *No way. What kind of girl do you think I am, Liam White? Do I look like a groupie to you?*

As we're stepping onto the elevator he says, "Would you like to come back to my room for another drink?"

"Certainly," I say.

Moments later he's opening the door to his suite and it's nearly one thirty in the morning. Kissie King would be laying her holy hands all over me if she had any idea. I take that back. The entire mother board of her church would be laying their holy hands all over me.

With his arm around me, we walk into a living room with floor-to-ceiling picture windows on two sides, overlooking both the park and the Hudson River. And I thought my room was gorgeous. There's a contemporary feel to his room that mine doesn't have, with clean lines on the beige sofas, the smooth straight tables and the accent pieces. An Asian flavor infuses his room, too, with subtle touches in the art, the orchids, and the Mandarin accessories. The blinds over the windows are raised and the view is magnificent.

"Take a look around," he says, before disappearing into his bedroom.

I drift over to the windows to get a better look at the skyline from the fifty-fourth floor. *Okay, Leelee, what are you doing?* I start lecturing myself. *You're in a guy's suite that you hardly know. Never mind the fact that you've had plenty to drink.*

I hear him behind me and turn around. He's pouring *more* drinks at a wet bar decorated with Bisazza tiles. "Do you like port?" he asks, as he's strolling toward me, two glasses in his hands.

"I love port, but I've had way—"

"I thought you might like it as sweet as it is," he says, handing me a crystal cordial glass.

Awkwardly, we both stare out at the skyline, watching the taillights of the cabs and cars blink red against the black night. It's mesmerizing. Looking for an excuse for any kind of small talk, I say, "I wonder if this city ever stops moving."

"Not since I've been playing here," he says, hooking his arm through mine and taking a sip of wine. I can see our reflections in the window, as we stand there with our bodies touching, side by side.

My heart is pounding and I'm just certain he can hear it. It's roaring inside my ears. He says something else, but I can hardly hear him. "I'm sorry, what did you say?" I ask.

"I said, you are beautiful."

It's very *very* difficult to resist a man calling you beautiful. It's another difficulty altogether to resist a man whose album cover has been beckoning you for over half your life. I hear the clinking of his crystal cordial glass as he sets it down on the glass table. He takes mine out of my hand and puts it down on the table, too. Reaching out to me, he grabs my waist, pulling me toward him. I can smell the sweetness of the port on his breath as he moves closer to my face, lightly kissing my right cheek and then my left. The whiskers on his chin brush against my lips when he moves across my face and it feels curiously sensual. I've never kissed a man with facial hair before and the sensation surprises me. Suddenly, I want him to tickle me with his beard all over my face.

When Liam's tongue touches mine, I can taste the port. That, alone, is titillating and at once we dive into a long, passionate kiss.

Standing in front of the windows I reach my arms around him and he pulls me even closer. I can see the skyline in the window and it's like I'm embracing New York, also.

"I can't help myself. I'm taken with you," he whispers in my ear. I feel his hands leave my back and move slowly toward my chest. I gently hold them at my waist before they ever make it to the front of my dress. When I reach up to run my fingers through his hair, he starts tracing his hands upward. I can't suppress the heat flooding through me, but without missing a beat, my elbows force his hands back down again. After a few more kisses, he takes my hand and guides me through the living room, around the coffee table, past the sofas, and around the wet bar. I'm a step away from his bedroom door when reality hits me with an image of Kissie King, with all the ladies from the mother board dressed in white, fanning me with palm leafs as I lay faint on the ground.

"No," I say in a rare, bold Leelee Satterfield moment. "I cannot go into your bedroom."

"Why not?" he says, enveloping me in his arms again and caressing the right side of my neck with his lips.

"Because we hardly know each other," I say, as I pull away from his embrace. "You might be used to having women fall all over you but I'm just not that girl. I'm not like that."

"Oh come on. You're a grown woman." The rolling of his eyes and the expression on his face is mocking.

"What difference does that make?" I push away from him. "I've never been that way, and I don't plan on starting now. Alice thought I was crazy to come here with you. So did Kissie for that matter, but I didn't listen to them. I was naïve enough to think you wouldn't expect something physical from this trip. But they were right. I shouldn't have come," I say, with surprising calmness. Inside though, I'm cursing myself for being so gullible. I start to gather up my things.

"No, don't say that," he says, dropping his eyes. "I'm sorry. I got carried away. Listen, I'm cool with whatever you want here. Honestly. I just think you're a special lady. And I don't get to spend actual time with many these days." If his sudden change of expression is any indication, I get the feeling he's being sincere. "Please. Don't leave upset."

"Tell you what," I say, "let's start over in the morning. It's really late and I need some sleep."

"If it's okay, I'll walk you to your room?" he asks, and winks . . . knowing it will make me grin.

Once at my door, he's a perfect gentleman, asking for my key. I'm a little embarrassed when he sees my room. My stuff is sprawled out all over the place. My yellow sheath is in a heap on the floor where I left it after running back for my quick change before his show.

"So are we going to the Statue of Liberty tomorrow?" I ask him.

"You bet. Anything you want to do."

"That's what I want to do."

"Okay." His smile is sweet. "See you in the morning, Leelee. I'll call you when I wake up. Or better yet—you call me. I wouldn't want to disturb your beauty rest," he says with a chuckle.

I nod my head and walk him to my door. He kisses my cheek and is gone.

After shutting my door, I check my cell phone. The first text message from Virginia reads, "Call me immediately." Followed by, "Okay, don't call me. I am smearing your reputation around town!!" Alice's says, "What in the hell are you doing? Don't come crying to me when you have an STD!" Mary Jule's reads, "Have so much fun, Leelee. Can't wait to hear all about it. I'M SO JEALOUS!!"

I decide not to call them back since it's so late, but I send all three of them the same text. "Bearded kisses are the bomb!"

Chapter Eleven

When I raise my head up from the pillow and turn toward the red illuminated numbers on the clock, it's past ten. I bolt straight up in the bed and fumble around for my phone. The heavy curtains on the windows have blocked all signs of daylight from the room and the light on my phone tells me that I have no missed calls.

Huh.

Then I remember that Liam said to call him first so he wouldn't disturb me. I could kick myself for sleeping this late. But, after all, it's only nine my time. Quickly, I punch in the numbers to his cell phone but it goes straight to voice mail. I can't remember his room number, even though I nearly pointed my moral compass in the opposite direction while staring at the view from his living room. When I call the front desk to be connected to him, the receptionist tells me there is no one by the name of Liam White registered at the hotel. I try arguing with her but the woman is adamant that they have no guests with the last name of White staying at the Mandarin Oriental. Admittedly, my mind charges off in all sorts of directions. Like any woman would do, I decide to think it over in the bathtub.

Melting down into the large tub overlooking Central Park, soaking in the Fresh bath crystals the hotel has luxuriously provided, I ponder the situation. If my not sleeping with him has caused him to be upset with me and turn off his phone to prove it, then so be it. I'll just make the most of this day. I'll drool over the shoes at Saks and tour the Statue of Liberty all by myself if I have to.

By the time I call Virginia and the others to fill them in on last night's escapade, and call home to talk with Kissie and the girls, who have been frantic for hours because Roberta dug up under the fence and escaped, but are fine now because the neighbor behind me had him the whole time, it's eleven thirty already. Part of me wanted to tell Kissie she was right about Liam, but since I'm giving him another chance, I didn't see the point.

When I call his cell phone again, and it still goes straight to voice mail, irrationality sets in. I half convince myself that he's left the hotel and moved on to the next city and the next girl. My message, on the other hand, calmly asks him to please call me. "I'm so excited about our trip to Ellis Island and Lady Liberty," I say, before happily telling him that I can't wait to see him.

Not wanting to venture too far from the hotel, I flip through the hotel's information booklet and learn there's a nice-size indoor pool on the thirty-sixth floor where I could munch on fruit, not to mention a spa that the hotel calls "an oasis of ultimate relaxation high above New York City." Mary Jule taught me a long time ago never to go anywhere without a bathing suit. When the girls and I go on trips together, we may not wear half the clothes in our suitcases, but if there's a pool or a spa nearby, it's got our names on the door.

I glance all around the pool area for Liam or one of his band members. As crass as they may be, it would be a relief to see one of them—positive proof that Liam hasn't taken his entourage and left me high and dry. There's no one around at all except a couple in one corner and an older man swimming laps wearing a Speedo and a bathing cap. I figure I'll hang out here a while and then head for the sauna.

I meander over to a stack of towels, grabbing two in case I decide to swim. I'm still holding out hope that Liam and I can eat lunch together before taking the journey down to the Statue of Liberty, but my stomach is growling loud enough for the couple across the pool to hear. The waiting only gets worse as the clock ticks and I find myself checking my cell phone every few seconds. When it does ring, while clutched tightly in my hand, I'm in such a hurry to answer that I accidentally drop it and watch as it crashes onto the hard, brick floor. I leap off the chair and scramble around for the battery, which is four feet away from the rest of the phone. My hands won't work fast enough and when I finally put it back together, the line is long dead.

Within two minutes it's ringing again and this time my heart leaps across the pool. When I check the caller ID it says, "Restricted." Thank god. It's finally him.

"Hey!" I answer.

"Leelee?"

"Yes, hey!"

"Hi, it's Wiley!" he says, matching my enthusiasm.

Well, crap. "Oh hi, Riley," I say, without even a hint of lilt in my voice.

"I haven't seen you for a couple days and I noticed Kissie is staying with the girls, is evwything all wight?"

"Yes, Riley, everything is just fine." My adrenaline is still racing from my near phone fatality.

"Are you out of town or something?"

"Yes. I'm out of town." My voice, I'm sure, has a bugged tone to it by now, but Riley Bradshaw is the absolute last person on my mind. "Why do you have a restricted number?"

"Why not? I pay a little extwa for it but it's worth it when you consider the time it saves you in the long wun. No one is asking for money, no political campaign calls"—I can just see him counting on his fingers—"the police academy leaves you alone. I'll be happy to show you how to get yours westwicted."

"I don't want mine westwicted, I mean *re*stricted. Excuse me, Riley. I didn't mean to say 'westwicted.' I'm just flustered right now and I'm expecting an important phone call."

"Who fwom?"

"A friend. He's . . . going to be calling me any second now so I should probably hang up."

"Okay, well, I'll see you when you get back."

"Fine, yes, I'll see you when I get back."

"When's that?"

"Sunday. I get home Sunday. But I have to go now, Riley. Take care."

"Sunday, huh?"

"YES, Sunday."

"Well, have fun in Flowida."

"I'm not in Florida."

"Then have fun in Alabama."

"Riley, I will see you when I get home."

"So you are in Alabama? Have fun at Gulf Shores."

"Good-bye, Riley."

"Birmingham?"

"Dang it, Riley. I'm hanging up now. Say good-bye, too, so I'm not hanging up in your face." I spy one of the guys in Liam's band, his bass player, spreading a towel on a lounge chair and I'm completely relieved.

"I think it would be smart if you told me where you are. Just in case of an emergency."

"*Okay.* I'm in New York City."

"New York City? What are you doing there?"

"Riley."

"Okay. I'll see you when you weturn. Good-bye."

"Bye-bye." I can't stand being impatient with him but I see what Kissie means when she says that he gets on her last nerve.

I order fruit and a water, poolside, and start another call, this time to Virginia. "Okay, what now?" I say, as soon as Virgy answers. "I still haven't heard from him and it's nearly one o'clock. I see one of his band members though, at the other side of the pool. That at least tells me he hasn't left town."

"Go talk to the guy. Better yet, flirt with him like there's no tomorrow and act like you don't give two cents about Liam White."

"But he knows that's not true."

"Not necessarily. That's what I'd do if I were you. Listen, when Liam surfaces, and he will, don't make it look like you've been pining away all morning."

"I'm not."

"Good," she says.

"Okay, I'll flirt with the guy. He's not my type, though, I can tell you that right now."

"So? Just go do it. And keep me posted. I'm not liking that you haven't heard from him yet."

"Don't tell Alice," I tell her.

"Are you kidding?"

"Or Kissie."

"I'm not."

"Should I wear my parero when I walk up to him or—"

"*Absolutely not.* If Liam walks out to the pool, you want him to regret the hell out of letting you out of his sight long enough to talk to other men."

"I thought that's what you would say, but I just needed to hear you say it."

"Trust me. Liam already knows how cute your figure is. Now get over there and let the other guy get a good look at it. Go. Right now."

"*Okay.* I'm going."

"And take that knot out of your hair. I know you've got it twisted up. Stop acting so nervous."

"*Okay.* Bye."

She knows me. Oh that girl knows me.

It takes five minutes for me to work up my nerve, so I straighten out my towel and tuck my purse up under my chair. Yanking off my ball cap, I lay it on top of the towel, remove my ponytail holder, and slide it on my wrist. After tucking my hair behind my ears, I bravely stand up, reminding myself that I deserve better than this. If Liam White is dumping me then I'll just, well I just don't know what I'll do.

As I'm sauntering toward the bass player I can see clearly that he's looking dead at me. I'm pretending not to notice him, though, by staring straight ahead. The closer I get to his chair I pick my spot and sit down on the edge of the pool dangling my feet into the warm water. After looking around nonchalantly, my eyes meet his and we smile at each other. My fingers flutter in the air and I mouth, "Hi."

He stands right up from his chair, only ten feet or so away, and strolls over to me. *Ahhh, it's working. I wish Virgy could see me now.*

"Hi," he says. "Mind if I join you?"

"Oh no. Of course not," I say.

He sits down next to me on the edge of the pool and plops his legs in the water. "Have fun last night?" he asks.

"Yes. Yes I did. Did you?"

"It was all right. I didn't do much after the gig. Pretty much just went back to my room."

"It must be so much fun to get to travel to all of these great places," I say.

"Yeah, it's fun," he says, dipping his hand into the water. "But it can get lonely at times. The road is a funny thing. It seems glamorous from the outside, but it's hard on the heart at times, too."

What a tender thing to say. "I hadn't really thought about it that way. I can see what you mean," I tell him.

He's the sensitive type, I can tell—not necessarily the best-looking guy I've ever laid my eyes on but he's not bad, either. I'm guessing he's about Liam's age, maybe a little older. His hair is dark, streaked with gray, and his five o'clock shadow is already making a show. He's pretty hairy and his nose is a tad big, but he sure is nice. When he speaks,

I can tell he's never worn braces. "The really crazy part about the road is that you lose track of what day it is. They all run together. There's nothing to differentiate between the days of the week, because our schedule is always the same. We travel, play, eat, and sleep on a Saturday or a Sunday as well as a Tuesday. I might not be explaining it well. You almost have to experience it to know what I mean."

"No, you've explained it very well. Have you ever thought about doing something else?"

He shakes his head. "Not really. When music's in your blood you can't *not* play. I don't think I could do anything else. Sitting behind a desk would never work for me. My brain's not wired that way. Where's White, anyway?"

"I'm not really sure," I say, with a wee bit of sarcasm in my voice.

"That's another thing about the road. If you're not careful your days and nights can get mixed up. White gets in his room, closes the curtains, and watches TV all night. Then he sleeps all day. It's a hard habit to break."

That must be it. I'm feeling so relieved I want to reach over and hug him as hard as I can. I opt for a big smile instead. "That makes perfect sense," I tell him.

"Me?" he says. "I can't do that. I get up early, go for a run, or head down to the hotel gym. But I also go to bed right after the show. It's Leelee, right?"

I nod my head. "Please tell me your name again. I'm sorry."

"Phil."

"Phil. Phil. I won't forget it again."

"No worries. You sure have a great smile."

"Thank you, that's very sweet of you to say." Slightly embarrassed, I trickle water over my knees.

"How'd you guys meet anyway?"

"At the radio station where I work." I glance over at him. "He came in for an interview when y'all had your show in Memphis."

He nods.

"And then he invited my best friends and me to come to the show, and then meet afterward in the green room. We got to know each other that night. And we met you briefly on the bus."

"Now I remember," he says. "You were a brave girl to hop on a plane and come up here barely knowing him."

He might as well have put a knife in my gut. Suddenly I see Alice's face on his body sitting right next to me, shaking her head. Even Phil, his bandmate, thinks it's a little strange for me to just hop on a plane, jeopardize my job, throw caution to the wind and run up to New York like a groupie. I've put my good sense on the back burner and compromised who I am. And the worst part is, I'm doing it all for a man again.

"May I ask you something?" My hands are resting on the pavement behind me and I'm leaning back so the sun, which is streaming in from the floor-to-ceiling windows surrounding the pool, can toast my cheeks.

"Sure. Shoot."

Turning my head toward him I ask, "Is Liam . . . a good boss?"

He pulls one leg out of the water, bending his knee. "Yeah. He's pretty cool."

Hmm, "pretty cool" doesn't seem all that convincing to me. "Pretty cool?"

A wry grin forms on his face before he takes a deep breath and slowly exhales.

What? I'm dying to say. *Why are you hesitating?* "Is there something wrong?" I ask.

"No, no. We just . . ." He shakes his head and it's obvious he's purposeful when choosing his words. "We just . . . look at some things differently." Now he's looking into my eyes.

"Really? Like what?" I can sense he's on the verge of telling me something important—something that might help me understand Liam.

I see his eyes leave mine and look up over my head, squinting from the sun. "Hey man," he says.

I feel someone's knee press into my back. I whip my head around and have the same trouble with my eyes staring into the sun. The person squats down next to me so we're at eye level.

"Hey," Liam says and smiles. He's wearing a white T-shirt with "Rick's Café" across the pocket, blue jeans, and brown leather flip-flops. I can tell he's freshly shaven—around his short-clipped beard—and his shoulder-length, blondish-brown hair is still damp. Rested, gorgeous, and twinkle-eyed. Green twinkle-eyed. *Wow. You are the sexiest thing I have ever laid my eyes on.*

"Sorry I slept so late." Unlike me, who's been frantic for hours, he doesn't appear to be in the least bit worried about it. I can smell a hint of cologne as gives me a quick kiss. "What'cha been doing?" he says.

"Eating fruit, reading a little. Just enjoying myself." *Liar, liar, pants on fire.*

"Well cool. You wanted to go to the Statue of Liberty, didn't ya?"

"I'm dying to go."

"Let me call Deke and see if he can get us a car," he says, digging his phone out of his pocket. He steps out of his flip-flops and rolls up his pants legs, dipping his feet in the pool. When he sits down, his eyes travel to my stomach. Now I'm happy about my spray tan.

"I went for a run all the way down there this morning," Phil says. "It's past Ground Zero, not far from Wall Street."

Liam glances at Phil with a smirk on his face. "Thanks, man." He shoves his phone back into his front pocket. Apparently Deke isn't answering. "Let's go." After jumping up he reaches out his hand for mine. "See ya, man."

"I enjoyed talking with you, Phil," I say. And then I throw in a wink—just for the heck of it. Virginia would be so proud.

"Would you like to change? Or are you comfortable in your bathing suit?" Liam says and laughs, as I'm gathering up my things.

"I always wear my bathing suit when it's sixty-something degrees outside," I say, resting both hands on his shoulders. "Don't you? It won't take me long to change. I can meet you in the lobby in ten minutes."

"Perfect," he says, walking me over to the elevator. "Are you sure you don't want me to come with?" He flickers his eyebrows.

It's hard to tell him no when he looks this cute, but I do it anyway. "I'll be really fast."

When the black Lincoln Town Car drops us off at Battery Park, we stroll over to the ticket office to purchase our passes. Liam leans into the ticket window and asks the woman behind the screen for two tickets into Lady Liberty's crown and two for the ferry. When she informs him that the last boat of the day left thirty minutes ago, I am sorely disappointed. After changing into my jeans, I still had to wait on him another fifteen minutes in the lobby. The car didn't even pick us up until two thirty. I can't help but feel hurt by his cavalier attitude about the day. Unfortunately, neither of us ever looked at the brochure to check the schedule. I shuffle away from the ticket booth wearing my disappointment on my sleeve.

"Sorry, baby." He reaches up to stroke my cheek. "I'll make it up to you. We'll go for a nice dinner tonight. Anywhere you'd like to go."

"Anywhere?" I ask, as we're walking back toward the street.

"Absolutely."

"I've always wanted to go to the Boat House in Central Park. What do you think?"

"It's a little touristy, and probably better during the afternoon when you can see the swans, but I'll take you there tonight if that's what you want."

When we walk under the shade of a tree, I notice a bite in the air. Unfortunately I've forgotten my jacket. I see him staring at my left bosom and I have to think about what kind of bra I'm wearing. "What are you looking at?" I say, giggling.

He lifts a chunk of my hair hanging on top of my breast. When he tries running his fingers through it the curl stops him. "Your hair. It's gorgeous. I love your curls."

"If you say so," I say.

"What? You don't like your curly hair?" he asks, genuinely surprised.

I shake my head.

"You are crazy, girl. Do you know how many—"

"People would pay good money to have my hair? I've heard it a thousand times."

He laughs and taps his forehead. "You at least like the color, right?"

"I started to appreciate it when my baby daughter, Isabella, was born with it. Seeing it on her makes me like it."

As we stroll through Battery Park, I'm enthralled by the mimes dressed as Lady Liberty and the street performers. Singers, cartoonists, jugglers—there's even a contortionist, about as talented as I've ever seen, stuffing himself inside a small clear box as he performs to the music of Michael Jackson. A thin, but tall, muscular African American man with dreads hanging all the way down his back, he calls himself "Yogi" and flips his legs over his head until he is completely flat with the rest of his body. Yogi has quite a following today, and the crowd shows their appreciation by stuffing the box once he's done. Liam strolls over and throws money in, too. It's worth every penny.

What if I were to marry Liam White? What would that be like? I picture myself with a gorgeous pale pink second wedding gown. Maybe something vintage. He'd rent a private jet and fly Sarah and Issie, Alice, Virginia, and Mary Jule, and their husbands, too, to our wedding in St. Barts or St. Kitts. Kissie wouldn't want to fly on a small plane, but he'd buy her a first-class seat on a major airline. Once she got to know him she would love Liam. I fantasize about the first time they meet. She would act all shy around him at first but after five minutes they'd be best friends. She'd cook for him the most beautiful Southern meals, just like she did for Baker. Baker never appreciated it, but Liam would. I just know he and Kissie would become fast friends. Kissie would tell him all the stories about me as a little girl. She'd get out my baby pictures and brag about what a smart child I was. She'd tell him all about my equestrian days and all of my ballet recitals—all the things a parent is supposed to do.

Liam's arm around my shoulder yanks me away from my thoughts. We meander some more, stopping at a few different tables where artists are displaying their wares—photographs of landmarks, sketches of the skyline, pictures of New York celebrities. When my stomach starts to growl, Liam laughs and says, "Hey, let's get out of here and go back to the hotel. By the time we get back it'll be late. I'll order us dinner in my suite. How's that?"

An evening holed up in a beautiful hotel with Liam White sounds even more romantic, and personal, than a public dinner at the Boat House. I turn up to his face and rub the line of his jaw with my hands, feeling his scruffy stubble. I lean into a kiss—a comfortable one, a relaxed one—that conveys my decision. When we separate, he drapes an arm around my shoulders and steers me to the street corner to catch a cab. He keeps it there the whole way back to the hotel.

By the time Liam digs into his jean pocket for the key to his suite it's past six o'clock and the two of us walk slowly into the entry hall. I can see the sky over the tops of the trees in Central Park on the right and over the Hudson on the left. The red and orange reminds me that I had had my heart set on watching the sunset while on the ferry returning to Battery Park.

The wet bar in Liam's suite is behind me and I can hear him uncorking a bottle of wine. I'm sure it's some kind of expensive vintage that I've never heard of. Peter has heard of it, though. When I hear the sound of the desk drawer opening and closing I turn around to see Liam walking toward me with two red wine glasses and the room service menu tucked under his arm. "Here, baby," he says, handing me a glass.

"Thanks," I say, and put the rim to my lips.

"It's a Beringer Private Reserve cab. Do you know it?" he asks, swirling the wine around in the glass.

"No, not really. I've heard of Beringer, though." I sit my glass down on the table. "I'll be right back, Liam."

Slipping into the powder room I take one look at my face—my cheeks are rosy from the waterfront, and the exposure to the sun during the afternoon; my freckles have popped out and my eyes have practically disappeared. It's been hours since I applied a fresh coat of mascara and without it I feel naked. With windblown hair and bare lips, I'm shockingly unadorned, undecorated. I debate going back to my room to freshen up; after all I'm with one of the most sought-after men in the country. Something tells me, though, that it doesn't really matter.

When I close the door to the bathroom behind me, Liam looks up from the couch, where he's strumming his guitar. Although it's not one of his, I recognize the song right away. It's one of my favorites from the Beatles White Album—"Julia." Once he finishes, he pats the couch next to him and hands me the menu. "Take a look at this and order whatever you like. I'm getting the filet." He goes back to strumming but it's not a song I know.

After studying the menu I say, "I'll take the filet, too. With béarnaise."

"Okay, sounds good." He balances his guitar against the side of the couch, grasps the menu and stands, looking out the window. As he's walking toward the telephone on the desk, the sound of his cell phone stops him. I watch as he takes it out of his pocket and glances at the number before answering. "Hey man," he says. "Now? Damn. I'll be right there."

"Hey babe, I've got to run down to Deke's room for a minute. Why don't you call in our order? I like my steak medium rare. And will you ask for another bottle of this cab while you've got them on the phone?" He picks the wine off the bar. "Oh, and one more thing, order about four shrimp cocktails. I'm starving," he says, with a forced smile and then he's out the door.

After calling in our room service order I change my mind and decide to go on back to my room to freshen up, especially now that he's down with Deke. Before leaving I scribble out a note in case Liam beats me back. I grab the room key, resting on the desk, and dash out the door. In my room I change out of my summery blouse and dab perfume on the deep grooves in my collarbone and alongside the veins on my wrists. I decide not to change into dressier pants; but keep on my weathered, form-fitting jeans. I throw on a white T-shirt and top it with a delicate pink cardigan with soft pearl buttons and three-quarter-length sleeves. I find mascara in the bathroom and reapply my gloss—but leave the rest of my face nude.

When I return, fifteen minutes later, Liam's still not back. I can see the sun beginning to set; later now that the daylight stretches into the eight o'clock hour. Allured, I go and stand in front of the floor-to-ceiling windows, where just last night I let myself be kissed by this mystery rock star. And kissed him back, too. I feel giddy and guilty at the same time. I worry what Kissie would think of me. Because Kissie is my parent. Always has been. She was the one who made sure I got a bath. Made sure I had a hot meal. Made sure my clothes were pressed and my sheets were changed. Even though my mother had everything money could buy, Kissie never once acted jealous or envious. Before I knew better, I asked her if she wished she lived in a bigger house or drove a nicer car like Mama. Anytime I'd ask her a question like that she'd say, "The Lawd tells me to be grateful for everythin' he gives me. Bible says, it's much easier for a camel to get through the eye of a needle than a rich man to get to heaven. That's because the rich man don't know his need for Jesus. He thinks he can do it all on his own cuz he's got so much money. He don't think he needs the Lawd. But I sure need Him."

Kissie somehow managed to pass along to me her values. Despite my parents' racist attitudes, despite the racial unrest still prevalent in the South, I don't see myself as prejudiced. And that's all because of Kissie. She'd say it's because of Jesus, but I say it's because of her.

Settling onto the couch, I notice his guitar and pick it up. The doorbell startles me and I lay it down quickly, in case it's him. After sprinting to the door, I'm disappointed when I open it. It's only the room service man. He wheels in a cart donned with a white tablecloth, heads straight for the round table in front of the windows, and transfers all the food. As he's leaving he asks for my signature.

"Thank you, Mrs. White," he says, and I don't correct him. It feels lovely to be called "Mrs." again. As soon as the door closes, I peek under the pewter dish covers and the smell of the sizzling hot steaks with béarnaise sauce folded over the top makes my weak stomach growl all the more. I have to force myself to wait for Liam.

Fifteen more minutes go by and he's still not back. I dial his cell phone but it goes straight to voice mail.

After a full thirty minutes have passed I call Deke's cell phone. He doesn't pick up so I dial the hotel operator to be connected to his room and he answers on the first ring. "Hi Deke, it's Leelee," I say.

"Hi."

"Would you please let Liam know that his food is here? I'd hate for it to get cold."

When Deke tells me that Liam had to go down to the front desk to take care of some business, it seems a little odd, I mean isn't that what Deke is for? Liam asks him to do everything else.

After a full hour, and no Liam I go ahead and sit down at the table. The quiet in the room is only interrupted by the sound of my knife as I set it down on the plate after each bite. I try and savor each piece of steak (by now, as Daddy would say, it's ice cold). But my shock at being left alone is quickly turning to offense—I feel like I'm giving this man a whole lot of second chances for only having known him a few weeks. My fantasy is fading and the dashing prince from last night's ball is not the nobleman I hoped him to be. As I chew the filet and watch the city slowly come alive for the night, I ponder leaving. Surely, there's a red-eye flight home to Memphis. And even if there's not, I'd rather sit in the airport all night than stay here any longer feeling abandoned and dejected.

I've nearly convinced myself to leave and take a cab to LaGuardia when the doorbell rings again. This time I take my time walking to the door. I look through the peephole at Liam with his hands in the pockets of his jeans. I slowly open the door to a man with a sullen look on his face. He's been gone nearly two hours.

"Sorry, forgot my key. I bet you're ready to kill me," he says, and strolls inside.

"I *am* wondering where you've been. Is everything all right?" Why can't I just act curt? Alice would have no problem putting on her bitch. She tells Richard exactly where he should go. She'll stare him down and relegate him to the laundry room for the rest of the night for washing and folding.

"Deke and I got into some serious business. He had to switch our hotels in Reno and needed my okay. Plus Sue, my keyboard player, can't finish the tour so I've had to hire another player. Sue's out in a week and a half and another guy, Steve, is in. We had a lot to rap about."

Calmly I say, "Huh. I called Deke when our food came and he said you had to go downstairs to take care of business at the front desk."

"Yeah," he says, not missing a beat, "that and I had to go to Sue's room. She's having a hard time with it all." He walks over to the bar.

"With what all?" I say, sitting on the end of the couch. My knee accidentally hits his guitar but I manage to catch it before it tumbles to the ground.

"Leaving the tour," he says, and returns with two wineglasses.

"Why is she leaving?"

"Family issues. She has to come off the road for a while. She'll be back though."

"I wish you had called to—"

He cuts me off, having spotted our dinner on the table with my plate half eaten. "You ate without me? How was it?" He hands me a wineglass, which I put down on the coffee table.

"Pretty good," I say, before adding, "I waited too long to eat, though, and it got a little cold."

"Why didn't you order another one?"

"I don't know. I didn't think to do that."

Liam sends his back without hesitation.

Within fifteen minutes his cold food has been picked up and a brand new filet is redelivered, and I'm sitting at the table next to him while he munches on a hot, sizzling steak. When he's done, and two of the four shrimp cocktails are left on the table untouched, I can't help but think about the terrible waste of food and money. He gives no thought whatsoever to overordering or reordering for that matter. Maybe Kissie's got a point about that camel and the eye of the needle.

After shoving his plate off to the side, he reaches across the table and takes my hand, entwining his fingers with mine. "I can't get over how pretty you are," he says. By the tone of his husky voice and his enticing smile I can tell what's on his mind. "Tell me more about you, Leelee Satterfield."

Two days ago, those words would have turned me upside down but tonight I'm no longer enthralled by his flattery. And I'm not really all that excited about holding his hand, either. His mystique, the wonder of his world has faded and if I'm honest with myself, I'm no longer captivated by what's inside that world. "What else would you like to know about me, *Liam White*?"

"Tell me something that not many people know about," he says, seductively squinting his eyes.

"Let's see, I hate turnips," I say, lifting my eyebrows and knowing full well that's not what he's after.

"That's not the kind of info I had in mind," he says, with a wink.

"Okay, how about this? I'm a great breakfast cook."

"How great?" Now he's caressing my hand.

"Pretty great." I nod and smile. "Peter taught me how to make maple cider French toast when I was in Vermont."

He rolls his eyes and retracts his hand. "Your sort-of boyfriend taught you to cook?"

"No," I say indignantly. "I *knew* how—but only the basics . . . I don't want to talk about Peter."

"You brought him up," he retorts.

"That's only because . . ." What I want to say is I brought him up in context of the question. My subconscious brought him up, actually. Because he is lovely. He is respectful. He is kind and I know for 100 percent certain that he never would have done the things to me that you have done in the last twenty-four hours. In nine months he never once tried luring me to his bedroom. *There's something I want to know about me, too. Why am I taking all this? Why am I allowing another man to treat me disrespectfully? What is it about me, or my past, that allows this to happen?*

When it gets right down to it, it's obvious. I just couldn't see it before. As much as I hate to admit it, I've put up with it because he's Liam White, rock star. Fame is the perfect trap, its insidious flame luring those unfamiliar with its powerful grip right into the threads of its silky smooth web. He's told me how pretty I am, he's bought me gifts, he's flown me first class on a fabulous trip to New York. And to make matters even worse, everyone thinks I'm sharing his room. Every single thing Kissie predicted has come true. Right down to his honeysuckle tongue. How did she know? And more importantly, why didn't I listen?

I get up from the table, pick up my purse, which is on the floor in front of the sofa, and head toward the door.

"Where are you going?" he says, from his seat near the window. I watch him take another sip of his wine and put the glass back down on the table.

"To my room," I say, and open the door.

"To do what?"

"Pack."

He looks down into his wineglass. "When are you coming back?"

"I'm not," I say, and let the door close behind me.

As I'm heading out of the hotel, wheeling my suitcase behind me, I see a man standing at the curb. From behind he looks familiar and when I stop to ask the doorman for a taxi to LaGuardia, I see his face.

"Phil!" I say, and step toward him. "How are you tonight?"

He whips his head around and smiles when he sees me. "Hi, Lee-lee." I see him notice my suitcase. "You're not leaving, are you?" he says, with a puzzled furrow in his brow.

"Yes. I've got to get home."

"Is everything okay?"

I nod my head. "Everything is just fine." I pause before speaking again, remembering his words to me earlier in the day. "But . . . I sure would love to know something before I leave."

He tilts his head to the side, inquisitively.

"When we were out at the pool today, what was it that you started to tell me about Liam? About the way you two see things differently?"

Hesitating, he presses his lips together. I can tell he wishes he'd never said anything by the way he falters.

"Please tell me, I need to know," I say.

Phil stares at the pavement and shifts his weight from one foot to the other. Finally he looks into my eyes. "You know, I think it's pretty simple when it boils down to it. Something happens to certain people when they become famous. Everywhere they go, they have folks falling all over them. No one ever tells them no. Everybody wants to be their friend. It's sad, actually. I've been in this business a long time, worked for quite a few celebrities and have only met a handful who are normal and don't buy into their own bullshit. After a while they start to believe their own PR. It's not really their fault, the world places them high on a pedestal and hands them a life free of accountability. It's the ugly side of showbiz, darlin'."

The evening air is chilly and the wind is blowing my hair all around my face. I can't help but draw my arms close to my chest. Phil moves nearer to block the wind. "White and I are different when it comes to women." He shrugs his shoulders. "It's a respect thing." He drops his voice to a step above a whisper. "Why do you think he's never been married?"

The cab pulls up to the curb and the doorman loads my bag into the trunk. I reach into my purse for a tip, pondering his words.

"Maybe I've gone too far, Leelee. This is really none of my business," he says, "but you seem like a classy lady."

I sigh and close my eyes for a brief moment. The doorman opens the back door of the cab and motions for me to step inside. "You haven't gone too far. You actually saved me from going too far. I appreciate your honesty," I say, before taking my seat in the cab. "Liam White should take a life lesson from you."

When the doorman shuts my door, I wave at Phil from the window before the cabbie edges onto Columbus Circle.

As I'm walking to my gate, I happen to notice a crowd of people waiting to board a flight to Albany, New York. When I spy most of them bundled up in winter coats I can't help but wonder if any of the passengers will be driving on to Vermont. Albany is the closest airport to anywhere in southern Vermont. Albany is only two hours away from Peter.

I pull my cell phone out of my purse to check the time. It's nine o'clock. It dawns on me that by the time I rent a car at the Albany airport I could be there by midnight. I'll appear at his door and he'll scream my name. He'll take me in his arms and twirl me around, telling me how much he misses me and that he thinks about me as much as I think about him.

The longer I stare at the word "Albany" above the gate agent's head, the more I convince myself to do it. I reason that I can still be back to work by Monday. Even if I just spend twelve hours with Peter, I'm sure he'll want to start his life over, move to Memphis and find a chef's position. And there's no doubt in my mind that he'll be able to find a good one. With all the people I know in Memphis, it shouldn't be a problem at all. I'm completely convinced of it. So much so that I run up to the lady at the ticket counter only minutes before the plane is due to leave. "Can you fit one more on that plane?" I ask, frantic to get inside.

"I'm sorry, ma'am, but the plane is full."

"Are you sure?" With my hands on the counter I lean over as if I can read the seating manifest on the other side of her computer. "It doesn't look all that crowded." I glance over at the forty or so people waiting to board.

"It's a very small jet, ma'am. And we're completely sold out. I just assigned the last seat to a standby passenger. If you had been here earlier, perhaps—"

Closing my eyes, I turn around and walk slowly toward the gate to Memphis.

Chapter Twelve

No one is milling around the halls when I put down my purse. I can see Will, our substitute deejay, through the glass window in front of my office and it appears he's the one on the air. It's perfectly quiet and since I'm my usual ten minutes tardy, I find the silence to be a little odd. After filling my mug with a bitter cup of stale coffee, most likely brewed before the morning shift began, I stroll into the control room to find out what's going on.

"Hey Leelee, how's it goin'?" Will asks, as soon as I walk in the door. "Hang on a minute." I watch him announce the name of the tune that's just been played, cut to a commercial, and then remove his headphones. "Why aren't you in the staff meeting?" he says, sipping on his own coffee cup.

"What staff meeting?" I ask, angst beginning to take hold. Go ahead and shoot me. It's official—Edward sent a spy to New York and has called an emergency meeting to discuss my insubordination.

"You know. The monthly staff meeting down in Dan Malcomb's office, the last Monday of every month."

"Aaaahhhh!" I cover my face with my hands.

He points at the clock on the wall. "It just started ten minutes ago. You're not that late."

I race out of the control room and down the back steps without so much as a wave. Dan Malcomb's secretary peers over her granny glasses when she spots me tiptoeing toward his office door, which by now has been long shut. I have a feeling she's never been late to anything. Although possibly, I suppose, she's only staring at the turtleneck sweater I'm wearing even though it's eighty-three degrees outside. Little does she know my spray tan underneath is still a radiant orangey-brown. I can't risk Edward asking why I'm tan all of a sudden.

This meeting is big. Not only does Dan Malcomb lead it, attendance is required by everyone, from Edward and all the full-time jocks to both the promotion and sales directors and even Sam, the production person, who voices and records all the commercials. Mr. Malcomb is discussing the value of branding when I slink into the room at 8:44 A.M. All eyes focus on me as I take my seat. It appears my chair is the only one empty. Mr. Malcomb doesn't stop to recognize my tardiness, thank goodness, but Edward glares at me from his seat next to Malcomb's desk. I'd rather wear a white faux-leather miniskirt with high-heel orange Candies to lunch at the club and sit right next to Tootie Shotwell, than be in this room right now sitting across from Edward Maxwell.

When the meeting adjourns I somehow manage to elude him, for the time being anyway. I engage the sales manager in conversation for a moment before stealthily slipping out unnoticed. Once back in my office, my day thankfully continues as if everything is back to normal. With one exception—the disc jockey's shuffled schedules. Because of the staff meeting Edward has decided to pull his own prank by moving each jock up a shift. The morning team will broadcast midday and Stan will take over Paul's shift in the afternoon. I'm the only one affected by the prank. My phone has not stopped ringing all morning from listeners more confused than amused.

When I slide into the control room before lunch, with the excuse of giving Johnny an urgent message from his dentist, he and Jack are in the middle of an interview with the guy who claims to have been in charge of bringing the *Lisa Marie,* Elvis's jet, back to Graceland. He says he was the one who actually drove it down the middle of Elvis Presley Boulevard back in 1984. That's the thing about Memphis. Almost everyone has a claim to Elvis fame. For instance, our family claim is that Elvis drove a truck for Daddy when he was a young man. The King was just out of high school and a truck driver for Crown Electric. He had dropped off some equipment at Daddy's cotton warehouse on Front Street and Daddy was highly impressed by his manners. When he asked Elvis if he would be interested in extra work, Elvis told him yes. So he delivered cotton for Daddy a time or two. Or so the legend goes anyway.

Once the interview concludes, Johnny smiles when he sees me and yanks off his headphones. "Welcome back, O Famous One."

"Shhhhh." I look behind me to make sure Edward is not hanging anywhere around.

"Feeling any better?" He winks twice, overexaggerating each.

I shake my head and wave my hand in the air, sweeping away his comment.

"Well? How was it?"

"I don't really want to talk about it, but I'll tell you that it started off good and ended terrible. I'm back to work and that's the end of that."

"*What?*"

"Fame is a funny thing, Johnny. There's a big bad ugly side."

"What are you talking about?" he asks.

Sighing heavily, I attempt to explain. "Liam White is a nice guy and his world is certainly intriguing but when it comes to women he doesn't know how to treat them." I continue, "I got the feeling he thought I should feel lucky to be with him. I guess there is something that happens to certain people when they become famous."

"Maybe so, but I wouldn't mind having his cash. Or his voice. Would you, Jack?"

"Show me the money, baby, show me the money," Jack says. His vocal repertoire naturally includes Tom Cruise.

Between commercials and during the songs, I do tell him all about how Liam slept till two on Saturday. I fill him in on how we missed the last boat to the Statue of Liberty and about how he left me in his room for nearly two hours while he conducted business in Sue's room. I finish by telling him how I'd just picked up and left the hotel with Liam staring into his wineglass.

"There's always Stan," Johnny says, and cracks up laughing.

The image of Stan and me as a couple may have him highly amused but as for me I'm not smiling. "Are you out of your mind?" I say.

"He wants to take you out."

"Don't you think by now I'm on to you? That is not true." I settle onto the stool across from him.

"Oh yes it is."

"And how do you know that?"

"He told me. And he's pretty sure you'll say yes."

"As my daddy used to say, it'll be a cold day in Cuba before that ever happens." Jack, who had disappeared from the control room for a minute, strolls back in with a stack of old records for the all request lunch hour. With a perfect Elvis voice he says, "Cute turtleneck you've got on there, little sister. Should we turn up the heat in here?"

"Very funny," I say, looking down at the front of my sweater.

"Why in god's name are you wearing a turtleneck?" Johnny says. "It's the first week of May."

"I'm hiding my spray tan. I don't want to give Edward any unneeded reason to be suspicious."

Johnny looks over at Jack and I watch the two cut eyes at each other.

"What? Why are y'all looking at each other like that?"

They continue flicking their eyes and eyebrows from across the room until Johnny says, "I haven't said anything because I'm hoping it all goes away."

"*What?*" By now I'm frantic and I practically yell. "WHAT all goes away?"

"Edward knows something's up," Johnny says.

"About my trip?"

He nods and positions his headphones. "Hang on. I've got a live spot coming up in five seconds."

As he touts the benefits of driving a Toyota, my mind travels ninety miles per hour down the interstate. What in the world could Edward know? How does he know and, most importantly, am I about to be dropkicked and punted down the highway? Jack disappears out the door again and I'm left counting the seconds until Johnny finishes his ad. The instant he presses the end button on the control board, I'm right back to our conversation. "How? How does he know something's up?" I say, biting my right thumbnail.

"Our resident bonehead."

"I didn't tell Stan anything about my trip." I'm twisting my hair behind my head so tightly I can feel my temples pulling. "You and Jack are the *only* ones who know."

"You didn't have to. I'm telling you he snoops around in everyone's business. He found out on his own."

"How?" My thumbnail is no longer a nail. It's a nub.

"He's jealous, I'm telling you. He likes you."

"But how did he find out my personal business?" I say, sliding off the stool and darting around the control room in a frenzied but futile attempt to make it all go away.

Johnny's head moves with every step I take. "He stopped by your house over the weekend. Some whack job with a lisp told him you were in New York. He was in your front yard picking up pinecones when Stan drove up."

I stop moving and peer at Johnny. "Riley's not a whack job, he's dear. And he doesn't have a lisp, it's a soft *R*. He is a tiny bit annoying at times, but he'd never hurt a flea. I never told him why I was in New York or who I was with."

"You didn't have to. Stan figured it out."

"Okay, now you're freaking me out. How?" I try sitting again but stand back up five seconds later, finding no comfort in taking a seat.

"He looked up White's tour schedule on his Web site. Found out he was playing a gig at the Mandarin Oriental and called the hotel to see if you were registered. Jackpot."

"You have got to be kidding!"

"Nope."

I mutter to myself, "The only reason I told Riley was to get him off my back, uuhhh." Exasperated, I throw my head back. That's it. I'm so done with Riley.

"I told Stan I'd kill him if he tells Edward. Let's just hope he doesn't squeal."

"Oh dear god. He better not," I say, closing my eyes and shaking my head. "Now I am petrified."

"Don't be scared. Just think up a good excuse in case you need it. You'll come up with something."

Weak kneed and scared stiff, I creep back to my office.

Back at my desk, prepared to bury my worries in paperwork, I check my e-mail, then my voice mail. Four new messages. The first two are from winners, checking on the status of their concert tickets. The third is from Edward. I hit the pound key, "Message skipped." The fourth call is from Stan welcoming me back to town. *Thank you,* Stanny. *Why do you even care?* "First skipped message," the lady says, and Edward's chilling voice is on the telephone. "Leelee? Edward. I'd like to see you in my office as soon as I return from lunch. I've been given some disturbing news and I'm hoping you can clear it up. See you when I return." *Click.* Dial tone.

I can feel my heart clanging in a way I'd only felt a couple of times in my life. The first was the day our principal, Mrs. Carrington, caught Mary Jule and me smoking on the roof of the gym at Jameson School and instead of *telling* us to come down she beckoned us down with her long, slender pointer finger. The other time was the night I fired Helga demanding that she leave my Peach Blossom Inn kitchen immediately, *with* her sacred hippo collection, and never step a foot back inside. Both times I'd had Mary Jule with me. This time I'm flying solo.

As the minutes tick by, my heartbeat increases and my pulse quickens. One glance at my watch lets me know it's close to one.

Edward left for lunch almost an hour ago and is bound to be back soon. I sneak into the bathroom to call Virgy and even she's at a loss. I thought for sure she'd be able to mastermind a scheme to get me out of this. "I'd tell you to tell him that you just happened to bump into Liam on Fifth Avenue but it sounds like he's too smart for that," is all she can advise.

"I'm scared to death," I tell her, huddled in the corner.

"Oh hell, Fiery, if you're gonna be fired anyway, just leave. Run out the door. Why put yourself through it?"

It was the only relief I'd felt since tiptoeing into the staff meeting this morning. "You're right. I can always e-mail him a letter of resignation from home."

"Definitely. Get out of there!"

I'm running through the parking lot when I spot Edward's bright yellow corvette turning in from Union Avenue. (Yellow is the FM 99 color by the way.) Darting behind another car, I hunker down and watch as he drives past, all the while praying that he didn't see me. When enough time has passed for him to make it safely inside the building, I zigzag to my old BMW, ducking behind and weaving in between the other parked vehicles. Just as I'm digging inside my purse for my keys, I hear a loud engine approaching. Determined not to look around, I click the remote on my keychain and quickly open my front door.

"What's your hurry?" I hear, and turn to see a blackened window rolling down. Edward's mug is staring straight at me.

"Oh, nothing. I just forgot something in my car." I'm surprised my voice isn't trembling.

"Why would you need your purse just to get something out of your car?"

"Because." My mind starts racing for an excuse. "Be-*cause*, I don't go anywhere without my purse. My mother taught me that. Never leave your purse unattended. It goes along with never leaving your diamond ring on the bathroom sink."

"Did you get my message?" he asks, sternly.

"What message?" If I act as if I haven't heard it, perhaps he'll just drop it.

"I'll meet you in my office."

I'm still planning my getaway when he parks two cars down and jumps out, walking briskly toward me. "So what did you forget?" he asks, turning toward the building, expecting me to follow.

"I . . . I forgot my phone."

"Personal calls aren't allowed."

"I know that, *Edward,* I just like to have it in case of an emergency."

He stares harshly and he and I, Dead Woman Walking, stroll in silence all the way back upstairs.

"I'll call you shortly," he says, and turns into his office. "After I make a phone call."

When I sit back down in my chair and happen to glace at the picture of my daughters in the simple silver frame on the corner of my desk, an overwhelming sense of taking responsibility for my own actions floods my thoughts. All of the reasons I used to justify my flight of fancy to New York no longer seem valid. Through the turtleneck, I can feel the sweat drip and then pool in my cleavage—I'm too scared to look in my compact, but I'm sure my face is bright red. Despite my nervousness, the phone calls keep on coming and it takes all my focus and concentration not to entirely snap at one of the contest winners. But when Stan pops his head in my office, all cheery and nonchalant, my eyes become poisonous arrows and I shoot them his way. It's not at all like me, but I honestly can't help myself.

Alarmed, he scurries in and shuts my door, honking an extra large something or other up his nose. "Hello, doll. How was the Big Apple?" he says, only seconds before Edward's voice booms through the wall. "Leelee. Would you come in here now?"

Stan's eyebrows pop up. "Ooops. That doesn't sound good. What's he so mad about?"

I'm so livid at Stan I want to shake him. "You know exactly what he's mad about," I say, with my hands resting on my hips. "What I'd like to know is why are you such a big tattletale?"

"If you're referring to your joyride to New York—"

"You don't know what I did last weekend, Stan. And what I can't figure out is, why do you even care?"

Fueled by rage, and indignant that my privacy was breached—not to mention being fed up with Edward's general sense of unpleasantness and self-importance—I'm suddenly furious. But this time, I'm furious with myself. Not only have I allowed myself to be bullied by a domineering doofus of a boss, I let myself be lured into a bad situation by one more charming, gorgeous man, under the guise that I was treating myself to an escape, a Cinderella fantasy worthy of telling my grandchildren. All along I knew the trip to New York was taboo—even if Edward's rules were inane, not to mention *so* hypocritical. But I let myself be convinced that this guy, Liam, would make it all okay. In reality, I'd known all along I was doing something wrong—and truthfully, I realize now that it would have been impossible to fully enjoy myself because of it.

During the first nor'easter in Vermont, I had been sans-Baker for only a matter of days—and no one had ever told me how quickly or vastly the snow would accumulate. Folks up there trade weather reports like gossip, and the town had been talking about it for days. It never once occurred to me to pay attention, though. I just assumed I'd be taken care of—that Baker, or Jeb, or *someone* would bail me out, the way Daddy always did. When the storm finally hit, the girls and I were left alone, and at first we were enchanted with the clouds of puffy snow. But when it started piling up one foot after another—to the roof in some spots—I made panicked phone calls to snowplowers begging for assistance. Naturally, they'd all been booked for days. When I finally sweet-talked one into helping me, his wife said that I'd have to shovel a three-foot alley around my car in order for her husband to clear my drive. It ended up taking me *four hours* just to shovel the way out to my car and once I'd finally made a three-foot clearance around it I noticed there was still another four feet of snow piled on top of it. It had to go somewhere and when I knocked it off in a rageful frenzy, and it filled back up my alley, I marched myself back inside and told that snowplower's wife that she could send in an eighteen-wheeler tow truck for all I cared but I was not shoveling one more inch of snow that day or any other day. In the end I paid the snowplower to do it. After all, there's only so much snow a girl can take.

All along I've been thinking I've grown up so much, matured, finally learned to stand up for myself. When in reality, I've made the very same mistakes again. I know that when I walk into Edward's office in a few moments, I'm going to encounter a nor'easter of my own—only this time, I'm determined to be prepared. I will not let myself be buried again.

"Shut the door and have a seat, Ms. Satterfield." Edward, who is already seated behind his desk, scoots his chair in tightly so he can rest his elbows on the desktop and clasp his hands together. My lips are silent but the pounding of my heart speaks for me as I settle down into the chair. I'm rubbing my thumbs together so hard I'm afraid I might rub off the skin.

With lips tightly pursed he stares at me a long time before ever uttering a word. Finally he says, "I have received a very disturbing report on you, Leelee."

"Edward," I say, jumping in before I lose my momentum, "I owe you an apology." Immediately his eyebrows rise. "I lied to you last week about having the flu, and instead took a trip to New York City with Liam White to hear him perform." I never meant to tell on myself to this degree but since it's all out in the open now I might as well proceed with my head held high.

Bursting with offense, he starts to expel what I imagine he'd been hanging on to all weekend, "I know all about it. Nothing around here gets past me—"

I cut him off. "I know. And you were very explicit that I was not to act like a star fornicator—and I bent the rules."

His eyes pop out of his skull.

"*Not literally!*" I say indignantly, standing up from my seat. "Just figuratively." Slowly I settle back down. Inside I'm dying to lean over his desk, point my finger in his face and say, Edward Maxwell, for your information, *you* are the biggest star-fornicator of them all! Instead I calmly say, "I'm sorry for going against your policies—I can only say, not that it matters, that I behaved with dignity and never did anything to reflect poorly on the station." I pause for a moment. Between the heat from my fury and this dang turtleneck I can feel a bead of sweat escaping my forehead, trickling down my cheek. And another. And another. I reach behind me and knot my hair to get some air on my neck before resisting the urge to fan myself with a *Billboard* magazine that I've spied on the edge of his desk. I'm not sure what to say next. Do I beg for my job? Do I tell him all the things I've wanted to scream back at him for the past few months? Or do I just quit? The more I look at his sun-dried tomato lips pressed tightly together and consider the anxiety he causes me on a daily basis, not to mention the vast amount of eggshells I must tiptoe across every time I step into his office, I realize it's not worth it. Working alongside Edward Maxwell falls in my "life is way too short" category. Dealing with him is not worth the exorbitant amount of distress required to wade through his daily dish of pompous malarkey. It's time to stand up for myself and find a new job.

"Edward," I say, surprised at my courage. "I feel I've learned a lot from this position; and I've thoroughly enjoyed working with many of the staff. But to be honest, I don't think we work well together—and I think my trip to New York was a way of showing that. Therefore, I'm tendering my resignation." As soon as the words escape my lips I grab the *Billboard* magazine off the corner of his desk and begin to fan my face. It's all I can do not to lift my sweater and fan up under my turtleneck. Confrontation is certainly not my strong suit.

Edward, naturally, had more to say—and clearly wanted to have the last word. I'm certain he was expecting tears and begging; and his displeasure at having been undercut was apparent—his face was nearly as red as mine had been moments earlier. I calmly listen as he reiterates everything I've done wrong. He goes on and on about issues of human resources and e-mails and leaving company information secure. All I can focus on are the neatly polished platinum records hanging on the wall behind him—the way his head is positioned, it looks as though he's been framed, next to his idols. It takes all my strength not to laugh out loud at the irony. In the end, we part as coldly as the day we met.

When I rise from the chair and abruptly swing open Edward's door, Stan tumbles in on top of me. Without uttering a sound, I step around him and walk calmly back to my office.

While gathering the few personal items I have in my desk, Sarah and Issie's faces pop into my mind. When I think about how I'm going to support them the actuality of my choice to go to New York grabs hold. At once I feel ashamed and can't help but question my motives, my choices, and even my ability to mother my daughters. But that's the good thing about finally owning up to yourself—if you admit you were wrong, there's really no point in beating yourself up over it. All I know is that I've got a ton of proverbial snow to get out from under—but at least I've got my shovel pointed in the right direction.

Stan appears in my doorway. "This is not my fault."

Completely ignoring him, I glance around my office one last time for any other personal belongings. I may have had a moment of enlightenment, but I know myself. I'm one calm breath from throwing my Southern upbringing out the window and taking a high heel to Stan's bustle of a rear end. Scooping up my purse, I head down the hall with Stan huffing behind me. I stop in front of the control room to say good-bye to Johnny and Jack but when peeping through the small window on the door I see the back of Edward's head and change my mind. So without saying good-bye to one soul, I push open the door to the back steps that lead directly out of the building.

Stan's trailing right behind me. "I'm sorry," he says, halfway down the stairs. "I got insanely jealous when I learned you were in New York with Liam White."

"Insanely jealous?" I say, scurrying down the last few steps. "Why? It's not like we're a couple."

"But we could be! I could make you the happiest woman on earth."

I hurry through the exit door and walk briskly toward my car.

Stan's right beside me now, trying his best to woo me as I pave my way through the parking lot.

Once at my car, I peer over at him and with my hand on the door latch I say, "Stan, I'm going to do you a big favor here. And I've got to tell you, normally I'd be the last person that could ever say something like this. But someone needs to tell you and it may as well be me—since we won't be working together any longer. First, I will say, there are some nice things about you. You have the potential to make a woman happy. But here's one piece of good advice. You can take it or leave it. I'm *not* trying to be mean, but if you don't stop honking snot up your nose, you are going to have a hard time making a girl feel like she's the happiest woman on earth. Go into the *bathroom,* for goodness sake, and use a *Kleenex*. You'll be surprised at how that one simple change can affect the romance in your life. Now go on back inside . . . bless your heart."

After settling down into my seat I flutter my fingers in his direction and back out of the parking spot.

While driving away a wave of clarity washes over me. It's as if I had been nearsighted and suddenly given contacts. Everything was more clear. I had made the perfect decision—I left on my terms, with dignity, and more importantly I took responsibility. I doubt I'd be able to get a stellar letter of reference from Edward, but at least I'd be able to walk around town, *and the club,* with my head held high. Sure, I'm sad about leaving FM 99, there's no doubt about it, and I may not know what's next in my life but I do know that I'll be just fine. I've stood up to two bullies in the last year and with the way I feel right now, I could do it again tomorrow.

Chapter Thirteen

In the four weeks since quitting FM 99—a move that sent Alice's chardonnay out through her nose. "Oh shoog, I never thought you had it in you," she'd said when I was done reenacting the scene and her wineglass had been refilled. I opted to dip into what was left of my savings and take a long hard look at what to next—personally and professionally. I'd reread *What Color Is Your Parachute?*, visited my pastor, and polled the girls each time we had lunch at the club. Currently, I'm finally succumbing to my absolute last, last resort—the one thing I've refused to do. Therapy. It's not so much that I don't believe in it—Richard and Alice swear by it, for example—it's just that I wasn't raised to share my opinions. Now that I think about it, no wonder I ended up in Vermont running a bed and breakfast—it never occurred to me to tell Baker I didn't want to do it.

My friends have always been my therapists, we tell each other absolutely everything with no judgment whatsoever. And most importantly, it's all vaulted in wine-fueled secrecy; I can't really see why I need to talk to a "professional." But they've finally convinced me to seek real help—"Fiery, you don't even take our advice when we give it to you anyhow," said Virgy—and now I'm in my car driving down Poplar Avenue past the quaint office building I've ignored for practically my whole life. I've driven past the blond brick building for as long as I can remember but have never stepped a toe inside. Until today.

I locate her name on the downstairs information board and step onto the elevator, riding only two floors up. I'd have rather walked but saw no sign of a staircase. Frances Folk's office is down the hall, all the way to the end. Once I reach my destination, I turn the knob but it's locked. So I tap on the door lightly.

"Be there in a moment," I hear a cheery voice say from behind the door.

"Oh, no problem," I answer, and wait a few feet back.

It's hard to believe I'm actually seeing a therapist. I take that back. It's hard to believe I'm having to spend one hundred and twenty dollars for *fifty* minutes of seeing a therapist. It's like having to spend money on a new air-conditioning compressor. Who in the world wants to do that?

When she opens the door, only a couple of minutes later, I meet a sweet round-faced lady, probably in her early sixties, who can't be more than five feet tall.

"Leelee? Won't you come in?"

I follow behind her and she points over to a flowery couch. A box of Kleenex is the only item on the brown coffee table in front of the sofa. Frances sits directly across from me in an overstuffed chair with a small analog clock on an end table next to it. There is a desk on the other end of the room with a phone and a bookcase brimming with books. By the names of the titles, I can tell they are mostly psychology related.

"Let's see now. Why don't you tell me a little bit about yourself," Frances says, and pulls her legs up underneath her.

Thirty minutes later she knows the high points in my life. Aside from telling her about resigning (getting fired) from my job at FM 99 and my weekend with Liam, she knows my parents are both deceased, I'm an only child, my mother had a drinking problem and that my husband left me with an inn to run and two daughters to raise all by myself. Phew. That ought to be enough information to keep her employed for the rest of the year.

"Let me get this straight," she says, scratching the back of her head. "Your husband came home one night and asked you to uproot your family and move to Vermont. What kind of business was he in prior to this?"

"The insurance business. It was his daddy's State Farm branch. He hated it though."

"Did you know he hated it?"

"Not until he wanted to move."

"Did you consider putting your foot down and saying no?"

I gave her question serious thought before answering. "My three best friends considered it. They told me I was crazy to move. Of course it wasn't any of *their* husbands who had a dream of becoming an innkeeper. None of my friends were ever faced with that decision. And I'm still not sure I wouldn't do it all over again—this was the love of my life telling me he wanted to fulfill a passion he'd had since he was a teenager . . . how could I say no?"

"Tell me more about your ex-husband. It's Baker, right?"

"Yes."

"Tell me about Baker. Because even though you were sympathetic to his wants, at the very root, that was a selfish thing to do in the first place. Moving his wife and young daughters to a place very different from home to satisfy his desires."

I shake my head as if I agree with her totally.

"And then especially to leave her to do it all. After only how many months?"

"Four."

"He left you for another woman to run the place all by yourself?"

I nod. "An older woman."

Frances smiles. "Did you consider coming home then?"

"Yes, but it was my father's money that financed the inn. I didn't want to lose it."

She slowly nods her head before speaking again. "No wonder it was that easy for him to walk away. It wasn't his money."

I hang my head in shame.

"Honey, you are not the first girl to let her husband talk her into doing something like that and you won't be the last. Plus you're what, thirty-two, thirty-three?"

I nod my head. "I'm thirty-four."

"You fit the pattern. A thirty-four-year-old young woman raised in the South by a controlling father, who has a hard time saying no. Not to mention an alcoholic mother. The South is the land of manners and perfect hostesses, pleasing others and acting graceful."

It's so obvious, I can't even say a word.

"If you'd been forty you might have thought twice about it. Fifty, you'd have said *hell no*."

We both laugh.

"How old were you when you married?" she asks.

"We were both twenty-four. I'd been in love with him since I was sixteen."

"Let me guess. He was on the football team."

"The captain."

"Gorgeous?"

"Drop dead."

"Fraternity president?"

"He didn't actually go that route. He was a University of Tennessee football star. Football was his first real love."

"What else did he love?"

"Fishing. And golf. He was a sports-aholic," I say, smiling.

"Was he ever a Leelee-aholic?"

I look away, studying the sterile window with a plain beige curtain hanging from a black iron rod. Hearing those words cut me to the core. Looking back over at her I can't help but hang my head. "No. I don't think he ever was, now that I think about it. I thought he was at first, though." I'm getting teary eyed.

"How was he as a lover? Did he please you?"

This is a tough one. "He did in the beginning. As the years went by he didn't seem as interested in my pleasure as maybe his own." As I hear those words leave my lips I start to cry. I've never admitted that to anyone. Not even my best friends, seeing as how they already felt about Baker.

Frances reaches over and hands me the Kleenex box. She reminds me of Mama the way she sits on her feet. "Leelee," she says tenderly, "are you familiar with narcissistic personality disorder?"

I shake my head. "No." I reach over for another Kleenex and blow softly.

"It refers to someone with excessive love or admiration of oneself. An inflated view of their own importance. When their weaknesses are brought to their attention it shatters their grand illusions of themselves. They also have envy for others who have what they don't, who are skilled at what they are not, who can feel what they don't, and who are happy just being themselves. Sounding familiar?"

"Very familiar."

"Leelee, the thing is, they're very attractive—most often they are good-looking people, and charming, and kind. They seek out partners who will complement them, add to their beauty. In turn, you become wrapped up in their definition of themselves. Baker could only love you for what you were together—not for you alone. Look, the point of this is not to talk about Baker, but to point out why your self-worth became wrapped up in his. From now on, it's you we need to fix."

I sit perched on the end of the flowery couch, squeezing the very last life out of the two tissues I'd grabbed earlier. It was a relief, to let go—to finally put a clinical name to what had happened to our marriage.

"Now. Your challenge will be learning how to stop the pattern. To change the kind of man you're attracted to."

"Has Alice been talking with you?"

Frances laughs and tells me she deals with this all the time. She says Southern women are particularly vulnerable to this type of man.

So now I have a label for Baker. And there is no way I would ever pick another guy like that. Oh yes—I already did. Liam. Just when I'm about to tell her that there is, *well was,* one man in my life that doesn't fit that description Frances glances at the clock and tells me politely that our time is done. It seems I've just gotten started. I guess I'll have to save that conversation for next time. After writing her a check, I make another appointment for two weeks.

How many bumps in this old popcorn ceiling can I count in one night? It's better than counting sheep or toe wiggling, I know that. Frances Folk has suggested that I try deep breathing and visualizing something peaceful. When pressed for other anecdotes, she claims sex does the trick but also recognizes that's not possible right now and even if it were the side effects might make things worse. She's been teaching me the benefits of thought and image blocking but as I'm counting the popcorn bumps high on top of me, someone's face keeps appearing in the patterns. Aside from the profound feelings of loss I feel over someone who's never going to be mine, I'm worried about my future and where I'm going to find a job. I've been putting in applications all over the place but I'm either underqualified over overqualified, depending on who's viewing my résumé. Even though I've been beating myself up about the choice I made to run up to New York with Liam, Frances has been trying to convince me to stick with my original thought and tuck it away as a memory to tell my grandchildren.

There *is* a big part of me that's excited about the next chapter in my life. After all, I am a dreamer. But there's definitely something missing. I can blame it on all kinds of things but when it boils right down to it I know it's Peter. He's what's missing. I can't help but think my pride has gotten in the way of calling him. Maybe it is my pride but I can't bring myself to do it. It's not like he ever calls me. I sit up in bed and cross my arms in front of me. After only a minute, I slide out and hunt down a pad and pen. After this one—I'm done. Frances Folk says I need to thought-and-image-block him out of my mind forever and finally move on.

Dear Peter,

How's your job going? I hope you're settling in. Did I tell you how happy I am that you got a big salary boost when you took the job? I'm not sure if I ever got a chance to tell you but when I think about it, it makes me smile. And that makes me think about your smile. Those gorgeous perfect teeth. Just like the old Dentyne ads.

Somebody winked at me today. Just like you used to do. But the only difference was it didn't give me goose bumps the way it did when you used to do it. I remember the first time. I had just interviewed you for the sous chef job and you were leaving the inn. You winked at me. I didn't realize it at the time but I was undone. You walked out the front door and I watched you walk to your truck while peeking behind the curtains in the front parlor. I had noticed your forearms in that T-shirt you were wearing. I had been sneaking peeks at them when you weren't watching.

I have one question for you. Why did it take you so long to tell me how you felt about me? Why did you wait until I was leaving? I had made up my mind already. When it came right down to it I felt like Sarah and Issie would be better off living back down South where they wouldn't have to spend most of their lives inside, trying to escape the cold.

Are you interested in why I left Vermont? Have you ever wondered why I didn't turn around and stay? I needed to be true to myself. Daddy had made almost every decision for me until I met Baker. Well, most all of them. I put my foot down when he tried to make me go to Hollins. Nothing against Hollins, it's just that I didn't want to go to school with only girls for another four years. He thought it might increase my chances of marrying a boy from a well-to-do family. In looking back on it now, maybe he was right.

But I ended up with Baker and I loved him. There was a time when he was good to me. I don't think a woman can go through pregnancy and labor with someone and not keep a place for them in her heart. Once I married Baker, he made most of my decisions for me. I just wanted you to know that my decision to move back home had nothing to do with you and everything to do with the fact that I needed to put myself first. Vermont was not my home. And it never would be.

I hope you are happy. I truly do. I don't think I'm going to be writing to you anymore but that's only because I've decided to move on. My therapist, yes, I'm seeing a therapist, thinks I need to open my heart and the only way I'll do that is to push you out of it. Don't be afraid to pick up the phone and call me, though. I still want to be friends.

Love always,
Leelee

After folding the letter, I tuck it in the drawer beside my bed with the others. If he never reads these letters, I can live with that. What I can't live with is never being able to express my feelings. Frances Folk says that it's very important that I write out my emotions and has suggested that I journal on a regular basis. For now, unsent letters seem to be the best way I know to express myself.

Chapter Fourteen

I'd assumed quitting my job would mean heaps of free time during which I could take a little time for some much needed rest, enjoy the Memphis summer relaxing by Virgy's pool with a spiked citrus beverage, and contemplate my next career move. Instead, I was too busy trying to find someone to patch the "accidental" damage in my powder room, tutoring Issie and Sarah for their new school year in the fall, and shuttling back and forth between therapy, swimming lessons for the girls, and walks with Roberta. I nearly forgot it was August until I spied a pair of overstuffed white polyester pants covered in sequins.

Thousands of Elvis Presley lookalikes descending upon your hometown during one week in late summer might be hard for the average person to imagine. Especially since the words "white," "handsome," "talented," and "male" are not prerequisites for the job. There are plenty of black Elvii (the plural of Elvis), Mexican Elvii, even Chinese Elvii floating around, not to mention a large number of female Elvis lookalikes who are making their own mark in the field of Elvis impersonation. They answer to Elvira.

As Memphians, we're used to it. During Elvis Week, held every August, you can't run down the street for a carton of milk without bumping into a black wig or a jewel-studded cape. These regal clotheshorses have become part of the city's fabric ever since the King's passing in 1977. We welcome them home with open arms, especially considering the amount of money they spend. Many are "official" Elvis impersonators, meaning they actually earn prize money from local contests, although the self-proclaimed "cream-of-the-crop" would dare anyone to call them impersonators. They are "tribute artists," thank you very much. And at the very end of Elvis Week the Orpheum Theatre holds the finals, the super bowl of all tributes, where one lucky artist is voted the winner of the Ultimate Elvis Tribute Contest.

Personally I think Memphians take Elvis for granted. Growing up in his hometown has blinded us not only to his talent and image but the money he brings into our city. It's a shame, but only a small number of us partake in the slew of well-planned activities swirling around Elvis Week. Elvis Presley Enterprises sanctions most of the events, which people pay a fortune to attend I might add, but there are a few local, off-the-Boulevard festivities that can be quite entertaining if you're looking for something more eclectic. One year we attended the Dead Elvis Ball at the P & H Café, a party poking fun at the hysterical Elvis fan. In our pre-children years we once attempted an Elvis Week 5K, but after Mary Jule spiked her water bottle with bourbon we abandoned any hope of finishing the 3.12 miles in a respectable time. We were just happy to cross the finish line.

But this year we're determined to experience the real McCoy, the granddaddy of Elvis events held every year in our own backyard—the Candlelight Vigil. "When in Rome," is what I say. Besides, due to my post-FM 99, post-Peter blues, the girls, though they won't admit it, have reached their limit when it comes to placating me. I have a feeling our little Elvis outing is as much for them as it is for me. So Virginia, Alice, Mary Jule, and I have unanimously decided not only to attend the Candlelight Vigil but do so in full Elvis regalia.

Virginia, the only true Elvis fan of our group, is dying to be an

Elvira. For weeks she's searched online for the perfect costume. Well, John searched and printed out the info. (Virginia's about as adept with Google as I was at snow shoveling.) And apparently, we'd all be shocked at how many girl Elvis costumes there are out there. "The only thing missing is the sweet potato bulge behind the zipper," Virgy said, when she called to tell me about the one she wanted. While searching the bounty of Elvis Web sites for Virginia's perfect EP getup, John found White Jumpsuit Elvis—with hotpants as an alternative instead of the traditional full-length one-piece; Sexy Black Jumpsuit Elvis with cleavage cut down to the navel, and Red Hot Elvis with or without a cape. To top it all off, she told us that each item was available in a variety of plus sizes for an additional ten dollars. The costumes range, she explained, anywhere from fifty dollars up to four thousand, depending on how fancy the Elvira wants to look, or just how seriously she takes herself. I couldn't believe that people would dole out that kind of money for a surely ill-fitting polyester monstrosity. But, true to form, Virgy settled on White Jumpsuit Elvis with a cape and promptly forked over two hundred dollars. Well, John did.

Alice has decided to dress like early Priscilla with a short sixties party dress and a ten-inch beehive that she's having done at a vintage beauty shop in North Memphis near the Millington Naval Base. Mary Jule has decided to be George Klein, Memphis deejay and Elvis's dear friend, since Elvis was best man at his wedding and especially since her dark hair is already short. All she would have to do is part it on the side, she said, and add a dab of Brylcreem. We suggested she also add dark circles under her eyes just so she'd be a dead giveaway.

I had the hardest time of all coming up with an idea for a costume. I wasn't all that thrilled about spraying my hair black and dressing as Lisa Marie for the night, so in keeping with my red hair I finally picked Ann-Margret—Elvis's costar in *Viva Las Vegas*. It was a little hard deciding on what to wear, to guarantee people would recognize me, but when I remembered that Ann had made a guest appearance on an episode of *The Flintstones* as Ann-Margrock I just went with that. I found a Betty Rubble outfit at a local costume shop, added a necklace with a dog bone charm, and called it a day.

So on a late Thursday afternoon, August fifteenth, the day before Elvis's actual death day, after a fresh peach daiquiri each (the peaches still have a little life left this time of year) the four of us set out toward Graceland. Although the vigil doesn't start until eight-thirty and goes well into the wee hours on the sixteenth, we've decided to arrive early to partake in some of the other activities.

Once we've all piled inside her car, Alice accidentally smashes her beehive on the inside roof. "Well crap," she says and pulls down her mirror on the sun visor to re-fluff. She turns on the air, full blast, and points the vent directly at her face. "I am hot as hell already," she says as she backs her car out of Virginia's driveway. "Damn this Memphis heat."

"At least your hair is off your neck," says Virgy, who is seated in the passenger seat. "How do you think I feel wearing this polyester stretch-suit and this hot black wig? I forgot all about the heat when I ordered it. Now I wish I'd bought the one with hot-pants."

"Better you than me," I say as cool as a Popsicle in my Ann-Margrock suit and high ponytail.

"I'm about to melt, myself," Mary Jule says. "What was I thinking when I chose this costume? Y'all know what I think about all the Elvis people anyway." She leans in toward the backseat air vent between Alice's console and lets the cold air blow the hair around her face.

"Oh, forget it. I've been living for this night," Virgy says. "If I get hot, I'll just dive into Elvis's pool. What can they do? Arrest me?"

It takes two hours to find a parking spot. Everything I'd read warned to expect big delays, but until we were inching down Elvis Presley Boulevard at five miles per hour for an hour and thirty minutes, I had no idea how jammed it truly would be. Finally Alice gets frustrated and jerks into a McDonald's, three long blocks away from the mansion. When we pull up, one of the workers motions for her not to park in the McDonald's lot but she just rolls down her window, inconspicuously fishes out some cash stowed away in her large, sprayed-to-the-nines beehive, and puts an unknown sum into his bewildered hands. "Shoog, I'm counting on you to look after my car," she says, matter-of-factly. He shoots her a toothy smile and waves us on through, no doubt curious as to what else Alice had hidden up there.

Elvis Presley Boulevard is closed off for two blocks in preparation for an estimated forty thousand people. As we maneuver through the crowds, we pass a Days Inn on the way down to Graceland. It's a motor-court motel, actually, and we notice hundreds of somber Elvis people milling about in the parking lot, as if actually waiting to attend a viewing. From wigs, to sunglasses, TCB (Taking Care of Business) gold necklaces, Elvis suits out the wazoo, and blue suede shoes, these people are paying their respects. Naturally, our combined sense of curiosity can't keep us away any more than a tornado could so we walk up to get a better look and mingle with the crowd.

Most of the doors to the motel rooms are standing wide open and the large windows above the air-conditioning units have been decorated as shrines, with flowers, signature Elvis photos, and homemade crafty items paying homage to the King. There are plenty of mementos for sale, as well. A little chuckle slips out when I see the ceramic blue suede shoes salt-and-pepper shakers. I immediately look around to see if anyone has noticed. Thankfully, my unintentional indignity has slipped by unnoticed. But when Virgy sees me inspecting an Elvis toaster, she holds up her own find—a clear shower curtain with Elvis heads scattered all over it—and asks the Elvira who is selling the merch for the price. Mary Jule gives me one of her "I'm about to lose it" looks as she squints her eyelids, presses her lips together, and lightly shakes her head. Whenever she does that, I know she's doing her best to temper a laughing attack. Clearly this is not the place.

"Are you thinking about it for the guest bath or the master?" I ask Virginia, loud enough for all browsers to hear.

"The master, of course. The King belongs nowhere else but," she says. And as the merch lady is ringing up her purchase Virginia adds, "And I'll take this EP toothbrush holder and wastebasket to go along with it."

Alice whispers under her breath, "And just where in the hell are you really going to put that? Your next garage sale?"

"I don't know right now. I might use it as a slip and slide for the kids. Here, Fiery, you need this." Virgy lightly taps the top of Mr. Potato Head Elvis.

"Now that's worth it," I tell her and pass over my money, too. Neither Alice nor Mary Jule make purchases. Alice said she'd already spent plenty on her beehive and Mary Jule thinks it's all ultra-tacky anyway and wouldn't be caught dead with something like that in her house.

We stroll over to a food court, which is set up in the middle of the parking lot with free tastings of all Elvis's favorite foods. Small portions of peanut butter and banana sandwiches, crunchy bacon, sweet potato pie and banana pudding are scattered among the tables. There's even one with samplings of meatloaf and mashed potatoes, cornbread, and small cups of ice-cold Pepsi colas. We all partake of the banana pudding but leave the rest untouched.

Despite the costumes, the general sense of Elvis Week revelry, and no doubt a few adult beverages, there's an honest-to-goodness air of somberness among the mourners. At the same time, they seem eager to reunite with the comourners with whom they've become acquainted during the yearly pilgrimages to Memphis. Instead of a high-spirited hello, they give each other a controlled hug, and lightly nod their heads to acknowledge their mutual state of bereavement.

The four of us, acting as if we're mourning right along with them, stroll through the motor court, stopping to chat with some of the fans, taste the food, and answer questions about our costumes. Naturally, Alice receives a discreet whistle or two as we pass, her natural beauty only intensified by the Priscilla getup. The sight of her in costume is most likely as close to the real Priscilla as some of them will ever come.

One man whistles at all of us as we pass and Virgy hollers out, a little louder than what would be deemed appropriate, "In your dreams, big guy."

"You are my dream, baby," he yells back.

"And don't you forget it," she says.

"Who are *you,* little darlin'?" he says to me.

"Before I can open my mouth, Virgy says, "Who do you think she is? The one and only Ann-Margrock."

"Where have you been all my life, Annie? Why don't you just Viva Las Vegas your way over here to Papa?"

We don't pause, even for a second, and as we're leaving he pleads, "Don't leave, ladies. I'm just taking care of business."

"Sorry," we all say in unison, as we're exiting the motor court.

We meander through the huge crowd bowled out toward the mansion to get in line for the vigil. On our way over to the gate, we pass the entertainment tent in front of the Heartbreak Hotel, which has a sign out front that reads "Elvis Bingo." Just outside the opening to the tent there's a small group of people surrounding a certain Mexican Elvis. The closer we get I could almost swear the big burly guy at his side is his bodyguard as he's standing dangerously close to the señor and seems to be making an effort to shield his body.

"Oh my gosh," Virgy says, outstretching her arms to stop us from moving a step further. "It's El Vez."

Alice grabs the back of her arm. "*Who?*"

"El Vez, the Mexican Elvis."

"How in the world do you know about him?" Mary Jule asks her.

"From TV or *People* magazine, I don't know. Everyone knows who he is," Virgy says, standing on her tiptoes to get a better look.

"I don't know who he is," I say to Mary Jule. "Do you?"

"Are you kidding me?" she says.

Without turning her eyes away from him, Virginia informs us, "I read an article about him in *Rolling Stone*. Here's the best: He claims he's running for president."

"Of America or Mexico?" I ask.

Mary Jule shakes her head. "This is almost more than I can take, to tell you the truth."

"El Vez!" Virgy screams. "Can we get a picture with you?" She's scrambling in her purse for her camera.

El Vez travels with an entourage and they all stop to see who adores him now. "But of course," he says, in his Spanish accent. "But I'll have to make it quick."

"Hurry, hurry," Virgy tells us, handing her camera to the bodyguard and we all squeeze in for a picture. El Vez puts his sweaty arm around my bare shoulder and puts the other around Virgina's. Alice and Mary Jule are on either side of us. I can hardly smile because I'm just sure my shoulder must smell like BO.

When the bodyguard stares at me and slowly peeks his tongue through his slightly parted lips, it churns my stomach. "Just take the picture," I say and shoot him a phony smile. When he hands Virginia back her camera, and we're walking away I say, "I hope that was worth it. I'm scared to sniff myself, there's no telling how nasty I smell."

Virgy says something but her voice is muffled due to an off-key voice emanating from inside the entertainment tent. When we get to the opening to sneak a peak, another Priscilla lookalike (this one must have spent the extra ten dollars on her costume) is belting out the chorus of "Jail House Rock" from the tiptop of her lungs. Bless her heart. She's awful.

"This is the hands down best thing about karaoke," Virginia says, "the people that think they're good when they're terrible. Let's find a seat."

We meander through the room and spot a table in the middle with four empty chairs. There's a White Jumpsuit Elvis, probably in his midfifties, sitting all alone, swaying his head to the performance. He's got the lip, the hair, the cape—with a large studded eagle on the back—and the TCB necklace. Since there's not another table to accommodate the four of us, Alice walks right up to him and says, "Excuse me, shoog. Do you mind if we sit with you?"

He takes one look at her, stands up and pulls out the seat next to him. "Why of course not, Priscilla dear."

As Alice is scooting into the table she says, "Would you please be a dear and pull out the seats for my other friends, Elvis darling?"

"It would be my pleasure," he says with a nod of his head. "Hello ladies, I'm Elvwayne. I know Priscilla is unaware, but a true tribute artist does not go by Elvis." First he situates Mary Jule and then helps Virgy with her chair. I notice him studying my costume while he's helping me with mine. "And who are you, little darlin'?"

"Ann-Margrock," I say. When he looks confused I remind him of *The Flintstones* episode.

"Of course," he says. "I'll look forward to your performance."

"Oh, I'm not performing," I tell him, shaking my head and waving my hand in the air.

"Why, anyone dressed as Ann-Margrock must sing 'Viva Las Vegas.'"

Alice slaps her hand on the table. "Leelee! Of course. You have to sing 'Viva Las Vegas.' You absolutely have to."

Without committing myself, I shrug my shoulders. I'm considering it; but I'm not telling them.

Elvwayne says, "The words are written on the screen."

I say, "Actually, you should be talking to Elvira over there." I point right at Virginia. "She's a much better singer than I am."

"Why don't we all do it? I swear it will be a riot." Virginia, who knows her voice is worse than terrible, insists that this will make it all the funnier.

Alice says, "You know, we should. Absolutely. I need wine, though, and fast." She looks around for the bar. "We'd like four wines, Elvwayne."

"Drinking is not allowed in this tent," he says.

"What! You mean those people get up there and sing stone-cold sober?"

"I don't know about that," he says and opens his cape to show us his flask. "But as for me, I'm never unprepared."

"Then we'll have four Cokes," Alice says and shoos him off to the bar. While he's gone, the show host, a woman dressed not as a certain character, but donned from head to toe in all things Elvis, stops by our table and hands each of us a list of songs. She wants to find out if anyone at our table will be singing, aside from Elvwayne who's already signed up. Virginia, who has now declared herself Elvween, lets her know that we all will be singing. The woman takes our stage names and says we can let her know our song choices right before we go on.

Elvwayne returns with four Cokes and proceeds to stiffen our drinks.

After studying the menu intently, Virginia slides it over to Elvwayne. "Poke Salad Annie," no question about it. What are you singing, Elvwayne?" She loves to use his name any chance she can.

"'All Shook Up.' It's my standard."

"I'm all shook up over that jumpsuit you're wearing. How much did you spend on that thing, shoog?" Alice asks him.

He stands up and slowly turns around in a circle. "If you consider that this jumpsuit is an exact duplicate from the *Aloha from Hawaii* concert from 1973, all hand-done with each stone costing two dollars apiece, and three hundred man-hours used to hand-place each one of them, it should not come as a shock that it set me back four thousand dollars."

"That would depend on your definition of shock," Mary Jule says, and kicks me under the table. "You must be a wealthy man, is all I can say. I wonder why Elvis wore those in the first place."

"Because of his love for Captiain Marvel, my dear," Elvwayne tells her. "Elvis wanted a costume that reminded him of his childhood idol."

"Oh good lord," Mary Jule says and exhales loudly.

After many more performances and another round of drinks, compliments of Elvwayne, not to mention a little person Elvis lookalike singing "Don't Be Cruel," the host steps onto the stage and takes the microphone. "Next up," she says, "is an Elvira from right here in Memphis. She's here with three of the four Jordanaires. Let's give a hearty welcome to Elvween!"

The applause begins as we scurry up to the stage. Virgy, who's plenty tipsy at this point, goes up to the karaoke machine and selects her song. The karaoke player flashes the lyrics across the screen just before the first chords of "Poke Salad Annie" are blasted through the tent. Naturally, at the last second Alice wants to be the leader. But in a bold move, even for her, Virginia says, "For once, you do not get to be the star. I'm the one wearing the Elvis suit, so you just get on back there with Mary Jule and Fiery and be a Jordanaire."

"Fine," Alice says, with a semipout, and backs into her spot.

Virginia whips her head back around and leans into the mic. "Down in Lou-zee-anna," she looks off to one side and throws her arm out to the other side, "where the alligators grow so mean, there lived a girl that I swear to the world made the alligators look tame. Poke Salad Annie." Within a few seconds she's so comfortable on stage that she's now holding her mic, gyrating and dancing, and making up her own karate moves. "The gator's got your granny," she belts out to the crowd.

With bourbon-fueled perfection, learned from years and years of having to be the backup singers, Mary Jule and I, along with Alice, dance right behind her, echoing "Chomp, chomp, chomp."

An even better sight is Elvwayne, who has moved up to the front of the stage and is gyrating right along with Virginia.

When the song comes to an end, Virginia makes large loops with her right arm and adds one final ad-lib, "Sock a little poke salad to me." She leans her head back as the music fades.

The crowd loves her. Right away Elvwayne walks onto the stage and takes the mic. "Ann-Margrock, Ann-Margrock, Ann-Margrock," he says as if it's a chant and sweeps his arms in an effort to get the rest of the crowd to chant along with him. Pretty soon the entire entertainment tent is calling for me to sing "Viva Las Vegas."

Thank goodness for bourbon. I take the mic from Virginia. The words crawl across the screen and the two of us duet to "Viva Las Vegas." At one point Alice can't take it anymore and dances up to the front to sing along with the two of us, which leaves Mary Jule as the only Jordanaire. I look back at her during the song and she just shakes her head. At this age, she's past the point of making an issue of Alice's bossiness. Once our number is over, and after another round of hearty applause, we say good-bye to Elvwayne and thank him for his hospitality.

By now it's almost pitch dark outside, and a huge crowd of thousands is lined up in front of the gates of Graceland waiting on the vigil's opening ceremony. "Dangit," Virginia says when she takes in the crowd, "We'll be here all night. We'll have to think of a way to break in that line."

There must be ten thousand people waiting at the gates. Tonight there is no admission charge. Once the opening ceremony is over, fans are invited to walk up the driveway to Elvis's gravesite, or the Meditation Garden as they call it, carrying their candles in quiet remembrance. The gates won't close until the last person has paid her respects, no matter if it's five o'clock tomorrow morning.

I can't help but wonder how many of these people have cashed in their life savings to attend Elvis Week, after all it's certainly not cheap. One of the fans we talked with back at the Days Inn told us that she had sent a funeral spray to the Meditation Garden with over one hundred red roses. She told us that hers would be one of thousands.

We have to walk around a sea of Elvis shrines scattered all over the boulevard. One fan has drawn a chalk rendering of Elvis on the asphalt underneath hundreds of votives in the shape of Elvis's personal signature. Others have pictures, candles, and other paraphernalia, but all have set up lawn chairs next to their respective shrines. We stumble upon a candle table and we all pick up a free taper, each with a drip guard.

When the ceremony begins, someone from Elvis Presley Enterprises stands at a podium in the distance, welcoming us and explaining the rules. He says it should be a solemn, quiet ceremony, and that we should keep our voices low. He further explains that the torches from the Meditation Garden will be brought to the front gates so each fan can light his candle. He reminds us that water stations have been set up throughout the property. It has to be ninety-two degrees outside and the sun went down over an hour ago. There's a misting tent dubbed Kentucky Rain, after one of the King's biggest hits, but we never saw it. There are more speeches by members of Elvis's many international fan clubs, and finally the musical tribute starts with "Love Me Tender."

Over ten thousand Elvis fans start the long haul up the driveway to the Meditation Garden, where they will have time to pause for a moment and pay their respects before they are led back down the drive and out the gate. Virginia leads us as close to the front of the line as she can, but it still looks like five thousand other mourners are ahead of us. People are quiet and they are dead serious. Their heads are hung in grief. Many are crying.

After an hour of standing in the same spot and never moving, we decide to move on ahead and squeeze in just behind the Elvis fan club from Denmark. The only way we know they are from Denmark is because their T-shirts say so in English. There are eight of them. All women. It goes without saying that they are decked out in Elvis garb, but none have gone to the lengths that we have. Not one of them is wearing a costume. Nonetheless, it's obvious that their blood runs true-blue to the King.

Virgy accidentally loses her footing and falls into one of them, which doesn't set well from the start. Even though Virginia says she's sorry, the woman does not seem to accept the apology. Instead she waves her hand in Virginia's face and utters something in Danish. From then on, any time one of us makes a sound, even a sneeze or a clearing of the throat, the ladies from Denmark turn around and glare at us. One woman in the group actually has the nerve to turn around and give us a loud "shush."

It's honestly not as easy as it seems to be totally quiet. Alcohol certainly has not helped the situation either. Not only has it turned the four of us into blabbermouths, but it's kindled our saucy streaks.

As hard as we try, we can't keep ourselves from whispering. Silence has never been any of our strong suits.

"Please be quiet," one of the women says and jerks her head right back around. At least one of them speaks English.

"I had no idea it was this serious," Virgy whispers, and I can tell she's on the verge of a laughing attack, which naturally sparks the same in the rest of us. Another minute goes by and Mary Jule has already forgotten she's supposed to be close-mouthed. "How long do you think it's gonna take for this line to even move," she says, much louder than she should. "I sure don't want to be here all night."

You'd have thought she'd damned the King himself by the way each woman in the Denmark fan club whips her head around. If looks could kill, all four of us would be lying out back in the Meditation Garden between Elvis Aaron and Jesse Garon (Elvis's twin).

Of course, this gets us all going, and it's a much worse situation than laughing in church. Much, much worse. At this point all of us completely lose it. Our shoulders start shaking and there's not a thing we can do about it. I'm afraid to catch Virginia's eye for fear I'll wet my pants. Pretty soon we are holding our stomachs and nothing can make us stop. Virgy hands her candle over to Alice and collapses on the ground.

When we see two of the fan club members storm off toward an Elvis Week official, we decide to break and run. Even if we found another place in line, the hours it will take, and the amount of perspiration it will require to actually make it to the Meditation Garden is simply not worth it.

Once we're back at Alice's car and we're pulling out of the McDonalds, Virgy leans over and lays on Alice's horn. She rolls down her window and screams, "Goodnight Elvis! See you next year."

While driving home from Virginia's the next day, I veer off through the historic part of town to stop at the Germantown Commissary for barbecue. I had called Kissie before leaving and told her not to cook and that I was treating her to her favorite food. She had spent the night at my house, yet again. When I told her our plans for the evening, she told me to just spend the night at Virginia's house. "I know you girls," she said. "No point in driving home that late by yourself."

As I'm leaving the restaurant with the yummy aroma of pit barbecue wafting through my car, I can't resist looping around over to West Street. I love all the town's history, especially the old buildings and homes. As I'm making a right onto Old Poplar Pike and crossing the railroad tracks, I notice a for-sale sign in a yard up ahead, so I slow my car down to a roll and stop in front of the cutest house I've ever seen.

I can't resist pulling in the driveway on the off chance this might be our ticket into a nicer home. After staring through my windshield at the blue Victorian with gingerbread on the screen door, gables, and the porch railing, I step out of my car and walk toward the house through a path of mature boxwoods. A wide set of steps leads up to a large front porch, which wraps around to the side.

The house appears to be empty so I run up on the porch and peek in the front window. Although there are no lights on, I can see through to the inside and make out a gorgeous, intricately carved old staircase in the entry hall and large rooms with fireplaces off to each side. The front door seems to be original and still has its charming, old turn-style bell. Just for fun, I turn the lever but no one answers the door.

Running around back, I almost trip over a hose that's been left out in the yard. There's another small porch and a parking lot just off the rear of the home. When peeking in the back door I instinctively place my hand on the doorknob and to my surprise the door swings open. After glancing around to see if anyone is watching, I steal inside to a small utility room. "Hello," I call out. "Anybody here?" I say, while walking into an outdated kitchen. It's large, but it's old and would need a total overhaul. From the kitchen there's another door that leads into a large dining room with a fireplace and as I walk on through my eyes are fixated on the high ceilings. I figure they must be twelve feet tall. The wide-board oak floors are original, too, it's obvious by the way they softly creak under my tiptoeing feet; and I can tell by a few old cracks that the walls must be plaster. The more I look around, the more I'm falling in love—it's absolutely charming.

I can't resist running upstairs for a brief run-through. It's equally as beautiful with three bedrooms and a bathroom out in the hall. The sound of my stomach growling reminds me of our lunch in the car and I run back down the stairs and out the back door, but not before imagining Sarah and Issie's little clothes hung in the closets and the sounds of cooking coming from the kitchen.

As I'm walking down the front porch steps, I turn around and look back at the house. Instead of blue, I see weathered peach with a shiny ivory trim. The more I stare at it, the more focused it becomes. I can't quite put my finger on what I'm feeling—it's like that moment when you take an old tired dress from its hanger and slip it on, and suddenly it fits in all the right places—transforming both the dress and you. But this isn't just the novelty of having found something new and pretty. I have an odd sensation that I'm coming home. Ever since leaving the house I shared with Baker—moving to Vermont, and now renting a temporary home—I haven't felt a sense of belonging.

I can feel the back of my head heat as the sun barrels through the trees, letting loose the deep summer rays. I'm sure to start perspiring through my T-shirt soon, and my hair is no doubt triple its normal size thanks to Memphis humidity. But I just can't seem to tear my eyes away. It's part cottage, part dollhouse—it practically oozes family and porch swings and peach daiquiris and a dog house in the backyard. Turning to the car, I take a final look and there it is—the Peach Blossom Inn sign.

Of course it's not really there, I tell myself. But I can just see it now, hanging there with the two peaches for the Os in the middle of "Blossom." I try wiping away the mental picture but each time I do it floods right back. I think back to my beautiful sign lying on top of the garbage heap behind my Vermont inn, exactly where Helga had thrown it, ready to be burned in the next trash fire. Now it's sitting in the garage with a few straggling boxes that were never unpacked after our return from the North.

What would Frances Folk say? More importantly, I ask myself, what would Frances Folk do? Ignoring all sense of rationality, I sink to the ground underneath the large pecan tree in the front lawn. Resting on its protruding roots, I stare into the layers of overhanging leaves, letting my eyes adjust to the incoming sun. When I shut my eyelids, I can still see the silhouette of the stems and branches and I turn off my mind to everything but the images.

When was I happy last? I mean, really happy—not just giggling with the girls, or bending over laughing with Kissie. I thought for so long it was when I was with Baker; sitting on our porch after we put the girls to sleep. My happiness was what I saw in his eyes—but now I've learned that was just a reflection, not the truth. So when was *I* really content? It comes to me more quickly than I thought. It was the night I opened the mail in Vermont, to find John Bergmann's review of the newly opened Peach Blossom Inn. It was a clipping from *Food and Wine* and he said: "Superb cuisine. Warm ambiance with real Southern charm. Call well in advance for a fireside table." It was the first acknowledgment that I had done something well, on my own.

It's all too clear. I'm so caught up in the possibilities that my mind is a hundred yards down the road by the time I open my car door. I'm picturing the grand-opening party. All of my friends will be there, Sarah and Issie will be dressed in beautiful hand-smocked dresses from the Women's Exchange and they'll greet our guests at the door. We'll be toasting with expensive champagne and photographers from *The Commercial Appeal* and *The Germantown News* will be there to snap our picture, which will end up on the front page of the living section. Kissie will be wearing her most beautiful Sunday suit, the one she wore to my going-away luncheon, and she'll accept accolades for her yeast rolls and other Southern delicacies she's added to the menu.

I imagine tables out on the porch for diners. And the linen tablecloths, and the dripless candles and the flowers and the . . . Have I lost my ever-loving mind? But the more I think about it the more I know that I was not half bad at it. Despite all the hard times I endured in Vermont with Baker and Helga, I learned how to run a business. I handled the staff, the scheduling, the payroll, the bills and taxes and I turned out to be a grand martini mixer after all.

All I need to do is to find another Peter.

Chapter Fifteen

CHEF NEEDED Peach Blossom Inn—small, gourmet restaurant in mint condition. Must have nice attitude, pleasing personality, GOOD HYGIENE, and expertise in classic and nouvelle cuisine. Historic Germantown, 462 Old Poplar Pike, Memphis, Tennessee 38108. Call 901-555-8912 or apply in person.

I have to give therapy a lot of credit. Well, I guess I have to give Frances Folk a lot of credit. Most people come to their senses when they seek professional psychological help. Me? I went utterly insane. In the ten weeks since I lost my mind, I fell in love with an old house, changed my life's direction (again), decided to open a Memphis location of the Peach Blossom Inn, and tackled everything from antebellum restoration to liquor permits. Still, I've yet to find a chef. The applications have flooded my mailbox and I've had a slew of people show up at my door. Why in the world I would include "apply in person" in my ad is beyond me. Every time I get in the middle of something important here comes somebody else looking for a job. And many of them, it seems, haven't even bothered to take the ad seriously. I've had more bad attitudes and stinky people show up here than I can shake a stick at.

Thinking back to when I was searching for a chef in Vermont, and happened upon Peter, reminds me that there could be another jewel in my large pile of resumes. After narrowing it down to six, three women and three men, I contact all of them to meet me at the restaurant the day after tomorrow.

The very first thing I did, after signing the closing papers, was hang my sign in the yard, right beside the old pecan tree. As soon as I knew my offer had been accepted, I ordered a large ivory post to hang the Peach Blossom Inn sign—my way of advertising the restaurant's opening. It was as much a sign of my personal comeback as anything else, my own way of telling the Tootie Shootwells of Memphis that I was more than just Baker Satterfield's ex-wife. The second thing I did was hire a designer to convert the old kitchen into a commercial one. I knew the girls would help me decorate out front but hiring someone who knew about installing the correct appliances, and to code, was mandatory. In just ten weeks, the kitchen is now ready and the drab blue Victorian home with cracked blue trim is now a gleaming peach painted lady with ivory spindles, spandrels, and gingerbread eaves. The inside is picture perfect, too, with both of the front rooms serving as dining areas. Porch seating will have to wait till the spring, when it warms up again, but as for the winter, I'm excited to have the fireplaces in the two front rooms to give the place a warm and cozy glow.

Cashing in a good chunk of my savings was one of the riskiest things I've ever done—but Frances tells me that no reward comes without some amount of personal skydiving. So, I've ordered tables and chairs and all the necessary table adornments such as salt-and-pepper shakers, flower vases, and sugar holders. Alice found a restaurant in Mississippi that was going out of business and we drove down in a Ryder truck and purchased their entire inventory. All the cutlery, china, glassware, and even the pots and pans. They even had a brand-new Viking stove and a walk-in refrigerator. I figured out that all of it combined gave me a savings of 50 percent. Although I'm happy for my gain, I can't help but feel bittersweet for the people who lost their business.

There have been lots of kettle corn moments these days—that's what Mama used to say when things are both happy and sad at the same time, like salty popcorn covered in burnt sugar. I can't help but pinch myself every time I really sit (not that there's time to *actually* sit) and think about starting another Peach Blossom Inn. As excited as I am, it's hard to be decorating a house, setting up a life, hanging our family pictures when it's just the three of us. Plus Roberta. And Kissie, of course. My entire definition of family has changed since last year.

I close my laptop after confirming an interview with the last potential chef. It's balanced on three boxes of linen napkins that I've stacked up to make a makeshift desk. I wipe my hands on my jeans and stare around at the half-filled spaces, freshly painted walls, and various mountains of tablecloths, utensils, and unpacked UPS boxes. Despite the melee of shipments, things have gone surprisingly well. I think it's a sign this was simply meant to be. Kissie's explanation is more spiritual. "When the Lawd wants somethin' to happen, there ain't no devil in hell that can stop it," she says. I can tell she's dying to take over the kitchen. I keep telling her she needs to be enjoying her golden years and no longer working but she tells me that if she ever really sits down she might as well die. Seeing as how that's the last thing I want to happen, I tell her there's plenty for her to do. Like supplying us with her yeast rolls, at least until a new chef learns how to make them.

Alice and Mary Jule have decided that they will be happy to be on my waitstaff, *one night* per week—and Virgy said she'd act as cohostess. When I first showed them the house, they were beside themselves and could not wait to begin the decorating. "I couldn't have come up with a better idea if it hit me in the face," Virgy said, when I told her. She also wanted to know why I wasn't hiring the Yankee Doodle. I reminded her, yet again, that he has a good paying job in Vermont and that I haven't heard from him in seven months. Besides, I told her, I'm moving on, something Frances Folk has been completely supportive of. She, like Peter, is not a fan of long-distance relationships.

Since I'm having to spend every day, all day, here at the Peach Blossom Inn, Kissie has had to move into my spare bedroom. She's used to it though. When my grandmother got sick, Kissie moved into her home to care for her. When Daddy was sick, she did the same thing for him. Of course, Mama, in her final stage of cancer, had in-home health care nurses, but Kissie supplemented all the extra care. There's always been a thing in my family to be able to die at home, away from a nursing home. Although I'm far from needing nursing home care, I'm in major need of Sarah and Issie care. If not for Kissie taking care of them during this transition time, I would never have been able to open this restaurant. Nor would I have wanted to.

I'm leaving the house early for my extra full day of interviews when I spot Riley in his driveway. His face is buried in the trunk of his car and Luke is perched right next to him. My car engine startles him and I watch as he leaps across the grass divider between our driveways, yelling my name as he's running. "Leelee, Leelee, woll down your window." My coffee splatters on the console as I try rolling it down and positioning my mug into the cup holder at the same time. Growing more panicked at the distressed look on his face, I'm just this side of yelling myself when he reaches my car. "What's wrong, Riley?"

"Nothing's wong." Now he's leaning in my window.

Oh for gosh sakes. I slap my hand on the steering wheel and sigh heavier than I had intended. "Then why did you run across the yard screaming my name?"

"Because I have something vewy important to tell you."

"What is it?"

"I feel howible about this but I'm going to have to cancel our Pampa'ed Chef Pawty."

It takes me a second to realize what he's talking about. Naturally, I'd forgotten all about it. For months, I cringed every time I saw him for fear he'd bring it back up. Either that, or he'd offer to help out on another home improvement project. Not only have I not had the holes in the bathroom wall fixed, I'm quite positive I can't trust my friends to take Riley seriously while he's performing his cooking demonstration. Poor Riley would be one soft *R* away from Virgy breaking into hysterical laughter. It's hard to conceal my elation but I try.

"Oh Riley, don't you worry about that one little bit." Of course, I have to admit I'm a little shocked. It's not like him to cancel anything. I'm almost afraid to ask why. "Well, I'll see you later," I say. "I've got to get to work."

"The weason is I've decided to let go of my Pampa'ed Chef consultancy."

"You have?" Now I'm more than a little shocked. I'm flabbergasted.

"Guess what line of work I've decided to go into now," he says. Ah, the other shoe drops.

"You've decided to become a member of the paparazzi," I say with a touch of sarcasm—starting a business has shortened my patience bandwidth.

"*No,*" he says, catching on to my joke. "Too much work. To tell you the truth I've decided there's more money to be made in Amway. Not to mention more fun. As a matter of fact, I'm headed wight now to Gwand Wapids, Michigan, to the Amway Gwand Plaza Hotel for a confewence."

Naturally, I had no idea that an Amway Grand Plaza Hotel even exists.

"You won't believe the cool pwoducts we have for weight management, energy drinks, vitamins, and supplements. And we have pwoducts for skin care, hair care, body care, cleaning supplies, and an automotive line. They even sell wightbulbs and battewies. Twust me, you will be much happier in the long wun having an Amway wep in your life."

Bless his heart. "Well, have fun, Riley. See you when you get back."

"Say, would you mind checking on ole Lukey boy a time or two? I have a pet sitter coming to take him out and go on walks but it would be nice if he could come to your backyard at some point and play with Woberta."

"That would be fine, Riley. I'll be happy to bring Luke over. Or take Roberta to your backyard. Either one."

"That would be gweat. See you when I get back."

"Yeah, see you soon, Riley. Enjoy your trip." I pat him on the hand and drive off down the drive. Through my rearview mirror I see Kissie peeking through the front dining room window. As I'm turning out of my driveway I look to my right and watch as the curtains close.

Just for kicks, I decide to open a bottle of Rombauer chardonnay. It's a bit self-indulgent, and I can't help but be a tad melancholy because of the connection to Peter—but the real truth is, it's the only chilled wine I have on hand. The wine fridges arrived yesterday and were easily installed. Before I left, I'd opened a mixed case of wine and unloaded the bottles of red into their shelves in one fridge. In the other, I loaded up the whites—but the only kind that had arrived was the shipment of Rombauer. After a day of interviewing six chefs—whose talent will pretty much determine the failure or success of my restaurant—I'm in need of some serious therapy, and I don't mean the kind that Frances provides. I still have one more interview to go, but my energy, enthusiasm, and even my faith in this venture is nearly as frazzled as my mess of hair, currently knotted in a loose bun at the nape of my neck.

The cork slides out with ease and just for fun I sniff its end, letting the crisp, biting scent hit my nostrils. Grabbing the glass and the bottle, I shuffle to the table and collapse into the worn wooden chair. After pouring an obnoxiously large serving, I take one delicious sip and check my watch—if the next guy doesn't show up soon, I'm going to be loopy when he arrives.

As much as I'm the one conducting the interviews, a skill I'm far from mastering, I've been aware that my applicants were evaluating me as well. The Peach Blossom Inn looks full of potential but there are too many unpacked boxes, loose wires, and odds and ends lying about to really look like anything at all. So, to make things a little nicer and certainly more businesslike, I set up a table with a couple of chairs in the middle of the east dining room. But despite my best efforts the day started off poorly.

When I first arrived in Vermont, I spent months trying to deodorize the Vermont Haus Inn. It not only stunk from Helga's stale cigarette smoke but the entire place smelled like a mélange of garlic and old, musty upholstered furniture, with a profusion of BO. Rolf was the reason for the latter odor and he left a trail of it wherever he went. The first guy I interviewed this morning stunk to high heaven himself, and honestly, he may as well not have bothered applying. After Rolf, I swore I'd never work with anyone again who had so little regard for his, *or her,* personal care. I even put that in my ad. "Must have good hygiene." But Mr. Dan Dunwoody from East Tennessee must have completely ignored that part. I could smell him the second he stepped his big toe into the foyer. The stench of body odor permeated the entire room. I was so terribly distracted by the reek that I couldn't concentrate on a word he said. How in the world he thought I'd ever consider him for my head chef is beyond me. Obviously "smelling like a goat," as Daddy would have said, didn't bother him in the least. People never cease to amaze me.

I suppose the woman with long brown hair who I spoke with around lunchtime might be a possible candidate. I'm guessing she's in her twenties by her I'm-out-to-prove-myself-to-the-world attitude. Fresh out of Le Cordon Bleu College of Culinary Arts in Miami, she even wore her checkered chef pants and white chef coat with her name embroidered on the pocket to the interview. Gung ho and confident, she had a PowerPoint slideshow of her "art"—her culinary creations, left me with a folder of references, and had already taken the liberty of designing a menu, with wine pairings, for the Peach Blossom Inn. Her ambition was nearly as overpowering as Dan Dunwoody's perspiration. Honestly, I'm not sure that I like her well enough to hire her, but there is nothing to dislike about her, either. When she left I told her that I'd be interviewing a few more applicants but that I did consider her to be a top candidate.

The only other person besides Miss Gung Ho worth a second look is an older gentleman with a résumé a mile long. He even worked at the Four Flames, a high-end eatery in Midtown that closed several years ago, suffering the same fate as many of the older restaurants in town. He had a fatherly way about him and I found myself warming up to him right away. Not only did he have a nice attitude and pleasing personality, his hygiene was impeccable. I'm almost tempted to call him back right now and offer him the job but I promised Mary Jule that I'd interview one of Al's old college buddies.

All she knows about him is they went to school together at Georgia and that his name is Rod McLain. As a favor to Al, she says, I have to at least talk to the guy. But if he's not here in the next five minutes, I'm leaving. He was supposed to be here a half hour ago and I'm absolutely ravenous. I haven't been able to put a morsel of food in my body all day. Actually I take that back. I ate the last two Tropical LifeSavers that were hiding in the bottom of my purse about three hours ago. Thank goodness for Kissie. She picked up the girls from school and I'm sure has dinner ready and waiting. Just thinking about what she has on the stove makes me all the more eager to get this day over with right now.

I pick up the phone and call Mary Jule. "He's not here," I say, as soon as she answers. My voice is weary and soft—and a little bugged. I'm sure she senses it.

I can tell she's peeved, too, by the way she's sighing on the other end of the phone. "Let me call Al," she says, as if she's ready to kill him. "He took a half day off and took Rod to play golf at the club. I can't imagine where they are."

"Golf? I thought you said he's a chef. Honestly. I don't know about another chef who plays golf. It reminds me too much of Baker."

"Now Leelee, you can't expect your chef not to have any other outside activities. I can see hiring someone who's not a football star but any man worth his salt is bound to have other interests."

"I know. But he was supposed to be here by six and it's six thirty. I'm sorry to sound abrupt but I'm starving. I haven't been able to eat a meal all day because of all these interviews. They've each lasted over an hour and they've pretty much been back to back. The last person just left here thirty minutes ago."

"You know what. I don't blame you. If this guy is not taking the chef position seriously enough to be on time for his interview, forget it. Just go home. Don't you have enough résumés anyway?"

"Probably so. I interviewed a girl this morning that might work and an older man this afternoon that I'm almost ready to call and offer the job to right now."

"Go on home, Fiery. I'll tell Al that you couldn't wait any longer. Why don't you come over tonight? Have a nice glass of wine. It'll relax you."

"I'm already working on the wine, don't you worry. I'm just so tired. I haven't been sleeping well. And this whole thing is driving me crazy. I'm starting to wonder why I did it."

"Why you did what?"

"Open up another restaurant. I'm not sure I'm meant to be a restaurateur. This ordeal about hiring a chef is the kind of thing that always happens in the restaurant business. Murphy's Law I'm telling you. It had to have been invented in a restaurant."

"Actually I think its origin had something to do with aviation."

"Smarty pants. You and Kissie."

"You just need to get some sleep tonight. I know you're worried about it, but you'll hire a chef, the place will be a huge success and all will be well."

"Whatever. I'm just having a hard time keeping my eyes open right now. And what about this weather? What's the deal?"

"I don't know. I heard the weatherman say the normal high is eighty and today it only reached sixty-one. The low is supposed to get down in the forties. I told Al he's building me a fire tonight."

"And here it is mid-October. I wonder if it will get warm again? Oh well, thanks for understanding. I'm going to head out before it gets too cold in here. I haven't even turned on the heat yet. I'm trying to keep the power bills down. Talk to you tomorrow," I say, and hang up the phone.

I turn on night lamps and shut off the overhead lighting, resigned to having been stood up by this Rod character, who must really be enjoying the golf course at the club—from the view *in the men's bar.* When I open the screen door and feel the chill in the air, it reminds me of a happier time. Football season at Ole Miss. Several of us sorority sisters, all dressed up in fabulous fall outfits, would be waiting for our dates in the living room at the Chi O house. There was something about seeing a boy in the foyer wearing a sport coat, khakis, and penny loafers that still makes me happy to this day. Life was easy then.

I shut and latch, and then lock the newly stained wooden front door with its brass sign that reads the Peach Blossom Inn and lists our soon-to-be hours of operation. I decide to call Kissie and tell her I'll be home earlier than expected. Spotting my purse on the table, I start to dig for my cell. Not unlike the rest of the house, it resembles a mobile Dumpster these days. Mounds of crumpled-up receipts, coins, old lipsticks, and loose sticks of gum lining the bottom, are just a mere tasting of the superfluous clutter that lives inside. I sigh and remove my wallet, hairbrush, checkbook, and the small bottle of hand sanitizer.

Ready to give up and just head home anyway, I am interrupted by a knock at the front door. Oh, so now he decides to show up. Well, buddy, you've aready got several strikes against you. You better smell good is all I have to say. Marching over to the front door, ready to show him who's boss, I'm suddenly scared stiff. Mary Jule may have already told Al not to bother sending over his tardy golfer-chef friend. Here I am, all alone in this house, and it's pitch dark outside. As much as I love my hometown, it's not the safest city in Tennessee. Just last week there was a bank robbery in Germantown—in broad daylight! Instead of answering it I creep back to my purse and frantically dig around again for my cell, which I finally find hiding in a side pocket. I dial Mary Jule and when she answers I'm whispering so low it'll be a wonder if she can hear me. "Did you get Al?"

"What?" she says, loud enough for the burglar outside to hear her. "I can't hear you."

"Shhhhhhhh." My voice is panicky. "Did you get Al?"

"Yes, *why*?" Now she's alarmed. But at least she's whispering.

"There's someone outside." Another hard knock comes from the front door, followed by the ringing of the turn-style doorbell and my fear intensifies. "I'm scared to death. Hold on. I better get a weapon." With nothing else in sight, I grab a Swiffer mop and creep over to the front door. Without a peephole I'm not about to open it. "Hello?" I finally say in the deepest voice I can muster. It comes out sounding more like a circus clown than a burly he-man. I hear someone chuckle.

"I thought Memphis was supposed to be warm this time of year," a voice says.

What in the world?

"At least that's what you always told me." I hear a shifting of feet—then he clears his throat and coughs.

Both the cell phone and the Swiffer fall out of my hands and crash to the floor.

"This ad says I can apply in person." I hear paper rustling. "Let's see here. *'Must have nice attitude.'* Check. *'Pleasing personality'* . . . most of the time, but I'll still give it a check. *'GOOD HYGIENE'*? Most definitely. Can't say I blame you there," he says with another chuckle.

My eyes slowly close as I breathe in the voice.

"*'Experience in classic and nouvelle cuisine.'* Looks like I've got that one covered, too . . . unless the position has already been filled."

I whip open the front door and look through the screen at the most gentle face I've ever come across. It takes me a moment to unlatch the outer door, my fingers catching on the metal, weary from nerves and lack of food. I open it wide and, losing my balance, stumble slightly forward. He's there to catch me, and when his arms wrap around my back I melt into him. The woodsy aroma of his fleece jacket immediately sends me back to February, when he last held me in his arms. The only time he held me in his arms. Stroking my hair tenderly, he kisses the crown of my head. To be enveloped in Peter Owen's mighty arms after months and months of longing feels like an apparition. I rear my head back to get a good look at him. "Is it really you?"

He strokes my cheek with the backs of his fingers and nods his head. Tears pool in the corners of my eyes and for the first time in a long while they're from pure joy. I take in a deep breath before slowly exhaling and suddenly the anxiety of the last year and a half escapes. Naturally, a million questions take its place. "How did you know?" I whisper.

He digs in the back pocket of his jeans and pulls out a newspaper clipping with my chef's ad circled in black.

"Who sent that to you?" I say, my eyes growing larger.

He digs in his other pocket and reveals a pale pink envelope, which has been folded in half. When he hands it over I see Mary Jule's handwriting on the front and when I turn it over her personalized embossing is on the back. "Wait a minute. Where did she get your address? I don't even have it."

"Something about the Kravitz Agency," he says, with a furrowed brow.

"She told you about that?" I cover my embarrassed face with my hands.

He reaches up and pulls them away. "What? Am I not supposed to know about it?" he says, with that adorable smile of his.

"No, it's fine. I just had no idea they had written to you. And I'm a little shocked, that's all." I lean back into the door frame. "So there's no Rod?"

With a deep chuckle he says, "Nope, there is no Rod."

Peter takes the envelope back, reaches inside and hands over the rest of its contents. "You should read their letter." When he contorts his face into a whacky grin, I remember how much I love his silly facial expressions.

I remove a piece of Mary Jule's pale pink Crane stationery from the envelope and read aloud.

Dear Peter, aka Sam Owen, h.t.b.k.a. (hopefully to be known as) Yankee Doodle Dixie,

If, on the outside chance you have not found your job at the Sugartree Inn in Vermont to be completely perfect, please consider applying for the one enclosed. While it may not be perfect, either, and might seem inordinately far away as far as job applications go, we can guarantee it will be fun, familiar, and forever Fiery.

If you have any questions, please don't hesitate to give us a call. Although you're welcome to contact any of us, Mary Jule hopes you'll contact her. The Gladys Kravitz Agency has uncovered your address and is in complete support of your candidacy for the position. We sincerely hope you'll consider a move down to Dixie. Please don't wait too long to apply. This position is highly coveted around Memphis and the proprietor is anxious to fill it.

Sincerely Yours,
Mary Jule, Alice, and Virginia
901-555-2266—MJ

After reading the note, I can't help but shake my head. "Who is Sam Owen?" I ask, snuggling in closer to him. Until now I had forgotten all about the chill in the air.

"Actually, I do know the answer to that one," he says, and wraps his arms around my waist. "But first, can I come in?"

Stepping over the Swiffer mop and my cell phone, which is strewn all over the place, in the lamplight of the main dining room, I walk him toward my makeshift conference table and we sink into two chairs on the same side. He scoots my chair closer to him and drapes both my legs over his, resting his hands on my knees and sending startling warmth up and down my legs. He glances at the Rombauer bottle sitting on the tabletop, with condensation dripping down the smooth body. I reach for my glass of wine and offer it to him. His smile grows, and he takes a sip from the glass.

"This ought to be good," I say, fingering the embossing on the stationery. "There's no telling what they did. Tell me."

"A couple of weeks ago I got a mysterious phone call. The girl on the phone said she was looking for Sam Owen, her old college boyfriend. Right away I could tell she was Southern, even though she tried to disguise her voice . . .

"I'm so proud of her. Who would have actually thought she'd have the courage to do it?" Virginia said.

Mary Jule piped up from the backseat. "I couldn't do it. No way."

"Personally, I think I could. But we're not talking about me," said Alice, who was sitting in the passenger seat of Virginia's car. "Let's get down to Agency business. Mary Jule," she said, turning around to face her, "did you sneak into Leelee's address book?"

"Yes, I did. No address, only a phone number."

"No address? That's odd, how are we gonna find it?"

"We can call Roberta," Virginia said. "Who knows her last name?"

"I don't remember. Do you, Alice?" Mary Jule asked.

"Heck no."

"How about Jeb? What's his last name?" Virginia asked.

The other two shrugged.

"Don't tell me we've hit a dead end."

"I've got it!" Alice squealed. "Mary Jule, what's his phone number?"

"You're not gonna call him, are you?"

"Just give me the phone number and watch the master at work."

"I don't know about this, but okay: 802-555-9998."

"Thank you very much, may I have total quiet please?" Alice pulled out a Virginia Slim, cracked the window and took a puff before punching in the numbers. "I did a star-sixty-seven, just in case." Alice put a finger to her lips. "Shhh, it's ringing. Still ringing. Hi-eee," she said in her best Yankee voice, "is this Sam?"

"You've got the wrong number."

Alice held the phone out from her ear so Virginia and Mary Jule, who were huddled toward the phone, could hear every word. "This isn't Sam Owen?"

"Nope. You've got the right last name, but my first name is not Sam."

"Oh well, that operator must have given me the wrong Owen. I'm looking for my old college boyfriend. He lives in Vermont on Acklen Road and I'm desperate to find him. Do you have a cousin named Sam Owen?"

"No, I don't have a cousin named Sam."

"Is your middle name Sam?"

"No, Sam is not my middle name."

"Are you sure you're not pulling my leg? Sam, this really is you, isn't it?" Alice pinched her two fingers together and glided her hand through the air, pretending to be writing. Mary Jule quickly dug in her purse and handed her a pen.

"It's not Sam," he said with a giggle. "And I'm not your old boyfriend. What's your name anyway?"

"Shauna."

"Nice to meet you, Shauna."

"You, too, Sam, I mean, whatever your name is."

"Peter."

"Okay, nice to meet you, Peter. Listen, would you please do me a favor?"

"I'll try."

"If you ever meet Sam Owen up there, will you tell him I'm trying to find him?"

"You bet."

"Thanks. Hey, what's your address? Maybe I'll send Sam a letter in care of you."

"It's 415 Forrest Drive, but I doubt I'll ever meet him."

"In Willingham?"

"No, Dover."

"And that zip?"

"05356."

"Alrighty then. Thanks, Peter Owen. Good talking to you and have a greet day." When she got to the "day" part she accidentally lost her accent. She recovered, though, when she said good-bye. "Byeeee." She closed her cell phone and blew two smoke rings. "And that's how it's done."

"I gotta say. You never cease to amaze me," Virginia told her.

"All in a day's work. I can't believe we actually caught him at home. What are the odds of that?"

"Ooooh, I'm getting excited," squealed Mary Jule.

"Who's got the letter?" Alice asked.

"It's in my purse," said Virginia.

Alice ruffled through Virginia's pocketbook and opened the unsealed envelope. She took out the newspaper clipping, which had one of the want ads circled with a black Sharpie, and read aloud:

> CHEF NEEDED Peach Blossom Inn—small, gourmet restaurant in mint condition. Must have nice attitude, pleasing personality, GOOD HYGIENE, and expertise in classic and nouvelle cuisine. Historic Germantown, 462 Old Poplar Pike, Memphis, Tennessee 38108. Call 901-555-8912 or apply in person.

"Leelee's left us no choice but to take matters into our own hands, and we're all in agreement, right?" After nods from the other two, Alice folded up the ad and stuck it back inside the envelope. She gave it a lick and under Peter Owen's name she copied down his address.

"Here's a stamp," Mary Jule said, leaning over the front seat. "I've only got a love stamp. Do y'all think that's too obvious?"

"So what if it is?" With a quick lick, Alice placed the stamp on the letter and handed the envelope to Virginia.

They pulled into the post office and got in line for the drop box. Virginia rolled down the window and reached out to place the letter on the edge of the mail slot. "Okay. It's worth a shot."

She gently let go of the envelope and let it slide down, deep into the mailbox.

"So here I am," Peter says.

"I can't believe they hid this from me," I say, waving the envelope in the air. "They are the craziest three women on earth. I'd tell you I'm surprised but—"

"You don't have to. I've met them, remember? Believe me, they are *quite* memorable. I'll never forget my first day at the inn when they helped you out in the restaurant. It was a miracle the meals were delivered hot."

"Or that the wine was ever poured without cork pieces floating in the glasses. I remember every detail of that night. It's the night I fired Helga, *remember*?"

"Do you think I could ever forget that?"

"Probably not," I say. I can't stop smiling at him.

"So, I've got a question for you," he says.

"Okay."

"What exactly *is* the Kravitz Agency?"

I slowly shake my head. "It's just a little something we made up in the seventh grade. Remember the nosy neighbor on *Bewitched*, Gladys Kravitz? And how she always spied on Samantha and Darrin? She knew everything that was going on."

He nods his head. "Yeah, I do remember her."

"We named it after her. The agency is the way we get our information. But it's top secret, you know. You mustn't ever tell anyone else about it. To tell you the truth, I can't believe they confessed it to you. You must rank high on their list."

"As long as we're on confessions, I've got one for you."

"Uh-oh. I don't know if I like the sound of this."

He reaches in his coat pocket and pulls out a stack of yellow lined legal papers folded business style. "These came from the girls, too."

I recognize them immediately but I distinctly remember throwing them in the trash a few weeks ago. I can't help feeling embarrassed.

If I had wanted to send them to him I would have. Clearly having the girls help me unpack boxes and redecorate my rental house granted them access to the more personal areas of my life.

"Why didn't you ever send them to me?" he asks.

I reach out for the wineglass and he hands it over. After taking another sip I breathe deeply. Fingering the rim of the glass, I look into Peter's soulful eyes. "When you told me on the phone that you couldn't move down here, that you didn't think a long distance relationship would work, I wrote the letters as a way of getting everything off my chest. It didn't seem like you wanted to talk to me, and I didn't know any other way of telling you how I felt. I didn't mail them because I didn't think you cared."

Peter slowly closes his eyes and he's silent long enough for the moment to feel awkward. If not for his arms resting on my legs, I'd be afraid he might be contemplating leaving. Finally he opens his eyes. "It had nothing to do with not caring about you. In fact I cared too much about you to move to Memphis without a job. Uprooting my life without the guarantee of an income is not something I've ever done. I'm too practical for that. It had nothing to do with you and everything to do with me. When you were leaving, even though I was wrecked by it, I didn't want you to feel like you had to stay in Vermont for me. I knew you wanted to go home to Memphis. Who would I have been to try and stop you?"

"That's exactly what my friends have been telling me all along."

Peter looks into my eyes an extra-long moment. Lifting under my knees and around my back, he hoists me onto his lap—cradling me as if I were a small girl. Our faces are level and I move my hands around his neck, clutching them together at the base of his scruffy hair. I come so close to his mouth, our breaths moving back and forth, I can smell and taste chardonnay and Peter all at once. No other words are spoken, nor is there a need, the reunion of souls speaks loudly enough.

In the pale lamplight of the darkened house, with the moon shining in from the open door, his perfect lips smile radiantly only inches from mine and his crystal blue eyes glisten. Peter opens his mouth to break the silence but stops abruptly, choosing to brush my lips with his and in an instant we rediscover what it's like to kiss. With no one in the world watching this time, we set out on a journey, exploring each other's faces and necks, scents and tastes, kissing as if our lips have never been touched before. Twenty minutes pass before either of us is willing to let the other go.

Out of nowhere, my stomach growls loudly and Peter places his hand on top of it. "Sounds like you need some dinner."

"I have not eaten one morsel of food all day. That's how busy I've been."

"Why don't you let me take you into the kitchen and fix you whatever your heart desires?"

"I have a better idea. How about we let someone cook for you for a change? Kissie's at my house and has dinner waiting."

When we drive up to my house, with no porch lights and the drapes and blinds blocking any sign of life from the street, Peter comments on it right away. "Is anyone here?"

"Yes," I say, rolling my eyes. "Kissie likes to keep all the windows covered and most of the lights out."

"Is Memphis that dangerous?"

"No, it's not that." I point to the house next door. "My next-door neighbor drives her a little crazy."

"Uh-oh."

"He's actually very sweet. It's sort of a long story."

Once in the carport, he turns off his engine. I had ridden with him, deciding to pick up my car in the morning. When we stroll inside to the dimly lit kitchen, the irresistible aroma of Kissie's cooking permeates the whole room. There are several pots on the stove and when I glance over at the oven, I can see a roast warming. The sound of the TV is wafting in from the den. I put my fingers to my lips and motion for Peter to creep in behind me. When we peek into the room, Sarah and Issie are on either side of Kissie, playing with her long hair. They've taken it out of the plated bun and she's leaning back with her eyes closed while Issie brushes and Sarah styles. Roberta lifts his head and I duck back inside the kitchen, pulling Peter with me. "Yoo-hoo," I call, before switching on the light. "Is anybody here?"

"Mommy's home," I hear Issie say, and the girls bound into the kitchen, right behind Roberta, who tries his best to jump up in my arms. I lean down to pet him and he covers me with tongue licks. He's quite a jumper, that little dog. After a visit to the vet we learned he's part Jack Russell. And part poodle.

Sarah and Issie's faces look as if they've just seen Santa Claus. "Mr. Peter," they both squeal at the same time. He squats down and my little girls fall into his outstretched arms.

"You guys have gotten so big, I don't know who's who," he says, pulling them closer. "Who's this?" he asks, and rubs Roberta's back hard enough to make his foot thump.

"Roberta. He's a boy but Mama wanted to give him a girl name," Sarah says, rolling her eyes.

Peter looks up at me and I shrug my shoulders. "I needed a reminder of my dear friend."

"What's all this commotion?" Kissie says, strolling in from the den. She's twisting her hair back up into a bun and has just taken the last black hairpin out of the side of her mouth when she spots Peter. "You don't mean it!" she exclaims, inserting the hairpin back inside her bun. "Is this Peter?" When she holds out her big, cushiony arms Peter lets go of the girls and folds right inside. "Ooo-wee, you are a nice-lookin' man, Peter. Let me take a good look at you." She takes a step back. "Leelee's bragged about you so much, I guess I just didn't know what to expect." With hands in his pockets Peter glances down at his feet before shooting Kissie a bashful smile.

"What took you so long to get here anyway?" she says.

"I had some things I had to work out first. Some business to get out of the way."

"That's right. Nothin' wrong with gittin' your business straight."

She runs her hand through his hair, which is hanging a little past his collar these days. "Look at all this pretty blond hair. You've got a plenty of it, too."

"Well, thank you, Miss Kristine," he says.

"Lawd, chile, you might as well call me Kissie. Everybody else does. Okay now," she says as she's heading over to the fridge. "We've got company, girls. Not just any company. There's a *good-lookin'* man in this house. And he seems like a mighty fine one to me. Sarah, why don't you set another place at the table? When a man has been driving for hours like Peter's done, he's got one thing on his mind. We are gonna serve him a fine Southern meal. *Hm, hm, hm.*" She opens the refrigerator door and studies the inside.

"I will never object to that," he says, touching his stomach.

"Dinner is ready, I'mo just heat it up. Won't take long." Now, she's got eggs in one hand and milk in the other, which she sets on the counter. Next I see her pull out the sugar canister, and the vanilla out of the spice drawer. When she's got everything she needs, she strolls over to Peter and places her hand on his shoulder. "Why don't you let me take your coat so you can stay awhile."

When he removes his jacket, I can't help staring at him. Tonight he's wearing a hunter green flannel shirt that he's rolled up at the cuffs with a white crew neck T-shirt underneath. His jeans are, as usual, a little raggedy but he's wearing a pair of new brown leather work boots and he is probably *the* most beautiful thing I have ever laid my eyes on.

"Now Peter, why don't you go on in the den there and put your feet up. Let the girls play with that fine head a' hair of yours. 'Fore you know it you'll be fallin' asleep it feels so good."

"That sounds nice," Peter says.

"Come see our room first, Mr. Peter." Issie pulls on his hand.

"Is it any bigger than the one you guys had in Vermont?" he asks.

Both girls laugh. "It's waaaaay bigger," Sarah says.

Peter takes Sarah in his other hand and I watch the three of them stroll down the hall.

Kissie turns on the eyes of the gas stove. "It won't take long to heat up this gravy," she says. "Mashed potatoes, neither." Into a metal bowl she breaks four eggs, pours milk straight out of the carton, the sugar out of the canister, and adds a dash of vanilla. I can't remember ever seeing her use a measuring cup or measuring spoons. After whisking the ingredients together, she pours the mixture into one of the heavy copper pots I brought back from Vermont.

"What are you making now?" I ask her.

"Banana puddin'," she says. "I ain't met a man yet not crazy about banana puddin'." While she stirs the custard with a long wooden spoon, I remove an extra table setting from the drawer and place it on the table. Sarah's too busy having fun to call her away.

"I told you the Lawd was gonna give you another chance at love," she says. "You just had to be smart about it. See what happens when you wait? Ole Kissie knows what she's talkin' about."

Kissie's back is to me and I walk up behind her and reach my arms around her waist. "I've always known that," I tell her. With my chin on her shoulder I watch as she stirs figure eights in the custard.

"*Hm, hm, hm. Hm, hm, hm. Hm, hm, hm.*"

"How can you tell when it's ready?" I ask, moving around to her side.

Kissie lifts the wooden handle from the pot and runs her finger down the back of the spoon. "When the custard stops seepin' back into the middle, it means it's ready."

Loud squeals suddenly ring in from the other room and Issie screams, "Hurry, Mommy and Kissie, come see Mr. Peter."

Without taking the time to remove the wooden spoon from her custard, Kissie grabs my hand and we dash into the den, rocket speed, freezing at the sight of my girls with their hands in Peter's poofed-out pompadour. He's got another of his silly looks on his face and when Kissie sees him, she lets loose one of her famous belly laughs and bends over, clutching her middle. It's the kind where you can't speak or breathe. The kind where your face hurts from smiling, and you're afraid you might spit Coke out of your nose or wet your pants or have to get your stomach operated on it's in so much pain. Watching Kissie gets the rest of us going and pretty soon all five of us are hunched over howling, with Roberta darting in circles around our sprawled-out bodies.

From over the top of Sarah's head, with Issie clutching at his flannel shirt, I catch Peter's eye for a brief moment. He winks.

Acknowledgments

It's hard to imagine that I'm actually to the acknowledgment stage and thanking certain people for their help and encouragement on a second novel. But I am, thank goodness, and I'd like to shout their names from the nearest mountaintop or, more appropriately, from the nearest hill, as is the case here in Nashville.

I love to quote John Lennon: "Life is what happens when you're busy making other plans." While I was writing this book, stuff just kept happening and there were days when it was hard to be creative, much less funny. But in her forever tenacious and encouraging fashion, Katie Gilligan, my gorgeous, talented editor, never gave up on me. Her sense of humor kept my shoulders shaking and inspired me to climb ever higher. I thank you for your ingenuity, your guidance, and especially, your dear friendship. Your belief in me is a gift that I will always treasure. Holly Root, my equally gorgeous and talented literary agent, your belief in me is the reason I had the opportunity to write a second book. Thank you for your faith, your friendship, your eternal optimism, and that wonderful young brain of yours.

To all the lovely people at Thomas Dunne Books and St. Martin's

Press who work triple-overtime to make sure my name gets in front of readers, I owe you a huge debt of gratitude: Sally Richardson, Matthew Shear, Thomas Dunne, Pete Wolverton, Matthew Baldacci, Anne Marie Tallberg, Lisa Senz, Sarah Goldstein, Rachel Ekstrom, Sarit Schneider, Meryl Gross, and the supremely talented Michael Storrings for two gorgeous book covers.

Michael and Will, thank you for believing in me. What a joy and privilege it is to watch you evolve into honorable men. You continue to inspire your mama. Dream big and dream often. You were both created to accomplish magnanimous things. I love you with all my heart.

My sisters, Laurie Patton and Leslie Davis, thank you for your unyielding ears, not to mention the hours of encouragement you have lavished upon me. And heartfelt thanks go to their daughters, Madeleine Patton and Elise Davis, my precious nieces, who list me as their favorite author.

I am blessed to have friends who stand by me and keep loving me, even when I disappear into oblivion to do this thing writers do. I can't thank y'all enough for understanding. . . .

Kathy "G" Peabody, my steadfast and faithful friend, how can I ever thank you enough for standing by me through the thickest and the thinnest of times? I can't. Just know that I am grateful from the bottom of my heart. The same goes for my sweet friend Penny Preston. What would I do without either of you?

Linda Yoder, my cussing coach and dear, dear friend, your gifts of encouragement and hospitality are just two of many. And to Wes Yoder, thank you for your friendship, publishing expertise, and guidance. Thank you both for the privilege of eating from your table.

My childhood girlfriends, who are really more like sisters, mean the world to me. We love to laugh, the harder the better, and after a forty-eight-year friendship, the hours we've spent doing so have certainly given me great inspiration and luscious material for writing. Lisa Murphey Blakley, Cary Coors Brown, Katy Collier Creech, Elise Norfleet Crockett, Nancy Jett Crutchfield, Becky Goodwin, Wilda

Weaver Hudson, Emily Freeburg Kay, Linda Abston Larsen, Katie Kittle Powell, Amie Todd Sims, Mimi Hall Taylor, Lisa Earp Wilder. Y'all are my soul sisters.

Stuart Southard, you carried me through this time in my life. Even when the waters became cloudy and murky, you encouraged me anyway and held my hand as I waded through the mire. Thank you, too, for that stellar business brain of yours, time outs of fun and laughter, your sense of adventure, and your wit. I'm so very grateful.

Fannie Flagg, I won't ever be able to thank you enough for your guidance and inspiration, not to mention your words of encouragement and praise. You're *my* Eudora Welty . . . not to mention my Paul McCartney.

Steve and Sarah Berger, my precious faithful friends, I owe you a huge debt of gratitude for whistlin' the names of my books all over the place. Vicki Olson, you've done the same thing, and I thank you from the bottom of my heart.

Leann Phelan, you understand the artist in me. You get me, no doubt about it. Thanks, dear friend, for all the hours of encouragement and "good for you."

Gail Chiaravalle, what would I do without your doggie day care? Thank you for watching Rosie ad infinitum while I traveled around promoting my book, and especially for your dear friendship. Bernie Chiaravalle, my sincerest thanks go out to you for a gorgeous Web site and, of course, your friendship.

Michael McDonald, Susan Gregg Gilmore, and Karen White. I owe you a huge amount of thanks for taking the time to read my book and offering up your praise. My head's still reelin'.

Ron Olson, Steve Conley, Karen Perrin, Preston Davis, Dan Barron, and Angie Whitfield, thank you so much for sharing your stories and radio-station expertise. Fun, fun, fun is all I can say.

Three important people were inadvertently left off my acknowledgments for *Whistlin' Dixie in a Nor'easter*—Donna Boone, Kathy Cheathum, and Anna McNeal. I'm not sure what happened, but I am sure of my deep thanks.

There are others who invested time encouraging and or helping me, and I want them to know how important they've been: Allison Allen, Liz Alexander, Becky Barkley, Cristy Beasley, Emily Bell, Alice Davis Blake, Carolyn Brigham, Genie Buchanan, Teasi Cannon, Kim Carnes, Mary Gaston Catmur, Sara Beth Cline, Steve Conley, Gigi Crichton, Jan Cross, Lyn DiGiorgio, Gail Donovan, JT Ellison, Shannon Harris, Jennifer Hart, Kim Jameson, Tammy Jensen, Lindsey Kennedy, Jodie McCarthy, Joyce McCullough, Shana McLain, Genie McCown, George Merrifield, Mary Lou Montague, Mary Norman, Penny Nelms, Erica Nichols, Anne Marie Norton, Teresa Ofman, Peggy Peters, Terry Robbins, Rosie, Lyn Simpler, Whitney Sorenson, Jay Stockley, Margie Thessin, Guy Wallace, Sallie Wallace, Leelee Walter, Ed White, and Kathy White.

To Julia Black, Devonia Crawford, and Christine King, thank you for loving me into adulthood. You showed me not only what it's like to be a good mother, but the Love of the Father. The color of our skin may have been different, but you treated me like I was your own. I am eternally grateful.

I lost two loved ones while writing this novel: my sister, Melanie Ann Orpet Winand, and a beloved young, close family friend, Josiah David Berger. Heaven has never shone brighter.

To all the Franklin, Memphis, Nashville, and other book clubs around the country who have read my first book and convinced me to write the sequel. You rock!

And thank you, dear reader, for buying and reading this book. A portion of the proceeds will help struggling single mothers and their children in Williamson County, Tennessee.

Above all, I give all the glory to God my Redeemer, who makes anything possible.

1. When the book opens we find Leelee headed home to Memphis. She heads straight to Virginia's house and when she can't reach her, Leelee turns her car around and drives to Kissie's, knowing full well she will not only be home but probably awake, despite the late hour. Kissie's house is in a part of town some would deem unsafe. Unfazed, Leelee decides to move in with Kissie, happy to be near her second mother. When Virginia learns of Leelee's plans she does not hide her disapproval. Would you think twice before taking your two young children to an unfamiliar neighborhood, even if it meant someone you loved lived there and would care for you in your time of need?

2. After making the decision to come home to Memphis, Leelee never considers that she would step into a gossip bed where she is the hot topic. Have you ever had to eat humble pie and endure a situation where you were talked about or even ostracized for a decision you made?

3. Leelee is devastated by Peter's decision to not enter into a long-distance relationship. He is not willing to pick up his life and run off to a place where his job security hangs in the balance. As hard as she tries she is unable to forget about him in the months following. Have you been in Leelee's situation before: A relationship that seemed to have all the makings of happiness but one of the partners makes the decision to end it because of distance or job security?

4. Leelee takes a step backward when she moves back home to Memphis; she falls right back into old patterns. Once again it's hard for her to stand up for herself, especially when it comes to her job. It's been said that old habits are hard to break. Just when we feel like we've learned something, that old demon comes back to roost. Do you find this to be true?

5. Leelee's friends think she is a doormat because she has a hard time saying no. Do you agree? Are you able to tell someone no and be okay with it?

St. Martin's Griffin

6. Southerners are often criticized for not saying what's on their mind and Northerners are often accused of being too blunt. Do you agree with this? What are the pros and cons of both sides?

7. If truth be told we are all a little starstruck, well maybe for some a lot starstruck. It's easy to criticize some of Leelee's decisions from afar. If you are older than Leelee, try to remember back to when you were in your late '20s and early '30s and did not have all the wisdom you've earned today. If a rock-star invited you to join him in New York City, would you accept? If you are close to Leelee's age and single, is this something you would go for? Why or why not?

8. When Leelee quits her job, she has decided working with Edward Maxwell is simply not worth it. Should you stay in a job even if the conditions are intolerable? Would you consider Edward's personality intolerable?

9. Leelee and her friends still enjoy their shenanigans together. What is the craziest thing you've ever done with your adult girlfriends? Are you ever too old for pranks?

10. Leelee and her girlfriends are more like sisters. They certainly take matters into their own hands when they send Leelee's unsent letters to Peter. Would you be mad at your friends (or sisters) if they had done the same thing? Would you do something similar for one of your closest friends?

11. How much influence do your friends have over your life? Do you consult them first; or your husband (or wife) first when making big decisions?

For more reading group suggestions, visit www.readinggroupgold.com.

Lisa Patton's novels are
"Southern to the core... funny to the bone."—Fannie Flagg

"Reading this book is like sipping a peach daiquiri on your best friend's porch. So pull up a chair and stay awhile."
—Karen White, *New York Times* bestselling author

"Sweet, sassy, and very entertaining!"
—Lee Smith, *New York Times* bestselling author

St. Martin's Griffin